Louisa
Meets Bear

Louisa
Meets Bear

Lisa Gornick

Sarah Crichton Books

Farrar, Straus and Giroux

New York

Sarah Crichton Books
Farrar, Straus and Giroux
18 West 18th Street, New York 10011

Copyright © 2015 by Lisa Gornick
All rights reserved
Printed in the United States of America
First edition, 2015

Library of Congress Cataloging-in-Publication Data
Gornick, Lisa, 1956–
    [Short stories. Selections]
    Louisa meets bear / Lisa Gornick. — First edition.
        p.   cm
    ISBN 978-0-374-19208-2 (hardback) — ISBN 978-0-374-71026-2 (ebook)
    I. Gornick, Lisa, 1956– Instructions to participant.   II. Title.

    PS3607.O598 A6 2015
    813'.6—dc23

                                                            2014029306

Farrar, Straus and Giroux books may be purchased for educational, business, or promotional use. For information on bulk purchases, please contact the Macmillan Corporate and Premium Sales Department at 1-800-221-7945, extension 5442, or write to specialmarkets@macmillan.com.

www.fsgbooks.com
www.twitter.com/fsgbooks • www.facebook.com/fsgbooks

1   3   5   7   9   10   8   6   4   2

To all my Js and Ss . . .
and
In memory of Candida Fraze

We are stardust
Billion year old carbon
We are golden
Caught in the devil's bargain
And we've got to get ourselves
Back to the garden

—JONI MITCHELL, "Woodstock"

Contents

1961

Instructions to Participant

When I was five, my mother, like all the other mothers I knew, slept each night in pink curlers so her dark hair would flip up at the ends. She had carefully plucked brows, a pear-shaped figure that looked skinny when seated and plump when she stood up, a closet full of polished pumps that I played grown-up in, and an unused Vassar degree. Then, my parents, who still lived together and, I imagine, believed they'd always do so, shielded us, my brother and me, from what they must have viewed as the provinces of adult life. We were not told about the Bay of Pigs or the arrest of the Freedom Riders. We were not told about grand-parents' cancer diagnoses or our father nearly (but not in the end) being passed over to become a partner in his law firm. We were not told about the desperate attempts of my Aunt Anna, my mother's year-older sister, to win the respect of my scientist uncle, or about her having fallen in love with a sheep farmer in Mendocino County. We were not told—and I would not learn for another thirteen years until, flat on my back with my own calamity, my mother slowly uncoiled the tale—about what happened to my mother that year.

At the time, I still suffered considerable confusion about where my mother stopped and I started and a terrible anxiety about being apart from her (*Off, off, my little kangaroo*, my mother ordered those first days of school when, at the kindergarten door, I clung to her belly), so that the changes that took place in my mother seemed to me bigger than a person—more like weather or a sea shift, akin to lying on a hot, still beach when suddenly there are black clouds overhead and a wind lifting sheets off sand and soon people are packing their bags, glancing every few seconds at the dark sky and the water whipped with whitecaps. In my memory, one day my mother was all hustle and bustle, packing lunches, leaving directions for our after-school babysitter, stuffing books and shoes into a maroon canvas tote she kept under a mahogany table in the front hall. The next day, she was lying on the living room couch, staring out the ceiling-to-floor glass windows, her face bloated and pasty, a bead of blood on her lip from a place where she'd bit the skin. Although she would not have stayed on the couch for more than a few days, she never fully returned. When she got up, it was to quietly drive us to school, to a routine of laundry and carefully prepared dinners and supervising my brother's and my evening baths.

•

My mother, I would later learn, had quarreled with my father about going back to school. To him—or so she remembered—it seemed like a lot of disruption for, in the end, very little money. As he put it, they'd have to pay nearly as much for a babysitter as she'd ever make as a social worker.

My mother, however, insisted. Her sister, Anna, worked. My cousin, Louisa, born a few months before me, had not been harmed. My mother's first semester, she took three courses, traveling into Manhattan two days a week for the classes. Your father softened, my mother told me, when I brought home all As. I think he was as proud as if it had been one of you.

In the second semester, my mother signed up for an interviewing class. As part of the course, each student was required to interview a family on public assistance, the visits arranged by one of the school's casework instructors. My mother could have selected a family closer to home, but she chose to go to East Harlem.

I still remember that morning, my mother told me, how I'd wadded my money into one of your change purses, a plastic thing with Donald Duck on the top that I hid inside my raincoat. It was the first time I'd taken the subway north of Bloomingdale's, the first time I realized I was scared of people who were poor.

Coming out of the station at 103rd Street, the vista before her came as a surprise. My mother had not known there were hills in Manhattan. There it was, a gentle decline from 102nd to 103rd, the length and steepness of the bunny slopes on which she and my father had taught my brother and would soon teach me how to ski.

My mother headed down the hill. Everywhere there were signs in Spanish: CARNICERÍA, FARMACIA, PAN RECIÉN HECHO. Christmas lights flashed over doorways and windows. Behind the rolling storefront gates and on tables dragged onto the street were fish dried and salted into leathery flats, bunches of green plantains, plastic shoes the colors of jelly beans.

At 105th Street, my mother turned east. Some of the buildings had boarded-up windows. A carton of milk and a stick of butter sat on a sill.

I remember the number, my mother said—235. A house dweller all of her life, it hadn't occurred to her to ask for the apartment number too. She climbed the steps to look at the names posted by the bank of bells, but most of the labels were too faded to read or missing altogether.

A boy with black hair poking out from under a hooded

sweatshirt came through the front door. He sat on the stoop and took out a pack of gum.

My mother gave him her mother-smile. "Excuse me, do you know where the Hendricks family lives?"

Slowly, the boy unwrapped three pieces of green gum.

"A lady named Jacqueline and her two children?"

A green bubble emerged from the boy's mouth. He pointed to the roof.

My mother rang the top two bells and stepped back to wait. She folded her hands over the belt of her raincoat and smiled again at the boy.

The boy darted his tongue in and out to gather the gum back into his mouth. "Bells don't work."

My mother could feel herself perspiring beneath her dry-cleaned blouse. The casework instructor had told her that the Hendricks family didn't have a phone. "Can you let me in? I'm here to interview Miss Hendricks. I can show you my ID card."

The boy wadded the gum and stuck it on the sleeve of his sweatshirt. "Door ain't locked."

The hinges made a nasty creak when my mother turned the knob. The light was out in the hallway. Not until she reached the elevator could she see the OUT OF ORDER sign.

Before her fears could gel, she pushed the door marked STAIRS and started to climb. At the third-floor landing, she froze. Had something scampered out from behind the piles of newspapers, Pampers boxes, garbage bags?

On the highest floor there were two apartments, one with the name TORRES taped over the bell. My mother knocked on the other. She turned her ear to listen. Had she knocked loudly enough? How long should she wait before trying again?

She gave the door two more raps.

"Hold on, Jesus, I'm coming." There was a clumping noise and then what sounded like locks and chains being undone.

The door swung open and a teenage girl appeared with a baby on her hip. A toddler holding a bag of Fritos trailed behind.

•

When, the summer after I turned fourteen, my mother sat my brother and me down to explain that she was moving out of the house, it seemed that her decision was somehow connected to those shadowy memories from when I was five of her laid out like a mummy on the living room couch. We lived in Dobbs Ferry, a river town fifteen miles north of New York, and my mother was heading three thousand miles west to Berkeley, where she had enrolled in social work school for the fall. They've accepted my credits from nine years ago, she told my brother and me—as though this were an explanation as to why she was moving across the country, across the bay from where her sister had lived until her death five years before in a car accident.

That summer, my brother had ditched the name we'd always called him, Josh, for Jay. Taller and broader than our wiry father, with gray eyes that already hid his emotions, he acted blasé, her decision peripheral to his real life. He'd been the vice president of his junior class. In the fall, he would be captain of the football team. He had two girlfriends: one a popular, freckled cheerleader who kept a horse in the north part of the county; the other a secret girlfriend, a Latina from Mount Vernon with a job modeling for the catalogues.

As for me, under siege by breasts and hips erupting on my large frame at a rate that had left me feeling both exposed and terrified that my destiny was not to be what my best friend Sandra optimistically described as statuesque and curvaceous but rather big and fat, my mother's announcement felt like a bomb had blown the roof off my precarious life. I was mortified, certain everyone would look at me with horror and pity. It took me a week to tell Sandra, who responded by bursting into tears and then saying my name over and over—*Lizzy, Lizzy, Lizzy*—which I interpreted as evidence that what my mother was doing was shameful, a blight that would affect even Sandra, her place in the world threatened by her proximity to me.

My father couldn't or wouldn't talk about it. All he said was, It's your mother's decision. The week after my mother left, he hired a housekeeper. Whereas he had always worked until ten or eleven three or four nights a week, he now managed to make it home most evenings by seven or eight for forcedly animated dinners during which he and my brother would discuss politics—Nixon's invasion of Cambodia, about which my father attempted to take a balanced view; Kent State, which Jay, just two years younger than two of the murdered students, experienced as a personal assault, evidence of a fascist undercurrent—after which he would retreat to his study to resume his work. A year later, with Jay already off to Yale, my father began dating a divorcée: a pleasant, buxom woman who seemed to be endlessly whipping up mushy casseroles out of what I still thought of as my mother's kitchen.

As for my mother, she wrote—or, rather, typed—my brother and me weekly letters, addressed to the two of us together. At first I made a show of not even looking at the letters, on several occasions ripping the paper into confetti when my brother tried to hand it to me. After Jay left for college, my mother took to sending one or the other of us the carbon copy and, with no witness for my little dramas, I took to carrying my copies around, back and forth from school, the envelopes growing dog-eared in the bottom of my book bag, until, giving in to what I told myself was simply curiosity, I'd lock myself in the bathroom and read two or three at a time.

Through the letters, I learned that my mother was doing her social work internship at a state prison, where she provided substance abuse counseling to first-time offenders. I learned that my mother was living in a small apartment in Oakland. (That's where the Black Panthers are based, my brother would later say, knowingly.) I learned that my mother had taken to the California landscape: that she had driven north to Mendocino County to see the redwoods and the wild, rocky coastline and then south to see the sequoias and Kings Canyon; that she and a friend were planning a five-day backpacking trip into the more isolated parts of the Tuolumne Meadows. I learned that every Sunday she took my cousin, Louisa, out to lunch and that sometimes Louisa would bring Corrine, her babysitter when she was younger and now her best friend, and the two of them would go shopping afterward at the vintage clothing stores on Telegraph Avenue.

In the letters, my mother invited us, my brother and me, to visit her, anytime, well, anytime except April or May or December or January—then, she wrote, she'd be too preoccupied with her exams and papers to really show us around—but neither of us did. The first summer after she left, she came east for a month, staying with my grandmother in Hartford, but I refused to see her, refused to even discuss it with anyone, and although I heard hushed conversations between my father and her over the phone, I surmised that she'd decided I was old enough to decide for myself if I wanted to see her, an awareness that left me even more miserable than had she or my father insisted.

My mother's second visit, prompted by my grandmother's hip operation, came the fall I began college—having managed to graduate from high school a year early by taking senior English and honors calculus in summer school but then, secretly afraid of going too far away, following my brother to Yale. Jay must have received our mother's letter a day before me because I remember hearing from him first about her request to visit the two of us in New Haven. It was a hot Indian summer afternoon, the kind of day when complexions look oily and sallow, half the campus still in sandals, the other half with long-sleeved shirts stuck to their backs, and my brother and I were having coffee together at Naples, sitting in one of the worn wooden booths etched with initials, a fan whirring above, the smells of oregano and pizza dough wafting around us. I must have been silent in a sullen, aggrieved way after Jay told me about our mother's request, because he spoke to me sharply, saying something about how it was time to cut the crap—Christ, Lizzy, can't you give her a break?

The words of my usually unflappable brother fell like a slap, and I remember him reaching for a napkin from the dispenser for me to wipe my eyes and ending up with a wad two inches thick and then, a few weeks later, sitting in the same booth with my mother and brother, the three of us sharing a pizza while Jay talked about his plans for a semester in Grenada and I tried not to stare at my mother, who in the three years since I'd last seen her seemed to have grown younger—thinner, with her hair cut short in a way that elongated her neck, golden against a white peasant blouse—and who, I could tell, was using every ounce of self-control not to stroke my arm or push my hair off my forehead.

After that visit, I took to answering my mother's letters and she took to writing separately to my brother and me, and even though things were not what any of us could call okay, it seemed that we were on the path to rediscovering some kind of connection and even planning for me to visit her the following Christmas. Which I would have done had I not, the fall of my sophomore year, gotten pregnant.

·

How and why I got pregnant at eighteen the first time I had sex, the unbeknownst father the husband of my history professor—Benita Frosch, a brilliant German woman with wild hair secured on top of her head by lacquered chopsticks, whom I worked for as a research assistant and who had pushed her timid husband, Hans, on me so she could pursue what was, I learned later from my brother, a scandalous affair with a female graduate student—has always seemed to me less significant than what ensued. Dumbly, I let two months go by, missing two periods, chalking up the nausea to nerves, finally taking a pregnancy test, which came back falsely negative, then waiting another week for a blood test, the results arriving in my eleventh week.

My roommate, Miriam, a modern dancer with a pointy nose and an obsessive crossword puzzle habit, came with me to the appointment at Planned Parenthood.

You're cutting it close, hon, the abortion counselor told me. Another week and we wouldn't be able to do a D&C.

Always efficient, Miriam took notes on everything the counselor said. *A long tube connected to a vacuum aspirator is inserted into the cervix. You'll hear a sucking sound for about five minutes. Imagine it as a mini-vacuum cleaning out the tissue attached to the walls of your uterus.*

I came back to my dorm room with pamphlets and mimeographed instructions. The *procedure*, as it was called in the pamphlet, was scheduled for two days later. *Don't eat anything that morning. If the cramping and bleeding continue for longer than three days, <u>immediately</u> contact your doctor. Bring payment in full in <u>CASH</u>.*

Miriam and her premed boyfriend disappeared into Miriam's room. I flopped down on the couch in the suite living room, the pamphlets perched on my stomach, my arm sweeping the floor for distraction. Then, in one of those coincidences that seem too fantastical to be true but that determine more of our lives than we would like to think (years later, when the evolutionary biologists would rewrite Darwin, moving randomness from background to fore, I knew from my own minuscule experience in the stream of evolution that they were right to give chance marquee billing), I picked up one of Miriam's boyfriend's books, dropped in a heap on the floor.

Perhaps it was not, in fact, as creepily uncanny as it seemed. Perhaps I had registered subliminally that it was a human biology text—not an accident when my hand landed on that book rather than the paperback of Machiavelli's *The Prince* or the organic chemistry text between which it was sandwiched.

Flipping pages, I reached the chapter on embryonic development. Seven color pictures showed the fetus at various stages. In the eleven-week photo, the fetus rested on its back in an orb that looked like the sun. Little hands played with a nose. A black eye stared out from the page. At three months, I read, the fetus is the size of a mouse.

I sat up. I felt queasy. They were going to vacuum something the size of a mouse out of my belly and into a bottle labeled medical waste?

The bed creaked in Miriam's room. Miriam, I feebly called. Can you come here? Please come.

•

When I started to bleed in my fifth month, the doctor I'd been seeing in New Haven ordered bed rest. I really should insist on a bedpan, he told me, but I'll let you get up to go to the bathroom. Otherwise, flat on your back. I withdrew from the spring semester, and the deans, encouraged by Benita Frosch, in whom I never confided the paternity of my baby but who must have suspected, granted me a leave of absence.

Miriam packed my things, and my brother and his roommate Tom, a theater kid from New York whom I'd had a bit of a crush on but realizing that he knew everything about my situation could now hardly look in the eye, loaded my things into my brother's car. Good luck, Lizzy, Tom said after my brother had settled me into the back seat with a pillow. He gave me a little salute and then a deep bow.

Jay and my father carried my boxes to my old room. Although we had talked about what I might do when the baby came—my father had arranged for a possible adoption, the cousins of one of his partners, a nice childless couple from the city, the husband a Yale graduate too, as though that somehow linked us in one big family, just an option, my father said, careful not to push me, you'll have up until the delivery to decide—this newest flat-on-my-back twist had come too quickly for me to think further than getting home.

We ate dinner, the three of us, in my room: me lying down with my dishes on a bed tray, my brother and father on chairs with their plates on their laps.

What the hell are you going to do on Monday? Jay asked. Who's going to bring you food while Dad's at work?

I looked helplessly at my father. I imagined him leaving a bowl of food by my bed.

My father cleared his throat. Afterward I thought maybe his eyes were damp. Your mother, he said. Your mother's coming home.

•

Although my mother had known that Jackie was eighteen and black, one of the few black families in the largely Puerto Rican neighborhood, my mother was, she would tell me (I was by then in my eighth month), taken aback at the sight of the girl—tall, with big arms and broad hips, a burnished Rubens, all volume with beauty and delicacy delegated to her almond eyes and bow lips. *She's so young*, my mother remembered having thought. And yet, the girl with her lushness, her full body and taut skin, seemed to my mother more fecund, a closer replica of Nature's Madonna than herself.

My mother extended her hand. Should she introduce herself by her last name or her first? Uncertain, she used both. "You must be Jackie," she added.

"Yeah."

"And this must be Brandon."

"That's the little bugger."

My mother leaned down to coo at the baby. Yellow crust rimmed his nose. The baby looked away, uninterested in my mother's feeble sounds.

Jackie led my mother in and motioned her toward a brown plaid couch with tufts of foam sticking out through the fabric. My mother caught herself about to dust off the spot where she would sit.

Jackie lowered herself into a metal folding chair facing the couch. From the back of the apartment, my mother could hear music like she'd once heard in a nightclub on a trip with my father to a hotel in San Juan. The toddler carried her bag of Fritos over to my mother and began dropping the chips one by one into my mother's canvas tote.

"Denise, you stop that or you'll get a smack," Jackie said. The child kept on with her game. My mother reached down and lifted the tote onto the couch. She touched the little girl's arm, and then fished around in the bag until she found her keys with the fuzzy animal ring. (You'd given it to me for my birthday, my mother told me. That was when you still thought that if *you* liked something, I would too.)

The child picked up the key ring and wandered over to show it to her mother. Brandon had started to cry, and Jackie put a bottle in his mouth. Denise yanked on her mother's pant leg.

Jackie jerked her leg back. "Girl, you been getting on my nerves all morning."

Now Denise was crying. Feeling somehow responsible— really, she thought, the only adult in the room—my mother leaned forward and beckoned to the little girl. "Come, you can sit with me. Mommy's busy with Brandon."

Denise next to her, my mother took out a legal pad from

the tote. Folded into the pad was a sheet titled "Family Relations: Interview Assignment." My mother glanced over the list of questions she'd so carefully reviewed the night before: *Who do you consider to be the members of your family? With whom do you discuss your problems? Who do you turn to when there's an emergency?*

Brandon had stopped sucking. His head rested now on Jackie's shoulder. She reached into her pocket for a cigarette pack.

"Before we begin," my mother asked, "do you have any questions?"

Jackie lit a cigarette and inhaled. For a second she closed her eyes and an expression of calm passed over her face. "Yeah, who's gonna see what I say?"

"No one. I mean, no one outside my class."

"My caseworker ain't going to see this?"

"No. This is for my educational benefit only."

"You mean like homework."

"Yes. It's one of my assignments."

Jackie leaned back in the folding chair so that her shoulder blades rested against the metal back and her legs, crossed at the ankles, stretched in front. Brandon lay belly-down on top of her. "Just the Welfare thinks that my gram watches the babies. She does a lot, but like today and some mornings she cleans this lady's house."

From the casework report, my mother had learned that Jackie, her two sisters, and her brother were raised by their mother's mother, Faith, after their own mother had disappeared. Now this gram at fifty-two had a third generation of kids in her home. "So, who watches the children?" my mother asked.

"I do, mostly. Or when I was going to school, I'd leave them with the girl downstairs."

My mother wondered if she should ask more, but child care was not on her list of questions and it seemed like prying to inquire further. "Well, maybe we should start," she said. Clearing her throat, she began reading aloud the lines typed under the heading "Instructions to Participant": "These are all questions about family relations—how you and your family work as a unit. Answer them as honestly and completely as you can. Remember, there are no right or wrong answers."

Jackie rubbed Brandon's back with her free hand. Denise sucked on the fuzzy key-ring ball. "What's *relations* mean?" Jackie asked.

My mother struggled to find a way to explain. "You know," she said, "it's like relationship, how people get along."

Jackie looked bored already. "Sounds okay. I'm just gonna put the baby down first." Jackie got up with Brandon and walked toward the back of the apartment. The music stopped and then my mother heard the familiar rattling of crib rails lifting.

When Jackie returned, she took the cigarettes out from her shirt pocket, turned the pack over, and tapped another one out.

"All righty," my mother said, embarrassed at how unnatural her voice seemed. (Something about the way that *all righty* came out, my mother told me, sounded like the Mr. Rogers imitations your brother used to do. Do you remember? He'd tease you, going on and on in that singsong voice, until you were so overexcited you'd start to cry or pee in your pants.) "Could you list for me the members of your family?"

Jackie took a drag on her cigarette and blew out three silvery rings. "Well," she said, "there's my gram and my two sisters, but they're both out of the house. And then my brother, but we're not sure where he's at."

"Anyone else who lives here?"

"No. Sometimes my uncle sleeps over, but that's not too much. And my kids."

Jackie looked at Denise. Her face softened. *She really is awfully pretty*, my mother thought about Jackie. As though sensing the shift in her mother's mood, Denise went over to her. She rested her head on her mother's knee. Jackie leaned down to pick up the child. She cuddled Denise in her lap.

When my mother finished writing down what Jackie had said, she moved on to the second question. "Who do you turn to when there's an emergency?"

"An emergency," Jackie repeated.

My mother could hear Brandon starting to cry. For a moment she thought about telling Jackie that probably he needed a clean diaper after having drunk that bottle, but then she realized that Jackie would, of course, know this.

"Hold on." Jackie put Denise down on the chair and walked to the back.

My mother looked over at Denise. She was reaching a hand toward Jackie's still-burning cigarette.

My mother jumped up. "No, no. Cigarettes aren't for children." She put out the cigarette and carried the child and the soggy key ring that had slipped out of her mouth over to the couch.

The crying stopped and Jackie returned.

"I put out your cigarette. I was afraid Denise would burn herself."

"Thanks." Jackie patted her shirt pocket and pulled out the cigarette pack. She turned it upside down, but nothing came out. "Shit." She covered her lips. "Pardon my filthy mouth." She sniffed, wiggled her nose, and looked around the room as though willing more cigarettes to appear.

"You mind if I run to the corner and get a pack?"

My mother wondered if it was against the rules for her to be in the apartment without Jackie, but it was hard to think of what or whose rules and it seemed silly to say no. "Sure," my mother said. "No problem."

Jackie took a jacket from a nail near the door. When Denise

spied her mother with her hand on the bolt, she wailed. "You stay with the nice lady," Jackie said. "I'll be right back."

Denise's wails turned to shrieks.

"Jesus, this kid's driving me nuts." She picked up the screaming child. "Okay, okay, I'll take you."

Jackie turned to my mother. "Brandon's out cold, but if he starts to cry, his bottle's on the dresser next to the bed."

My mother nodded.

Jackie zipped the jacket so Denise was swaddled inside. "I won't be but five minutes."

•

In fact, my mother's coming home was not the way my father's look that night suggested. She moved into the house the way a boarder might, taking the guest room, bringing only a few things with her: a trunk of clothing, two boxes of books, her typewriter. (She had, by then, decided to get her PhD in social work and was at work on the dissertation—a comparative study of the relationship between the availability of an array of social services and infant mortality in thirty-six countries.) She and my father talked to each other politely. Could he move the television into my room? she asked. Perhaps she might like to look in the attic for some rain boots? he wondered.

By the end of the first week, my mother and I fell into a routine. I'd wake to the sound of her typing or her chair making a squeaking sound against the floor, as she got up from the card table she'd set up as a desk, in search of a book. She'd break to bring me cereal and juice. At two, she'd stop writing and we'd have lunch together—me in bed, she seated in the armchair my father had carried into my room. After lunch, my mother would wash the dishes, change the sheets on my bed while I took a shower, bathe herself, and then, in the dove afternoon light, we'd talk.

While we talked, my mother knit—first a vest for my brother, then a scarf for me, and, in the last month, a pair of yellow booties. I'd never seen my mother knit, hadn't even known she knew how. My mother smiled when I told her this. How could you, she said, I haven't knit since I was pregnant with you. I knit matching hats for you and Louisa. Of course, I didn't know that my sister and I were both having girls, we didn't do amniocenteses in those days, so I made them both yellow like these. After that, with two young children, there was hardly time to brush my teeth. And then, well, I lost interest.

It was my mother who always determined how long these conversations would last, sometimes half an hour, sometimes two or three, the house growing dim around us. There seemed to be no pattern to when my mother would signal the end—stretching her thin arms over her head, arching her back, rolling her neck, and then saying, depending upon the hour, I better get to the store before it's too late, or, My goodness, your father will be home any minute, time to start dinner—and I'd be left, still flat on my back, to think over the things my mother slowly told me.

•

We circled backward and forward—backward to my mother's childhood in Hartford, she and her sister left to entertain each other while their mother retreated with her migraines to a room with the dusty velvet curtains drawn closed. Their father had worked as an insurance actuary, thirty-nine years with the same company and *never* a sick day, a point, my mother said, he often repeated, as though the mere fact were a virtue. He'd insisted upon no talk during meals due to his belief that silence aided digestion.

We circled forward to my mother's Berkeley life and her new friends, each quirkier than the next, in whom my mother seemed to take pride, and then back to the numb, really desperate, my mother said, state she'd been in when she'd left my father five years before.

My mother looked up from her knitting. It was May and the sweet, tickly smell of lawns cut for the first time of the season wafted in through the open window. I was in my seventh month, my legs swollen like zucchinis left too long on the vine.

Of course, my mother said, I didn't realize then that I was depressed. *Clinically* depressed, as my friend Harold would say. I just thought I was losing my mind. I felt like I was someone else, like I was floating above looking down at this other woman scooping food onto plates. It got so bad, I'd wait for you and your brother and father to leave in the mornings so I could crawl under the desk in your father's study, all balled up with my arms hugging my knees, trying to squeeze back into my body.

In my eighth month, I began bleeding again and the doctor banned even bathroom trips. I wept when he told me that I would have to give up this last thread of autonomy: the toilet and shower to be replaced by bedpans and sponge baths. Driving home with my mother, me lying on the back seat, still sniffling, I complained that I felt like a junked refrigerator.

A beached whale, my mother countered from the front seat.

A paralyzed elephant.

Mount St. Helens, she said.

That eight-hundred-pound man who could only leave his apartment lifted out the window by a crane.

Although my mother managed the bedpans with no more fuss than she did my trays of dishes, although she knew not to talk as she sponged the lower half of my body, beyond my mountainous belly and out of my sight, it felt, nonetheless, like a terrible intrusion. Perhaps in recompense, I began asking her bolder questions, which she, perhaps also in recompense, seemed to feel obliged to answer.

Do you have a lover? I asked on a hot June afternoon.

My mother reached for one of the tall glasses of herbal tea. Ice clinked as pink splotches of embarrassment rose above the neckline of the old football T-shirt of Jay's she was wearing. Not now, she said. But I did.

Before you left Dad?

No, after.

And then, on another afternoon, Did you love Dad when you got married?

Of course, she said. Of course I did. My mother paused as though trying to remember. She ran her fingers through her hair. Her lids fluttered. Your father was terribly handsome and bright and filled with promise. Like a young Jack Kennedy.

When did you stop loving him?

She squinted as though peering through time. I don't think I stopped loving *him*, she said. I just stopped loving.

My cheeks burned with nearly unbearable suspicion: My mother hadn't come home to take care of me. She'd come home to make me, roped to this bed, listen to her explanations for why she'd left. My temples throbbed. I closed my eyes, the thought dissolving, like a drop of colored oil in a pool of water, into the pounding in my head.

When? I asked the next day. When did you stop loving?

My mother furrowed her brow. Her hands rested on the yellow booties, done except for the heels. Your father thought it was when my sister died. But the truth is, it was long before.

When? I demanded.

You were five, she said. In kindergarten. Your brother was eight.

•

After Jackie left, my mother sat perfectly still as though there were a store camera pointed at her, watching what she would do.

Don't move, my mother thought, and then, *That's ridiculous,* but still she felt odd as she got up. Just stretching my legs, she said to herself as she headed toward the back of the apartment.

It was a railroad flat with two small bedrooms behind the front room where my mother had been, and then a kitchen and bathroom at the rear. The first bedroom was small, with a linoleum floor and a window that faced brick. There were two single beds, a dresser, and a curtain rod mounted between the side of the dresser and the wall for hanging clothes. From the items that hung there—plaid shirtwaists, two white uniforms like nurses' aides or cafeteria workers wear, a nightgown, some cardigan sweaters—it seemed like the clothing of an older woman, probably Jackie's grandmother, Faith. In the back bedroom there was a crib where Brandon lay and a mattress where, my mother supposed, either Jackie or Denise must sleep.

I was so taken up in those days, my mother said, with the struggles with your father about his belief in a natural division of labor between men and women, I think I was looking for clues to bring home about how they lived together, Faith and Jackie. Who was in control? Who decided who'd bathe the children, or did it just happen: the children cried, wet their pants, got dirty, and someone then scrubbed or did not scrub a tub before drawing water?

In the kitchen, my mother opened the refrigerator: milk, cookies, peanut butter, a plate covered with wax paper with what looked like chicken underneath. In the bathroom, she opened the cabinet, examining the vials and reading the prescription labels. She cracked the smoked window and peered into the alley of trash cans, the acrid odor floating up to the top floor. She closed the window and went back to the room where Brandon lay in the crib.

My mother felt dirty, as if she needed to scrub grime from behind her ears and soot from the bony protrusions of her ankles. She could hear her mother instructing her the first time she'd spent the night at a girlfriend's house, *Don't touch anything, don't open any of the people's drawers, don't snoop*, as she leaned down to look at Brandon, to inspect him too.

The baby lay facedown. He was perfectly quiet. *He's small*, my mother thought, *really very small for three months.* Hardly bigger than her own children had been as newborns.

My mother put her hands on Brandon's sides to pick him up. Lifting him, it was as though he had no muscle tonus, as though only the part of him that touched her fingers yielded, the rest heavy and limp.

Not until my mother had Brandon turned toward her and fully in her arms, his head resting on her breastbone, did she realize she could not feel or hear his breath. Her heart pounded, hard, hard, as she jerked Brandon away from her body until at arms length she could see his open motionless eyes. *Oh my God, oh my God, oh my God*, she heard herself saying, and then she pulled Brandon back to her chest and began banging on his little birdcage of a back, small sharp thumps with the flat of her hand.

There was still no breath.

Holding the baby tight to her chest, my mother ran to the front room. She pressed her nose to the window, *Please, please, Jackie, be there in the street, on the stoop, footsteps on the stairs*, but there was no Jackie and then my mother remembered that there was no phone. She dropped to her knees, laying the baby on the floor, and tried to breathe into his mouth, her thumb pumping the spot she best guessed to be near his tiny heart in vague memory of a lifesaving course she had taken years before when she was pregnant with my brother.

My mother could not say how long it was that she knelt over Brandon, her mouth over his, whether it was two minutes or five, only that her breath floated up over her cheeks, bathing her own face, the baby refusing to drink in her air, and that at one point she jumped up, grabbed her raincoat from the couch, wrapped it around and around Brandon, and ran down the stairs.

She screamed when she reached the street, "Help! Help!" but, whereas before it had seemed like there were people everywhere, now there was only a little girl bouncing a ball.

"Telephone, I need a telephone, an ambulance," she yelled at the girl, but the girl looked at her uncomprehendingly, picked up her ball, and ran.

My mother clutched Brandon to her and ran too. Wrapped in the raincoat, he felt more like a sack of flour or a bag of gardening soil than a baby. She ran to Lexington, short mincing steps in her pumps and narrow skirt, panting from the pressure in her lungs and the weight of the baby in her arms, a small sound like a whimper or a yelp coming from her throat.

At the corner, she paused to look, and then ran left toward a storefront.

Jackie will be there, my mother thought, *Jackie will be there hanging out in the store, smoking cigarettes and joking with the other young people. She will take Brandon, unwrap him from the raincoat, and once in his mother's arms, he will breathe.*

But there was no Jackie inside the store, only the smell of rolls warming in golden lines on bakers' trays laid out under a picture of Jesus, cases of cakes decorated with pink and yellow and blue sugar roses, a small crowd of people waiting for cups of coffee mixed with steamed milk and rolls stuffed with melted orange cheese.

"An ambulance," my mother cried. "Please, please call an ambulance."

The woman behind the counter wiped her hands on her hips, shook her head, and stared at my mother.

"Ambulance, I need an ambulance," my mother half panted, half screamed.

The woman lifted her hands so her brown palms were revealed and her fingers pointed at my mother. "No speakes English," she said. She rubbed her hands together, and little torrents of flour fell through the air. "No speakes English," she repeated, shaking her head slowly from side to side and then tapping her lips with her floury fingers.

My mother leaned against the counter to steady herself. A man in worker's garb pushed toward her. "Miss, miss," he said, "what's the problem?"

"The baby. He's not breathing." My mother stared at the clock on the wall. Everything felt slowed down and speeded up all at once. Mostly what she was aware of was that too much time was passing. She started to cry. Brandon no longer felt human. She had the fleeting thought of setting him down amid the napkin dispensers and the boxes of coffee stirrers and running out the bakery door.

The man touched her arm. "Lady, lady, calm down. It takes a very long time for an ambulance to come to this neighborhood. It is better to go right to the hospital."

The man pointed. My mother followed his finger with her eyes. "This way. Up two blocks. Then you turn left."

No one, not the man, not the lady, was going to take over. They weren't going to take the baby from her. *He's one of yours*, she wanted to cry, *you take him*, but instead she ran. Out the door, with Brandon still wrapped in her raincoat. Lexington to Park. Park to Madison. Everything's okay, she repeated over and over as she ran, a blister now burning on her heel. Everything's okay, okay, okay. He's just asleep. *Dear God*, she prayed, *let him just be deep in sleep.*

At Madison, my mother turned left. Ahead of her, she could see the hospital marquee and then green arrows for the emergency room. A fleet of red-and-white ambulances sat silently in the circular drive.

Once inside, my mother halted: a blur of signs and lights, a television bracketed to the ceiling. People with bandages on their arms and ice packs on their ankles, and one man with a patch on his eye peered up at a game show.

There was a drum roll, and the game show host was asking, Will the real Someone-or-other please stand up? while the camera zoomed in on three men, all dressed in what looked like mechanics' garb. The man to the left stood, Brandon a lump inside the raincoat, and then my mother screamed. Pure sound, voice swimming through larynx, panic transmuted into tone, my mother screamed over and over until the security guard and a nurse rushed her, the nurse grabbing the bundle of raincoat and baby, pulling Brandon's cold, stiff body out from inside, and then the nurse's voice rising over my mother's, "Code Blue, ER waiting room, Code Blue."

•

The casework instructor volunteered to attend the funeral with my mother, but the night before the funeral my mother bolted out of sleep with a terrible nausea. From then until dawn, she vomited, more food than it seemed she could have possibly consumed during the three days since Brandon's death ("Most likely, he was dead before you found him," the doctor had told her at the emergency room), and by morning it was clear that the stomach virus would prevent the train trip from Dobbs Ferry to Grand Central and then the subway ride to the church on Third Avenue and 107th Street. Afraid there would be no delivery to Jackie's apartment, my mother sent flowers to the church—an arrangement of white lilies ordered through FTD.

Lying on the living room couch, music from the classical station blanketing the room, a cold drizzle dotting the bay window, my mother told herself that she would visit Jackie the following week and that, in fact, they would be better able then to talk about Brandon and what had happened when the police took my mother back to 105th Street to find Jackie after Brandon had been declared dead, about Jackie smashing her fist on the side of the police car and my mother then holding the big wailing girl while Denise crouched by the rear door, her thumb in her mouth, urine running down her legs.

But the following week and then the weeks after that, my mother said, things kept coming up. You caught my stomach virus and were home from school—her words jogging my memory so that vaguely, vaguely, some dusty brain cell firing after fourteen years on the shelf, I remembered coming into the living room, where my mother lay on the couch, her eyes fixed on the huge glass window, afraid to let her know that my stomach felt funny and my head hurt. Then it was Thanksgiving and the trip to your grandparents'.

The dean of the social work school gave my mother a leave of absence for the remainder of the term, allowing her to take incompletes in her courses until the spring. The week before Christmas, my mother mailed a red hooded jacket with white fur on the edges of the hood and the cuffs of the sleeves for Denise and a card with a hundred-dollar check inside for Jackie. The check was cashed but Jackie never wrote back.

On the first day of the spring term, my mother dressed in wool slacks and a sweater and packed the maroon tote with her notebooks and an umbrella. I remember standing in the foyer, my mother said (pointing at the floor to make sure I realized that she meant here, in this house where I'd been flat on my back by then for three months), looking at the front door, unable to bring myself to push it open and go outside.

My mother stared at the heavy wooden front door, at the frozen lawn with its patches of grimy snow, and then at the accoutrements of the front hall—the mahogany table she had inherited from her grandmother, the beveled mirror she and my father had found in a Poughkeepsie antique store shortly after they were married and then paid an exorbitant amount to have refinished, my yellow rubber boots, my brother's ice hockey stick. She stood there for a long time looking, it seemed, at her life of little contentments, satisfaction and dissatisfaction perfectly balanced for that one morning moment, thinking about Jackie and Denise and Brandon. I hung up my coat, my mother concluded, stashed the tote under the mahogany table, took off my pearl earrings, telephoned the dean's office, and withdrew from school.

My mother smiled—a sad, wry, self-deprecating but knowing gesture that seemed to contain all of her then-forty-five and my nineteen years. We looked at each other, my belly and how little I'd known about her rising between us. I rested my hands on my stomach. My baby would know even less about me, only what the childless couple from New York themselves knew— that I was a college student who couldn't, no, wouldn't raise a child—and it was only then that I realized that I'd decided to do it, to give up my baby.

My face buckled and my eyes filled. All I remember, I said, is your face, lying there on the couch.

My mother nodded. She took my hand and stroked it from wrist to fingertip, as though my hand were something separate, a wounded thing. Tears slid off my cheeks, dampening my neck. I wiped my nose on my shoulder.

Well, she said, you were very young. Only five. Then, *whoosh*, my mother was up, the yellow booties dropping from her hands onto the chair as she mumbled something about the store and dinner.

•

My father made a respectable attempt to discuss with my mother her decision to drop out of school, but my mother could sense that secretly he was relieved. She stirred a leek bisque, a recipe she'd clipped from the Sunday magazine, while he queried her, answering each question matter-of-factly but briefly.

Within a few weeks, my mother resumed what she'd come during her eight years of motherhood to think of as her life: tennis twice a week, an occasional coffee with a friend or neighbor, involvement in various of her children's activities (a rummage sale for my ballet school, rotating driver for my brother's ice hockey team).

Still, the other mothers noticed changes. She'd lost weight— the pear bottom gone—and the gray had begun to overtake the brown in her hair. They envied the thinness. How had she done it? A diet center, a powdered shake mixed in the blender, an exercise machine bought mail-order? My father suggested a rinse for her hair. My mother bought new clothes, a size she hadn't worn since college, but she kept the gray in her hair and stopped using curlers to make it flip up at the ends.

Sometimes, in the middle of the night or during a shower, my mother would be seized with the thought that what she must do was leave my father. Looking at the French lace curtains that hung in their bedroom or the floral wallpaper that covered their bathroom, she would yearn for a simple room, whitewashed, with a mat on the floor and a bamboo shade, a room where there would be no objects to tend and her mind would be free. *To do what?* she would think, but then my mother would draw a blank and she would think of her children and how, with their toys and their books and their kicked-off shoes, no room could ever be spare like the monks' quarters she'd seen in a book.

A week or two before I went into labor, both of us worn out from the July heat during which I sweated so badly that sponge baths and a change of sheets morning and night were required, my mother told me she'd had the thought during those first months after Brandon's death that it would have been easier, more just, if it had been her own child who had been taken. (Seconds after saying this, my mother startled, as though she'd just realized to whom she was talking.) My mother continued: I would feel overcome with guilt. Dear God, I would say, I didn't mean that, please don't think that's what I want. Thank you, dear God, for sparing me and mine.

At other times, more often than not during a domestic moment, her family circled around the oak kitchen table, my brother, my father, and I excited and all talking at once, a pan of lasagna or a roast in the center, my mother would feel a vague anxiety, as though she might be punished for having wished for something heightened: years ago, for something different between my father and her; more recently, for an involvement with something outside herself or her family. For having been gluttonous for life. Wandering through the house after we were all asleep, wiping off counters, picking up toys, she would wonder, even though she knew it was illogical, if it had been her greed that had led to Brandon's death.

When the leaves began to fall, Dobbs Ferry turning gold and orange and red, my mother became aware that she had been tracking time as the days passed since Brandon died, with the approach of one year bringing an increased sense of dread and an accelerating feeling that she should take some kind of action.

At night, after you and Jay were in bed, my mother told me, I took to pouring brandy into a snifter, wrapping myself in an old blanket, and then moving outside to sit in one of the Adirondack chairs at the far edge of the lawn.

For a long time, my mother said, I stuck to that one snifter of brandy every night. Then, that last year before I left, it crept up—two, then three snifters before bed. Your brother, I'm sure, had noticed.

My mother sighed. For a moment, I thought it was about some conundrum concerning the nearly finished yellow booties.

What would Dad say? I asked.

Oh, your father was hardly ever home. And he'd long lost patience with me. Time to let it go, he said to me around the time of the second anniversary. Time to let go of this obsession with those people. The kid died. These things happen.

•

Once, near the end of my pregnancy when I was too big to sleep well, I woke in the middle of the night to hear something that sounded like groans and creaks coming from my father's room. A few moments later, a toilet flushed and I thought I heard my mother's voice. If so, if indeed my parents had resumed love-making during my mother's stay, in the end it didn't change anything between them in a permanent way.

I had the baby, a girl, at five o'clock on a Sunday morning. I saw her for only a few minutes. Then she was gone.

•

I named my daughter Brianna. When my mother asked me what name I'd put on the birth certificate, her eyes welled and I could hear her in her mind whispering the two namesakes: Brandon and her sister, Anna.

A few days after I left the hospital my mother flew back to Berkeley, and in the fall I returned to Yale. Because I'd left school before I had begun to really show, all but my closest friends assumed I'd been on a semester abroad or some such thing.

That first year, I woke every morning at four. Lying in my dorm room bed, Miriam lightly snoring across the hall, I would wonder why I'd given up my daughter. It wasn't as though either of my parents had pushed me to do so. It wasn't as though a Yale degree were a necessity. Then I'd feel a surge of anger at my mother for having told me about Brandon, as though learning about his death had tipped the scales.

Did she think we owed a baby back?

Did she put the yellow booties on my baby's feet or have the social worker hand them over with the paperwork?

The nice couple from New York—it was a long time before I could call them her parents—wrote me that they had decided to keep the name I'd chosen so that later in life, if Brianna were to decide to meet me, they and I would both know her by the same name. In the only letter I ever sent them, forwarded to them by my father's law partner, I wrote that when they thought Brianna was old enough to understand, I hoped they would tell her that I would always love her and always welcome seeing her but that I would leave it to her to make that decision.

The summer after I graduated, my father remarried—a stylish (but I thought hardened) woman in her thirties who was an associate at his firm. A couple of months later, my brother followed suit, eloping with a Brazilian model whose parents opposed the marriage due to Jay not being a Catholic. My mother finished her degree and took a faculty position in the school of social work at Sacramento State.

After two years kicking around at odd jobs in various parts of the country—editing a trade publication for the Idaho Association of Plumbing Supplies Distributors, keeping the books for an ostrich-breeding farm outside of Austin, teaching English as a second language at a Korean community center in Spokane—I came back East to go to law school. I direct a program that runs halfway houses for women with chronic mental disabilities. We pride ourselves on finding them meaningful work and fostering in the houses a sense of family. As for what my alumni fund questionnaire calls my "personal life," I live with a man who has an odd sleep disorder such that he sleeps during the day and stays awake all night. He supports himself on the interest from a trust fund and is working on a book on probability theory and games of chance. Our living room is stacked with DVDs of people playing roulette and blackjack.

Until Brianna was fifteen, I received a letter from her parents every Christmas. In their last letter, they told me that Brianna played on a travel soccer team, sang in her school choir, and loved to read. In the summer, they would go to Italy. They planned to show Brianna my letter around her birthday, and after that it would be up to her if she wanted to be in touch with me.

Although my brother and I both followed our father into the practice of law, my mother is fond of remarking how much my brother is my father's son—the implication being that I have in some way taken after her. It's not that I'm dismayed that she is, in fact, right (the area of law that I practice is essentially social work) but rather that I am troubled that this is so—troubled that those fourteen years the four of us lived together could have set the direction of either my brother's or my pursuits.

None of us have had more babies.

1975

Louisa Meets Bear

We meet awash in a Princeton drizzle, the fountain turned off for the winter, the lights dripping yellow in the grayness, everything a stately concrete or gargoyle Gothic. You are with James, that sickly boy who with his dirty oversized sweaters fancies himself a typhoid poet. Always before when I've spotted you, you've been in a horde of muscular boys like yourself—boys who play on sports teams and are so loud about everything that they leave me sometimes intimidated by their mass and sheer beauty, their hair wet from showers and glossy as horse hide, and sometimes, I must admit, filled with disdain (the old brains-versus-brawn thing)—so that it surprises me to see you with James, whom I know only for his incomprehensible poems with their references to T. S. Eliot and the Greek dramatists, the footnotes often three or four times longer than the verse.

What I will most remember about you this night is how you try to smell me through the dusky drizzle, your nostrils distended with the effort, and how I am certain you must be able to detect the scent of Professor Boyd plastered between my legs. Later, when I tell you about him, you grow angry. "Louisa, the guy's a pervert," you say, unable to grasp that Boyd, the nearsighted academic rising star whose op-ed pieces on geopolitics have twice

appeared in the *Times* this past year, had been less spider than
fly, and that I, interested both in the marijuana he offered and
what would be my first experience with a married man, un-
zipped my own jeans.

•

It takes you two days to find me after that night. I know that you
are looking. I don't hide, but neither do I help. Instead, I frequent my usual reading spots—a green couch in the basement
of the art library, a leather chair in the back room of the Eastern
Studies collection. You find me in the leather chair. You lower
yourself into its mate. Between us are my diet soda can and a
bag of red licorice. "You don't make it easy," you say.

I like that you don't pretend to be looking for a book on
Buddhism in Chinese history. I like that when I offer you my
red licorice, you take a whole handful and then another while
we talk, first about whatever we have in common, that being
mostly James, the roommate assigned you your first year, he a doctor's son from a gentleman's farm in Virginia, you a plumber's son
from a Cincinnati row house.

When you ask about me, where I sprang from is the way
you put it, I tell you about my father. A "biomedical scientist" is
how I describe him. You look slightly lost.

"Genes. The chemical directions on how to build a person.
Adenine, thymine, guanine, cytosine."

I stop there because that's about as much as I know about
what my father does in his San Francisco laboratory. What I
mostly know is the way the fog settles into the pocket where the
hospital lies so that taking the bus with my father east to our
sunny Mission District home is like changing seasons. "Micro-
climate," my father calls it, cheek to window as he studies how
the clouds catch on the ocean side of the telegraph tower. I could
describe where my father's office is in the corridor of laboratories, a skull-and-bones sign posted on the door, the acrid metal-

lic smell that hovers over the beakers, counters, and various, always ticking, measurement dials. But I can't explain what it is that my father researches, only that I think about it as unveiling the machinery in the magic, the molecules that make your eyes look like a deer's and mine the pale green, you later tell me, of leaves yet unfurled.

"Think about Dorothy pulling back the curtain on that old geezer who made the Emerald City," I say when you inquire further. "It's something like that."

What you tell me about your father, *my old man* you call him, which seems at first awful but then kind of wonderful, is about a shrapnel wound during World War II, a scar that cuts from under his armpit to close to his heart, and a time, fifteen years or so ago, before he found God and started going to mass every Sunday, when he drank too much. I ask if he resents it, your coming east to this fancy place, and you say mostly he thinks about it as a character flaw in you that you'd spend four years sucking up to rich people. It's your brother-in-law, you say, who knows enough to really resent you, having gambled on an ice hockey career instead of college and then coming up empty-handed when his back gave out before he turned twenty-five.

"And what made you the frog-prince?" I ask.

"Celia Healding, whose old man was an alum and sent the recruiter my specs."

"Celia Healding?"

"In Cincinnati, if you're Ohio All-State, the rich girls give you rides in their cars."

•

When I call Corrine, my best friend from San Francisco who lives out by the beach with her two-year-old daughter, Lily, and her jazz drummer and cocaine addict boyfriend, Alfie, she says, "Bear, what kind of name is that?"

"His real name is William. William Callahan. But his friends,

I don't even know if they're really his friends, all these guys he knows, that's what they call him."

"He sounds like a jock. An Irish jock."

"His mother's parents came from Sicily. His father's father was born in Ireland. The jock thing, that's his meal ticket. How he got here. Like Alfie playing weddings."

"So where can he take you?" This is Corrine's and my special question, the question we have asked each other about the boys and then men each of us have had in our lives since we began to realize that something about our necks and breasts did something to the rate of their heartbeats such that we could get them to do things for us. At first, when Corrine wore her blond hair so it touched her waist, her face the kind you'd see drawn in a children's book in pale watercolors, me with dark hair and the air of something mysterious (Italian? Arabic? boys would ask), we had meant the question literally.

"He has a car," Corrine would say. "We drove to the top of Twin Peaks and just sat there, looking out at the lights."

"He has a motorcycle," I'd say. "He's going to take me to Point Reyes."

Later, "Where can he take you?" meant what can he show you. "He's into acid," I remember Corrine telling me about this skinny guy with a ponytail and a squinty way of looking at people. "He knows these guys who make it out of Menlo Park, but the way they do it, it's not really drugs but more like a religious experience." Or it might have been me saying, "He's older. He had a girlfriend he lived with for a while. He reads poetry and talks about writers I never even heard of before."

About you, I pause. It's hard to put into words for Corrine where you will take me. I imagine Corrine curled on her bed, the TV on without the sound, books piled on the crate at her side, Lily's toys strewn like bread crumbs across the floor.

"Don't tell me it's something stupid like sex," Corrine says.

"No, it's not that. We haven't got there yet. It's something about purpose. It's almost old-fashioned—kind of the way I imagine my father having made himself a scientist, determinedly moving himself from one world into another. You can feel it in him, like something chugging. We don't have that. Your parents will always be richer than you. I'll be lucky if I do half as well as my father. Does that make sense?"

"Best I can make out, the guy's a goddamned race car."

•

You have a red VW that has no heat. You take me for Chinese food at a place outside of town. You drive with the window open and only a sweater, and I am too timid, too ashamed to tell you how cold I am, my toes clenched, my shoulders hunched so my arms can steal some of the warmth from my chest. I don't tell you that I barely know how to drive, that watching you shift gears, drink a Coke, fiddle with the radio, and wind us through the back roads to the highway, all I can think of is I must be missing some gene you have—that whereas I have learned from my perpetually lost father to transpose spatial relations into words ("Let's see," he would say as we stood at a street corner ten blocks from our house, "I think we made a right here at this burrito place"), you move with an internal map of your body through space, your limbs generating their own heat.

At the restaurant, you cup my stiff hands between yours, and rub. "You have no blood," you say. You keep my hands pocketed inside your own while you tell me about your afternoon drinking scotch with the Ivy Club members who are recruiting you.

I raise my eyebrows.

"Working-class boy comes to the country club," you say, and even though I disapprove of the eating clubs, many of which don't admit women and one of which, I was told, hung a blow-up of my photo from the freshman directory as one of the top ten coeds of the year (Screw them, Corrine said, only losers waste their time going through those books, but it had left me humiliated, like one of those dreams in which you realize you're walking around without any pants), it tickles me to think of you breaking into the ranks of these pale and anemic third- and fourth-generation Princeton men with their land-grant Virginia and Connecticut families.

"I made first string this year, that's why," you say. "They always take one football player. It's affirmative action for jocks."

Your laugh sounds like an engine rumbling, and I understand why the Ivy boys are courting you: so that they, self-conscious and mannered like me, might imbibe something about you, about your uncomplicated maleness, about the way you stretch out on the couch with an arm crooked behind your neck when you watch TV and yell, "Go, baby, you got it!" at the players on the screen, the way you drive a car as though it were an extension of you, the way your outside and inside coincide. Rumor has it that there are entire departments of investment banks that are all Ivy men, and I know that for you, being admitted into their circle is more valuable than an inheritance. The advantages will go on and on.

You bite into a spring roll. Still chewing, you lift my hand to under your nose and inhale. "God, you smell good," you say.

•

It's a Saturday night, a month later, and we've gone on my suggestion to see *Last Year at Marienbad*. You're still on good behavior with me—we've not yet slept together—but I can feel your irritation at the pretentiousness of the audience, everyone jammed together on metal folding chairs, pretending they understand what the trancelike actions of the characters signify and the meaning of the mathematical game, which I recognize from my father as Nim, that they play.

Walking back, we both know that we're headed into bed. You've told me that James is visiting a girl in Philadelphia; I've not told you that I'm not a virgin, that Corrine and I have gathered an anthology of sexual adventures, often reported to each other with greater relish than we had in the acts themselves—she, being four years older than I, having more entries, but I, with Boyd, having held my own.

Your room comes as a disappointment, not the room itself but that you have no aptitude for creating an environment. I think of Corrine's and my theory: a man who does not appreciate color, who cannot arrange objects so they create balance in a room, will have no talent for sex.

You motion me to sit on the edge of a bed dressed with a nappy blue blanket and brown plaid sheets while you pour wine into paper cups. You sit next to me. I make a show of sipping a few times. You take two gulps, put your empty cup on the floor, and lean over me, pushing my shoulders backward, your mouth covering mine. For a moment I am stunned by the size and weight of you, but soon there is so much commotion, your hands under my sweater, my hands on your belt, that I stop focusing on the mass of you.

"Condom," I whisper, thinking of my cousin Lizzy, pregnant her very first time, she told me, shaking her head in disbelief.

You reach for the bedside stand, fumble with what sounds like the wrapper. Then you go soft. I panic. I am losing you. I can't track what you are doing, only that you are trying and trying, rough waves crashing against me, and it is a relief when finally you roll onto your back.

It's dark but still you shield your eyes with your hands. "Jesus," you say. "I feel like such a pussy."

I pull the sheet over me and move onto my side. Propped up on an elbow, I kiss and kiss the knuckles of your hands.

"This has never happened to me before."

You turn your back to me.

I run my fingers across your shoulder blades—big, beautiful angel's wings. "Shhh," I say, "shhh."

"All I've been able to think about for weeks is how much I want you. It was too much to actually have you here."

I wrap my arms around you and spoon myself behind you. I imagine you are my baby and I can hold you inside of me.

"It was strange," I say to Corrine the next day over the phone. "But I liked that he lost it. It made me feel that I mattered to him."

"You're a weird one," Corrine says. "What happened after that?"

"He fell asleep. I dozed off after a while. Then in the morning we tried again."

"And?"

"That decorating aptitude–sex talent theory—wrong, wrong, wrong."

•

By spring, we are playing married. I am nineteen and you are twenty; we embrace the idea for that reason. You buy a double mattress for your room and we move the dorm bed into the hall. When summer arrives, we rent an apartment in New Brunswick and cart the double mattress up four flights of stairs. You get a job in a lipstick factory, a gig, you call it, that one of your coaches arranged. I tutor two little boys, one a whiner, the other a screamer, both dumb but rich. You buy us a hibachi. I learn how to grill eggplant brushed with olive oil.

In August, we go to San Francisco even though at the last minute my father calls to say he is off to Argentina that week.

"Something's come up," my father says mysteriously.

"What?"

"I have to help a friend with some matters in Buenos Aires."

"A friend?"

"Well," my father says, "a lady friend. Her mother just died, and she needs to wrap up her financial affairs. It's a big mess. I said I'd help her straighten it out."

It seems useless to complain. I did a lot of that with my aunt, my mother's sister, when she first moved to Oakland and would take me or Corrine and me most Sundays to brunch. Enough that I now understand the complaints only confuse my father. Instead, I ask the lady friend's name. "Juanita. She's an urban anthropologist. She just published a book on the street children of Buenos Aires."

We stay at my father's house. You are fascinated by your glimpses of him: the First Nations wood carvings he brought back from Alaska, the fossils from Mongolia, his study with floor-to-ceiling books and a library ladder. That there is no TV. Snooping around, I see women's clothing in my father's closet (bright silks, a size ten, bigger than I am) and a vial of an expensive eye cream on the medicine cabinet shelf.

Although my father has left the house unchanged since my mother's death, her presence has been blurred by the slow accretion of his clutter: papers piled on the dining room table, a beach chair stashed next to the sofa, cans stacked on the kitchen counter. Only their, his, bedroom feels the same—the sheer curtains, the rose-colored dhurrie, the white bedspread with the knotted bumps.

We sleep in my father's bed. It is a clear, cool night and the curtains billow in the breeze. My mother lingers near. I realize how little I've told you about her: only that I was nine when she died in a car accident, north of the city.

You rub your nose across the top of my arm. "What are you thinking?" you ask.

I hesitate, unsure if I want to open this door. "About my mother."

"What about her?"

"Right then, when you asked, I was thinking about the day she died. Corrine was my after-school babysitter. She was thirteen." I can see Corrine with her dirty-blond hair caught high in a ponytail. "My mother wanted to hire someone older but I begged for Corrine because she was so pretty and she talked to me about junior high and having boyfriends and the music she and her friends listened to."

You nuzzle my shoulder.

"Corrine was showing me how to paint my toenails. Chinese-red. I remember the phone ringing and Corrine telling me to sit very still so I wouldn't ruin the polish."

I study the hair on your chest, the way it fans out like a spray of water. Not until I was older, maybe thirteen myself and Corrine was no longer my babysitter, did she tell me that my father, weeping on the phone, had blurted out the news to her. "When she came back in, she took a cotton ball and wiped the red off my toes."

There's an image that often comes to mind of my mother. It's from a photo album that's mostly filled with green-tinted pictures of me as a baby. A chubby bundle held high by various adults. Near the back of the album, though, there's a photograph of my mother from the year before I was born. She's crouched by a tree, her eyes raised toward the camera, an expression of full deliberateness on her still-childish face. Her hair is cut in a pageboy, swingy and shiny, her skirt encircling her in the crouch. In the look she gives the camera and my father, who says he took the picture, she is both coy and bold, as though saying to my father, *I know you want me and I know you want me to act like your sweet girl.* When Corrine and I would flip through the album, she would always pause to stare at that picture of my mother with her appearance of innocence and boldness all at once. "What a tease," I once said, afraid that if I didn't say it, Corrine would.

•

Later that week, I take you to visit Corrine. On the bus out to the beach, I try to prepare you. I tell you that Corrine lives in varying intensities of chaos, that she thinks of herself as a painter, sees the world as a tableau in Matisse primary colors, but that aside from the butterflies she painted on Lily's bedroom walls, she rarely actually finishes anything, her apartment littered with canvases in different stages of completion.

Sitting on pillows in Corrine's living room, you surprise me by your obvious disapproval, your pointed silence. Corrine grows nervous, talking more and more. She offers us cocaine. You refuse and then walk out of the room while I partake. Corrine whispers to me, "That Bear of yours, he sure is overbearing." I giggle nervously.

Afterward, we fight. "The chick lives like a slob," you say. "I feel sorry for the kid."

"She's a wonderful mother." My voice sounds tight and closed even to my own ears. "Lily is happy and healthy and open with everyone. Her teacher says she's one of the most empathic children she's ever known."

"Reports who? Corrine?"

That night, you sleep turned away from me. In the morning, I have this idea of homemade English muffins. Not until the ingredients are mixed do I realize that they take an hour to rise. Anxiety I cannot explain creeps in.

The muffins are still rising when you come into the kitchen with a towel wrapped around your middle. Your hair sticks up and you haven't brushed your teeth. You reach for a box of cereal and head to the refrigerator for milk. "I'm making English muffins," I announce.

You pull your hand back from the refrigerator door in an exaggerated gesture and sit down at the table. I pour you a cup of coffee the way you like it, black and sweet, and give you the newspaper. I hull strawberries and scrape the seeds from a cantaloupe.

Ten minutes pass before you shoot me a look.

"A few more minutes," I say. "Then I can put them in the oven."

You roll the paper into a tube and slam the table. Coffee sloshes onto the floor. "Jesus Christ, can't I just have a bowl of cereal? Or do I have to stand on ceremony for this production of yours?"

I start to cry. You get a sponge and wipe up the floor. You lean against the counter with your arms folded across your chest and your chin jutted forward. You seem to be inspecting me: skinny arms and legs poking out of a nightshirt. You shake your head back and forth and glare. "Don't you know how to fight?" you say.

In the fall, we move back onto campus. We both take singles, though mostly we sleep in your room, where you have installed the double bed. I learn to fight back. Sometimes after an argument, you poke me in the ribs and grin. "Good job," you say. "A real contender."

•

When I tell you about Andrew, that I met him on an expedition to New York to visit Juanita, east for her book tour and by then my father's live-in lover, that I had not wanted a man to get up from his café chair to come talk with me, you look at me with disdain. "You fool," you say. "You arrogant little fool. Do you think you're so astounding that men can't control themselves with you? You invite it. You fucking invite it."

Once you say it, I know you are right: there had been something open, available, in the way I held my head while I waited for Juanita, in the way I carefully folded my magazine, crossed my legs, sipped my cappuccino, lit cigarettes. I had watched myself as though I were blown up on a movie screen, twenty times life-sized, lifting my eyelids ever so slightly to glance around the room, careful not to reveal my unfamiliarity with the scene before me, my uncertainty as to how to find my way back to Port Authority should Juanita not arrive—which she did not during the hour before I left with Andrew.

And, if I am honest, I noticed him before he noticed me, recognized in him even though I did not then recognize it in myself that he was posing: a pack of European cigarettes on the table, a copy of *Le Monde* spread out before him, a leather bomber jacket across the back of his chair. I'd seen both that he was posing and that it was an interesting pose, one that Corrine and I might dissect over a long telephone conversation and a string of cigarettes, and now I can see that I must have arched my neck in a way that would have invited a tiger to bite.

Later that night, after Andrew had taken me uptown for Japanese food and then downtown for Brazilian jazz, I called Corrine.

"Did I wake you?"

"No. Lily's been driving me crazy, climbing in and out of my bed. I just got her to sleep."

"I met someone."

"Shoot, girl."

"He's a law student, here in New York, but he grew up in Berkeley. He looks like a California boy, tall and blond, but there's an edge to him. He seems to be always on the road. He spent a year after college running some kind of weavers' collective in Guatemala, though it sounded like there was money in it for him too. This summer he's off to South America. He carries a beeper in his pocket."

When it comes to men, Corrine is a mistress of distinctions. She can talk about men with the same level of refinement that her mother can discuss upholstery. About Andrew, she asked what his hands and shoulders were like and what kind of car he drove. Does he listen? What does he read? What does his father do for a living? She wanted to know if I let him kiss me and what kind of kisser he was.

"Long and thin, broad, an Alfa. How he listens, that's hard to say." I paused to think it over. "I'd say he listens for the gist of things, and he gets that quickly, but he's not too interested in the details. I don't know what his father does, but his mother is a hotshot feminist professor at Berkeley, though maybe there's some kind of family money because he has that rich-kid way about him. The kiss—he didn't ask if he could kiss me, he just did it, but he did it so fast, a brush of the lips and with this air that of course he could kiss me, that it was as though it was nothing."

"Did he pay for your meal? Did he talk about girlfriends?"

"He paid. American Express. No talk about other women, but I'm sure they exist."

"I'll sleep on it," Corrine said. "It's the beeper that's got me. Sounds like a guy with a taste for dirty business."

I was still in bed when Corrine called the next morning. In the background, I could hear Lily asking for cereal and the canned laughter from a children's show. I looked at my clock. It was 11:00, 8:00 a.m. Corrine's time. All I wanted was to get on a plane and sit in Corrine's kitchen, drink coffee, and wait for the fog to break so we could ride over the Golden Gate to the beach, Lily singing in the back seat, a raft sticking out of the trunk.

"You're in big trouble," Corrine said. "He found his way into my dreams. I could see his bomber jacket and there was an Alfa too."

"Why trouble?" I was thinking of you and how long it had been since I had slept alone and how you must be wondering why I didn't come last night to your room.

"You got yourself a heartbreaker. One of those too-dangerous-to-resist guys."

Everything felt stale. My hair smelled of cigarettes. There was dirt under my nails.

"Listen, Louisa, I'm not saying don't go for it, just know what you're doing."

Corrine and I rarely call each other by our first names. It made me sit up and listen. "I'm just going to forget it, a one-night misguided adventure."

Lily was laughing at something.

"Bets are you're already sunk."

●

After you tell me that I am a fool, an arrogant little fool, you punch a wall. We are in bed, in my dorm room, and little pieces of plaster fly onto the sheets. For a moment I think you might punch me too, and even though I know it would break my jaw, I wish that you would, that it would be you hurting me and me being comforted by you instead of you yanking on your jeans, grabbing your keys, and slamming the door.

You are down the stairs before I start to cry. You pretend not to hear me calling, "Bear, Bear," through the open window until it is clear that people walking by are stopping to look up and I have to duck behind the curtain. In that moment, all I want is to take it back, my words that have, you tell me, wiped out all of your happiness in me, in my smell, in my touch, in our talks, in your certainty as you hike from gym to classroom to club that I am yours and the world is right. I want to take it all back, to say it's nothing, truly, nothing. Nothing has happened, just a guy I met in a café, nothing will change, but I know that by evening I will board the train to the city, even more the fool than you know.

A week later, you let yourself into my room with the extra key we had made for you. It's early morning, not quite light, and I am still asleep. I open my eyes and look at your face. I haven't seen you since you punched the wall. Already I have slept with Andrew.

You're wearing a green sweater and in the gray light it looks as though the muscles have wilted from your face. Your mouth is loose and your eyes are drooping. You look post-operative, like someone whose chest has been torn open so a surgeon can tamper with his heart.

You sit on the edge of my bed, and I take your hand. For a long time, we don't talk. I stroke your hand over and over. Then you lay your head on my chest and I stroke the angel wings in your back.

I kiss your hair. You sob, wetting the sheets and my skin. I pull you into the bed with me, shoes and all. I am crying too. When we make love, it is hard to tell which of us is making what kind of sound.

Afterward, you prop yourself on an elbow and study my face. "Your eyes are crooked," you say.

"Thanks for telling me."

"They are. And you have a pimple on your chin." You stare at me as though you are studying a map. "There are a dozen other girls on this campus who'd take up with me in two minutes, a lot of them a hell of a lot less morose than you."

I run my hands over your enormous arms. All you'd have to do to end your misery is press your thumb to my windpipe and snuff out my breath.

"Don't cut me off," you say. "Do what you have to do, but don't cut me off."

I draw you into my arms, spider and prey.

•

It's a hot May day when my father calls to explain about the conference in Helsinki and the paper he's presenting on variations in the architecture of the genetic code and how he must have completely overlooked my graduation when he promised to attend. I hold the phone from my ear as he gives me the details. Outside, everything is a Technicolor green. Two bare-chested boys throw a yellow Frisbee on the lawn. A girl in an apple-red T-shirt reads with her back against a tree. My father has never visited me here, never met you. Listen, you brat, I say to myself. He paid for your four years here. It's too late for a pity party.

I place the phone closer to my ear and wait for a break in my father's stream of words. "Fine, Dad, no problem, no big deal."

"I sent you a little present in the mail. It's not much, but it's the best I can swing for now."

Although you think Andrew buys me the car, I buy it with my father's check, which arrives two days later. On a bulletin board at the Wawa market, I see a file card for a used Datsun wagon, $650. Because I do not want to ask either you or Andrew to drive me to the owner's house eight miles outside of town, I buy the car sight unseen.

The week before graduation, I mail my books and three cartons of winter clothes to Corrine. I call the dean's office and arrange for my diploma to be sent to my father's address. I leave you a note that I am going to Ocean City, Maryland, to look for a job. *Please believe me*, I write. *I am going alone. I hear it's easy to get a job if you get there before Memorial Day. My father canceled coming to graduation and everything has turned so complicated that I no longer want to wear robes and go through the ceremony.* I add, *I love you. I know that sounds crazy but I do.* Then I telephone Andrew, who I think is in Martinique for the week, to leave a message on his machine.

A girl answers the phone. "I'm housesitting for Andy," she says and then giggles. "Is there a message?"

•

I remember only a few things from the three weeks I spend in Ocean City before you arrive. I remember driving in from the north that first night, past the white high-rise condominiums, past the seafood restaurants that line the highway in the center of town, into the original resort of peeling clapboard houses, little stores with umbrellas and beach towels and suntan lotions, and then, at the south side of town, a honky-tonk boardwalk with rides and haunted houses and, at the end, a pier.

I don't remember how I find the room in Mrs. Ford's boardinghouse, whether there is a vacancy sign in the window or an ad in the paper, only that Mrs. Ford is wearing nylon support knee-highs under her sandals, her white hair so wiry you can see each strand. "I'm not going to lie," she says about the room, "it gets hot up here. But then you get the best view in the house." I peer out the small window. In the dark, I can't tell what I am looking at.

"My Harry loved this room the best," Mrs. Ford says. "He'd always say, 'Don't rent that attic one.' Mornings, I'd find him sitting up here staring out, he'd say, at the blue, blue sea."

When I wake, sunshine is splattered over the bed, across the little desk at the window and around the pile of my typewriter, suitcases, satchels, and book bag. In the morning light, I can see that the floor, scrubbed until the wood is almost white, slopes toward the door. It's like being on a ship. From the bed, I can hear the gulls and smell the salt air and the residue of things being fried. Standing at the window, I can see Harry's blue, blue sea.

By noon, I have a job at Mattie's Schnitzel Haus, a German restaurant twelve blocks to the north. Arlene, the hostess, interviews me. "Ever waitressed before?" she asks.

"No," I admit. Arlene looks me over and then smiles. "Well, at least you're honest. Most girls come in here with baloney stories about having worked for some uncle in his French restaurant in Baltimore." She wets her lips and then pulls them back to check in her reflection on the chrome cash register that she has no lipstick on her teeth. "I'll give you a try. Just remember, mornings and lunches, this is a family place—pancakes, eggs, burgers, and Monte Cristos. Lots of kids, lots of spilled Aunt

Jemima's. After dark, we get the middle-aged crowd. Then we do steaks and seafood and the German theme stuff: Mattie's Wiener schnitzel, apple dumplings, that kind of thing. Thursdays through Sundays, there's a three-piece cha-cha band and Mattie's wife sometimes sings. Dinner's served till twelve, but you don't get out till two since you got to do the breakfast setup. Night's the good money, but if you're fast on your feet you'll do all right on the seven-to-three too. And don't tell anyone I hired you without experience."

The first night, I spill ice water in someone's lap and keep two tables waiting over an hour for their dinners. The cook, an old albino guy with skin so pale it hurts to look at, yells at me, and when a lady asks, "What exactly is the Wiener schnitzel?" I realize I have no idea. The second night, a man with an open shirt and lots of gold displayed against his chest hairs pinches my butt and a woman screams when I serve her a lobster platter with a cigarette butt smashed in the claw. A few days later, they give me the breakfast-lunch shift, and I slip in the kitchen, the plates crashing around me, egg yolks running yellow down my calves and blood from my palms staining the white uniform.

I want to cry, everything hurts so much, but I feel too humiliated to let the tears come. "What did I slip on?" I whisper as Arlene peels a butter pat from the bottom of my shoe and Mattie starts to yell, "Who the fuck is dropping butter? What you trying to do, kill this gal?" One of the other waitresses wipes syrup off my knees with a warm damp cloth, and the cook hands me a plastic cup with some whiskey in it and says, "All right, kid. Just take it easy." I swig. My heartbeat slows.

"You're christened, love," Arlene says. "A bona fide waitress."

•

Then, one lunchtime, I look up and you are there, sitting big and beaming in a T-shirt and shorts at one of my tables. You're suntanned and your arms look like tree trunks. For a moment, I feel irritated that you've just arrived without giving me any notice, but then you wink at me, raising your eyebrows in mock appreciation of my legs, and I smile.

I pretend you're one of my customers and bring you coffee and a menu. "How'd you find me?" I ask.

"You said a German place. Lots of Wiener schnitzel in Cincinnati." And so we resume, without the bother of words or discussion about the terms of our arrangement: why you, who should be beginning a training program at a Wall Street bank, are running a beach stand; why I, who should be, well, I don't know quite what but something other than carting platters of sauerbraten. Nor do we mention Andrew (off somewhere, Peru would be my closest guess), Andrew by then mostly an idea, an idea linked with a fantasy of exotic adventure: the medina in Tangier, the casino on Lido, a train cutting through the Andean clouds.

You move in with the younger brother of an Ivy Club friend, a skier and party kid from the University of Colorado who through a college buddy of his own landed a job at a fancy restaurant, the kind of place you hate, with a circular drive and valet parking, JACKET AND TIE REQUIRED FOR OUR GENTLEMEN GUESTS. The apartment is a summer version of a fraternity house, with girlie posters on the walls, the bathroom a swamp of wet towels, the refrigerator empty except for beer and packets of sweet-and-sour sauce. When I stay with you, which is most nights, I bring my own towel and carry a roll of toilet paper.

Within days, you have fallen into a routine. You paint your nose with zinc oxide, grab your fins from under the bed, and then walk to the corner, where you buy a pile of newspapers, two carry-out coffees, black and sweet, and three cherry Danish. You blow up the rafts, lay out the beach chairs, and stack the umbrellas. After the flurry of morning customers, you settle into whichever of the rental chairs is left to read the papers and have your breakfast. Midday, you get someone to watch the stand while you bodysurf for an hour: in and out of the water, your arms flung straight before you, your concentration as complete as the hour when you study the stock pages. Days that I work the dinner shift, I man the stand for you—watch you skim the waves, sometimes thirty yards or more before you crash into the sand, picking yourself up, shaking the stones out of your swim trunks, pushing your hair from your eyes, squinting to see if I am watching, and then grinning at me before you head back into the sea.

The night you arrive, we make love. For me, it is as it has always been between us since that first morning in your dorm room: languorous, satisfying in a more reverent way than Corrine and I had imagined sex might be. Afterward, you lie on your back with an arm stretched out as a bolster for me. You stare at the ceiling while you talk. "I feel like an animal with you," you say.

I turn on my stomach so I can see your face. I touch your cowlick. "Why is that?"

"Because I want you in this primal way. You're pining after some other guy. And yet here I am. It's like eating the leftovers off somebody's plate."

You crinkle your nose in disgust. "It's amazing, fucking amazing. Laney's old man has offered me a training position at Lehman Brothers as a trader starting whenever I'm ready. Those guys are making eighty, ninety grand their first year, upwards of two hundred by the second. Carrie Carston, who's probably sitting on ten million just from her trust fund, has been chasing me all spring, inviting me to visit her at her family's place outside of Rome, sending me perfumed letters, and yet here I am in Ocean City, Maryland, with no money, no plans, blowing up rafts just to have some crumbs of your time."

You laugh. It's a cruel laugh, mocking of both of us. In that moment, I can see that you hate me as much as you love me. I think of Carrie Carston, who was in my sophomore English class, always dressed in a pastel cardigan and a white turtleneck, little pearls in her earlobes, always, it seemed, in tandem with some other similar-looking girl. Carrie was considered a catch— a rich, popular, cute girl, petite with big breasts and hair cut like Dorothy Hamill—but I know that for you, she seems shallow and somehow ordinary, that what you are smitten with in me is my foreignness to you, that you don't know the authors I read or the painters I admire or the places I've traveled with my father. You say it's the length of my limbs, that I am, you say, "a long, cool drink of water I can't get to the bottom of," and although it sounds both vain and simpleminded, I have to admit to think-ing that you are right, that something about my arms and legs makes me elusive, that the nineteenth-century physiognomists understood but then overstated something true about how our bodies form the outlines of our selves—that with my kind of fingers and neck I had to aspire to a certain kind of thought, just as you, with your towering height and bouldering shoulders, had to find a trail and blaze your way through, that my body would no more allow me to giggle like Carrie Carston than yours would permit you the footnoted shuffle of James.

You want what is at the bottom of the glass but I want what you have, what my father had in his youth: a belief that one can find a path and fashion a life by sticking to it. I long for your faith in an order to the world, the analog to my father's faith in science. My father's faith was born and bred in his skin— not shared by his father, not passed on to me. Now my father complains that science has become no more than a cog in the technocratic machine—the romance of Crick and Watson buried under anxiety about grant applications, the degree of specialization having reached such absurd proportions that a developmental embryologist will look at my father, now classified in the annals as a theoretical geneticist, as though he were talking Urdu.

After this, after you paint us as the cruel mistress and her dog, you sleep curled around me but we don't make love. Each night you climb into bed in a pair of clean gym shorts; I keep on my bikini underwear. You breathe with deep even sounds, your arms folded over my breasts. Often, I lie awake, staring out the window, listening to the sound of the waves hitting the shore. I think we could be Hansel and Gretel huddled under a tree. I think I am the wicked witch and you are Hansel trapped in my garden. Bound in the lock of your arms, I think you are the wicked witch and I am Gretel caught in your cage.

•

Midsummer, my father forwards a letter from Andrew. Andrew writes that he has reached Machu Picchu and that trekking the Inca Trail is like walking in the footsteps of God. *Next week,* he writes, *we head to the Indian village of Chichicastenango in Guatemala to meet up with some silver merchants from southern Mexico.* It is unclear who the "we" are or what exactly Andrew is buying on this three-month journey. Indeed, his apartment is filled with native textiles, but then the money being made and the aura of intrigue suggest something more contraband. When I told this once to Corrine, she said, "What a taste you have for being a moll." I must have grown silent because she then said, "Don't act indignant. Being a moll is exciting."

I read on. This letter could be to anyone, I think. A generic travelogue. Maybe he has sent it to two or three other girl-friends and his mother too. Because I am only interested in the subtext (how Andrew feels about me, what I might expect from him), the details about Lake Atitlán and the community of hippie women who run the Blue Bird Café and have taught the Indians how to make yogurt bore me. I skim forward, looking for what Corrine calls the good stuff. At the end, there's a morsel: *I'll be back in New York the last week of August. Call my answering machine to let me know where you can be reached. And don't leave the country whatever you do. I think it's time we start to get to know one another. Thinking about you more than I wish, Andrew.*

Leave the country? Where does he think I'd go? Thinking about me more than he wishes—what the hell does that mean?

I read the letter three times. The words might as well be a local bacterium; they have left me jittery and on edge.

He must be traveling with a woman, I think. I imagine straight ash hair and expensive tooled boots, Andrew with his leather camera bag and Gitanes cigarettes. The business must have something to do with drugs. It all seems sordid in a Euro-trash kind of way. All I can think of is that by comparison you seem so clean, every pore washed by the sea, and that I, bad child, want only to play in the dirt.

•

One Saturday, I walk out of work to find you leaning against your car in the parking lot. It is three o'clock, hot and sticky. There are ketchup stains on my uniform and coffee spots on my shoes and what I want is a shower and a nap and then to go to a movie with you.

"What's up? Why aren't you at your stand?"

"I closed it." I can see your duffel in the backseat of your car. You reach inside for the bottle of Coke in the cup holder. "I'm headed out for two weeks."

My insides speed up. You've not asked if I've heard from Andrew. I've not volunteered about the letter, stashed now at the bottom of my underwear drawer. I think of something Corrine said after I told her that you had moved to Ocean City to be with me for the summer. "Be careful, he's going to give you your comeuppance." Despite the nights worrying what will happen between us once Andrew returns, it shocks me that I now feel so panicked about your driving away. "Where to?" I ask.

"North Carolina. A guy who bodysurfs at Ninety-fourth turned me on to a fast-money job. It's a two-week carnival, and they're paying a hundred bucks a day under the table plus a three-hundred bonus if you stick it out to the end. No hours. You just sleep and eat and work."

You stare straight ahead. Could there be another woman? For a moment, I wonder if it might be Carrie Carston.

"I'm broke. It's almost August. I'm not Einstein, but then again it's not dog food between my ears. Your lover-boy will reappear from wherever he's been by September. You don't expect for me to stick around after then?"

You swig from your Coke. I am silenced by the flint in your voice, by the glimpse I have that, to you, I seem like a prima donna, only worse, since I hide what I do under a layer of reserve. "What I like about a whore," Corrine once proclaimed as we walked together down lower Market, home to San Francisco's prostitutes and derelicts, "is she makes a clean contract."

"I need to borrow some cash to get there."

Everything is shifting without warning, as though a storm has unexpectedly blown onto shore and you are taking down umbrellas and deflating rafts while I lie still on my beach towel, unsure if the raindrops portend real danger or a momentary shower. You've never asked me for money before, and I wonder if maybe you don't realize how delicate and private money is for me after four years of carefully parsing the allowances my father sent each semester, carefully budgeting the money I saved from my summer jobs, and now depositing my waitress tips in a checking account every other day, watching the balance rise even after the rent and expenses by two hundred, sometimes even three hundred dollars each week. I have not thought about what

I am saving for, only that, like you, I too will at some point need to get out of here.

"I'll pay you back in two weeks," you say. My waitress tips are wadded in my apron pocket. It was a good morning. One family left fifteen dollars after I helped them with their tantruming three-year-old. As always, I had counted the money, exchanging the ones and the quarters and the dimes for bigger bills. Today, Arlene gave me back a fifty, two tens, and a five. I reach into my pocket, hand you the two tens and a five. You stuff the bills into your jeans.

"Thanks."

I feel a twinge of guilt. I should have given you more. If you're asking, you must really need it. But I earned it, I think. You spent all day sitting on the beach drinking coffee and reading the papers while I carted around trays of greasy food.

We brush lips. I watch while you pull up to the edge of the parking lot. I finger the fifty in my apron pocket. How will you get down to North Carolina on twenty-five bucks? I run toward your car. "Bear, Bear," I yell, my arms flapping like an agitated goose. For a moment I am certain that you are looking at me in your rearview mirror, but then the light changes, and you pull out onto the road.

•

A month passes before I go to your apartment. It's late August, the end of the season. The kid from the University of Colorado is sitting on the porch reading a ski magazine and drinking a Slurpee.

"Hey, Louisa. What's happening?"

"Not much." I look around, half expecting you to walk through the screen door. "Anyone seen Bear?"

The kid rubs his eyes and leans back in his chair so he is propped on the back two legs. He fiddles with the Slurpee straw and then sucks hard, making vacuum cleaner sounds. I'm sure he's checking me out for clues as to what I do and don't know.

"Nope."

I feel in a state beyond foolish, dangerously close to the dreaded desperate woman, stringy hair falling over her face, kids clinging to her skirt as she goes bar to bar in search of her alcoholic husband and his dwindling pay. "I was in the neighborhood and thought I'd drop by. Could I use your bathroom?"

"Sure. Help yourself to all the toilet paper you want."

I push open the screen door and walk back toward your room. The door is open. Inside, the bed is stripped and the pillow lies on top of the dresser. I look in the closet. It's empty save for some bent hangers and a crumpled paper on the floor. I uncrumple the paper and read a circular for a grocery store's weekly specials. I drop to my hands and knees to look under the bed: bare, your collection of running shoes and bodysurfing fins gone.

•

You call me two years later. It's Christmastime, early morning, and I'm sitting in my father's kitchen, poring over cookbooks, planning a Christmas Day menu. My father has requested duck. Juanita has taken up lacto-vegetarianism. Corrine wants plum pudding and Lily loves anything with apples.

"Louisa," you say. Your voice is low and gravelly.

"Bear?" My own voice sounds like a squeak. "Where are you?"

"New York. My apartment." You laugh. You sound like you've been drinking.

You tell me that both of your parents died last year: your father first, and then, a few months later, your mother.

"I'm so sorry," I say, feeling terrible that I had not heard.

"Well, it was good for my nephew, at least. My sister was able to move them out of their trailer."

Before I can say anything more, you change the subject to your job. You are trading bonds for one of the big investment houses. Seven of the guys in your group are Princeton boys, as you put it, four from your eating club. You tell me that Laney's old man got you the job and that you slept on the floor of Laney's apartment for two months before you could afford your own place. You tell me that right this moment you are fingering a check for one hundred and twenty thousand dollars, your Christmas bonus.

You laugh again and I can feel you filling the room. I imagine you stretched out on your bed, the pillow bent in half under your head, one arm folded under your neck, the sheer length of you. You rub the check between your forefinger and thumb, a line of running shoes against the wall, your fins thrown under the bed. I wonder what floor your apartment is on.

"Jesus," I say. "What will you do with all that money?"

"Lots of guys put it up their noses. Can't say I've never done that either. What a fucking waste. But with this mama, I don't know."

I'm surprised to hear you say this; not that you're a teetotaler, just that you were so critical of Corrine. I tell you that I have been living with Corrine and Lily for the past year, working at a bookstore in North Beach, housesitting for my father during his frequent trips out of the country. You don't ask where I'd been before, and I don't tell you about the time living with Andrew or how I moved west after finding him in bed with a woman who called herself Cat-Sue. Nor do you tell me about Carrie Carston, who someone told me you'd been seen with.

"Why are you calling me?"

It takes you a while to answer. I can hear your breathing. Even though we are a continent apart, it feels like we're talking in bed. "I don't know. Holding all this goddamned money makes you look at your life." You pause. For a moment I think you're going to fall asleep with the phone cradled to your ear. I want to ask about North Carolina and whether it was before or after you stuffed my twenty-five dollars into your jeans that you decided not to come back.

"I'm falling out, baby. Got to go."

•

A year and a half later, I'm sitting in my kitchen in New Haven, my first year of graduate coursework in English almost completed, flipping through the mail. Looking out the windows, I can see the top of a white clapboard church framed by a frill of green treetops. It's late May, hot but not yet muggy. I'm debating my summer options: teach high school students in mandatory summer school, work on the Emerson project (awful, I've been told; long hours in a windowless room in Sterling Library checking the punctuation and spelling in the now-typed version against the original handwritten correspondence), cocktail waitress at a new hotel out by the wharf.

The mail is a department store catalogue, an appeal from a world hunger organization, notification of an electric rate hike, and the Princeton alumni magazine. I flip through the catalogue, looking at jackets and shoes I could never afford, stash the hunger appeal and electric notice in the salad bowl, and turn to the alumni magazine. Like everyone else, I look first at the column listing news of our class: law firms joined, medical schools attended, babies born. As always, I scan first for your name.

When indeed it is there, for a split second I think I am hallucinating, a desert trekker conjuring water spilling over wet rocks into a deep, cold pool. It's an announcement that you've been promoted to vice president at Goldman Sachs. Although I have never had reason to read the business section in the paper and couldn't explain what a margin is, even I know that you have reached the big league.

I call Corrine. Lily, now eight, answers. "Hi, Lily Pad."

"Hi, Louisa."

"What are you up to?"

"I'm eating a Popsicle. Then I'm going to wash my pink troll's hair."

"Is your mom home?"

"She's taking a bath."

"Ask her to call me when she gets out, okay?"

"Mommy, it's Louisa," Lily hollers.

Corrine hollers something back and then Lily whispers, "She said to bring the phone to her in the tub."

"Don't do that!" I say, but Lily must already be holding the phone away from her ear as she marches down the hall to the bathroom.

"Oh," Corrine moans, and then, "Lily, honey, I don't want you to get in here with me. We'll give you your own bath later."

I can hear Lily fussing in the background.

"Scat. Let me talk to Louisa."

"Call me later. You shouldn't have the phone in the tub."

"Thank you, Mom. You know I always talk on the phone in the tub."

"You're in a mood."

"She won't let me out of her sight. When I woke up, she was sleeping next to me."

"I hope you were alone."

"Just barely. She must have got up when she heard Danny leaving."

Corrine goes on to tell me about Danny. As usual, he's an artist, this time a sculptor, with a day job doing something else, this time substitute school teaching.

"He's great with Lily."

"I can't imagine that's the real draw."

"He's awesome. His hands. Oh my God. But he is good with kids. So, what's up?"

Corrine has been disapproving of my celibacy since Andrew. I've tried to explain to her that between you and Andrew, I've been worried about the condition of my soul—that I think about my soul the way that my father thinks about genes: over time we acquire a map of where our ancestors have been, who they lay down with, so that we carry both in our chromosomes and our soul the history of these couplings. "Listen to this," I say, and then I read the lines about you.

"He must be fucking rich."

"It's so weird. I had a feeling he'd be in that column. Though I guess it's not the first time I've thought that."

Corrine and I have talked at length about why you are still so much on my mind. We've gone through the guilty-party theory: I did you wrong and am waiting to make amends. We've gone through the wronged-party theory: you did me wrong and I am waiting for you to make amends. We've gone through the purity-versus-squalor theory: after the squalor of Andrew, I am eager for the purity of you. What I have not told Corrine about is the image I sometimes have of the strands of each of my chromosomes slowly untwisting, each gene a twirling ballerina, the motion choreographed like Balanchine, the strands floating across the stage toward the leaping, bare-chested dancers who make up the untangling strands of you.

"Do you think I could call him? I mean, what would I say? It's not as though he ever called me back that time two Christmases ago."

Corrine and I go over the options: calling, writing, doing nothing. We settle on calling you at your office, just calling to offer congratulations, I will say. I will suggest a coffee or a beer the next time I'm in the city—with coffee or a beer, you won't have to refuse if there's a woman in your life. Corrine instructs me to be warm but cool, to make the invitation sound sincere but nonchalant, as though it just occurred to me as we were talking. We practice, she playing you, me playing me.

For the rest of the week, I do both parts in my head. Then I dial. When I hear your voice, my mouth goes dry. I put my finger to the receiver and think about hanging up, but I've given the receptionist my name. "It's me, Louisa," I blurt.

You respond as though we had spoken yesterday, as though you had called me. "Come down for a weekend," you say. In the background, I can hear a lot of commotion. I imagine you in a gray-carpeted room with screens all around you like the cockpit of an enormous plane. Perhaps you have your feet up on the laminate surface that serves as your desk. Perhaps you are high enough that you can see the water, the tugboats heading toward the Narrows.

"The city's great this time of year," you say. "We can catch a movie, go out to eat." You tell me about a restaurant in Tribeca where they sauté soft-shell crabs like in Maryland and serve a Kobe steak with truffles that tastes like you're in Tokyo. You are flexing your muscles, showing me your newfound urbanity, telling me that you have left Cincinnati and your plumber father and fisherman brother-in-law in the dust.

"Come Saturday," you say. I wonder who you have booked for Friday or if you have to move someone from Saturday to make a slot for me.

•

On Saturday, I dress carefully in a short skirt with a back vent and a sleeveless silk tee Corrine sent me for my birthday. I add a light jacket with padded shoulders, take off the tee and jacket, try a blouse, and then put the tee and jacket back on. On the train, I thumb through a book on the politics of interpretation lent to me by a comp lit guy. The debate, as far as I can glean, has something to do with whether the world is parsed by class or by sex. Riding to meet you, rising capitalist or is it capitalist tool, my breasts poking against the silk, I have the urge to add my scrawl to the margins. *This is bullshit*, I would write. *What purpose does this serve other than the aggrandizement of the writers and their careers?* I feel vicious, and then I realize that already I have put myself in your shoes, the viciousness of the commercial man toward the intellectual and, for that matter, of the intellectual toward the commercial man. Or, for that matter, I continue, of you toward me and me toward you. Then I drift off.

When I wake, I'm in the tunnel between the 125th Street station and Grand Central. I pull out a compact, powder my nose and chin, and brush out my hair. It's been nearly four years since I last saw you in the parking lot of Mattie's Schnitzel Haus. Time has left me more svelte, I've been told, and my hair now sports a better cut, but there are also small lines that web out from my eyes.

You don't rush forward when you see me. You stand still, arms folded across your chest, in a lean against the ledge of the information kiosk. You watch me approach, your face open and appreciative as you look. When I reach you, you encircle me with your arms, lifting me a little in your embrace. You place your hand behind my shoulder and guide me toward the street and then into a cab that you direct to a place on the East River with a deck over the water. We drink and then we leave and go downtown to eat. You tell me about your work: what a bond really is, who buys them and why, what arbitrage and futures mean, where you stand, as you put it, as a player, the way that the business flows into basketball games at the Downtown Athletic and houses on the North Shore. Reading between the lines, I can see that it is Ivy Club redux, and that again you are courted because you, who were a boy's boy, are now a man's man, that men like men with a boom to their voice, that you assuage their anxiety about what a life manipulating money does to their muscles and the length of their dicks.

Afterward we go to a movie. It's an artsy foreign thing about a priest who falls in love with a beautiful woman. I have the sense that you have chosen it deliberately, a way of communicating that you know what I will like and how to partake of the cultured platter. I am embarrassed by how erotic it is. The priest undresses the woman. Her skin is pink and moist, like the inside of a conch shell. "You are my proof of God's existence," the priest says to the woman.

"I've often thought that about you," you whisper in my ear.

From then on, I realize we are beginning again. When the movie ends, you hail a cab, this time to the lot where you store your car. It's a metallic-gray Mercedes. Your second German car. You unlock the door. I've never been inside such an expensive car and for a moment I am scared to get in, scared of the car, scared of you and all about you that I no longer know.

You drive north on the Henry Hudson and then up the Hutchinson River Parkway. You still drive with the window open, and although I am cold, I am relieved that you have not taken to using the climate control. We talk, but not about Andrew and whomever it is that you've been with. I wonder if you're driving me back to New Haven because her things are still in your apartment or if maybe she herself is there.

When we get to my apartment, you push me onto my bed before I've even turned on the lights or taken off my jacket. You are the first man I have had in this bedroom. You yank my skirt over my hips.

Afterward, I cry. I can't tell if I am crying because there is something brutal about the way you touched me or because you've stripped my nerves bare or because you feel new and shiny and strange.

You lie on your back. I pull my skirt back over my hips and

lie on my stomach looking down at you. You run a finger along the line from the base of my throat to the hollow of my breastbone. "I'll do this," you say. "I can't stop myself. But we're star-crossed."

"Why is that?"

"You'd find the people I see, the people who are my friends, a snore. Stupid. Ignorant. Some of them are the same Princeton guys you dismissed five years ago. Others are punks from Brooklyn College who've made their way to the floor from the mail room. They don't read the kind of books you've got around here. They're dirt Republicans. They watch football in the fall and basketball in the winter and baseball until the last World Series game. They drink a lot of beer and they belch and they laugh when somebody farts."

Are you sneering at me? You trace a star on my forehead, pull my head down to your mouth. "Star-crossed," you say before you kiss me again.

•

Once, I try to get you to talk about what happened between us that Ocean City summer. It's September, early evening, and we are at Sachem's Head beach, the sun an orange ball sinking into the glistening water, the colors sharp and full-hued. All afternoon we've been lounging on beach chairs, reading the *Times*, snacking on the fruit and cheese I buy each weekend before you drive up.

I angle my chair so I can see your face. "We should talk about it," I say, "what happened before you took off for North Carolina."

Your eyes narrow. Since we've been back together, you bristle at anything I say that hints at a demand. "Why is that?"

"Because," I say. "Otherwise it will seep back in and poison what we have now." *What we have now*: the words feel awkward in my mouth. What do we have now? You drive up Friday nights or I take the train down Friday afternoon. If we're in New Haven, we go to the beach and eat lobster from a place that serves them broiled over a pit. If we're at your place, we sleep late and then eat Thai or somewhere downtown, since you have a rule that outside of work you wear only sneakers and jeans. Other than one day at your friend's summer house in Bay Head, we've never seen anyone else during these weekends.

When we go out, you always pay. At first I tried to pay for at least a few things, a breakfast here and there, but always you'd object. "You're a student," you would say. "It feels odd," I've complained to Corrine, "having all the bills whisked away. Unreal, as though I'm Peter Pan refusing to grow up."

"What happened," you say, "is you left me for a rich-kid drug dealer who'd been off screwing some other girl all summer."

"I don't mean with Andrew. I mean with you."

"I've told you. I told you that first night in Ocean City. You made me feel like an animal. Like a dog who can't control himself from sniffing the backside of a female. That's what I felt like, Louisa. Like I was crawling around sniffing your butt. How much more graphically do you want me to put it? You want me to get down on all fours and demonstrate?"

I bite my lip to keep myself from crying. You are enjoying hurting me. I put on my sunglasses so you can't see my eyes.

"How about you?" I ask. "Why won't you tell me who you were with these past four years?"

You roll the business section of the paper into a tube and swat at a fly on your leg. "I was with Carrie Carston for about a year. She was in a training program at another bank. We spent a lot of time at her parents' villa outside of Rome. It was hot as hell and everyone drank too much and pretended we didn't know her old man snuck off every afternoon to fuck his mistress. Then Carrie got pregnant, wanted to get married, have the baby, the whole nine yards. It was the year my parents died, and I was completely wrapped up in that. We broke up. Then I met this girl Susan. She lived in my building. She was an actress, had a part in one of the soaps. I was infatuated with her, with how beautiful she was. When she lost her part, I let her move in. But she wouldn't get out of bed. I'd come home and she'd still be in bed with all this food spread out around her—boxes of cookies, bags of potato chips, cartons of ice cream."

You reroll the paper and whack the arm of your beach chair. "One night I found her sticking her finger down her throat. After that I couldn't stand to touch her. I don't know, maybe I just didn't want to be bothered with her problems. I told her I'd help her get her own place. She got hysterical and threatened that she was going to jump out the apartment window. I had to call her mother in Philadelphia, and she came and put her in Gracie Square Hospital."

I look out at the horizon. There's a sailboat silhouetted against the sky, too far away to see any people. It looks like it's sailing itself. I can hear you swatting at another fly.

"What else do you want to know?"

"Nothing," I say. "I got the picture."

•

In January, we decide to take a trip. You suggest Hawaii, an out-of-the-way island you'd been to with Carrie Carston. I look in the travel section of the newspaper. There's no mention of this island, but round-trip to Honolulu with seven nights' lodging is two thousand dollars. I don't have two thousand dollars.

"Should I let him take me?" I ask Corrine.

"Of course. It's nothing for him."

"But he hasn't offered."

"He'll offer," Corrine says. But you don't offer. I wonder if you just assume that you'll take me or if it never occurs to you that I wouldn't be able to take myself or if you're waiting for me to ask. Is that it, I wonder, cat and mouse, and then, smelling danger, I call you and suggest Vermont. "It would be simpler," I say. "We can just throw our things in the car and go."

I reserve us a room in what looks from the picture (gabled roof covered with snowdrifts, a tree-lined drive leading up to the door) like a storybook inn. What is left out of the picture, we discover, is the highway on which the inn sits. You refuse to look at me. I comment on the few redeeming features: the large color TV with cable in the middle of the guest living room, the library of discarded paperbacks, the chocolate mints placed on each pillow. You punch the mattress and declare it filled with sand. We try taking a walk, but it is painfully cold. The hairs inside our nostrils freeze and my toes grow numb.

"All right, it's awful," I say. "Should we go somewhere else?"

You snort. "You think they're going to give back the deposit?" The deposit is on your credit card; I let the subject drop.

That night, you complain that the mattress is injuring your back. I try to interest you in simply holding me and ignoring the bed but you carry on, finally dragging a blanket from the bed and sleeping on the floor. I come and lie beside you. You turn away. I remain awake until I hear you fall into sleep.

In the morning, we pack up and leave. Back in New Haven, I make pasta with a pesto sauce I keep in the freezer and that you have always told me you love. You eat without talking and don't finish what's on your plate. "Look," I say, "I'm sorry. I obviously didn't realize the place would be so horrid. But what can I do now? It happened."

"It's not your fault," you say, but still, after we do the dishes, you tell me that you're going to leave.

I am close to tears. I'm sure you can sense this. I count backward from a hundred subtracting threes. I am on the verge of grabbing your coat, telling you that it's unfair, that you're punishing me, that you agreed to go to Vermont, that it's not a sin to make a mistake. Instead, I keep counting. If I make a scene, I say to myself, I will make myself the problem.

I watch you through the window, unlocking the Mercedes, throwing your bag on the back seat. I hear the engine turning over, see you fiddling with the radio. Then the car door opens and you step out onto the street. My heart pounds and for a moment I think you're going to come back upstairs, you'll put your arms around me, and this will all dissolve into a funny story.

You take off your coat and get back into your car.

●

In the morning, you call me. From the sounds of many things clicking, I call tell that you're back at work. "You went back," I say.

"Yeah, the market's hot. No point missing out." You pause. "Listen, I'm sorry. I was a real bastard." I hear another phone ringing. "Hold on, I've got to take this." Three minutes pass before you get back on the line. "There's a big play about to happen. Can I call you tonight?"

So we continue. Over the summer, I move in with you. By the fall, we've settled into a routine. On Tuesdays and Thursdays, I take the train to New Haven. Tuesdays, I stay over with a friend. Thursdays, I take a late train back to the city. Mondays and Fridays, I work in the apartment.

I learn your trader's habits as I had once learned your Princeton and then your beachcomber rhythms. I watch as you rise every morning at exactly ten of six, never playing games with the alarm, never pressing the snooze button three, four times as I do. You listen to the news while you shave, hum while you select your tie, lean over to kiss me goodbye before leaving and double-locking the door. I learn that you buy three papers at the newsstand on the corner, thumb through all three on the subway ride downtown, buy a large black sweet coffee, a carton of orange juice, and a bagel with cream cheese from a blind vendor, and are at your desk before seven. On the days that I'm home, you call me midday, inquiring about the progress on whatever course paper I'm writing or the work on my dissertation proposal, giving me the lowdown on what is happening on the floor. "The Turk is leading a raid," you might say, or "I've got this guy by the balls but he refuses to holler uncle and close the goddamned deal." I learn that after work you walk to your gym, that on Tuesdays, Thursdays, and Fridays you lift weights and climb the stair machine, and that on Mondays and Wednesdays you play basketball with a group of Catholic kids from Brooklyn who have found their way onto various trading floors. You call them the Toddlers. You telephone at nine, asking what I want for dinner, and when you arrive, you're minty-smelling, your hair still damp from the shower, a bag of take-out Chinese, calzones, or roasted chicken under your arm.

"The only problem," I say to Corrine, "is sex. We hardly have sex. Is that normal?"

"What do you mean, 'hardly'?"

"I mean hardly," I say, not wanting to let even Corrine know how little *hardly* is. "Part of it is we barely see each other. If I add up how much time we spend together in a day, not even counting the night I'm in New Haven, it's not much more than an hour."

"Them's the breaks, sweetheart, with one of those fast-track guys. You don't think I choose the grungy, wannabe artists for no reason, do you?" Corrine has a point. Although none of her boyfriends lasts more than a year and even the ones in their late thirties seem still like kids, they are there. They listen to her dreams and her thoughts about how the woman with the floppy hat is her anima and how the robber with the stocking cap is her animus. They are interested in what foods she would choose if she could only take three to a deserted island and her ideas about what happens to your body after it's buried under the ground. With you, in our snatches of time, these things never come to my mind. The agenda is full: catch up with the events of the day, plan for tomorrow.

After the winter break, I find myself thinking about one of my professors, a young guy with a reddish beard and a certain flair for clothing—an enfant terrible, I've been told, always au courant on the latest theoretical discourses and renowned for his sexual escapades. I know that really his passion is for the sound of his own voice, his greatest fascination with the meanderings of his own mind. Still, I can't help noticing during his Tuesday seminar on French literary theory how he seems to appreciate everything I say or how at the departmental cocktail hours he hovers near. Or how my hand flutters from my glass to push back a strand of my hair, my chin tilting slightly up.

When I think about it, though, riding the train back to the city, what his kisses might be like, they are, I realize, patterned after yours when we first met, long exploring kisses that moved from my mouth to my throat, kisses that have evaporated, it seems, in the savage light of this, our adult life.

•

I can imagine many endings to our story. In one version, I go on to have an affair with this rakish professor. There is an explosive scene. You throw a plate. Lo mein hits the wall, pieces of broccoli and broken dish cover the floor. One or the other of us packs up. Mostly, I imagine it is you emptying drawers, throwing underwear and socks in a bag, grabbing an armload of suits.

In another version, we go ahead and marry. We buy an apartment. By the time, though, that we paint the walls, sand the floors, select the Oriental, order the couch, frame the pen-and-inks, plant flowerpots for the terrace, and assemble the grill, we have lost the language of love, the cadences of tenderness permanently transformed into communications about delivery-persons and summer rentals. In this version, I pray for magic. I accumulate slim volumes of poems, piling them each night by the side of the bed, hoping that the words (arms encircling bellies, tongues probing palates) will find their way into our sheets. In this version, I keep trying to turn our story into that O. Henry tale in which she cuts her hair to buy him a watch chain and he sells the watch to buy silver combs for her lovely long hair. I keep trying to explain to you how our apartment is something like this, that in the story the lovers exit with even greater devotion to each other, only the analogy doesn't make sense and, in the end, I take the rug, you take the couch, we divide up the pen-and-inks, and the gay couple who buy from us get the freshly painted walls and beautiful floors.

The real ending, though, is nothing like either of these. The real ending begins with the phone ringing in the middle of an autumn night. You reach to answer it and I hear you saying, "Who's this? Who's there?" You turn to me and say, "I can't understand a goddamned thing. It's some woman sobbing and sobbing." I bolt awake. I know it is Corrine.

I grab the phone from you. "Corrine, Corrine, honey, what is it?" Already I am crying too. I struggle to grasp a word between her sobs. "Is it Lily?" For a long time, I can't untangle any words. Then I think I hear, "Yes," before it is again only wails. "Corrine, I'm coming," I say, "I'll be there as soon as I can."

I call my father. For once, he is home. "Daddy, please," I say. I am almost yelling. "It's Corrine. Something's happened to Lily. I think she's in a hospital. Probably UCSF is where Corrine would take her."

It's been a long time since I've called my father Daddy. "Do something," I whisper.

You telephone airlines for me and book me on the next

flight. I pack some things, get dressed, and wait for my father to call back.

"You were right. She's at UCSF." My father clears his throat. "I'm there now. It's not good. A vein burst in her head. It happened in her sleep. Corrine went to check on her and found her vomiting, with blood coming out of her ears."

I can feel my bowels contracting. I hold on to the edge of the kitchen counter. "How bad? Is she going to live?" I can't tell if I am screaming or not.

It takes my father so long to answer that for a moment I wonder if he's still there. Then I hear his voice swimming toward me. "I don't think so." I rest my forehead on the counter. "They've still got her heart going with a machine but she's brain-dead."

"How's Corrine?" I manage to ask.

"Hysterical. They just gave her some Valium to try to calm her down. She's got some boyfriend with her who looks like he's had a handful himself."

You help me get a cab and kiss me on the cheek. You don't offer to fly out with me and I don't ask, not because I don't want you to, I desperately do, but because of Corrine, because she will need me in ways I can't manage if I am with you.

On the plane, I sit next to a rabbi whose job is to say the blessing to make horseradish kosher. He's young, probably younger than I am, with skin that looks like it's never seen sun. During takeoff, he prays, swaying forward and back, but after that he talks on and on about the convention of industrial rabbis he's headed to in Oakland, about a childhood trip to San Francisco and a baseball game he saw at Candlestick Park. He refuses the meal, eating instead two meatloaf sandwiches he unfolds from a tinfoil wrapping. Although nothing about him feels holy to me, still I tell him about Lily.

"I will pray for the child." He refolds the tinfoil around the remains of his sandwich and bows his head. I listen as he murmurs words I can't understand. It occurs to me that I have not heard Hebrew since my mother's funeral when my father nearly punched the rabbi who had been hired to appease my mother's parents and who had slunk from relative to relative the hour before the service to learn something about my reclusive mother only to then bungle the eulogy by referring to her as a devoted wife who would be missed by not only her three children but the entire community.

By the time I get to the hospital, Lily has been taken off of the machine. Corrine is wild-eyed. A button has popped off the front of her shirt and her fine blond hair is tangled as though she has been pulling at it all night. Her brother, Marc, who lives in Connecticut but has somehow arrived before me, is there, and some guy who looks like he's eighteen. Corrine won't let me hug her. I take her by the shoulders and try to hold her still. She smells like vomit. "Corrine," I say. I am struggling not to break into sobs. "Tell me what to do."

"Get rid of him," she whispers, pointing to the guy. "I can't stand to have him here."

I go up to the guy and walk him down the corridor. "Listen," I say, "I don't know how to tell you this, but you've got to go now. Now is only for family and close friends." The guy nods. He looks relieved to be dismissed.

"Should I say goodbye to her?" he asks.

I pat his hand. "I think it's best if you just leave from here."

"I was there when it happened. I brought Corrine some pot, and she went up to check on Lily and then she just started screaming."

"I understand." I feel old. Old enough to be this boy's mother. He nods at me and turns toward the exit.

When I get back to the waiting room, Corrine is standing in the middle of the room kicking one of the chairs. Marc is talking to everyone, the doctors, the nurses, people on the pay phone.

I can hear him making arrangements, funeral parlor, flights for his parents who now live in Florida. He tells someone on the other end of the line to wait a minute, and then beckons me to come over. "Take her home, okay? They just gave her some more Valium and the doctor said she'll probably crash."

Corrine lets me hold her hand in the cab. With her other hand, she pulls at her hair. "Stop it," I say. "Give me that hand." I keep both of her hands between mine. When we get to her house, there are bloody dish towels in the hall. Corrine ignores them and heads up the stairs. I follow her into Lily's room with the butterflies Corrine painted on the walls. The bed is clotted with vomit and blood. I try to strip off the lavender sheets but Corrine won't let me. She climbs into the bed, shoes and all. She curls up on her side. I follow, fighting off nausea, putting my arms around her until we are spooned together. I hold her as she rocks and howls, low like a wolf, over and over, "My baby. My baby. My baby."

When the Valium takes hold, I untangle my numb arms and go downstairs. I put the bloody towels in a garbage bag, and then call my father. "What caused it?" I ask.

"It was probably congenital. She was probably born with a weak blood vessel. It's like waiting for a time bomb to go off." I start to cry again, thinking of Lily walking around with her Popsicles and trolls and a time bomb ticking in her head.

"You mean it was in her genes."

"Maybe. Or it could have developed from some fetal problem."

I'm afraid to ask the next question but I force myself. "Did she have a lot of pain?"

"I don't think so. Not more than a moment or two." I want to say, *Do you swear that, do you swear on your life that it wasn't more than a minute or two, can I tell that to Corrine, that her baby suffered at most, absolute most, one hundred and twenty seconds?*

After I hang up with my father, I think of calling you but suddenly I'm terribly tired. I go upstairs, back to Lily's room, reeling at first from the stench of her vomit and dried blood, acrid now like a discarded menstrual pad, my eyes welling as I think how Lily never even had a period. I manage to get the sheets off the bed without waking Corrine, then crawl back in, pulling Lily's quilt over the two of us. I listen to the rhythms of Corrine's breath, so different from yours, letting myself join her in sleep.

•

It's the part about Corrine's hair that undoes us. I tell you about it ten days later, the night I arrive back in New York, when we sit up until the sky turns slate, something we haven't done since our beginnings, while I try to describe to you the days before the funeral.

Corrine begged me to tell her parents they had to stay in a hotel. "I can't have them in the house," she cried. "Lily might be trying to talk to me. She might not talk to me if they're around." So she and I stayed at her house, Corrine sleeping in Lily's little bed, punching my arms and screaming when I insisted on washing the sheets before she put them back on, me in Lily's Barbie sleeping bag at her feet.

The night before the funeral, at the funeral parlor, Corrine's mother whispered to me, "Louisa, darling, see if you can get her to do something with her hair for tomorrow." Corrine had pulled up a chair so she could sit next to the coffin. She was holding Lily's hand, talking softly to her. I knew that she was telling Lily not to be scared. From across the room, Corrine's hair looked matted, as though it were knotted and then stuck to her head with something sticky.

In the morning, I laid out clothes for Corrine and told her to be sure to wash her hair. I heard the shower go on and then, a minute later, go off. When Corrine walked into the room, her hair was dry. I swiveled her around, back toward the bathroom, turned the shower on, and guided her under the water.

"Close your eyes," I said, pushing her head under the nozzle. Something that looked like brown rust flowed over her shoulders. Jesus, I thought, is that Lily's blood still in her hair?

I got into the shower with her, squeezed shampoo into my palms, and lathered her scalp. I rinsed, lathered again, and rinsed. Then I surveyed the mass of her hair. It was horribly knotted. I reached for a bottle of crème rinse, put a handful in, waited a minute, and rinsed. I could hardly see or feel any difference. I continued adding crème rinse and rinsing until I'd used the whole bottle. Then I took a washcloth and started washing the rest of Corrine: her feet, the back of her knees, between her legs, under her arms.

By the time I got her out of the shower, she was sobbing. I dried her off with a towel, wrapped her in a second one, pulled down the toilet seat cover, and sat her down. For fifteen minutes, I tried to comb the knots out of her hair. Then I went down to the kitchen and got a bottle of vegetable oil. I rubbed oil into Corrine's hair and attempted again to comb. Slowly, I got out some of the tangles. She never stopped crying and I was sure that some of it was because I was tearing at her hair.

"It was awful," I tell you. "I finally got a scissors and cut out the remaining knots. Then I had to wash her hair again because of the oil. I tried to make her look presentable by using mousse and hair spray to cover the spots where her scalp showed through, but by the time we got to the funeral parlor, she had undone all my work by pulling again at her hair. She looked like someone from the back ward of a loony bin. When her mother saw her, she nearly fainted."

We're sitting at the kitchen table. You're drinking beer. I'm sipping tea. My suitcase is still by the front door. You're staring at me as though you're not quite taking in what I'm saying.

"How did you get in the shower?" you ask.

"What do you mean?"

"Did you have your clothes on?"

I look at you, trying to figure out what it is that you're getting at.

"Answer me. Did you or did you not have any clothes on?"

"Of course not. I wouldn't get into a shower with my clothes on."

"You mean you were washing Corrine while you both were naked."

"What the hell are you suggesting?"

You get up from the table and head to the bathroom. The toilet flushes, and then I hear our shower running. I bang on the door before letting myself in. "Listen," I say. I am yelling. "You can't make wild accusations like that and then walk out of the room." I am so enraged, I'm near to tears.

You don't respond. For a moment, I think you are singing. Then I realize that you have the shower radio on. "Who do you think you are? I've just come back from my best friend's child's funeral and you pull this shit!"

It's not a song; it's a dog food commercial. I pick up a bottle of your very expensive aftershave and hurl it at the side of the tub. The glass shatters into glistening green shards and a sickly smell mixes with the steam.

•

Of course, we make up. "I was tired," you say. "You know how irrational I get when I'm tired."

I buy you a new and even larger bottle of the aftershave. "I'm sorry," I say. "I shouldn't have thrown it no matter what you said."

But I can't shake it, the sense of something debased and dangerous between us, the feeling of betrayal that you used what I told you about Corrine's grief against me, the sound of the bottle shattering, the shards of sticky green glass. What if you hadn't headed into the bathroom? What if we had stayed in the kitchen? Would I have reached for the teapot filled with boiling water?

I play this scene over in my mind. You say, *You mean you were washing Corrine while you both were naked.* I say, *What the hell are you suggesting?* Your hands rest palms down on the table. I reach for the kettle. You track my arm as it moves through the air.

•

Once, during the month before I pack up my things, you say about Lily that it was God's will.

We're sitting in an Indian restaurant. You're dangling a forkful of vegetable samosa next to your mouth.

"God's will? It was God's will to have a blood vessel burst in her brain?"

You bite and then put your fork down with a clank. I watch you chew. "Yes," you say. "That's what I believe." You set your jaw and stare at something behind me. I can't tell if you really believe this or are saying it to provoke me.

The waiter arrives with a tray of chapatis and chutneys. A doughy mist rises between us.

If I had to put my finger on when I decided to leave, it would have to be that moment before the chapatis when you evoked the possibility that reasonable people, and perhaps even you yourself, could view Lily's death as redeemed by her ascent into heaven, whereas I could see only the dumbness and bruteness of nature—the only redemption if I excise that dumbness and bruteness in myself. And, for me, this bruteness has been most bald-faced with you, in this love of ours that had become, if we are honest with ourselves, an exchange of cruelties.

Your father bequeathed you this God when you were a child and I think this is what you love most about him, that he gave you this idea you might turn to later in life of a God who could shepherd you, as he believed he'd been when he stopped drinking—an inheritance richer than all the T-bonds and blue-chip stocks you gather now in your portfolio. My father has no God. No stories of Jesus washing the feet of Mary Magdalene or throwing the money changers out of the temple. What my father has are concepts, concepts that, despite his own failings with my mother and then me and I suppose now Juanita to imagine another person's experience, he did try to teach me: tolerance, compassion, justice. For the most part, he succeeded, and, for the most part, I have learned to be grateful to him for showing me that one can fashion one's life at whatever ethical level one chooses. At other times, though, it seems that my belief in the origins of human life in a primordial soup leaves me with only my bestiality. At these times, I understand why the fundamentalists have fought so hard to keep the theory of evolution out of the schools—that what's at stake are not the scientific facts but how we see ourselves and what we aspire to be.

•

You already know that at first I went back to New Haven because when I sent you a letter asking you to forward my mail, you did. What you probably don't know is that I've since moved back West, into Corrine's house by the ocean, and that I'm living alone there now since she's in Puerto Rico with a man she met when her brother and I insisted she get away for a few weeks. Her parents have been a wreck, calling me when they can't reach her, and I spend a lot of time reassuring them that the change of scenery, not living here where Lily died, is good for her.

I never finished my degree. "ABD," as my father says, "Louisa's All But Dissertation." It just seems unnecessary for my work (I'm now the manager of the bookstore where I worked when I lived here after you left me in Ocean City and I then left

Andrew in New York), which, unfortunately, involves more time handling accounts and dealing with salespeople than reading books. "What I need," I tell my father, "is not a PhD in English but a bookkeeping course." In the little spare time I have, I've been working on some poems, a handful of which I've published in journals that no one except other poets ever read. From time to time, I hear from Andrew. He's married, though the way he writes about his wife makes me think that the marriage won't last long. Don't worry—I know better.

I've heard through someone who knows someone who works with you that you have a serious girlfriend and that she is tiny and smart and some sort of doctor. The news hurt (actually, it hurt a great deal), but it came also as a relief, a relief to know that you have moved on and that somehow that must mean that I have too.

As for me, I have friends, some of them men who I know pine for more, and on the rare occasion I go to bed with one of them. I am for now, though, too frightened of my capacity to pour boiling water on someone's hands to do more than a one- or two-night sort of thing.

What I miss most is sleeping with you. Not sleeping with you as it was at the end but sleeping with you as it was at the start, before we hurt each other, when you adored my smell and I could see your angel wings.

Now I sleep in Lily's old room with her troll collection and the butterflies Corrine painted on the walls. I have thought about moving, out of the fog, to the sunny side of town, out of Lily's bed, to a clean white room with a bed meant to hold a man and a woman. Just not now. Not yet.

1978

Lion Eats Cheetah
Eats Weasel Eats Mouse

At first, we named everything: the apartment, Andrew's leather jacket, my car. Andrew's leather jacket, we named Raoul. "Raoul and I will be home around ten," Andrew would say, and I would imagine Andrew and some unbearably good-looking Latin male, narrow-shouldered, long-torsoed, with a shade of stubble and a lot of bruised lip, both of them wearing leather jackets with collars of chocolate fur. My car—the Datsun I'd brought from Ocean City to New York, which had developed a crack in the dashboard (the crack we referred to as the San Andreas Fault) and rust seeping up into the trunk—we called the Quake. "Gotta get the Quake some new shoes," I'd say. Or, "Time to give Quake a bath."

In the winter, the kitchen became infested with mice and I became consumed with Percy Green, a black kid whose story was spattered across the papers. Deathly afraid of mice, I would not go into the kitchen in the mornings until Andrew had gone before to remove any carcasses and hide the traps. As for Percy, in the beginning the story read scholarship kid from Washington Heights, shipped off to Hotchkiss on an alumni fund grant, gunned down on the street by a brutish white cop. Standing on a footstool to do the dishes, afraid a mouse might scamper out from under the cabinets, I would study the countertop TV, flipping channel to channel for more local news, and then turning the faucet off and wiping my hands on the sides of my jeans when the pictures of Percy Green floated onto the screen.

"They're more scared of you than you are of them," Andrew swore about the mice. It was morning and I was crying. "I feel so stupid," I said. "I can't stand to even think about them, the way they slip through cracks and have those soft flexible bones." Mostly, though, what I was crying about was me: that since moving in with Andrew I had become a person who had to do the dishes standing on a footstool and who huddled in a ball on top of the bed.

Andrew fingered the fur on Raoul's collar, and then swung the jacket over his shoulders. Leaning into the bookshelf, he blew dust off a tiny pre-Columbian figure—an animal man with a distended belly and no eyes—he'd brought back from his summer travels and that now stood guard by his turntable. Already his mind was on the next thing. "When will you be home?" I asked, hating my whiny tone.

"Late." Andrew lifted his book bag. Taxiing for takeoff, he moved into the hall.

"How late?"

"Late. Don't pressure me, Louisa." He enunciated the three syllables of my name as though it were something distasteful he was picking up with a crumpled paper towel. "It's ten days to exams."

I'd known Andrew was in his last year of law school when I moved in with him but I'd not known there were mice in the apartment. Afraid I might break into a messy gurgly sob, I chewed the braided silver chain dangling over my nightgown, comforting myself with the memory of the night Andrew had given me the necklace. He'd lit candles, long shadows blanketing the room as he laid the silver over my breastbone, explaining how the necklace had been made by a man who lived in the same village as the shaman Don Juan in the Carlos Castaneda book. When he'd lifted my hair to fasten the clasp, I had felt linked to the mystery at the center of the universe.

"You're acting like a baby." Copper wind chimes clanged wildly as cold air rushed into the apartment. "A colossal baby," he added, before shutting the door.

•

At the private girls' school where I worked as an assistant librarian, two of the girls looked at me blankly when I asked what they thought about the Percy Green story, and a third, her eyes outlined in purple, said, "That guy who shot a cop?"

"No, I mean, yes." I tried to explain. "But he didn't shoot the cop. He was shot *by* the cop near Riverside Park." Then, later in the week, the story began to shift. Reports came that Percy was apprehended in the midst of an assault, the victim a Pakistani man visiting his engineering-student brother. Percy had a knife; the Pakistani man had a camera and a subway map.

Although Andrew would never say so publicly (at his law school, he associated with the leftists who handled the appeals for prisoners on death row and the feminists who wrote amicus briefs for keypunch operators whose hands had turned puffy and stiff), I knew that secretly he viewed Percy's death as justice executed. Once, he had told me about a Guatemalan man who'd ratted on someone who'd sold corn to a guerrilla band. "When the villagers found him, they killed him." I winced. "He was a worm," Andrew said. "A *gusano.* That's what happens to a worm."

Since finding mice droppings in the silverware drawer, I had avoided the kitchen altogether. I climbed the stairs to the apartment, a bag with a tuna on pita hanging from my arm, and unlocked the door. There, not even a yard from my shoe, was a little carcass splayed on the floor, the tail pointing stiffly at me.

Rooted in the doorway, I covered my eyes and peeked through my fingers. It would be hours before Andrew came home. I knew my neighbors well enough to talk about the news (Mrs. Fabrizio on Percy Green: "What do you expect, the young people, these days, they are animals. It comes from the welfare and the drugs and nobody going to church no more") but not well enough to ask them to remove a dead mouse from my floor.

Exiled by a rodent, I headed for the street.

•

Two days later, I came home early to let in the exterminator and found Raoul thrown over the couch and Andrew in bed with a classmate who called herself Cat-Sue.

Cat-Sue wriggled her fingers at me. Andrew shoved a pillow over her head as though he might still hide her. She slithered under the sheet. I ran toward the kitchen, unsure if it was to retch or to grab the butcher's knife. From the bedroom, I could hear Andrew calling my name. I closed my eyes. Plastered to the back of my lids was the afterimage of Cat-Sue's tiny breasts, the nipples staring out like two raisin eyes. I pressed my lids to try to erase the picture. Then, hearing a swooshing sound, my hands flung out and my eyes bolted open. A mouse darted across the linoleum, its body long and flat on the floor.

I rushed for the front door, grabbing Raoul both for revenge and for warmth. Andrew stood naked next to the couch. I heard sounds but there was too much noise in my head to make out the words. Knowing Andrew, he was probably telling me that I had misunderstood everything—that he and Cat-Sue were studying contracts law together, that she'd just popped by to take a friendly nap.

Looking back, those three minutes with Andrew and Cat-Sue fall into scenes: bedroom, kitchen, living room, slamming the door behind me, yelling over my shoulder, "There's a mouse in the kitchen," and then jutting my chin high—brave heroine—as I ran down the stairs.

•

Four months before my mother died, my father took us on a trip to the Soviet Union. Memory is odd, since of course I hadn't known then that my mother would soon die, but somehow the trip, the last time I spent any length of time with her (in fact, I hardly remember anything from after we returned—some neuronal quirk, or was she actually then hardly home?), seems like both the first and the last glimpse I ever had of my mother, the images especially vivid to me, as though after her death they were quickly resuscitated, outlined in black and cold-pressed to my mind.

During the days, my father and the other scientists (we were with a group of European and American geneticists) visited laboratories and hospitals, while my mother and I toured the museums. The guides let the two of us roam freely, assuming, I suppose, that a slight woman with glossy black hair held back from her face with a scarf folded into a headband and tied at the nape of her neck and a nine-year-old wearing Mary Janes and a tent dress were harmless. My mother must have read up on the museums before we left, because I can still recall standing with her on one of the palatial platforms of the Moscow subway, en route to the Pushkin, her thin hand encircling mine, while she told me about the entrepreneur collectors and how they had filled their cavernous dining rooms with paintings and sculptures from modern artists at a time when hardly anyone else recognized the value of Picassos, Cézannes, and Bonnards. "Picassos, Cézannes, and Bonnards," I repeated, knowing these were names of painters but unable to conjure even one of their paintings.

For years after, when I thought of my parents, what I thought of was a painting by Matisse that hung in one of the back rooms of the Hermitage in Leningrad. My father had come with us on our first visit there, explaining to me that the museum had been a palace, the home of czars, and joking after we were instructed to put paper slippers over our shoes, "They have us polishing the floors."

I don't remember, though, seeing the Matisse that first day with my father—my father leading us from room to room, translating from his German Baedeker, giving little lectures about various of the objects before us. In my memory of viewing the painting, I was alone with my mother, my father off with the other scientists. My mother was carrying a French guidebook, and we stopped while she pointed for the guards at one of the pictures. When she finally found the painting, she snapped shut her guidebook and planted us in front. I rested with my bottom against her kneecaps.

"It's called *The Conversation*," my mother whispered. "The man is Matisse. He's in his pajamas. The woman is his wife, Amélie. She's in her bathrobe."

The man had a small pointed beard that stuck out and seemed to be pointing at the woman's toes. "He looks like Daddy," I whispered back. My mother spread her fingers over my breastbone and pulled me gently toward her. I reached my hands backward to hold on to her thighs. The woman in the painting had long black hair, shiny like my mother's. Her mouth was firmly shut as though refusing to speak. The man looked like he was talking at her, perhaps even raising his voice. Even at nine, I could see that it wasn't much of a conversation.

•

There was the beginning of a lipstick-colored polluted sunset as I left the city, driving the Quake north on the Saw Mill to look at an apartment. Donna, the headmistress's secretary on whose couch I'd slept for two nights, had brought me a tear-off tag for the apartment from an ad she'd seen on a bulletin board at the supermarket near her mother's house.

"Where's Hastings?" I asked when she handed me the scrap of paper over breakfast.

"On the river. It's nice—kind of funky and laid-back."

"Is it near Dobbs Ferry? My aunt and uncle used to live there in a big house with Adirondack chairs on the lawn."

"No, it's not like that. Go see." Donna examined me. "I can see you there in faded jeans, not too tight but still well-fitting, and an oversized turtleneck sweater." Donna considered it her particular talent to figure out people's underlying style. "I'm a gamine," she'd told me about herself. "The Coco look with lots of pearls and a flippy skirt. You're a classic with a hint of bohemian and an undertone of the sensual in the fit of the clothes."

The rest of breakfast had been spent listening to Donna's description of a Lacroix imitation she'd bought for her cousin's wedding. "It's pink with black dots, not really dots, but little telegraph dashes with dots that droop from the lines. It's off the shoulder, except that it has tiny sleeves, and then there's a big crinoline skirt that comes straight out like this." Donna whooshed her arms out and then up and around. "My accessories will all be pink, but different colors of pink. Pale pink stockings, hot pink shoes, pink pearls that I'll wear like a dog collar."

I rested my head in my hands. Imagining all of that pink so early in the morning was nauseating. I thought about Andrew and how his butt turned pink from the bathroom steam and how embarrassed I'd felt the first morning I woke in his apartment when he'd insisted on showing me the pleasures of showering à deux—embarrassed to have him see me in the blaze of lights, embarrassed by his ease with its implication that he'd showered with any of a dozen other women before.

Donna patted my elbow. "Don't worry. The Cat-Sues will

be as outré as lime green by next year. You're like a little black dress: you can use it forever."

•

It's odd how you can detect how old someone is from their voice on the phone, from the way their vocal cords resonate in their body, and I was not surprised, when Mr. Pryzwawa opened the door, to see a slight man with a concave chest and a shock of white hair.

Mr. Pryzwawa led me through his living room and up the back stairs to the third floor. Looking around, I could tell he was widowed, his house with the same untended look as my father's, the dining room table covered with things—a stack of grocery store circulars, a pile of bank statements, a clump of stray socks—that women would not leave out for company to see.

Like the beach apartment I'd rented right after college, it was an attic apartment: a large room with dormer windows that faced the river, a prefab unit with a miniature stove, a sink, and a half refrigerator on the opposite wall.

"It used to be my daughter's room," Mr. Pryzwawa explained. "We made it into a studio apartment after she moved out to go to nursing school. I'll let you look around without me underfoot. Just turn out the light when you're done."

I opened the closet and peeked into the other, which had been converted into a bathroom with an undersized shower stall. In the kitchen area, the sink was clean but lined with black scratches, everything grim but functional. I crossed the room to look out the windows. The view of the river was stunning, the road hidden by the treetops, the water cold and still, shimmering like a piece of metal laid into the earth.

I'd first seen the Hudson with Bear. It was a month or so after we'd met, the evening charged in the way of two people who haven't yet slept together but know they will, just not when. We'd driven to New York in his VW and he pulled off the West Side Highway at the Seventy-ninth Street exit to show me the houseboats and the New Jersey skyline silhouetted on the horizon. Having never seen an ocean before he'd come east for college, Bear had found Manhattan with its various waterways as exotic as Venice. For his birthday, I took him on the Circle Line around the island and bought him a navigator's map of the channels. Not until we went together to San Francisco could he understand why the New York water vistas looked to me tame, almost quaint—closer to the Old World of my grandparents than the West of my parents, where the Pacific pounded the raw cliffs and the bay loomed wide and wild as a sea.

I sat on Mr. Pryzwawa's daughter's twin bed and bounced gently up and down. I looked at my watch. It had been nearly one hundred hours since I'd left Andrew with Cat-Sue. Once on the street, I'd given Raoul to a man asking for quarters and then walked for hours, aimlessly wandering through Lord and Taylor and then Saks and Bergdorf's, letting the bird women at the cosmetic counters test sherbet shades on the back of my hand. When the department stores closed, I headed up Fifth Avenue toward the museums and checked into the Sherry-Netherland—terribly expensive, I discovered, but the only New York hotel I'd ever seen from the inside, years before with Juanita, my father's not-yet wife. My usual frugality dissolved, as if money had lost all value in the face of this gaping hole in my chest, I ordered a bottle of wine and crawled into bed to call Corrine, the alcohol taking its effect, the tightness in my throat easing as with Corrine's voice on the other end of the line I was able to cry.

"Just let it all out. Everything's going to be okay," Corrine cooed, and it reminded me of the way she had rocked me during the weeks after my mother's death when she'd still been my after-school babysitter, not yet my best friend. By one in the morning, I began to laugh, uncontrollable paroxysms, as I remembered Andrew standing at the front door, his penis still half erect, yelling as I headed down the stairs not to take Raoul.

"It looked like that damn mouse tail, pointing at me."

"Fuck him. None of them's worth crying over."

"What a jerk. And with a woman called Cat-Sue!"

Lying in the enormous hotel bed, sloshed from the wine but too agitated (where, it dawned on me, would I be able to afford to live?) to fall asleep, it was my mother, not Andrew, whom I couldn't get out of my mind: my mother, whose little car, lifted by the wind, had veered into a guardrail that buckled from the force, sending her down an embankment between Route 1 and the rocky coastline below.

One Christmas when I'd come home from college and Juanita had made us an Argentinean holiday meal and my father had drunk too much California wine and then too many snifters of his prized French brandy, he bitterly commented, "For your mother, everything was play. That summer when we went to the Soviet Union, she wandered around Moscow, you in tow, wearing dark glasses, excited that there were KGB keeping tabs on our whereabouts. She thought it was a spy game." My hands had grown clammy, and I'd turned away, anxious that my father—who, with Juanita, I felt, had abdicated his right to discuss my mother—was going to say something more, something about how for my mother death would have seemed an adventure.

The river glinted like the blade of a knife. I could see Andrew's face—seasick green when I walked in on him with Cat-Sue but then, after I took Raoul, splotched red with rage. *What did you expect?* I asked myself. *You betrayed Bear with Andrew, Andrew betrayed you with Cat-Sue, Cat-Sue will betray Andrew with God-knows-whom. Lion eats cheetah eats weasel eats mouse.*

•

When I came downstairs, Mr. Pryzwawa was in the kitchen making tea. He unfolded the cellophane wrapper from a column of saltines he sat on a tray with a plate of jaggedly sliced cheddar cheese and a tin of sardines. "Here, let me," I said, carrying the tray into the living room.

I looked down at the little fish heads, six of them lined up in a row. I hadn't seen tinned sardines since my grandfather, whose sweaters had smelled like a potpourri of the oily brine and sweet Virginia pipe tobacco, died. Because I couldn't tolerate the fish eyes on my plate, my grandfather would cut the heads off with a fork and then with his pocket knife make me tiny fillets.

I lowered the tray onto the coffee table and went over to the fireplace to look at the photographs displayed on the mantelpiece on either side of a Chinese urn: to the left, a squat woman and gaunt man in wedding garb—Mr. Pryzwawa's wedding picture, I assumed; to the right, a picture of the squat woman with a little girl standing beside her; on both sides, many pictures of what appeared to be the same girl growing older. In one of the photos, the girl held a kitten close to her face. In another, she sat on the floor hugging a German shepherd.

Set off a bit from the others was a large photo: three rows of young women, all dressed in khaki pants and long-sleeved white shirts, in front of a jeep. I picked out the girl. She was in the front row, thinner than in the other photos. Without the puffiness in her cheeks, her features looked more intelligent. She appeared slightly worried. To the right of the jeep there was a black man who looked like a guide, to the left a huge crate with the slats covered with wire mesh and some kind of animal inside.

Leaning closer, I made out the face of the beast, the eyes dark globules, as though the pupil had overtaken the iris and then all of the white. They reminded me of a painting my mother had shown me during one of our visits to the Pushkin: two animals in a field of lush grasses and red day lilies with black dots for eyes. "It's a Rousseau," she'd explained. "The speckled animal is a jaguar. The white one is a horse." The animals had appeared to be in some kind of embrace. The horse's eyes, though, had made me uneasy. Although only dots, they seemed anguished. When I pulled on my mother's sleeve to ask what the animals were doing, she bent down to brush her lips over my forehead. "The jaguar is kissing the horse," she'd whispered into my ear.

Next to the safari photo was a small crucifix: the Jesus with tilted head and blood dripping down his forearms and calves. Given Mr. Pryzwawa's age, the girl should have now been middle-aged, with nearly grown children of her own, but there were no later pictures, no new cycle of mother and child.

Mr. Pryzwawa came in with mugs of tea while I was still looking at the photographs. It occurred to me that maybe the girl had died.

Mr. Pryzwawa put the mugs on the tray next to the sardines. He lowered himself onto a hard-backed chair and I sat across from him on the couch. From years of people avoiding asking me about my mother, I knew that I had to inquire— the added pain when someone senses your grief and treats it like leprosy.

"Is this your daughter?"

"Our Judy." Mr. Pryzwawa's eyes had a burnt dry look, years beyond tears. My mother's death had taught me that *time heals all* is a stupid platitude. Wounds change: a crushed bone turns into a limp. An arsoned building becomes a home for rats.

Once, when Bear asked me to tell him something more about my mother, I told him about the trip to the Soviet Union: how my mother had taken me to see the Impressionist paintings at the Pushkin and the Hermitage. "I remember standing in front of her, little enough to lean against her knees. There was a picture of a jaguar kissing a horse. The horse's eyes looked like the button ones on some of my stuffed animals."

"A jaguar kissing a horse?"

"Yes," I said, bristling and then recoiling as it dawned on me how strange that would be.

For my birthday a few weeks later, Bear bought me a book about modern art in the Soviet museums. Not until I had leafed through it several times did I see the Rousseau—the white horse and the jaguar drawn as though for a children's story, the day lilies a brilliant red backdrop. Goose bumps broke out on my arms as I read the title: *Jaguar Attacking a Horse*. I've never asked my father if my mother had known the title and not wanted to tell me, but I can imagine his response: *For your mother, kisses and bites were the same.*

Mr. Pryzwawa shifted his gaze from the mantel of pictures. "Last summer made twenty-three years since our Judy died." He studied my face. "She was about your age." I held myself very still, hoping he wouldn't ask how old I was. I didn't want to find out that I had been born the year his daughter died. "She died in Africa."

Mr. Pryzwawa took off his glasses. With one hand on his forehead, shielding his eyes, he inhaled sharply. "She'd just graduated from nursing school. A group of them went to work for the summer in a village in Tanzania. At the end of their trip, they went on a weekend safari."

My head was nodding up and down like a bobbing doll.

"They stopped to photograph a pride of lions. Seems that Judy walked away from the jeep to take a picture of one of the cubs. The mother lion looked up and made a run for Judy. The guide shot the mother lion, but he only wounded her."

I stared at Mr. Pryzwawa's skin, parched white as desert sand.

"The mother lion must have been in a rage from having

been shot because she jumped up and dug her claws into Judy's face. Ripped out her face."

Mr. Pryzwawa put his glasses back on. He adjusted them on his nose and focused his gaze on me. "That's what my wife was never able to stand—that our Judy lost her face. Me, I was relieved. The doctor told me the claws went through her eyes, directly into her brain. She died in an instant."

Although I'd been countless times on the telling end of the story of my mother's death, I couldn't remember what anyone had ever said in response other than Bear, who'd asked where my mother had been going and I'd realized that I didn't know.

"What use do the dead have for a face was the way I saw it, but my wife, she didn't want her buried without a face, not even in a closed casket, so we had her cremated."

Mr. Pryzwawa pointed to the Chinese urn on the mantel. "That's her," he said. "She's in there."

•

I took the apartment. There was no lease and I told Mr. Pryzwawa that it would be for only a few months—until the end of the school year, when I'd already decided I was going to move back West. He didn't ask me any questions but I could tell he knew I was in some kind of trouble because when I asked if he wanted a month's deposit, he patted my shoulder and said, "No need. I see you're a nice girl."

I drove back to the city on a local road that ran next to the river. For a stretch, there was a wall covered with graffiti, and from a distance I caught sight of a heart with *Percy Green Forever* written in large bubble letters. When I got closer, though, I saw that I was wrong—the bubble letters spelled *Peter and Gretchen Forever*. I hadn't heard any news about Percy since B.C.: Before Cat-Sue. In the lull of the car, Percy's story distilled to a sentence: cop with gun got Green with knife got Pakistani tourist with subway map.

Though I didn't know the road, not even its name, I assumed that if I followed the river, I couldn't get lost. Wandering at dusk through an unfamiliar neighborhood in Moscow, my mother had taken my hand, declaring, "If John Speke could find the source of the Nile, we can find our way back to the hotel." Then, with no idea of what or where the source of the Nile might be, I'd been aware only of the descending dark and that my mother's hand, a shell over my own, was cold.

Not until I was a teenager, old enough to know about Lake Victoria but not old enough to have stopped pretending that my mother was not really dead but rather away on a long trip, had I discovered that my mother, who must have imagined herself a kindred spirit to Isak Dinesen and Beryl Markham with their brave but syphilitic lovers, had had a passion for these European explorers of the wild continent. In the attic of my father's house, Corrine and I found my mother's underlined copy of the memoirs of Vivienne de Watteville, a woman who had traveled to Kenya with her father in the twenties and then continued her journeys alone to photograph the regal animals after her father, like Mr. Pryzwawa's Judy, had been killed by a lion. Corrine and I wept when we read how Vivienne's father, whom she'd called Brovie, pulled the lion's claws out of his own flesh and then walked bleeding to the camp where Vivienne had been left behind with spirillum fever, and how Vivienne, never mentioning her own febrile state, nursed him for thirty hours, cutting the pus from his wounds, spooning him broth, until he died. When we got to Vivienne's description of Brovie's death, "I cannot tell you how unbelievably heroic he was," our cheeks had become waterfalls, each of us imagining ourselves the brave and beautiful Vivienne alone with our father in the Kenyan wild.

With the Palisades cast in a pinkish glow, the Hudson looked cold and deep. It occurred to me that there are two kinds of people: those who die of needing others, die attempting to rip open their skins so as to snuff out the emptiness with someone else, and those who, like Andrew, maneuver through life as though the purpose is to avoid being touched more deeply than the dermis. Despite the Cat-Sues and the baker's dozen of my shower predecessors, Andrew would undoubtedly die believing he never needed anyone. I'd be a dot on the time line of human traps he escaped.

My father would claim my mother was like this too. "Your mother," he'd once told me, "lived like an egg sliding over a Teflon pan." This, I know, is my father's conceit—though I never would have said that to him or told him that Corrine, inflamed with the intuition of a thirteen-year-old first apprehending the full powers of the body, had folded the newspaper from the day my mother died into a pillowcase she gave me on my own thirteenth birthday, or that, studying the yellowed weather page, I read it had been a hot and humid day, the boating report for calm and placid waters. No wind.

•

It was nearly nine o'clock by the time I reached the Kappock Street bridge that crossed into the city. Looking west at the lights reflected on the water, it seemed as if I were peering into the future—into the weeks and probably months of trudging through the days, putting one foot in front of the other, while I waited for the afterimage of Andrew and Cat-Sue to fade.

The way Mr. Pryzwawa had dunked his tea bag up and down, over and over, until the water in the mug turned the color of the river, had left me feeling afloat in something terribly but also preciously human, and even though I could still taste the bile from the moment when Andrew had jumped up from the bed and Cat-Sue had dived under the sheet, for an instant in Mr. Pryzwawa's dusty living room there had been a real and almost soothing quality about it all.

The sky was speckled with a smoky white haze, the stars hidden by the city excrement. In the dark, I could see the George Washington Bridge lit up ahead. As part of our naming game, Andrew and I had called the bridge Martha. "George wouldn't have bothered with bridges," Andrew had said. "Martha's the one who would have wanted a clean dry path." Now, though, the bridge looked more shapely and elegant than a Martha, like an unworldly animal with an arched back and a million diamonds sewn into its pelt.

When I'd first learned that there had been no wind the day my mother died, I'd not yet known about my mother's sheep farmer—that I would learn years later from my cousin Lizzy after my aunt eventually told her—but I had understood in that moment with the yellowed newspaper in my hands that it must have been a great but unbearable passion, not unlike the passion that lifted the lioness onto her hind legs when she'd seen Mr. Pryzwawa's Judy approaching her cub, that had driven my mother's car off a cliff.

Salty tears cascaded over my cheeks, the car echoing with a cacophony of sniffles and gulps. Sniffles and gulps because in the back of my mind I had been looking for an apartment so I could pack my bags so Andrew would fall to his knees and declare that even though nothing had happened with Cat-Sue, it all served only to confirm his eternal love for me. Because with Mr. Pryzwawa probably at that very moment ripping down his ad for the apartment from the bulletin board at the A&P and planning to run the vacuum cleaner through the room of his daughter who lost her face, nothing Andrew could say would let me pretend Cat-Sue had been taking a nap.

Because no jaguar ever kissed a horse. Because no wind blew the day my mother died. Because by the weekend I would be sleeping in Judy's old bed—the bridge no longer Martha, no longer a bejeweled brontosaurus, just pilements of concrete buried deep in the silt.

1990

Misto

Richard watches his wife, Lena—at forty-four, still obsessively thin, with bones so tiny that Richard used to tease her that a cannibal would pass her by, and skin so delicate that on days like today when she is angry or overtaken by strong emotion, the blood vessels seem at risk of breaking the surface, Lena who has lobbied against smoking in places populated by children or public employees, Lena who now lights an Italian-packaged Marlboro and inhales with her chin jutted high into the damp Venetian air, her neck arched slightly backward, her lips pursed in the way that inspired her father nearly forty years ago to nickname her La Principessa.

"It's a *joke*," Lena says. "Fourteenth-century Walt Disney that the tourists think is High Art."

Richard looks over the café railing at the queue of people waiting for the vaporetto: children with black satchels going to school by boat, women with net bags crossing the canal for morning errands, tourists laden with suitcases headed to the train. Across the canal, the wall of palaces appears one-dimensional, the facades a pastiche of colored patches of peeling paint, water lapping over the doorsteps, like a huge movie set behind which no one expects to find bathrooms and kitchens and couches and rugs. Despite Lena's disdain, Richard feels the elation that the city has always induced in him. At times, walking through the narrow cobbled streets, he has had the sensation of stepping into a wrinkle in time, as though he might turn a corner and be lifted backward eight hundred years or outward into another reality where pigeons sing and gondolas fly through the air.

Lena raises her index finger to beckon the waiter. *"Vorrei un caffè macchiato caldo,"* she says in her excellent Italian. The waiter wipes off their outdoor table and scribbles on his pad. He seems to register nothing about them, and Richard is certain if they were to return in twenty minutes, he would again wipe their table without a flicker of recognition. This is part of what Lena abhors about Venice—that two centuries in which the city's major commerce has been displaying its rotting facades have left an insurmountable gulf between the Venetians and the foreigners upon whom they depend.

Richard watches as Lena breaks off a piece of bread, picks up a butter knife, and then puts them both down. After nineteen years of marriage, he knows she is struggling not to gobble the entire basket of bread, all of it eaten so quickly that afterward she will stare miserably at the remaining crumbs and say she hardly tasted a calorie. She taps the table with the butter knife. "This city," she says, "it's like watching an aging call girl decked out in garb even she knows looks ridiculous."

Richard resists the impulse to grab Lena's wrist and say, *Stop, you're making it worse,* it's only one day, Cubby's an old friend, Brianna will enjoy riding the vaporettos. Instead, knowing how Lena likes setting up the verbal trap and then watching her opponent take the bait, he says, "So that makes us the johns?"

Lena smiles—the smile that Richard thinks of as her shy-arrogant smile, her pleasure at her own intellect overtaking her usual reticence. Were Lena not so consumed with a torrent of black feelings, she might jab his arm and say, *Ahhh, I should have been the lawyer instead of a hospital administrator,* to which Richard would reply, *Absolutely, my dear. And I should have stayed in Eureka and run the biggest dry-cleaning establishment in the county,* to which Lena would retort, *You mean the only.*

Again, Lena reaches for the bread and then withdraws her hand. "It's been nearly half an hour. Where the hell is she?"

Richard turns his metal chair so he can see the archway through which Brianna should have come. Two backpacking students tear off chunks of bread while they examine a map. Yesterday, on the train from Milan, Richard and Brianna had studied maps of the city while Lena read a catalogue from the Uffizi Gallery in Florence—a missive, Richard knew, directed at him to indicate Lena's refusal to participate in the planning for the day in Venice.

Despite Richard's imposing paunch about which skinny Lena and athletic Brianna tease him mercilessly, he sports the most sensitive stomach of the three of them. When, an hour out of Milan, Brianna pulled from her shoulder bag a traveling backgammon set and asked Lena, "Mom, be a team with me against Dad," and Lena coolly refused, Richard had felt his stomach clench and a cramp take hold in his lower abdomen. Although he knew that Lena's ill humor had nothing to do with Brianna and that most mothers and fifteen-year-old daughters oscillate between distance and fireworks (last night, when Brianna wanted to wear her black mini-mini skirt as opposed to her black regular mini out to dinner and Lena banned the mini-mini for the duration of the trip, there were fireworks), he has never overcome his profound nervousness when Lena expresses irritation with Brianna.

At these times, when each side of the triangle that Lena, Brianna, and he form seems charged with high voltage, Richard feels acutely aware that Brianna—who matches Lena's pale fragility point by point with a robust, muscular beauty—is not their flesh and blood. At two days, when they first got her, Brianna's olive skin had looked lush against Lena's white hands. At eight, her firm, round arms had stopped in wrists already wider than Lena's; by twelve, she had towered four inches over her mother. Last night, photographing his wife and daughter on the Rialto Bridge, Richard had been struck how, from a distance, Brianna, with her broad shoulders and large breasts, looked like the parent; not until he zoomed the lens in close did the perfection of Brianna's skin and the still-unfocused quality to her eyes, as though she is not yet quite hatched, make the age relations clear.

"Where did you tell Cubby we would meet him?" Lena asks.

"At Harry's Bar, at noon. I thought we could show Brianna the islands—make a tour of Murano, Burano, and Torcello. Cubby's probably never been farther than the Campanile."

"Which means he'll be there at two." Lena breaks off another piece of bread. This time she has it nearly in her mouth before she hurls it at a pigeon skirting the canal wall.

On the eve of their departure, Cubby had called from Dallas, presumably to discuss some legal snafu concerning his divorce but, Richard thought, desperate-sounding in his insistence that he would meet them in Venice. Richard had, of course, anticipated that Lena would be annoyed. In the moment before saying yes, he had not, however, added up the pieces: that for Lena, rerouting their meticulously planned trip to Florence (Lena never does anything that isn't meticulously planned) to meet Cubby, who she claims is the only man she knows who has reached the age of forty without developing a single virtue, in Venice, a city she despises, would be intolerable.

"It's twenty-four hours. Twenty-four hours out of our vacation so I can give my college roommate a pat on the back before his divorce goes through."

"It galls me that you jump through hoops for him. Is there anything, other than the fact that he's going to inherit fifteen million dollars, that is interesting about Cubby?"

Richard sighs. He and Lena have had this conversation countless times. On each occasion, he has explained to Lena that his attachment to Cubby has nothing to do with Cubby's money—that it has to do with their freshman year rooming together at Yale, with their weekend visits to Trinity College where they both lost their virginity on the same night with the same girl, with the trip they made together cross-country the following summer during which the car was stolen and they were held up at knifepoint in Cheyenne and Cubby never let on that he'd flunked two classes and wouldn't be returning to Yale in the fall. To Richard, reared on a diet of caution by his father (always worried about bills, about taxes, about slick roads and tire treads and worn-out refrigerator coils, about what his dry-cleaning customers might think), Cubby had seemed fearless—undaunted by challenges, liberated from concerns about the mundane, from concerns about what Richard's father always referred to as *consequences*. For Cubby, bones could be set, dented front ends pounded smooth.

Whereas Richard now usually negotiates with ease—times and places, which restaurant, what weekend—with Cubby, whose generosity seems free of inhibition and the alloys of calculation, Richard has always felt reluctant to refuse a request. With someone who would literally give away the car he is driving (while in law school, Richard had admired a red Triumph Cubby had bought on a whim; "Take it," Cubby said, punching Richard's arm. "You know what a lousy driver I am. You're doing me a favor"), how could he say no for less than dire reasons? This, of course, only further enrages Lena, who sees Cubby's guilelessness as part of his unquestioned privilege. "Yes, it's great that Cubby's so generous, but it's nothing for him to give you a car. For him, it's of no more significance than my offering the plumber a cup of coffee. But in return, you feel like you have no right to ever have a say. It's like he's the benevolent monarch and we're supposed to be the loyal serfs."

Richard had been pained to realize that Lena had accurately diagnosed the problem. This time, he hardly had the phone receiver back in the cradle after having agreed to meet Cubby in Venice before his neck muscles gripped and he realized he'd done it again—inflamed Lena's view that he is a coward with Cubby. In the two days since, Lena's anger has moved through its characteristic phases: from a silent but palpable rage to yesterday's brittle politeness to this morning's tentative but still distant banter. Now Lena raises a hand over her head. Catching the waiter's eye, she points at her empty coffee cup.

"I know. I know. I should have talked with you first. I should have suggested he come to Florence. I got swept up in feeling sorry for him. He seemed so excited about the idea of Venice, I didn't have the heart to say no."

Once he's said it, Richard senses that he's made a miscalculation, that Lena is not ready to discuss the incident any further.

"If she comes down with that skirt on, I'm going to kill her."

Then Richard gets it. This is Lena's revenge for Cubby: she'll torment him by fighting with Brianna. "Please, Lena," he blurts. *"Don't."*

He is taken aback by how shaky his voice sounds, by the strength of his reaction—as though the timelessness of the city has erased fourteen years.

Lena's eyes contract and then fill with tears. She winces and Richard realizes that she's been unaware of what she has been doing. He imagines Lena's brain clicking as she surveys the events of the past day, feels guilty to have thought Lena would purposefully wound him by hurting Brianna. She takes his hand between her own two and lifts it to her lips.

She murmurs into his fingers. Richard reaches over and kisses her lowered forehead. "Forgive me," she whispers.

Lena lets go of his hand and dabs at her eyes with a napkin. "There she is," she says.

Looking over his shoulder, Richard can see Brianna wending her way toward them. Dressed in black leggings and an oversized T-shirt, her thick hair falling loose over her shoulders, she looks like a Thoroughbred horse with strong, well-defined limbs. Richard watches while the vaporetto ticket man turns to get a better view of his daughter.

When she reaches their table, Brianna gives them a big smile. She kisses Lena and then laughs as she wets her finger in her mouth and rubs at the smudge of lipstick left on Lena's cheek. "Spare me," Richard jokes, backing away from Brianna's brightly colored lips.

Brianna gobbles hungrily on the bread and takes a long gulp from Lena's water glass. "Cubby called," she says. "He missed the flight from Rome but he's going to take one this afternoon. He said he'll call us at the hotel around six to make a dinner plan."

Richard braces himself for a torrent of I-told-you-so's. When Lena remains silent, he steals a glance in her direction. In return, Lena flashes him the second of her shy-arrogant smiles for the day—more pleased, Richard sees, to have been so easily vindicated about Cubby than angered by Cubby having missed his plane. Relieved to not discuss Cubby in front of Brianna, Richard realizes that Lena is not going to comment: she considers it beneath her to land such an easy blow.

Lena pushes back her chair and strikes her La Principessa pose.

•

It's Lena who suggests that they go ahead with the plan to visit Murano. Richard knows that this is, in part, a ploy to keep them out of the Piazza San Marco with its associations to her father, Guy, and the three summers they lived nearby while he worked on his biography of Canaletto. Now Lena views Canaletto as plebeian ("Quotidian!" she once neighed), her father's interest in Canaletto flowing from the same character eddy that had led him to Frankie, the library cataloguer for whom he left Lena's mother, Isobel, by then diabetic and obese with an unpleasant odor that emanated from her skin, three months before Lena and Richard were to be married.

Although Lena has not been able to excise her childhood love for Italy, she has funneled it into a passion for Florence and Tuscany, dismissing as crude anything that came before or after the Renaissance—Canaletto, St. Mark's (referred to by Lena as *that ode to the Byzantine barbaric*), and most of Venice relegated to the ash heap. From the venom with which Lena delivers her proclamations, Richard can detect the extraordinary effort it has taken her to destroy the sense of wonder she once felt about this city under siege from the sea, its palaces and churches decorated with the plunder of the East. Last night, watching Brianna, mesmerized as they headed south to the hotel by gondola, Richard could only extrapolate from Brianna's glazed fascination, from the way she clutched his arm, how Lena, so much more high-strung, must have first experienced this place under Guy's tutelage.

Even at twenty-four, Richard had felt transfixed by Guy. The first time Lena took him to her parents' house, Guy had given Richard a tour of the paintings that lined the walls. They'd paused in front of a Canaletto reproduction in Guy's study with its alphabetized ceiling-to-floor library of books. Guy pointed to a tiny round sign in the painting that marked the same Hotel Sturion where he, Isobel, and Lena had lived the summer Lena turned ten. In Richard's own parents' home, there had been one bookshelf that held a set of *World Book* encyclopedias, the King

James Bible, the telephone book, and a dozen or so best sellers acquired over the years as Christmas gifts from his father's sister, who belonged to a mail-order club. Except for a painting of an oceangoing sailboat that hung over the living room couch and a deer's head mounted in the basement rec room, the walls of his parents' home had been bare.

At Murano, they get off the vaporetto. Lena dodges the guides hawking tours of the glassworks and then ducks inside one of the shops that line the main street to look at a blue glass bowl she's spotted in the window. Richard holds up a finger, signaling he'll be back in an hour, and Lena makes a cross with two of her own, meaning make it half an hour. Richard nods, and Lena smiles in return, her mood softened, he senses, by the salty air and the glimmer of sun now pushing through the clouds.

He takes Brianna's arm, leading her away from the commercial bustle and toward the church of San Donato. Tomorrow and during most of their first week in Florence, he will be occupied with lawyers representing the Swiss and Italian bankers he is trying to interest in financing an electric power plant outside Nairobi. Lena will attempt to get Brianna to spend as many days in the Uffizi Gallery as Brianna can tolerate while Lena raves about the transcendent qualities of Botticelli and Raphael, unaware, Richard thinks, of how like Guy she sounds. In exchange, Lena has promised Brianna that she'll buy her a pair of ankle-high Italian boots (though in private she has worried to Richard that the Italian footwear won't come in Brianna's size). When Richard is done with his business, they'll rent a car and spend a week touring the Tuscan hills to the east and the Chianti district to the south.

Inside the church, Richard shows Brianna the intricate tile work of the floor and points to the mosaic of the Madonna, her head encircled in gold, floating over the altar. Brianna gazes dutifully at the floor and then sinks into one of the pews. She leans back and stares at the ceiling. Her mouth relaxes, and for a moment she looks again like a child with a drooping lower lip, her newfound composure dissolving in the blaze of gold.

Richard first saw the mosaic four years ago, a few months after Guy was diagnosed with brain cancer. Although Lena had never forgiven Guy for abandoning Isobel to her swollen ankles and wrists, for fracturing Lena's until-then-unbroken childhood loyalty to her parents, leaving in its wake a coolness inside her, at base, a skepticism about the nature of love, she had been beside herself at the idea of Guy's welfare being in Frankie's hands. "I don't trust her," Lena cried to Richard. "She'll have his will rewritten with everything in her name and then she'll tell the doctors to turn off the lifesaving machines. I *won't* have it," Lena cried, pounding the pillow.

Perhaps because Frankie thought of Richard and herself as similar, both from families where no one talked about the Renaissance, perhaps because Richard watched sports on TV the two or three times a year when they brought Brianna to New Haven to visit Guy and Frankie, so that Frankie had the feeling that he wasn't "stuck up like that wife of yours," Frankie had agreed to let Richard assume the guardianship for Guy. The papers hadn't been inked a week when the neurologist informed Richard that Guy had a new tumor in the frontal lobe of his brain. Each choice had been worse than the next. If they didn't operate, Guy's chances of living a year would be slim. If they did operate, Guy might die from the surgery. If he survived, he might be severely impaired—"impulsive, like a child of six or seven," the neurologist said, "prone to fits of temper and unable to plan more than a day or two in advance."

"Christ Almighty," Richard responded.

"Yes, Christ Almighty," the neurologist echoed.

A week later, the decision still unmade, Richard boarded a plane for Venice, where he was scheduled to present a paper at an international conference on the debt issues of African nations. He gave his paper the morning of the third day of the conference, then played hooky from the afternoon proceedings. Too distracted for museums, he took the vaporetto here to Murano, his first time to the island. He arrived at dusk, and as he descended the gangplank, the streetlights flashed on and patches of yellow haze infiltrated the gray mist. Uninterested in the glassworks, he wandered away from the stores toward San Donato. When he opened the heavy wooden door, he'd been stunned by the golden Madonna arched over the altar. Like Brianna now, he sank into one of the pews. Having lost religious belief long before he left Eureka, he'd been surprised to find himself praying: *Please, tell me what to do about Guy.* He heard a rustling and his heart turned wild like an animal caught in a cage as he imagined a miracle, the golden Madonna whispering a response, but then the wooden door squeaked and a blast of cool air hit the back of his neck and a group of Japanese students poured down the aisle, breaking the spell.

Brianna points to the mosaic of the Madonna. "Is it from the Renaissance?"

"No, from long before."

"Then Mom wouldn't like this, would she?"

"No."

"Barbaric!" Brianna whispers, in imitation of Lena.

"Crude," Richard teases, pinching his nose and jutting his chin into the air.

Brianna giggles. "Kwo—what's that word Mom uses?"

"Quotidian," Richard says in falsetto.

"Well, I think she's beautiful."

Richard feels a surge of love for Brianna as he adds Byzantine Madonnas to the list of *b*'s—backgammon, burritos, Bond movies—that he and Brianna enjoy without Lena. He leans back in the pew and gazes at the Madonna.

•

At five they return to the hotel. Brianna flops onto the cot that's been added to their room with *Franny and Zooey*. Watching Brianna sprawled on the couch lost in a book or playing soccer or singing with her school choir, Richard and Lena will sometimes look at each other with a secret smile of triumph: victory over the skeptics, or maybe some part of themselves, who had presumed an adopted child, without their genes, would never have their talents. The truth is neither of them believes they could have with their own genes produced such a magnificent child.

Richard opens the window and leans out. Without reservations, they had been unable to get a second room—hence the cot for Brianna—or a room facing the canal. He looks down at the courtyard fed by half a dozen passageways and festooned with clotheslines and clay flowerpots, then draws the lace curtain, the pattern casting a wobbly shadow over Lena's slender arms as she unbuttons her blouse and reaches for her robe. Lena plumps the pillows on the bed and lies down with the Uffizi catalogue balanced on her knees.

Richard lowers himself into the armchair by the window and unties his shoes. He is struck by the incompatibility between the exquisite scene before him—his wife and daughter resting on a late afternoon in Venice, Brianna propped on her elbows, Lena with her lovely limbs gracefully arranged atop the plum-colored bedspread—and the tightness in his gut as though a metal vise were squeezing his bowels.

Lena studies the catalogue plates one by one, fixing, it seems, each painting and the information printed beneath in her mind. Richard wants to shake her, to yell, *What the hell are you doing, you'll be in the Uffizi in two days, why are you studying the god-*

damned catalogue? Then, abruptly, she gets up from the bed and goes to the sink. She fumbles through her cosmetics bag until she finds a bottle of Tylenol. Richard feels a cramp in his stomach. He watches while Lena swallows the caplets without water, then raises her eyebrows as though to ask, *Do you want one?* before putting the bottle back in her cosmetics bag. He shakes his head no, afraid that any utterance would pull the loose thread that unravels the entire garment.

•

Lena had refused to tell him what she wanted. By then, Guy—woozy and disoriented, with toothpick limbs and white wisps where only weeks before there'd been a head of thick, still mostly black hair—seemed to Richard only abstractly connected to the man who had once taught him how to transform thoughts in the head into thoughts on the page. "You're the legal guardian," she said. "It's your decision."

"But he's your father. I need to know how you'd feel if we operated and he then lived for five more years like the neurologist said—maybe with fits of rage, unable to plan ahead. Or if he died from the operation. Or if we don't operate and he then dies in a year."

"I don't have any feelings about it." Lena turned off the light. "Ask Frankie and Caitlin." When Richard asked Frankie, she responded with a torrent of tears and then wiped her face on Richard's sleeve. Having moved from her parents' home in Waterbury directly into Guy's home in New Haven, having, Richard was alarmed to learn, never written a check and with no idea as to what assets Guy had or what debts they owed, Frankie was panicked by all of the alternatives. Richard didn't ask Caitlin, Guy and Frankie's then-eleven-year-old daughter, though watching Caitlin—whose resemblance to Lena (the same deep-set gray eyes; the same high forehead and pale skin) always caught Richard by surprise—scramble eggs for the three of them for dinner, warm rolls in the microwave, and wash lettuce for a salad, he had wondered if he should.

Richard had pled with Lena to come with him to the Venice meetings. "Brianna can stay with a friend. I know you don't like Venice, but it'll be good for us to have some time together."

"I can't." Under Lena's eyes, there were dark hollows—the telltale sign of the insomnia that wrecked her during bad times.

"Do you want me to cancel? I can do that. I can say there's a family emergency."

"Don't be ridiculous. You've worked for months on the paper. It's only six days. I will be fine."

Onstage with the other members of the panel, Richard had been overcome with a feeling of gratitude toward Guy, who, when Richard was five years out of law school and trying to find a way out of a transactional group at a big firm, had taught him how to write an article. Sitting at Guy's kitchen table, Guy had explained, "An article is like a painting. First and foremost, you have to get the audience's attention. Without that, all of your ideas will go to naught. That's the difference between a first-rate and a second-rate Canaletto. With the second-rate Canalettos, the canvas looks shadowy and uninviting. Most museumgoers will walk right by. Second, there has to be a central topic. After-ward, the reader has to be able to say in a sentence, *That was an article about such and such*. Similarly with a painting. Look at a Titian. Novels could be written about what's going on in the corners. But when the viewer leaves, he has a central image: Mary rising to heaven." Two weeks later, Richard had taken the train back to New Haven with the first draft in tow. While Guy read, he'd wandered through the house, looking for the hun-dredth time at the Venetian art on the walls. Afterward, Guy rolled up his shirtsleeves and reached in his desk drawer for a blank pad of paper. "Very good, very good start," he'd said before proceeding for the next two hours, the two of them seated side by side at his worktable, to cajole Richard into distilling the fundamental ideas while he scribbled reams of notes, all with such calm and good humor that it wasn't until Richard was halfway back to New York that he'd realized that the article had to be entirely rewritten.

His paper in Venice had been met with applause. It had been just hours later that he'd been foiled by the Japanese tourists as he prayed to the golden Madonna of San Donato for guidance about Guy. Afterward, he'd spent most of the night at the hotel bar getting drunk with the Nigerian minister of finance and two members of the Swedish delegation and then almost gone to bed with a young woman translator with bad skin but fantastic legs who had been flirting with the group of them. Standing at the door to her room, his hand on her hip while she dug through wads of tissues in her purse for the key, he'd felt his intestines turn hard with gas. In an instant, he turned stunningly sober as he realized what he was a hairsbreadth from doing. Unable to remember her name—was it Inghild or Ingvild?—he took her balled-up hand, inside of which was a clump of tissues. "I'm sorry," he said, "I don't know what came over me. I have to go," and then nearly ran to the elevator.

Back in New York, Richard called Dr. Bussmann, the psychiatrist he'd taken Lena to see when Brianna was an infant. Talking into Dr. Bussmann's answering machine, Richard had feared that the psychiatrist would not remember him, but when Bussmann called back to make the appointment, he'd said of course he remembered Lena and him.

"Now, is this an appointment for just you?"

"Yes."

Richard's prior visit to Bussmann's office had been with Lena, who had come under duress, Richard having threatened to leave if she didn't. Brianna had been five months old. Once in the office, Lena had refused to talk. Furious and frightened, Richard had been beside himself. Bussmann had taken a long look at Lena, then terribly thin, with bruised skin under her eyes, and turned to Richard. "Why don't you tell me what is the problem?"

So, Richard had told the story. How they had tried for four years to conceive a child. How Lena had had five miscarriages. How they had decided to adopt and had been so lucky to get Brianna when she was just two days old, the mother a Yale undergrad who wasn't prepared to raise a child. How happy he and Lena had been with their beautiful, healthy baby—always smiling, easily comforted, sleeping through the night since she was one month old. Everything going so well until last week when Guy called to say that Frankie was pregnant and Lena—here, Richard looked over at his wife—"just completely fell apart."

Lena had cried and cried, railing at Frankie and Guy "always trying to *ruin* whatever I'm doing—first, telling us they're getting married right before our wedding, now having a baby when we've just got Brianna." She'd locked herself in the bathroom, turning on the shower to block out his voice, when he tried to get her to think about it from Frankie's perspective—that Frankie, four years older than Lena, would have been nervous about waiting much longer. Two days later he'd come home to find Lena in bed with the shades pulled and earplugs stuffed in her ears and Brianna with her diaper soiled, her room foul with the smell of a day's feces.

As Richard talked, Bussmann had taken notes, pausing on occasion to look over his bifocals at either Lena or Richard. When Richard reached the part of the story about how he had put Brianna in a warm bath, had cleaned her and fed her, and how during the entire time she just whimpered, "couldn't even cry, as though she was too worn out from hours of screaming," Richard's voice faltered and Lena began to weep.

For nearly five minutes no one said a word, while Lena sobbed and shook and blew her nose. Then Lena looked up, first at Richard and then at Bussmann.

Bussmann had instructed Richard to arrange for a nanny. For the next two years, Lena had seen Bussmann on Tuesdays and Fridays. After a month, she had told Richard, "You can let the nanny go. I've discussed it with Dr. Bussmann and he agrees." Richard had looked into Lena's eyes—sad but resolute. He closed his own to listen to the words in his head; what he heard was, *You have to trust her.* He had, and Lena had not broken that trust.

Richard hadn't seen Bussmann since that visit with Lena a decade ago. The office seemed unchanged—the same worn Oriental rug, the same smell of eucalyptus about which Lena used to say she couldn't tell if it came from the office or Bussmann's skin. His head felt filled with cotton as slowly, laboriously, he tried to explain the situation with Guy: how he'd been appointed the legal guardian, the neurosurgeon's claim that the operation might leave Guy with the knowledge of a professor and the temperament of a child. "Lena refuses to tell me what she wants. I can't figure out if she's refusing because she's furious about the whole thing or if she can't let herself even think about it. Guy's wife is so hysterical it's useless to talk with her. The only one who it seems I could talk to is their daughter, Caitlin, who's eleven but acts like she's eighteen."

This time Bussmann didn't take notes. Over the couch, there was a painting that looked like the Grand Canyon framed in a mysterious light.

"What are you thinking?" Bussmann asked.

"About light. Guy used to say that Canaletto showed his debt to his Venetian predecessors by his use of light as a character in his paintings."

"What do you think Guy would decide if he had all of his faculties and were able to make the decision himself?"

Although Richard had asked himself this question before, consumed with the struggle with Lena about her refusal to tell him her thoughts, he'd been unable to concentrate sufficiently to really imagine what Guy would think about the possibility of living like a child.

"Guy is deeply logical. Or was. Now he's dazed and seems to only half recognize any of us."

Richard looked off; in his mind's eye, he saw Guy the way he'd been that day in his study with Richard's awful first draft of the article spread out between them. "Guy would say it's unnatural to return to childhood, that he wouldn't want his daughter, daughters, to know him that way." A man who spent his life honing his sensibilities like a perfectly ground magnifying glass, he thought, wouldn't want to live with them dulled or dissipated.

At the end of the hour, Richard reached in his pocket for his calendar. Bussmann didn't move, and for a moment Richard had the eerie sensation that Lena's stillness, now manifest in Brianna too, was an imitation of Bussmann.

Bussmann raised his eyebrows.

"The next appointment?" Richard asked.

"I don't think that's necessary." At the door, Bussmann touched Richard's shoulder lightly, with two fingers. Outside, Richard walked into the park and sat on a bench watching a boy feed pieces of bread to some pigeons. It was November, and a faint heat emanated from the sun. When he closed his eyes, a reddish light darted across the back of his lids. What matters, Guy would say, is the vision, not the year count.

With the wan light on his face, Richard had felt a moment of calm. In his book, Guy had discussed the influence of Giorgione on Canaletto. Giorgione had died at thirty-three, but he had, Guy wrote, left his mark, his way of seeing passed from generation to generation of Venetian painters.

•

Cubby calls at a quarter to seven. Richard is lying next to Lena, who is still studying the Uffizi catalogue plate by plate. Brianna, asleep, pushes her book to the floor and turns on her side. Cubby suggests a restaurant near the Church of Santa Maria Formosa. Richard opens his map and searches for the piazza. It's in the Castello, on the other side of the canal, a fifteen-minute walk from their hotel. Lena looks over, following as he traces the route with his forefinger. She lays the catalogue on her stomach and massages her left temple in tiny circles. *Here it comes*, Richard thinks.

"I'm going to beg off. I have a miserable headache."

Richard glances sideways at Lena. Like a batter readying for the swing, he calculates the dimensions of Lena's pitch: her dislike of Cubby, her annoyance at Cubby's unreliability, that they are in Venice, the disruption of their travel plans, her headache. He feels tempted to lob an indignant tirade—how many times has he been a good sport with one or another of Lena's friends?

Richard can hear Brianna stirring, the little purrs that mark her transition out of sleep. He runs his hand down Lena's cool arm. Please, he says silently, please come. *No*, he imagines Lena's reply; *I'm too angry.*

"Are you sure? Maybe the walk, the fresh air, would help."

Lena widens the circles she is making over her left temple. *Let go*, Richard says to himself; *it's a done deal.*

"I don't think I'd be much fun. You go with Brianna."

Brianna dresses in the regular black mini (doesn't even take the mini-mini out of her suitcase) and a long-sleeved red cotton blouse. From the way she vigorously brushes her hair, pulling it back from her face with a wide headband in a style that Lena always compliments, skipping all makeup except for some shiny stuff on her lips, Richard can tell that she is trying not to raise Lena's ire.

"Won't you be hungry, Mom?"

"There's the fruit and biscotti we bought at the market."

"I'll bring you back a gelato. *Cioccolato!*"

"*Fragola*," Lena says, brightening as Brianna draws her into their old flavor game.

"*Vaniglia!*" Brianna says, clearly pleased that she remembers all the names.

"*Misto*," Richard adds.

"What's that?" Brianna squeals. Lena smiles.

On their first trip to Italy together (before Brianna, before Lena's five miscarriages, before, Richard realizes, they were even married, since Lena had bought a print for Guy and Isobel), Lena had teased Richard by ordering him a *misto* and then watching for his grin of delight when the chilled glass arrived with two perfectly formed mounds—one chocolate, one vanilla— and a long-handled silver spoon.

Richard winks in return.

•

Crossing the Rialto Bridge, Brianna pauses to look down at the reflection of the lights on the water. Standing next to her, Richard can smell the floral scent of her shampoo, the musky residue of sleep that lingers on her skin.

While he and Lena and certainly he and Brianna never discuss it, Richard has been profoundly aware this past year that Brianna was adopted. Even more than her appearance ("Those shoulders," Richard's mother whispered to him the last time she saw Brianna. "She looks like a young Judy Garland!"), he is struck by the mystery of Brianna's talents: her natural athleticism, her musical memory, her deep intelligence so that even at eight she'd been able to beat him at chess, a game he'd prided himself on until he'd seen the way his daughter could effortlessly visualize six steps ahead. Watching Brianna grow, Richard has often thought, has been like moving in winter to a house where no one knows how the prior owner planted the garden and then waiting while green sprouts poke through the soil and stalks grow and leaves form to discover the blooms.

Shortly after Brianna's fifteenth birthday last month, they showed her the one letter they'd ever received from, Lena's phrase, *the woman whose tummy you came out of.* In the letter, written when Brianna was just a few months old, the woman—girl, really, just nineteen—had asked that, when Brianna was old enough to understand, they tell her that she would always love Brianna and always welcome seeing her, but that it would be Brianna's decision. Brianna had read the letter slowly. At one point, it had looked to Richard as though she were mouthing the word *welcome.* She'd turned the letter over to look at the handwriting from all directions, smelled the paper. Then she handed it back to Lena, who'd begun to cry. Richard moved onto the couch, next to Lena and across from Brianna, who sat perfectly still on the edge of a swivel chair. With an arm around his now-weeping wife and a hand reached out to touch his daughter's knee, he said, "Every year, at Christmas, we've written her, telling her how you are. Now, pet, it's up to you if and when you want to be in touch with her." Brianna nodded and then asked if she could be excused. Her friends were waiting for her to play Frisbee in the park.

Brianna leans her head on his shoulder. "Mom doesn't like Cubby, does she?"

Richard moves into alert as he contemplates how to navigate between this Scylla and Charybdis—how not to betray Lena or Cubby by saying too much, how not to betray Brianna by not telling the truth. As a little girl, Brianna had adored Cubby, who had showered her with presents. For her third birthday, he'd bought her a five-foot-high stuffed panda from FAO Schwarz whom Brianna promptly named Cubby. Annoyed by the extravagance, by the way Cubby's gift dwarfed all others, Lena announced they could have paid for a month of Brianna's preschool for the cost of the gift. "Probably the best way to sum it up," Richard says, "would be that your mother finds Cubby immature."

"Is he very upset about getting divorced?"

Richard tries to make out Brianna's expression, but her face is shaded by his own body. He doesn't really know how to answer. Cubby and Penny were married for ten years but never had children. Penny managed everything in Cubby's life, from the meetings with accountants and lawyers to buying his clothing through the Nieman Marcus catalogue. Lena had quipped that Penny probably marked on Cubby's calendar which nights he could drink himself blotto and end up in bed with a model or cocktail waitress he then never saw again—"out of respect for Penny," Cubby once explained to Richard. Still, Richard had been surprised when Cubby called to say that he and Penny were getting a divorce. A week later, Cubby flew in from Dallas, where he and Penny had been living in a Gothic monstrosity situated on a two-hundred-acre farm that they had converted into an unprofitable cattle ranch. After two Jack Daniel's, Cubby said things that left Richard thinking that the problem had something to do with sex. After two more, Cubby spilled the news: Penny had gone to Mexico with a cowhand who used to work on the ranch.

"I think he's pretty upset. He was pretty dependent on Penny."

"Do you think he'll cry?"

Richard wonders what Brianna is really asking. Is she worried that he and Lena will divorce? "I don't think so. But he'll probably look sad."

Brianna is quiet for the rest of their walk. Twice, Richard stops next to a lit store window to look at his map. Slowly they move away from the Grand Canal, through narrow walkways that lead to tiny waterways, over delicate footbridges, into the interior of the city that Richard has always found so mysterious. When they reach Campo Santa Maria Formosa, Richard pauses to take in the imposing campanile and the Greek temple design of the church. They turn right at the north side of the square into a cobblestone passage. Ahead, Richard can see a string of pink lights adorning a striped awning. The sounds of forks clanking on plates and people talking and laughing float out the door.

Richard takes Brianna's elbow and leads her into the trattoria. A woman with thin gray hair that barely covers her scalp and a checked apron tied around her thick waist squints in their direction; for a moment Richard has the thought that she disapproves of something about them. She motions for them to follow her into the softly lit dining room. Unnerved by the inspection, Richard inhales deeply and concentrates on the pleasing smell of warm cream and garlic as he looks around the room for Cubby.

When Richard spots Cubby, seated at a table by the window, his stomach lurches. Sharp pains dart toward his sides. Leaning in to Cubby, with her head almost touching his chest, is a young woman. A very young woman with extremely large breasts visible in the V-neck of a peach sweater.

Cubby waves. Richard rests his fingers on Brianna's upper arm and guides her to the table. The woman sits up. She waves too. She has the meticulously put-together makeup and hair that Richard associates with the girls in his high school, girls who went on to become secretaries in accountants' and dentists' offices, with the department store clerks who have assisted him over the years in buying the purposefully unmade-up unmatched Lena countless scarves, pocketbooks, nightgowns, and earrings. It's a look that has always struck Richard as having an oddly asexual effect, as though each of the parts—the hair, the clothes, the lips—are sexy in and of themselves but the glue that holds them together—the hair spray, the coordinated accessories, the cosmetics—has destroyed the intrigue, the result too obvious and stripped of allure.

Cubby gets halfway up and then sinks back into his chair. "Hey, man." He wraps an arm around the young woman. "This is Baby."

"Cubby! It's Babs. Just Cubby calls me Baby."

Cubby laughs at the sound of Babs's voice. "She's from *Ar-can-saw*."

When Cubby doesn't reach over to kiss Brianna, Richard realizes that he doesn't recognize her. *Jesus*, Richard thinks, *who the hell does he think I'm with?* Turning to Babs, he says, "This is my daughter, Brianna."

Cubby raises the back of his hand to his forehead, feigning a swoon. "This beautiful lady is little Brianna?"

Richard feels Brianna stiffen. He pulls out a chair for her.

"Real nice to meet you," Babs says.

"Lena sends her apologies. She's feeling under the weather."

"The Lena, the Lena, the Lena."

Babs laughs and Brianna lowers her gaze. Richard feels light-headed, overtaken by the heat in the restaurant, the boozy smell of Cubby's breath, and the omnipresence of Babs's cleavage dipping in and out from the center of the table as she takes bread and then sways into Cubby. "I'm famished," Richard says. "Let's order."

He picks up a menu. Brianna looks over his shoulder. "What should I have, Dad?" she whispers.

"What do you feel like, pet?"

Richard translates from the menu, using his phrase book for assistance.

"How about you, gorgeous?" Cubby asks Babs.

"You got me. All I know about Eye-talian food is spaghetti and meatballs."

Brianna kicks Richard under the table. He gives two kicks in return. When Brianna was little, Guy had told her that there is no spaghetti and meatballs in Italy. For weeks, Brianna had solemnly announced this information to everyone she met.

Cubby shifts in his seat. For a moment he seems sobered— sad and double-chinned.

"Why don't I order for all of us?" Richard says.

"That's my man. And order us a bottle of champagne. Baby here and me need to celebrate our two-day anniversary."

The waiter arrives and Richard orders tagliatelle with prosciutto and baby peas for their first course, the house veal with polenta for their second, and a bottle of champagne. Afterward, Cubby wraps an arm around Babs and pulls her toward him. "Baby here and I met on the shuttle from Dallas to Houston."

"Do you work in Houston?" Richard asks Babs.

"Used to." Babs looks coyly at Cubby. "Till Cubby gave me a better offer."

"Yup. When I saw Baby carting around those airline trays, I thought, what a *waste* of talent. I offered her a job as my personal assistant—double your salary, I said, but you got to start immediately."

"I said, Cubby, I don't even have a change of clothes with me, but Cubby, he said he'd buy me all the clothes I need for the job when we got to Rome." Babs pats her peach sweater with her matching fingertips. "He bought me these clothes this morning!"

Richard starts to fit the pieces together: Babs, the shopping trip, the missed flight earlier today.

When the waiter uncorks the bottle of champagne, Cubby cheers and Babs giggles. Cubby finishes his glass in two gulps. His skin looks tight and pink across the expanse of his forehead, and his hairline, Richard notices, has crept back even farther since their last meeting. Cubby pours himself a second glass, and Richard considers saying, *How about slowing down?* but it seems pointless—twenty years too late. If Lena were here, he imagines, Cubby would be under better control. Richard can remember occasions when Cubby jumped up on a table or, once, wrapped a woman's bra around his face as mock sunglasses, only to drop the antic after being met by Lena's cool, questioning gaze.

The old woman who'd greeted them at the door brings the tagliatelle. Richard steals a glance at Brianna, who stares into her plate. She eats quickly, barely pausing between forkfuls of the creamy white noodles. Richard takes a forkful himself, but his throat feels tight. The food reverberates in his chest and for a moment he fears he will get sick. He pushes back his chair and takes a long drink of water. Cubby eats with his left arm over Babs's shoulder. His fingertips brush the side of her breast.

"Mmmm," Babs says. "What do you call this? It's so yummy."

When the veal arrives, Cubby orders a second bottle of champagne. Brianna again eats quickly, hardly looking up. Richard moves to put an arm around his daughter, but then pulls back his hand, appalled at the image of Cubby and himself, both of them with their paunches hanging over their belts and their arms draped around a girl.

Cubby pours Babs another glass of the champagne. Richard covers the top of Brianna's glass with his hand. Last night, he and Lena had told Brianna that she could have half a glass of wine with dinner. Brianna eagerly drank the two ounces and then pleaded for more. Lena had said absolutely not but then let Brianna take little sips from her glass. Tonight, Brianna has not even tasted the champagne.

Babs is talking about the hotel in Rome. "The bathtub was the size of a swimming pool."

"Babs here *loves* taking a bath."

"It was so deep, you had to climb up these steps to get in!"

Babs leans toward Brianna, her breasts an avalanche approaching, then touches Brianna's arm, as though her comment were something another female would naturally understand. Brianna startles, a forkful of veal in her hand.

It flashes through Richard's mind that he is exposing his daughter to something obscene. He shakes his head slightly back and forth to see if this makes sense. With Richard's articles, Guy had been fond of saying, if you can't figure something out, try to step outside and look at it as though you were a stranger. Richard looks around the room. No one seems to be paying any attention to them. He wishes Lena were here so he could ask her. Only, he realizes, if Lena were here, she and Brianna would be sharing their food and softly talking together and everything would be different.

Brianna lowers her fork, leaving the veal speared on the end. She picks up her purse. "Excuse me," she says.

Richard watches Brianna make her way across the dining room. Like Lena, she walks with her head absolutely still.

"Yup," Cubby says. "We were damn lucky. Snagged what they call the Royal Suite. An emirate from one of those Arab countries canceled at the last minute. There was a butler came with the suite and a private workout room."

"Cubby bought me a camera so I could take pictures to show my mother. Me, sleeping in the *same* bed where a queen slept! Honey, which queen was it that butler said had just been there?"

"The Queen of Sweden. Only I bet she didn't look half as good as you in that bathtub with bubbles up to your ears."

It occurs to Richard that Cubby and Babs are telling each other, not him, about their escapades of the past day—making a history out of their forty-eight hours together. When the waiter comes to clear the table, Richard glances at his watch and puts his hand over Brianna's plate to indicate to leave it. It seems to him that Brianna has been gone a long time, but then Lena always complains that the men's bathroom is invariably empty while women stand endlessly in line.

The food no longer under his nose, Richard feels his stomach relax. He takes a few sips of the champagne. The waiter returns to take their dessert orders, and Richard orders three coffees, a tisane for Brianna, and two servings of a fruit tart for the four of them to share. Again, he looks at his watch. Ten minutes have passed since he last looked. Could Brianna be sick?

"Excuse me." He heads out of the dining room the way he watched Brianna do, surprised at how unsteady he feels on his feet. The old woman—the word *crone* comes guiltily to mind—who'd brought the tagliatelle is back standing guard by the door. He keeps his eyes on the tiled floor and turns the corner.

At the end of the dark hall are two closed doors, SIGNORE and SIGNORI, each with a shadow portrait: a woman holding a parasol, a man in a top hat. Beads of sweat form at Richard's hairline. He presses his ear to the door marked SIGNORE. But what if she—the crone—rounds the corner? Quickly, he steps back.

Richard knocks on the door with the picture of the man in the top hat. When there's no answer, he turns the handle and enters. He locks the door and stands looking at his reflection in the mirror, his sandy-colored hair that remains his last vestige of youth, his eyes now hooded with age. Like his father, he'd lost his looks early. As a little girl, Brianna would pat Richard's stomach, saying, "My Daddy, my Daddy," over and over, as though her daddy were somewhere inside.

For a moment Richard stands lost in his memories of Brianna as a child. Then a wave of anxiety again rushes over him. *Jesus, where is she?* Feeling a pressure in his bladder, he unzips his pants and urinates: a hard, odorous stream. Afterward, he splashes water over his face and dries his hands and cheeks with a wad of toilet paper. Maybe the SIGNORE door will be open when he comes out.

But it's not. Richard knocks. "Brianna," he says, first quietly, and then, as he repeats his daughter's name, louder and with greater insistence. "Brianna, pet, are you in there?"

Richard waits. He knocks again. *"Persona?"* he asks. The corridor is silent. Now Richard is certain that the crone is watching him. He looks over his shoulder, expecting to find her, arms folded, at the end of the hall.

No one.

He turns the door handle.

No one.

Richard rushes down the corridor. The crone is at the door. Seeing Richard, she raises her hand to her throat. Instinctively, Richard checks his fly.

He can't remember how to say *daughter* in Italian. *"Mia bambina?"*

The woman looks confused. She rubs her hands on her apron. Then she waves them up and down by her face. Long hair. Brianna's long hair.

"Sì," Richard pants.

The woman points outside. She darts her hand in and out from her chest.

"Quanto tempo?"

The woman shrugs her shoulders. She looks at the clock on the wall. *"Mezz'ora fa."*

Richard clenches his fists to keep from grabbing her. He has the impulse to shake her or, even worse, sink to his knees and begin to cry.

"Capisce?"

Richard shakes his head no.

She moves to the clock and places a knobby finger on the

face. It's nearly half past nine. She sweeps her finger back to the nine. *"Alle nove."*

Richard holds up nine fingers.

"Sì, sì."

•

Richard runs—past an old man walking a dog, past a crowd of women with covered heads coming out of Santa Maria Formosa, past groupings of tourists, laughing and waving guidebooks and cameras. His breathing has shifted from panting to something heavier and rougher. Once, he stops to pull out his map, but his fingers feel thick and rubbery and he gives up before he has it half unfolded.

It had seemed too complicated to explain to Cubby and Babs that Brianna had left. "Her stomach," Richard said. "I'm going to take her back to the hotel." Richard pulled out his wallet, but Cubby pushed away his hand, saying, "Don't be a *moron*," and then Babs cooed, "Poor thing, tell her to drink a ginger ale, that's what my mother always says, nothing a ginger ale won't help."

As he runs, Richard tries to put out of mind the thought that he's made a wrong turn. Again he stops to look at his map; this time he gets the map unfolded before realizing that it's useless since he doesn't know the name of the street he's on.

When he finally reaches the Grand Canal, it's at a vaporetto stop north of the Rialto Bridge. He looks at his watch. It's been nearly an hour since Brianna left the table; if she'd retraced their steps and had not herself got lost, she'd be back at the hotel by now. He wonders if he should call Lena. If she's not there, though, Lena will panic. Then what? Would they call the police so soon?

Richard studies the map on the wall of the vaporetto station. Their hotel is five stops to the south. Farther south, after Santa

Maria della Salute, the vaporetto heads out to Lido. Brianna loves riding on the vaporetto. If she were to ride to the end of the line, she could be stuck on Lido for the night with no return boat until morning.

When the vaporetto comes, Richard walks out to the front deck. He zips his jacket. The boat is nearly empty and in the quiet he can hear the rumble of the engine and, in the distance, the lapping sounds of the water on the steps of the palaces. Many of the palaces are lit, the colors pale, aglow with yellow light, the rich tones of the striped mooring poles buried under the darkness of night. For a moment Richard has the terrible thought that Brianna has left them for good—that just as she came to them out of nowhere, she has now disappeared. Returned to her people, like a princess in an ancient fairy tale.

Once, a few years back, Richard had a sexual dream about Brianna. Despite all attempts to erase the dream from his mind, he still vividly remembers both the day before the dream and the dream itself. He had been changing his clothes before dinner when Lena came upstairs. "It *happened*," she whispered. "Brianna got her period." Richard felt a moment of confusion, uncertain if he should be concerned or pleased. He looked to Lena for guidance; she seemed thrilled and almost dewy-eyed. "Don't say anything to her. She told me I could tell you, but she doesn't want you to talk about it with her."

At dinner, he had felt shy with Brianna, who avoided his eyes. Lena had taken special efforts with the dinner. Classical music played in the background and an uneasy quiet fell over the three of them as they sat in the dining room (usually they ate in the kitchen) eating broiled lamb chops and lemon rice. Afterward, Richard volunteered to do the dishes. Brianna and Lena disappeared upstairs. Once, Richard turned off the water and listened. There were muffled sounds, something that sounded like laughter.

That night, Richard dreamt that Brianna came into his bedroom. In the dream, he woke as she was pulling her nightgown over her head, her small breasts with their dark nipples pointed up as her arms reached over her head. In the dream, he was surprised to see that she had a full triangle of hair between her legs. She pulled the covers off of him, leaned between his legs, and began sucking on his penis. He woke feeling dirty and queasy. It was the first wet dream he had had since college. For weeks, the dream flashed into his head: while shaving, while driving, once while talking with his secretary at work.

Richard watches the bow cut into the water and the navy ripples dancing out toward the edges of the canal. In the dream, as Brianna walked naked toward him, she said, "It's okay, you're not really my daddy." He rubs his eyes to erase the phantom Brianna, but she darts into his mind's eye. She tosses back her hair and laughs; Babs's guttural laugh echoes in the canyon of his head.

Richard presses his thumbs into his temples. The dream Brianna pulls back her shoulders, and her brown nipples float through the air. His stomach clenches, and then begins to churn, up and down with the motion of the boat. He leans over the guardrail and heaves tagliatelle with prosciutto and veal with polenta into the Venetian night.

•

Richard fumbles in his jacket pocket for the key, and then unlocks the hotel door. Lena is lying in the same spot as three hours before, a half-eaten plastic cup of strawberry gelato in her hand. On the bedside table to her left, the Uffizi catalogue is closed. To Lena's right, Brianna lies curled on her side. The crown of Brianna's head and the tips of her knees rest against Lena's torso and thigh.

Lena points at Brianna and places a forefinger against her

lips. She holds the cup of strawberry gelato out toward Richard. "*Fragola*," she whispers. Richard takes the melting ice cream from her. His mouth tastes foul from vomit and he feels light-headed and terribly thirsty. Lena reaches toward the end of the bed where a gray blanket is folded at her feet. She unfolds the blanket and spreads it over Brianna and herself. Then she turns out the bedside lamp.

Richard sits down on what had been Brianna's cot. He leans against the wall and rests the cup of gelato on his stomach.

In the end, with Guy's brain riddled with cancer, his body so weak that three shifts of nurses were needed to tend him, his voice gone after a bout of pneumonia left laryngitis in its wake, Lena and Frankie had agreed on one thing: Guy should be allowed to die at home. It was late February and an early warm spell had tricked some of the forsythia into bloom. Lena was in Guy and Frankie's yard cutting yellow branches to bring in for Guy, and Brianna and Caitlin were in the kitchen helping Frankie make sandwiches when Guy motioned to Richard. Slowly, laboriously, Guy wrote on a pad. At first Richard couldn't make out the word, Guy's formerly bold script now shaky and broken. Then it came to him: *Isobel*. Richard looked up. Guy moved his thin wrist up to his chest and made little knocking sounds with his knuckles on his breastbone.

"Bring my mother to the house, with Frankie and Caitlin here?" Lena said in amazement when Richard told her.

"Well," Richard said, "I hardly think he can go out." So, after lunch, Lena took Frankie and the girls to a movie and Richard drove across town to get Isobel, who, Lena reported, had not seemed surprised when Lena had called to tell her Guy's request. For nearly an hour Richard sat in the kitchen drinking coffee with the private nurse while Isobel visited with Guy. Then, worried that the others would return with Isobel still there, he went upstairs.

The door to Guy's room was closed. Standing in the hall-way, Richard felt timid, something akin to the shyness he had felt as a child on Sunday mornings, the one day of the week when his parents, not up at five to open the dry-cleaning store by seven, would keep the door to their bedroom locked. He knocked gently and then entered. Isobel was sitting on the edge of Guy's bed, her head resting on Guy's shrunken chest, her swollen legs barely reaching the floor. Guy was petting her thin hair and whispering, really more like a rasp, something that sounded like Italian.

Richard dips the spoon into the remaining gelato. Spoonful after spoonful, he lets the sweet strawberry cream bathe the in-sides of his mouth and the top of his tongue. In the distance, bells are chiming. He counts the rings. *Eleven.* In the morning, they'll take the vaporetto to the train, and then the train to Florence. In the afternoon, Richard will meet with the Swiss lawyers, who would have arrived midday with the loan proposals for the Ken-yan electric plant in tow. Either Lena will wheedle Brianna into going to the Uffizi or Brianna will wheedle Lena into shopping for the ankle boots.

When all that is left is a pink pool at the bottom of the cup, Richard raises the plastic to his lips and drinks. He places the cup on the floor and switches off the last light. In the dark, he listens to the familiar breathing of his wife and daughter— Brianna's slow and rumbling like a boat departing, Lena's shal-low and staccato with a little hiss like a teakettle coming to a boil.

Priest Pond

As far as Charlotte MacPherson, née Callahan, can remember, she's only told two lies in her forty-four years—the first, twenty-six years ago, when she told her mother she was going with Rachel Bigsby to visit Rachel's aunt in Loveland, when really she was going with Wen to the Cincinnati City Hall and from there to Niagara Falls, where in the morning they sent her parents a telegram to announce their marriage; the second, fourteen years later, when she told Wen there was forty-five thousand dollars left in her parents' estate with another twenty thousand put in trust for Eric's college, when really, with her brother Bill's share gifted to her, there was ninety and it was she who'd arranged for the trust—so she is surprised to find herself in the next five minutes telling in rapid succession another two.

"Is Dr. Rendell expecting you?" the epauletted doorman asks, and Charlotte is so taken aback by the *doctor* and by the marble counter behind which he is scanning four miniature screens, that she says, "Yes, yes, she is."

The doorman murmurs her name into a telephone receiver while Charlotte's mouth goes dry, and then waves, gold buttons flashing, toward the farthest elevator. "Ninth floor, south side."

"The apartment number?" Charlotte asks, her voice low, almost a whisper, and cracking—surely he will not let her pass.

But there is no censuring arm, only the doorman's thin eyebrows arching in tandem with his epaulets. "No numbers. You take the one on the right."

Inside the elevator, Charlotte glances at herself in the enormous gilded mirror that forms the top panel of the back wall. How simple and naive and maybe even poor she must have seemed to the doorman: the mousy hair still cropped into the pageboy she's worn since shearing her girlhood braids, the green parka with the hood that zips bulkily into the collar, the corduroy jumper the color of stewed prunes, the white cotton turtleneck, nappy from a hundred washes, the rubber-soled walking shoes ordered from a catalogue. She lost vanity so many years back, it is hard to remember when. Only about her eyes, still a large china blue, has she retained pride. Pride that they haven't sunk into her face like Wen's had, faded from wind and sand and sun and, she's always thought, from the years of humiliations—the feeling of defeat when his back wouldn't heal and he had to give up ice hockey and all his Icarus hopes; when, these last five years, the fishing gone bust, the fishermen having taken out more of the cod and mackerel and hake than the bay could reproduce so they'd gone from each boat bringing in upward of two thousand kilos a day to the whole fleet hardly hauling in that much, he'd had to take road work and then unemployment to make ends meet.

On the ninth floor, the elevator opens onto a foyer with a high-backed chair to the left and a pedestal table with a glass orb filled with white tulips to the right. In front, there is a door with a brass nameplate on which DR. MARGARET RENDELL is engraved in small script letters. As Charlotte steps out of the elevator, a chime rings and then a young woman—redheaded, ponytailed, crisply aproned—opens the door.

"Oh . . ." A hand, so freckled the white skin beneath is nearly hidden, flies up to cover her mouth. "Excuse me, only I

thought he'd said *Mr.* MacPherson. Is . . . did Dr. Rendell know
you were coming?"

"Yes," Charlotte says, this time the lie rolling smoothly,
without pause, off her tongue.

"Oh, dear. She just left, not even ten minutes ago. Said she'd
be out for about an hour." The girl seems flustered, which has
the effect of calming Charlotte. "Would you like to wait?"

"Please." Charlotte follows the maid down a long corridor
lined with sepia-tinted photographs of elegantly dressed black
people, and then through a set of French doors into a large room
with a blond oak floor and a rose Oriental rug covered in a
pattern of blue-gray vines. She motions Charlotte toward a
creamy couch with a fan of pillows against the back and a mohair blanket, also light, like the inside of an oyster shell, laid over
one arm.

Charlotte runs her fingers over the blanket and inhales:
the sweet decaying scent of gardenias. Across from her, a wall
of tall windows looks out over Central Park. There are no real
curtains, just a sheer voile, left loose on one side so a shadow
falls over the black grand piano, but pulled back with a braided
cord on the other so the late afternoon light forms a gold pool
on the floor. A ficus tree with shiny leaves brushes the ceiling,
and on the walls there are pastel canvases, one of silvery cubes
floating like bubbles, the other of what looks like a nude female. Folding her chapped country hands, she thinks of her
own living room with its centerpiece of Wen's television and
recliner. When they built the house, a prefab ordered from a
company in Ontario, they'd economized, putting in wall-to-
wall carpet instead of finished wood floors, but what with Wen
and Eric always coming in damp and muddy, the carpets had
mildewed and Charlotte finally had the rugs ripped up, resign-
ing herself to the linoleum underneath, which at least she could
keep clean.

The maid returns bearing a lacquered tray she lowers carefully onto a glass table. On the tray is a whimsical teapot, shaped like a Pierrot doll with an arm for the spout and a matching sugar bowl, creamer, and mug. To the side sit two oval plates: one with an array of sliced fruits—strawberries, oranges, pineapple rings; the other with a sampler of tiny bakery cookies—iced rounds, chocolate-filled straws, flowers with red jam centers.

"Milk or lemon, ma'am?"

"Lemon, please."

The maid pours the tea and lifts a lemon wedge with a pair of silver tongs. She points to a small bell on the tray—"If you need anything . . ."—and then disappears, closing the French doors behind her.

•

Three days before, on the morning she left Priest Pond, Charlotte woke thinking of her father. She hadn't seen her father in twelve years, and then he'd been in his coffin, the remaining strands of his jet-black hair plastered to his head, his thick arms straining even in death against the suit he'd worn only to church and other funerals, the scar he'd brought home from the war hidden beneath. Charlotte's mother, who would die less than four months later, had insisted that the wake be held at home, her father's coffin placed in the room her mother had called the parlor. Charlotte had stood next to her brother, Bill, a year out of Princeton and in his first banking job. She'd been struck by how fitting it seemed, how the room, which her father had always hated, seeing it as her mother's attempt at pretending that she wasn't a plumber's wife, had always felt like a funeral parlor, dark and heavy and stiff with the promise of chastisements.

It was early, the morning light filtering through the white bedroom curtains Charlotte had sewn herself. She lay still for longer than usual, knowing there was nothing to do. The car was packed, her neighbor set to pick the fall garden crop. (*Take it*, Charlotte had urged when she'd shown her neighbor the kitchen garden—the beans, the acorn squash, the onions, beets, kohlrabi, red cabbage—unable, now, to even imagine why she'd planted all of this or how, in years past, she'd spent weeks at canning, at preparing the root cellar.) Arrangements made to spend the two nights she'd stay in New York with her brother and his wife, their apartment, Bill had explained, not far from where she was going, just a short cab ride across the park, Charlotte too embarrassed to tell him that she would be driving the pickup to New York.

Twisting backward, she reached the window over the bed and pushed it open. Outside, the air was balmy, the island's secret, God's kiss, she used to tell Eric, the Gulf Stream that came from Florida warming the Gulf of Saint Lawrence, the water warmer than anywhere north of the Carolinas, like the Caribbean, she'd heard tourists say, as though there should be palm trees and coconuts instead of fields of barley and stands of pine and spruce tumbling into the sea.

She dressed quickly in her jumper and tights, made tea and a slice of toast from a loaf of bread one of her sisters-in-law had brought two days before. When she finished eating, she rinsed the cup, checked the stove, locked the kitchen door, and stuck her handbag on the front seat of the pickup.

Charlotte walked down the clay road lined with wild blueberry bushes, the outer bunches shriveled and dry, but inside, where she reached her long fingers, filled with the tiny tart budlets. Although their ten acres ran from the road out to the Gulf of Saint Lawrence, Wen had insisted they build away from the water, where in the winter cold gusts of wind blew in from the north Atlantic, so as to save on heating costs. Then, Eric had been in his fourth year of ear infections, and Charlotte, tired out from her fights with Wen that the boy would never get well if Wen refused to let her keep the trailer a decent temperature and scared too that Eric's keen sense of sound might be damaged, had gone along. Today, there was a warm breeze from the east and the field of hay that stretched west from the house made rustling sounds. On the dunes, the sea grasses would be blowing, soft, all in one direction, a lime-green animal's hide. This year, with Wen sick, they'd left the tract behind the house unplanted and wildflowers had grown, defiant, like children spinning wildly through a room where they know they should be still: yellow goldenrod, purple Michaelmas daisy, a spiky fireweed with leggy stalks and fluffed cabernet-colored flowers Wen's sisters called rosebay willowherb.

When she'd first come to the island, Charlotte had been amazed at the way the fields ran right to the edges of the bluffs, the land dropping off like those ancient drawings of the earth as flat. Before her, red clay cliffs abutted the gulf, this morning a sapphire blue stretching out toward a pale horizon, the water velvety with only the thinnest slivers of whitecaps toward the shore. Green lichen streaked the cliffs and, below, pools of water formed between the rocks. Floating in one, there was a wooden slat from a lobster trap, smooth, Charlotte knew from years of scrambling with Eric over these rocks—Eric, whose translucent skin she'd had to cover from head to toe with suntan lotion, the peaked white brow dotted with a tiny bluish star, the residue of a little piece of lead lodged under the skin after another boy had poked him with a pencil, eerily, in the exact spot where the mystics place the third eye. Eric leaning to examine each object that washed ashore: a starfish, a bottle embossed with Japanese characters, pieces of rope, once a braided gold chain he'd laid cold and wet against her then-still-young neck.

A quarter of a century before, sitting on the porch of her parents' two-family house, when Wen, a roguish boy she'd met at a street fair—Wen and the other Canadian ice hockey players loud and bold from German beer and a winning streak that had left money in their pockets—had told her about the island, she'd imagined it as something between Pocahontas and *Little House on the Prairie*. Wen had talked about first-growth forest: red spruce, white spruce, black spruce. Pine, cherry, maple, birch. He'd talked of beef chickens and lane chickens and how his father had sheared their own sheep and his grandmother and great-aunts had spun a coarse white wool his mother and aunts had dyed and knit into bulky sweaters. There'd been a double outhouse—frosted over or bee-infested depending on the season—and an orchard with apples, peaches, and pears. He and his brother had trapped beaver, mink, and rabbit for pocket money. They'd walked four miles each way to a one-room schoolhouse by a river, where, after school, the boys would saw a hole in the ice and then lower a torch to attract salmon, six man's hands long, they'd spear with a long spontoon. Winter nights, they'd drag his uncle's combine down to the river to generate electricity for lights so they could play ice hockey.

Before, before, Charlotte thought, gazing up at the white October sky, empty of clouds or color, and then out at the horizon, where she could see a tanker headed toward Newfoundland. That useless before.

•

On the ferry to Cape Tormentine, Charlotte sat in the second-deck cafeteria drinking tea from a Styrofoam cup. It was a forty-five-minute crossing over the Northumberland Strait, a trip Charlotte had made a half dozen times with Wen to shop in Saint John. A young couple sat at an adjacent table. The girl had long dark hair, stiff with hair spray, and athletic calves that peeked out between the bottoms of her Lycra pants and the tops of her slouchy socks. The boy, man really, had brought back a tray of food from the cafeteria line: two cups of coffee, a muffin for the girl, and, for himself, eggs, potatoes, bacon, and toast. The girl teased him, ignoring her muffin and instead taking nibbles from the crispest pieces of his bacon and the edges of his toast. He gave her hand a play whack and pushed the plate out of her reach. She giggled and lifted herself onto her knees, leaning over the table toward him, her sweatshirt falling forward so the tops of her large soft breasts were exposed.

Charlotte tried to remember if she'd ever felt that way, proud and in full possession of her body. It had been a different time. Her mother's brother had died in Honfleur, the first year of her own marriage. Her mother's hair had turned white within the year, her grief draining the color from everything it touched. Her mother's grief had not abated, it seemed to Charlotte, until Bill, her uncle's namesake and nine years her junior, had been born, so that Charlotte would always think that she and her brother had grown up not only in different eras but in different households with different mothers. She'd been eighteen and in her last year of high school when she'd met Wen. Wen had mistaken her heart-shaped face, blue eyes, and slender shape for angelic temperament; she'd mistaken his tight muscular arms, his rust hair, always falling forward into his eyes, and his laugh, boisterous and from the gut, for the outward signs of a deep pulsing vital force. The next day, watching him play, his flat butt almost parallel with the ice, his eyes fixed on a spot far ahead, Charlotte had thought of an animal, a leopard or a lion, a creature with natural grace. A week later, they had eloped.

The girl got up from her chair. Giggling, she walked around the table and plopped herself on the boy's lap. Her thighs spread over his and he reached his hands around her and moved them under her zippered sweatshirt. Fascinated and then embarrassed, Charlotte averted her eyes.

With Wen too, she'd been embarrassed at first, intimidated

by his experience: the many girls he'd gone to bed with on the road. After Eric was born, when he'd hardly wanted her, she'd wondered if the girls had continued, but he'd slept peacefully wrapped around her, hardly like a man racked with guilt. Later, she'd wondered if it was his back, the injury when Eric was five. Over the years, though, she's come to understand that it was none of these things—that it was simpler, sadder. Wen experienced himself as living on scarce resources. It took all he had to leave the house eight months a year at 4:00 a.m., to put on the damp yellow oilskins and head for his boat redolent with fish guts. After that, he could either love her or want her, and she supposes that if she'd been able to choose between his face pressed every night into her shoulder and something more like she'd imagined that first time watching him play ice hockey, she would have chosen what she'd had.

•

She must have dozed off, because she starts when she hears the chime ring in the hall, the fruit dish still balanced on her lap, the maid's high voice saying there is a Mrs. MacPherson here, *she said she was expected*, and Charlotte tastes her mouth, a bitter metallic from sleep, and for an instant thinks how foolish to have said this, certainly there will now be a scene. But if Margaret, Dr. Margaret Rendell, responds to the maid it is very quietly, because Charlotte hears no disclaimers, only the maid coming in to clear the tea tray, the red wisps tucked back into her ponytail.

A moment later, the rapid click-click of pumps announces Margaret Rendell's entrance. She is tall and large-boned, clad in a red-and-black houndstooth suit with a jacket that buttons on a diagonal up the front, just glancing her ample hips, and a short straight skirt. Her gazelle's neck is accentuated by her hair, slicked back from her face and secured in a chignon at the nape. What leaves Charlotte with her mouth ajar is Margaret's skin, a deep mahogany so beautifully cared for it looks almost polished, and the tortoiseshell glasses, large and round with the lenses so entirely opaque Charlotte can only see her own reflection in their face.

Margaret lowers herself into a white leather swivel chair. She crosses her long legs, and spins the chair in quarter turns with a tiny rotation of her ankle. "Would you mind," she says, "closing your eyes for a moment? I'd like to take a look at you but I don't let anyone see me without the glasses."

Confused but obedient, that obedient impulse she learned from the nuns at Our Lady of the Immaculate Conception, Charlotte closes her eyes. The chair creaks as Margaret stands, walking away from the couch and onto the bare floor by the windows. Charlotte hears the snap of glasses folding, and then what feels like Margaret's eyes running over her, that old tingly sensation from morning services when she believed she could tell if one of the sour-breathed nuns was passing her eyes over Charlotte's back, particularly Sister George, with her lashless lids and blue-veined temples, whose gaze would spark an electrical current that would spread across Charlotte's shoulder blades before racing down her spine.

Margaret laughs. It is a friendly laugh, but with a sharp edge to it. "You didn't know, did you?"

"Excuse me?" Charlotte's voice sounds small and weak and suddenly she feels panicky, an impulse to open her eyes and dash out of the room.

"That I'm blind. Well, ninety-five percent. I can make out large shapes."

With her eyes closed, the street sounds that before seemed muffled and almost soothing, a gurgle of human life so unlike the unpeopled silence that blankets the Priest Pond house, now seem amplified, what Eric would call a cacophony of horns and gunning engines.

"You're an ectomorph like Eric. All skin and bones, with cold hands and cold feet."

Charlotte can hear her own breath, short and hollow. Since Wen's death, now nearly a month ago, there's been a hard tight feeling in her chest, as if a piece of ice has broken off from a frozen mass inside her, drifting up toward her heart so that she has to breathe around it. She's been mortified to realize that this feeling is not grief for Wen—who'd been gone, really, for years, no, decades already—but the awareness of Eric's absence, Eric whom she'd thought of as only temporarily estranged from them, not so unusual for a boy in college, but who, when Wen went into the hospital, she'd not known how to even contact. It came as a shock, that old ache of longing for Eric, followed by a sudden and terrible sense of shame that they, she, had let so much time pass, three years now that he's been out of college, years in which their calls to Eric dwindled from once a month to birthdays and Christmas, his cards and letters growing less and less frequent so that the week after Wen's first heart attack, she was taken aback looking through the shoe box where she kept Eric's letters to see that the last she'd heard from him was six months earlier, a Christmas card in which he'd written only his name. With Wen's second heart attack and the ensuing days when she tried to locate Eric, his phone disconnected, the school where he'd written that he worked unable to tell her any more than that he is on leave until January, abroad, they believed, the curtain of pretense lifted, and she had to acknowledge that it has been five years, more than a fifth of Eric's life and all of Wen's final years, of only polite gesturing between them.

"And you didn't know that I'm black."

When Charlotte hears Margaret sit back down, she opens her eyes. Margaret has put the dark glasses on again. Her head is tilted in Charlotte's direction.

"I'm afraid I've intruded upon you. I . . . ." She doesn't know the end of the sentence. "I'm afraid I don't know myself why I came."

Margaret nods slightly. In the center of the opaque lenses, where her eyes should be, two circles, reflections from the crystal lamp on the table between them, glow a buttery yellow.

"I know Eric's out of the country. The principal at his school told me. That was in August, right after Eric's father went back into the hospital." She can't not look at Margaret's face, but when she looks, she's distracted by not seeing her listener's eyes. "He said he'd ask around if anyone knew Eric's itinerary or how to reach him. I got a letter from him saying one of the teachers had given your name as someone who might know."

The maid pushes open the French doors, her face flushed, a gray spot near the hem of her uniform suggesting a mishap in some distant room. Charlotte feels guilty, seeing something about Margaret's maid that Margaret is unable to apprehend. The girl sets a round teak tray on the table between them: a carafe of pale wine, a green bottle of sparkling water, a glass bowl filled with large crescent cashews.

"Thank you, Janie," Margaret says as the girl, ponytail flapping, hastens off.

"Eric's traveling in Indonesia." Margaret's hands rest quietly on her lap. "I think you have about as much chance of locating him there as finding a needle in a haystack."

"Wen, Eric's father, passed away a few days after I spoke to the principal. I'd already buried him before I got the letter."

A silence falls during which Charlotte feels relieved that Margaret doesn't say any of the expected things like how sorry she is—why should Margaret be sorry?—that would require Charlotte to evade or explain. Instead, Margaret laces her fingers together and extends them upward, making a steeple with the tips. A moment passes during which Charlotte wonders if

Margaret is silently intoning a prayer. Then Margaret leans forward. She wraps a hand around the carafe.

"Shall I?" Charlotte asks.

"I can do it. Wine, bottled water, or a spritzer?"

Wen stopped drinking after his heart began acting up, and Charlotte had stopped with him. At the reception after the funeral, she'd longed for a drink, but her sisters-in-law had served coffee and turkey and cheese sandwiches and pound cake they'd made themselves. "Wine," she says.

With one hand on the wine glass and the other circling the carafe, Margaret rests the lip of the carafe on the rim of the glass and pours. She angles an ear toward the glass, pouring, it seems, by sound.

"He, Wen, Eric's father, was sick for a long time," Charlotte says, surprised by her own words, since Wen died four days after his second heart attack. They are, though, in a certain way, true: Wen had never really recovered from the back injury nearly two decades before.

"Eric sublet his apartment, but didn't want to leave his electronic keyboard and his other instruments there. They're in my guest room."

Charlotte feels her heart pounding, knocking hard—her son's things here, just a few rooms away.

Margaret hands Charlotte the glass of wine and then pours herself half a glass, topping it off with the bottled water. *That must be a spritzer*, Charlotte thinks, her hand tremulous as she moves her own glass to her lips. "How do you know Eric?"

Margaret swivels toward Charlotte, and for a moment Charlotte is overcome with the suspicion that Margaret is tricking her, that she really can see. Her face grows hot, the awful red splotches of embarrassment that have plagued her since childhood, when they'd streak her neck and burn across her cheekbones toward her ears, as she wonders if Margaret is Eric's lover.

With the glasses hiding her eyes, it is hard to tell how old Margaret might be—certainly past forty. But Eric will be twenty-five in the spring.

"He saved my life. Brought me back from the dead."

Charlotte presses a damp palm over her heart. Perhaps, like her mother, she will quickly follow her husband to the grave. "What do you mean?"

"I was one angry son of a bitch after I lost my sight. It was six months or so later that I met Eric. I was supposed to be going through a rehabilitation program and I was giving them hell." There's a lilt to Margaret's voice, as though she is talking about a naughty child. "I couldn't imagine what I was going to do with the rest of my life. I'd spent eleven years training to become a surgeon—four years of medical school, four years of residency, a three-year fellowship in microvascular surgery—then two more years establishing my practice and *boom*, in an instant, it was gone.

"At this rehab place, they were trying to teach me what they called functional skills: how to navigate without sight, how to cut your food, how to fix your hair. There was an idiot psychiatrist there, blind himself—but from birth, that's different—who kept talking about letting go of the false expectation that life is fair. One of the other patients, a kid who was never going to walk again after a motorcycle accident, told me that the nurses rolled their eyes whenever this idiot opened his mouth."

Margaret reaches for a cashew, tracing the perimeter of the tray until she finds the bowl. The salt glistens on her lips. "One day, after I'd been there a good while, making no progress towards what they called my therapeutic goals, I had a temper tantrum over something and shoved my food tray across the cafeteria table. It flew off the table, landing with this enormous bang on the floor. The sound shocked me so badly I started to cry. I just sat there with my hands over the eye patches. This nurse peeled back my fingers—bloody around the nails, they'd told me, from chewing the cuticles. She held my hands in hers and said, Sugar, there's got to be something you can do with these hands other than make trouble, and that's how she came up with the idea of introducing me to Eric."

Charlotte lets her own hand drop from her chest. Outside, light is draining from the sky and a shadow, sharp, like a parallelogram, grazes the piano—dusk, that chimerical rupture between day and night when tree branches and leaves and even the veins on the leaves appear for a fleeting instant more distinct, the edges no longer blurred by glare. It has always struck Charlotte as a pensive time, light and dark held in balance, and now she remembers those quiet dusks in the trailer at Priest Pond, before her parents died and they built the house on the money she inherited, her brother insisting she take his share since he was by then in his second year at his bond-trading job and expecting a bonus twice the size of the inheritance. In the trailer, Charlotte's kitchen window had looked out over a field of emerald grass that stopped at a red mud cliff only fifty feet away, the Gulf of Saint Lawrence purple in the ebbing light, Wen seated on the banquette that served as a couch reading the paper, Eric at the fold-down kitchen table playing with pipe cleaners and humming so quietly that ten minutes passed before she recognized that he was humming Chopin's Polonaise in A-flat, a selection from an Arthur Rubinstein recording she'd brought home from the library and played that afternoon.

"This nurse's son was in Eric's class, a nine-year-old kid with a school chart three inches thick from smashing mirrors and stealing things and scratching obscenities on a teacher's car. One of those kids who looks like he's headed in a beeline for jail. It was Eric's first year as the music teacher at the school, his first job out of college, and he'd taken the kid on, kept him after school trying him on the piano and the tuba and the cello and the saxophone until one day the kid sat down at a drum set and Eric saw a look in his eyes, and now this nurse's son was doing great with the bad behavior behind him."

Charlotte's thoughts are breaking into fragments, darting every which way as she struggles to put this Eric—the nurse's, Margaret's, *he'd taken the kid on*—together with her own: a shy, dreamy boy with ankles that wobbled in the hockey skates Wen had bought him and large ears that the other children had teased him about.

"It was a humbling experience, letting your son teach me to play the piano. I wasn't used to doing things without a guarantee that I could succeed. We weren't poor when I'd grown up, there'd always been money for food and clothes, but there for damn sure hadn't been money for piano lessons. In college, I'd been single-minded. Anything I wasn't certain about, I avoided. It might lower my grade-point average. I was going to become a doctor and I was going to go to a top medical school. And it was easy. Not that it wasn't a lot of work, just it was predictable. If I went to all my classes and labs and did all the problem sets and read and then reread all the assigned reading, I'd get an A in the course. Effort was, as they said in my biostat class, strongly correlated with outcome. I'd never tried to learn anything that didn't work that way."

Charlotte's own music instruction had been limited to the recorder during grammar school and chorus once she'd reached high school, but she'd learned enough to know when she heard Eric humming that *he* could hear, that he'd heard every note of the Chopin polonaise.

"Of course, Eric didn't tell me that he'd never taught a blind person before—or that he was just twenty-two. I guess I was lucky I couldn't see how young I've heard people say that he looks. I was still living at the rehab center, and for the first lesson, we used this old clunker of a piano they had in the patient dayroom. Eric placed my right hand on middle C and said play. I banged. Banged like an angry four-year-old. Eric didn't say a word. I must have banged for a good half hour, but eventually, maybe I was just getting tired, I let up, allowed myself to feel my fingers on the keys and listen to the sounds they made. I experimented with a little ditty. After a while, Eric started humming along. He leaned over me and began to answer my ditties and I answered back. And then he asked, When are you leaving here? and I said by the end of the month and he said, Good, when you get home, rent yourself a piano and we'll start. So I did. Actually, I bought one. Not this one," Margaret says, pointing over her shoulder, "this I bought last year, but a used upright."

The day after Charlotte had recognized Eric humming the Chopin polonaise, she drove him the fifteen kilometers to the white-spired church in Naufrage. Sitting in the choir practice room, she placed his right hand with the thumb on middle C. Like Margaret, he banged until he was tired with the banging, and then slowly found his way to a melody. She sang her response and he answered with his fingers. There was no one on the east side of the island who could teach beyond the beginner level, so for ten years, until Eric was able to drive himself, every Saturday morning Charlotte drove Eric the hour and a half to Charlottetown for his lesson with old Mr. Fleitzig, a German Jew who'd left Bremen before the war and lived in a Victorian house by the harbor, the garden and exterior so overgrown and neglected the house appeared to be decomposing around him.

"So," Margaret says, and then she comes to a full stop like the silence between movements in a piano sonata, and Charlotte realizes that this is partly why Margaret feels so intimidating, this bluntness exercised at will. "Why do you have to ask me where your son is?"

Dazed, by the wine, by the opulent room, by the scent, stronger now of gardenias (could it be Margaret's perfume?), by

Margaret, by Margaret's Eric and the flood of her own memories, Charlotte fears that if she speaks, her wet eyes will overflow, a whimper escaping from her lips. But to her surprise, the next thing that happens is a yawn. A moaning yawn that pulls her eyes shut and casts her mouth wide. She raises her hand to cover her teeth. "Excuse me, I'm afraid I'm not accustomed to the wine."

Margaret stands, briskly rubbing her palms together. Grains of salt float through the air. "You need a nap. All that driving, the body wasn't made to be confined that way."

"Oh, no. That's not necessary. I'm fine, really."

"No arguments. Not a word more until you've had a nap. Besides, I have some phone calls to make. You can stretch out on the couch. There should be a blanket resting on the arm."

Again, Charlotte feels the heat rising up from her neck, and then, to her horror, she yawns again. Before she can think of what more to say, the French doors open and then close and there is the click-click of Margaret's heels receding in the hall.

•

Of course Charlotte dreams of Wen. She knows she will. She has dreamt of him nearly every night since he died. In the dream, he is as he'd been when she met him: jumpy, boyish, rakish—a big grin as he took her elbow and led her back to the racetrack stables, along the bank of the Ohio River, where he knew the Canadian trainers who winked exaggeratedly at him for having a girl on his arm. Then the dream changes and he is as he'd been when Eric was a boy: grim, dour, because they never saw him until dusk, always with a shadow on his lip and jaw. He is standing at the bow of his boat, his back toward her and naked from head to toe: his forearms a leathery brown, the rest mushroom white. On his back, there is an ugly red gash, and even in the dream, Charlotte, the dreamer, knows this is wrong, that Wen's injury is two disks compressed together, not anything she could see. Wen turns and there is a long gleaming knife in his hand like he might use to clean the hake in the silver pail by his feet, but then the scene shifts and Eric is crouched by the pail, his large ears pink and wiggling, his bony ankles flanking his hips. Charlotte rushes toward Wen but the dream grinds to a stop, Charlotte bolting out of sleep at the moment she reaches Wen, just a millisecond before the fish knife would have cut her palms.

She sits up. Outside, the streetlights have been turned on, casting white globes on the blackened windowpanes. In the wake of the dream, the light is painful, leaving her with a hollow, empty feeling. She pulls the mohair blanket over her lap and closes her eyes again, her thoughts drifting to the last day the three of them—Wen, Eric, and she—were together. Really together, since Eric made two more trips to the island but they were more pantomimes of visits than visits.

It was Eric's second year at Oberlin, winter break, a Saturday, a few days before Christmas. Everything was frozen and bare, the trees, the roads, the fields all mud brown, waiting for the January snows. During the fall, Eric had veered from his piano studies, overtaken by what Charlotte had guiltily hoped (she'd always told herself that all that mattered was Eric do what he found interesting) would be a passing infatuation with musical anthropology. For his final paper, he'd programmed an electronic keyboard to reproduce a seven-note Javanese gamelan scale. He'd borrowed a portable keyboard from the music department and brought it home in a bulky black case to show them, though later Charlotte would wonder who he'd had in mind: his father and her, or Fleitzig?

Charlotte had placed a book of Renaissance Christmas carols she'd bought mail-order on the piano music stand, but Eric had set the keyboard up in his room and was occupied with only it. All morning, while she was baking Christmas cookies, strange music wafted through the ceiling. After lunch, Wen fell asleep in the recliner, exhausted from the roadwork he'd signed on for in November with the hope of logging in his twelve weeks on the province payroll so he'd qualify for unemployment in February and March, when it would be too blustery to either fish or repair roads. That year, the roadwork had taken its toll on Wen in a way Charlotte hadn't seen before. She'd been frightened by his ashen pallor and by the way he had to soak his hands in a bowl of warm water before he could feel his teeth on his fingertips. Wen, angry, defensive—probably scared himself, Charlotte had thought—had insisted the gray cast to his skin was soot, the numbness in his fingers the consequence of gripping a shovel seven and a half hours a day.

Around three, Charlotte heard Wen stir and then get up to use the bathroom. The music stopped, and there was a loud thumping as Eric descended the stairs with the keyboard back in its case. He came into the kitchen, Wen following behind. Charlotte smiled at the two of them—Eric looking like the spindly, elongated forward-cast shadow of his compact, muscular father. She would make cocoa, bring it into the living room on a tray with a plate of the cookies still soft and warm from the oven. Perhaps Eric would play the carols afterward.

But before she could heat the milk, Eric asked Wen to borrow the pickup; he wanted to show Fleitzig the electronic keyboard, to play him the gamelan simulation. Wen went outside with Eric to go over with him again where the safety brake release was on the floor and how to use the five gears, even though Eric had been home three days already and had already driven the new (really used, but new to them) pickup. Through the open kitchen door, Charlotte could hear Wen's litany: "Remember, there are five gears, not four. The old truck had four. Not that you should go higher than third—fourth is where reverse was on the old truck." Eric listened patiently, his head tilted slightly, but whether he was listening to the words or to the cadences of his father's voice, Charlotte wasn't sure.

That evening, Charlotte and Wen ate in silence, a familiar

silence, not hostile but rather the silence of people who've run out of things to say to each other, not because life doesn't provide an endless source of conversation but rather because the peace between them wouldn't accommodate Charlotte's ruminations: the memories set off by her mother's Christmas cookie cutters (the fir tree, the Santa, the elf, the reindeer, the stocking, the wreath), would Eric go back to the piano, how would Fleitzig respond to the electronic keyboard.

After dinner, Wen returned to his recliner to watch television. Slowly, staring out the window into the murky night, Charlotte washed the dishes. She lined two Christmas tins with wax paper, packing each with an assortment of the cookies. Twice, she heard Wen get up from the recliner, once to use the bathroom, the other time to open the front door and step outside, listening, it seemed, for the pickup. Around ten, he called out that he was going to bed. Charlotte placed the filled tins on the kitchen table, one for each of Wen's sisters whom she'd see in the morning at church. Then she curled up in her armchair to read. But she too had been distracted, listening for the pickup. At eleven, she checked the wood-burning stove, pushing the remaining charred log to the side, turning the knob for the flue so the air would dwindle, and went upstairs to bed as well.

It was after one when Charlotte heard the kitchen door open and Eric's footsteps, loud and heedless of whether he was waking them, on the stairs. Then Eric was knocking on their bedroom door.

"Come in," she called out. Eric stopped at the foot of the bed. She turned on the reading light. A small cut, covered with dried blood, crossed his chin. The piece of graphite in his forehead glowed blue.

Charlotte propped herself up on an elbow. "Eric, honey, what happened?"

"I had an accident. A raccoon ran out into the road and I

swerved not to hit it. There was a patch of ice and I skidded." Eric's lip quivered. "I hit a tree."

Charlotte moved over so her hip was pushed against Wen, asleep on his side with his back to her. She smoothed the blanket and curled her fingers in and out toward her chest, motioning for Eric to come sit beside her.

His hands were icy cold. She rubbed them between her own. "Are you hurt? Did you get hurt?"

"No."

Charlotte touched Eric's chin. Wen rolled over so he was lying on his back.

"That's from a branch of the tree when I was trying to see what happened to the pickup."

Wen opened his eyes. "What did you do?"

Eric looked down at the blanket. Wen sat up. "It's pretty bad," Eric said.

Charlotte reached out for Wen's arm. "He hit a patch of ice."

Wen jerked his arm away. He lowered his feet onto the floor, his torso slightly bent, his hand pressed over his lower spine.

"Don't be foolish. This can wait until the morning."

Wen reached for his pants. Eric covered his eyes.

"It's dark out. You won't even be able to see." Her voice sounded thin—weak.

Wen leaned against the bureau and stepped into his pants. Eric followed him downstairs. Charlotte heard the squeak of the kitchen door opening and then the bang as it shut. She drew back the edge of the curtain from the window over the bed. All she could make out were the bare branches of their pear tree. It was a pointless gesture, this peering out into the inky night; even if Wen had grabbed a flashlight or turned on the pickup head- lights, the driveway was on the other side of the house. A useless compromise between the old impulse to chase after them, to intercede, and the idea (where had it come from—magazines, radio talk shows?) that she should let them work it out alone.

Charlotte sank back under the sheets. She hated the women's magazines with their awful catchphrases—*empty nest syndrome, midlife crises*—their assumptions, never questioned, that life rolls neatly through its stages, that difficulties can always be overcome, that feminine beauty and marital passion and maternal perspective can with sufficient effort be preserved, but she was unable to resist flipping through them when they arrived at the library. Was she fostering Eric's childishness? Yesterday, after she'd twice run out to the driveway, once to hand Eric a hastily arranged plate of the Christmas cookies for Fleitzig, the second to call out to remember to go slowly on the stretch of road near Cable Head, the fog nestling between the gulf and St. Peter's Bay can catch a driver unaware, Wen had looked up at her with an expression that wed hatred and disgust.

A door slammed. Charlotte pulled her knees up under her flannel nightgown and listened for voices, but all she could hear was the wind rounding the corner of the house.

In the morning, Eric was gone. He'd taken the electronic keyboard, leaving a suitcase of clothes with a note taped to the side: MAIL TO and then his address. Wen was in the driveway, rubbing a rust repellent into the smashed panel behind the passenger's door of the truck.

Charlotte rushed out the kitchen door. "What?" Air wheezed through her nose, making a hissing sound. "What did you say to him?"

Wen didn't answer. He lowered himself onto his back so he could see beneath the truck bed. Under his breath, she heard him muttering something that sounded like, *Raccoon, wouldn't kill a fucking raccoon.*

Charlotte felt herself coming to a boil, her muscles clenching—jaw, fists, gut—to hold back the rising steam. Only once, years before, when Eric was a toddler and he and Wen had come in from the beach with Eric dangling under Wen's arm and screaming, loud piercing cries that had led Charlotte to jump out from the shower, certain that the child was hurt, had she raised her voice at Wen. Then, Wen had dumped Eric on the floor and grabbed her by the upper arms and shaken her, shaken her so hard the towel she'd wrapped around her had fallen to the floor so she stood naked before her husband and son. His words—"Don't you ever holler at me. You got something to say, you say it"—had echoed in her neck and spine for days.

That morning after Eric left, Charlotte frantically called Eric's aunts, Fleitzig, his two closest friends from high school, and then, for the rest of the day, every hour, his dorm room, knowing all along it didn't make sense, the dorms were closed for the winter break. She and Wen tiptoed around each other, barely speaking. On Christmas Eve, she went alone to church. Head bowed, her tears dropped onto the coat folded in her lap as she prayed: prayed that Eric was safe, prayed to be released from the anger at Wen. In the morning, she woke feeling calm. When Wen turned toward her in his sleep, she reached out a hand to run down his side and he stretched out an arm to pull her close. At noon, Eric called from the off-campus apartment of friends. Charlotte picked up the phone, and although she'd grown used over the prior year and a half to talking with Eric long-distance, it was the first time he felt far away, the first time there were awkward gaps between their words. Cautiously, they wished each other Merry Christmas, the caution even more painful than Eric's absence but now, after another five years, so familiar that her former ease with Eric—the way she'd scooped him into her lap as a baby, jostled him awake every school morning with her singsong *Rise and shine*, run out laughing to the driveway that last Saturday with the plate of cookies for Fleitzig, whispering, *Remember to take back the plate*—seems now like the memory of a dream.

•

Charlotte sits for several minutes with her eyes closed, fingering the mohair blanket, the images from the dream and memory mingling together: Wen's bleeding back, the dented pickup, Eric crouched by the silver pail. Leaning over, she retrieves her shoes, two ugly frogs, from under the glass coffee table. Gently, she opens the French doors. She finds the powder room, runs warm water, and washes her face. Turning off the water, she hears piano music, the notes so clear and clean it sounds like the speakers must be in the next room. She pats her face dry with a fringed hand towel, following the melody in her mind. It is Mozart's Sonata in F, a piece she recognizes from Eric's lessons with Fleitzig but played slower and with more feeling than Charlotte recalls.

When she returns to the living room, Margaret is seated at the piano bench, and it takes Charlotte a moment to comprehend that it is Margaret playing the sonata.

Quietly, she lowers herself onto the sofa where she dreamt of Wen. Margaret plays with her chin jutted forward, hearing, it seems, with her throat as much as her ears. The voile curtains have been drawn and a tall torchiere lit, casting a halo onto the ceiling and trembling shadows over the ivory keys. Through the curtains, Charlotte can see the lights from the buildings across the park.

At the end of the piece, Margaret holds her hands for a moment suspended in the air. The spell broken, she sighs and with a clunk lowers the piano lid. When Margaret turns, Charlotte realizes that she's changed her clothes: the houndstooth suit replaced by loose black pants and a long lavender silk blouse.

"That was beautiful. I remember when Eric first learned that piece."

"I've been working on it as a welcome-home gift for him."

Margaret cocks her ear toward Charlotte, as though listening to her unspoken question. "Early December. But you know Eric. He doesn't believe in timetables. I wouldn't be surprised if it's two days before he's due back at work."

Charlotte thinks about saying, no, she doesn't know, but it seems too jarring an idea to introduce into this exquisite room.

"Did you sleep?"

"Better than I have since my husband died." She is surprised to hear herself, usually so reticent, offering this information. Perhaps it is because Margaret hasn't said any of the inane platitudes favored by Charlotte's neighbors, with their casseroles and wreaths and hushed comments, and Wen's sisters, with their pat-pat to Charlotte's hand or shoulder and even once to her head as though her bereavement has reduced her to a pet, and even her own brother with his repetition of their father's refrain about how God chooses his time.

"It's not from missing my husband that I've been sleeping badly." Her fingers fly to her mouth, as if to stop the rebellious lips. She lowers her hand and holds it tightly in the other. "I know that must sound terrible—just he'd been gone so long I can hardly remember when he was here. Wen was like a turtle. He kept retracting further and further into his shell. These last couple of years, he'd come home so worn out from the roadwork, having to ask permission for bathroom breaks like a grade school child, all he could do was take a shower, get his dinner down, and then sit in that recliner watching the stupid TV."

With *stupid TV*, Charlotte's voice breaks, and her eyes fill again. Margaret reaches an arm toward a gilded Kleenex box. She hands it to Charlotte, who blows her nose twice and wipes her eyes, only then realizing that Margaret can't see the tears, that she has responded to the break in Charlotte's voice.

"Eric told me, about his father. About wrecking the truck. How he didn't come home for another year after that."

"Seventeen months." When Eric finally came home, he'd seemed altered. Taller, more filled out. More aloof. During his visit, there was a string of perfect days: the sky a cloudless periwinkle, the water warm enough to swim with comfort, the fields a riot of wildflowers, the bay so glutted with lobsters and mussels they feasted every night. But afterward, after Eric returned to school, she felt empty, as though she'd been entertaining a stranger. Except for the greeting and parting kisses, they'd never touched. Never exchanged looks of bemusement about certain things Wen said or did as they once had.

"I remember the day Eric told me about his father. It was at the beginning, when I was still banging the keys, refusing to let Eric teach me or to let myself feel the music. We were here, in this room, before I had this piano," Margaret says, running her fingers across the top of the music stand.

"He was trying to explain to me about flats and sharps and how they relate to scale intervals, but I was so filled with rage that I might as well have been deaf too for all I could take in of what he was saying. I'd hear the words but they'd bounce right off me. I'd sit on the piano bench with my hands clenched like baseballs, and I must have been doing it then because Eric just stopped what he was saying, literally, midsentence."

Margaret turns her head slightly—except for the glasses, Charlotte thinks, a profile like a schoolbook Cleopatra.

"He touched my fist, and Lordy, it was like a cloudburst. I cried so hard I soaked the front of my blouse. I don't know how he got me off the bench and over to the couch."

She points to the couch where Charlotte is sitting. "I just sat there, sobbing and heaving and then sniveling, with Eric holding my hand and not saying anything. After a while, a long while, he asked me if I wanted to tell him what had happened, how I'd lost my sight, and I realized I did."

Margaret gets up from the piano bench. Charlotte imagines Eric leading her over to the couch, his thin arm around her waist. Margaret lowers herself into the leather chair where she sat earlier, slipping off her ballet flats and crossing her stockinged long-toed feet on the matching ottoman. "So I told him. Of course, I'd told people before, the police, my lawyers, the staff at the rehab center, but never because I *wanted* to."

The lower half of Margaret's face loosens into a half smile; the top hidden behind the dark glasses—eerier, now, with the daylight gone. She reaches toward the table, where the maid has brought clean glasses, a fresh carafe of wine, and another bottle of sparkling water. "Let me," Charlotte says. Margaret nods.

"The first thing you learn is how little people want to hear. It scares them, scares them that it could happen to them too."

Charlotte hands Margaret a glass, half wine, half sparkling water, and then makes the same for herself.

So Eric sat on this couch.

"Eric took me on. I still remember his words. Look, Margaret, he said. That *Look, Margaret*, was a balm. I hadn't heard anyone say that to me since I was a girl. Look, Margaret, he said, there are two ways of living. One way you try to control everything. That's how you've done it up to now. You studied hard in high school and got a scholarship to college and then you studied hard in college and got into a good medical school and then you worked hard in medical school and got a good residency and then you impressed everyone there and were able to start your own surgery practice and make a lot of money and move into this apartment. But then someone, a crazy, jealous, racist kook—I think that's how Eric put it, a crazy, jealous, racist kook—someone whose life didn't work that way and who's decided that the reason he didn't get into medical school and you did is because you're black and a woman, throws acid in your eyes and it's all over."

Charlotte gasps. Margaret turns toward her and for the first time Charlotte notices the sliver of raw skin—thin, stretched, like the membrane between the shell and white of an egg—at the edge of her glasses.

"I forget," Margaret says softly. "I forget how shocking it must sound." She reaches for her glass and sips, the wine tipping golden toward her crimson lips. "That was when Eric told me about his father. How he hurt his back and had to give up playing hockey but was never able to accept it, to take it as an opportunity."

Charlotte's head is throbbing and she doesn't know if it is because of what Margaret is telling her or because it is as if Eric, but an Eric she's never known, is here in the room, or because it is true, so starkly true about Wen that it amazes her that she hasn't thought about it before. Never had she seen any signs that Wen felt any pleasure in the fishing, never had she seen any elation or contentment on his face, not on those cold March mornings when the sea would turn lazurite, the sky whitewashed from winter, not when he'd come in on June afternoons and the sun, still high in the sky, would dart off the metal pails and glisten on the silvery fish skins, not at dusk when he'd sit on the patio cleaning the hake and mackerel and little herrings, the cliffs looming in the violet sky, the smell of onions barbecuing in tinfoil, his cuts so deft that the only blood would be a thin crimson line down the belly of the fish. No wonder Eric never wanted to go with him. No wonder Eric retreated into a world of sound, at first the Old World sounds Fleitzig had brought with his leather-bound music books from Bremen—Bach preludes, Strauss waltzes, Mozart sonatas—and then, later, after he went to Oberlin, sounds so unrecognizable to Charlotte, she didn't know to what in the seemingly random jangle she should attend.

"I remember Eric once saying something about his father that astonished me. That really the ice hockey had been as much dictated by circumstances as the fishing—only with the hockey his father had had the illusion of choice, the feeling that his life was under his control."

Margaret raises her hand to her breastbone. An opal ring, the stone fat and cloudy, rests on her middle finger. "It occurred to me that the same was true for me with medicine. I'd felt like I'd chosen to be a doctor, but it had been more reaction than anything else. Math and science had seemed less intimidating than the humanities, where my Wellesley classmates were leagues ahead of me. With differential equations, it's irrelevant if you've ever seen the Joffrey or spent a summer in Avignon."

Margaret spins the ring around on her finger, and then presses it to her lips. "I was so agitated by the thought, I got up and started pacing. Back and forth across the room. Eric paced with me, holding my elbow to keep me from bumping into things. Talking all the while: that he didn't mean to sound like a Pollyanna, that he wasn't telling me to look for the silver lining, but that it had happened, my losing my sight, and I could rail and scream and make life miserable for myself and everyone around me and still I wouldn't be able to see."

Charlotte can feel herself straining forward—as though she might miss one of Eric's words. As though she has never heard her son speak before. And really, when she thinks about it, what she's always listened for in Eric is the sound from his fingers. There had been very few words, very few words from any of them, so that it seems all the more wondrous to learn that Eric has grown to be a man of so many.

"I'm not saying I was out of the woods after that day. There was plenty of hell still to come. I'm talking hatred. A hatred at white people like I'd never felt before." Margaret pauses. "I don't know why I didn't take that out on Eric. Maybe because I'd never seen him, maybe because he's so young. He felt to me like the Buddha in a body without color."

Margaret leans back in her chair. She runs a hand over her hair. "I felt something, that day, pacing back and forth with Eric holding my elbow, a sense of possibility, of going with what had happened the way they teach you in tai chi, that you move with the aggressor's energy, not against it. And it came back, at first so fleetingly it would be gone before I'd even recognize it had been there, but then, later, for longer stretches, even a few minutes. The agitation would subside and I could breathe."

The maid comes in with a new bowl of cashews. She wipes the damp spots on the tray with a cloth. Reaching behind the curtains, she pulls down the shades. Sealed from the streetlights, the room intensifies, each object gaining the gravitas of things late in the day. She waits by the windows, her red hair electric in the artificial light.

"That's fine, Janie. We won't need anything else."

After the girl leaves the room, Margaret continues. "Of course, it got worse before it got better, since once I stopped ranting and raving I had to face how frightened I was of the darkness, that it was dark all the time."

Charlotte closes her eyes. On the inside of her lids are shades of black, a shimmering red aureole.

"And then there was the trial. Having to listen to that sorry excuse for a human being and his sleazy lawyer arguing temporary insanity. That set me back. It was then that I'd think about Eric's father. Your husband."

In the dark, Margaret's voice seems to Charlotte both lower and more distinct, the words silky and abundant with meaning. "That Eric had told me about him as a warning."

Opening her eyes, Charlotte sees Margaret's face as a triptych: the smooth brow, the opaque glasses, the tranquil mouth.

"Eric never talked about him again. Later, I'd wonder if I'd imagined the conversation. But then I'd be struggling with some new piece I'd spent all week memorizing from the Braille, practicing it phrase by phrase, and I'd go blank and do something stupid like start to kick the back of the console and Eric would hold my shoulders and exhale deeply and I'd know that he was instructing me to let go, let the music enter me, let myself understand what he was teaching me. Then I'd wonder if he'd told me about his father because he truly believed I was going to be able to play the piano if I let myself or if he just took a risk."

Margaret laughs. "That would have been something—if, after all that, it turned out I had a tin ear." The pleasure in the thought sweeps across her cheeks. She runs her thumb over what Charlotte realizes must be a Braille watch. "Good Lord, is that right? Is it nearly seven thirty?"

Charlotte looks at her own watch. "Yes."

"I wish I could invite you to stay for dinner, but I have a date."

"I'm so sorry, lingering on like this." A date. Charlotte has never known a grown woman to have a date.

"We're meeting at the Museum of Natural History. They're open late tonight. Will you walk with me? It's only a few blocks south."

Charlotte nods and then—flustered because of course Margaret can't see the gesture and anxious too about the evening and finding her way to her brother's apartment, figuring out how to park the pickup overnight—blurts, "Sure, I mean yes, of course."

Margaret rings the silver bell.

"Our coats, Janie, please." A moment later, the maid returns with Charlotte's stiff green parka and Margaret's soft camel's hair.

•

Once inside the museum, Margaret switches her hand from atop Charlotte's arm to beneath so that she is now leading them.

They're in a rotunda surrounded by murals of scenes from primitive cultures: loinclothed men, women with sleek hair that falls to their waists. Two enormous dinosaurs fill the middle of the room, one with an elongated neck, arched like a great giraffe, the other thick and compact with an immense pointy-toothed jaw, its left leg bent in preparation for attack.

"Oh, my," Charlotte says.

"It's called *Barosaurus Defends Her Young*. They've redone the models so the tails arch up like birds'. Before, when I was a kid, the tail of the barosaurus—that's the taller one—dragged on the floor like a lizard's."

Her young? Charlotte looks more closely. Crouched behind the barosaurus is a smaller dinosaur, its legs astride the mother's tail, its head no larger than the mother's ankle bone.

Margaret squeezes Charlotte's arm. "Come, I'm meeting my friend on the fourth floor in the old dino room."

Margaret leads them to the left of the admission booth toward a wide staircase. Whereas the rotunda was bright and cheerful, the stairwell has the musty smell of old buildings where even new paint every two years fails to foil the dankness. She releases Charlotte's arm, grips the banister, and marches up the stairs with Charlotte following two steps behind.

At the top of the stairs, Margaret takes Charlotte's arm again. They walk down a corridor with no doorways, no exhibits. Could Margaret be lost?

"Here, to the right," Margaret says, and suddenly they are in a room as sprawling as a high school gym. Glass cases line the walls and, in the center, there is another grouping of dinosaur skeletons—even larger than the ones below. There are no other people save for an elderly guard with broken blood vessels on his cheeks. He sticks his thumb in the book he'd been reading. "Evening, Doc," he calls out.

"Jim, how are you? Your wife?"

"Fine, fine. The missus is doing better. Up and about like her old self." He taps the book against his thigh. "You just tell me when."

Margaret steers Charlotte to the center of the room. "You have to walk all the way around to really see them."

When they reach the railing surrounding the dinosaurs, Margaret lets go of Charlotte's arm and moves ahead. Late Cretaceous, Charlotte reads on the placard, from North America. Looking more carefully, she can distinguish the three different specimens: the sad, cow-faced anatosaurus, a water-loving beast, she reads, who feasted on the plants along the river and lakeshores; the three-horned triceratops, also a vegetarian but able with its armored back to fight off attackers; and, the largest, the bullying snake-clawed tyrannosaurus, with carving knives for teeth and an appetite for meat.

Margaret stops by the skull of the tyrannosaurus. The yard-long jaw gapes, the hind legs thick as tree trunks, the tail a magnificent cord, stretching back the length of five men.

"That jaw!" Charlotte says.

"When I was a kid, my father took us here the first Sunday of every month. We'd travel in by train from Newark. Always, he'd say the same thing: Now, children, don't get the old daddy mad."

Margaret waves a hand at the guard.

"Okay, Doc." He walks to the entranceway, where he stands with his back to the room.

"Now I come here nearly every week, to this room. I don't know if it's because this guy's so big or because it's something I'd seen so many times, but when I take off my glasses it feels like I can see him."

Margaret touches the arm of her glasses. "If you'd close your eyes," she says.

Charlotte turns away from Margaret so she is facing the

duck-billed anatosaurus. She squeezes her eyes shut, then opens her lids a tiny fraction. The anatosaurus looms toward her, the spaces between the bones occluded by the haze of her lashes. Viewed this way, the dinosaur seems almost full-bodied, as though flesh has found its way back onto the skeleton.

Charlotte leans against the rail. A warm heaviness seeps down her limbs. How had these tremendous creatures been vanquished? What could have extinguished them? And then, as if set loose from the bottom of an old deep well, an image, static like a photograph, comes toward her: Wen in a racing stride, his weight on his right skate, the left held tautly behind, her first sight of him moving over the ice, she and Rachel Bigsby huddled together in the stands. Unable to see Wen's face under the helmet, she'd studied his body: the tremendous compression, an economy of concentration and action, eyes locked on the puck. A determination, Charlotte had thought, not simply to win that game—which they had—but to triumph over his own muscles, over that sweet, soporific sluggishness beckoning, always, release, release and die.

"Done, Jim," Margaret calls out.

Jim turns, ushering in a short man, clad in a belted black raincoat, too crisp, Charlotte thinks, to have ever been used in the rain. Bald but with a plump babyishness in his face, he beams as he moves toward them.

"Looking at the old tyrant, Margaret?"

"Yes, poor Charlotte's had to stand here with her eyes closed." The man tilts his face upward and kisses Margaret on the cheek. Margaret's fingers graze Charlotte's back. "This is Eric's mother."

The man's eyebrows dart up but his look of surprise quickly disappears behind another of his beaming smiles. "Well, well," he says to Charlotte, "When will our peripatetic musicologist be back?"

Charlotte stiffens. "December," Margaret answers for her.

"Or January or February," she adds, her voice bouncing over the words. The man glances at a large gold watch. "My dear," he says, tapping Margaret's nose, "I'm afraid we'd better scoot along. Our reservation is for eight forty-five and they're Nazis about the time."

Margaret takes Charlotte's hands between her own. "Cold hands, warm heart." She bows her head and kisses Charlotte's fingers. "Thank you for coming to see me."

The baby-faced man encircles Margaret's waist. "Good to meet you," he says, and then they are off and Charlotte is so taken aback by the sight of the two of them from the rear, Margaret towering above, her dark hair glossy next to his pale scalp, his black raincoated arm swept around her camel's hair coat, that it isn't until they are already at the door, their goodbyes to Jim echoing behind, that Charlotte realizes she and Margaret never discussed what Margaret will tell Eric.

Fleetingly, she feels an impulse to chase after Margaret, to catch her and her date halfway down the stairs, but it no longer seems to matter. Wen died, Eric will be told.

Facing the grouping of dinosaurs is a well-worn mahogany bench. Charlotte lowers herself onto the seat. From here, the tyrannosaurus looks even larger, perhaps how it appeared to smaller animals creeping through the grasses. Larger, though, in an absurd and vulnerable way, like the story she recalls from high school about Xerxes's ships defeated when they couldn't turn around in the channel. Was this how Wen had seemed to Eric, not simply bullying but also pitiable? Helpless. Blinded. Doomed. Always, when she's thought about them, about their threesome, she's seen Wen coiled to pounce, Eric and she hidden in retreat. Her remorse has always been about Eric, that she didn't intervene, that she let him be driven out. Now, though, this seems wrong. What she sees is Eric, his face easy and relaxed, a hand resting on the piano, his torso curled over Margaret.

In the distance, an electronic bell sounds, a long ring followed by two short blasts. Charlotte tries to picture Eric and
Wen as they are at this instant. Eric, his skin golden from the
Indonesian sun, a batik shirt, palm trees—are there palm trees?
Wen, so shrunken the undertaker had to pin the back of the
brown suit she'd buried him in, the white cords of his neck visible over the unfamiliar tie, his face—hadn't she read that the
hair keeps growing underground?—covered with whiskers.

Behind her, Charlotte hears the guard's voice, "Closing in
fifteen minutes," and then softly, or is it shyly, "Ma'am." They
seem far away, her husband and son, apparitions that require
conjuring. Her mind drifts to the awareness of her own heart
beating and the feeling brewing inside her: fear—trepidation
about moving from this bench, from this room of bones, about
venturing out, alone, onto the darkened city streets—but underneath, swimming low, tremulous, quivering, excitement too.

Raya in Rapahu

Shortly before midnight—eighty-seven days after her mother, Raya, walked in front of a bread truck that sent her soaring diagonally across the street, her flight halted only by the crash of her head into the door of a parked car, leaving her locked in another reality that Marnie imagines sometimes as a long deep sleep during which the body tends to itself (though, in Raya's case, with the help of tubes going in and out of her orifices) while the mind wanders through a cineplex infinitum, and, at other times, as a terrible and lonely claustrophobia, akin to being trapped in a mine shaft with limbs pinned by the walls and air sweet from lack of oxygen—Marnie lifts her rather substantial leg over the edge of the tub and dips a big toe into the steaming water.

When the doorbell rings, Marnie, still soaking, is jolted from a reverie (her work: the way she finds the kernels for her children's stories) about a creature, swift and cunning like a wood thrush with a crest of plumules a peacock would envy, who flies into a dank, bat-ridden cave to retrieve a key to . . . to the universe. *Damn you*, she thinks, both about Ben, her ex-husband, and the only person who would visit without calling, and Julio, the night doorman for whom Ben once did some free printing work, who lets Ben come up without announcement.

Damp under her terry-cloth robe, Marnie pads through the living room with its bay window from which if you lean far out and look west you can see a patch of the Hudson and unlocks the sequence of bolts Ben installed before moving out nine years ago. Then, at twenty-six, she'd been a young divorcée; now the building houses a half dozen other women of Marnie's age also with a marriage behind them.

Ben hands Marnie a bag of kosher Chinese takeout. His dark hair is flecked with snow. With the collar of his leather jacket turned up over his thick neck, he looks like a Jewish version of an Irish thug from a thirties movie, only an inch or two taller than Marnie but with shoulders twice as broad; indeed, some of Ben's printing shop clients (Marnie thinks of Mesoni— a guy rumored to have used Mob connections to get the contract to grind the city's used subway cars into spools of wire) suggest something B-grade, a world where the action passes in warehouses, landfills, and container-ship yards.

"Ellie?"

Ben nods and follows Marnie into the kitchen. He leans against the counter while she fills a teakettle.

"What happened?"

"She's back to wanting to keep it. The social worker told her they take the baby right after delivery—to make it easier on the mother. She came home bawling her eyes out, that she can't go through with it, can't let them cut the umbilical cord and then that's it." Ben shudders.

"Is she just upset or do you think she means it?"

"I don't know. She's got that midwestern bullheadedness where there's a right and a wrong and nothing in between. It was that way with the abortion; she wouldn't even consider it."

Ben helps himself to a beer from a six-pack he left in Marnie's refrigerator last week. Marnie refrains from commenting on the irony of Ben talking about Ellie's bullheadedness given that it is his refusal to marry a woman who's not Jewish despite his loving Ellie and her tearful pleas that she'd happily convert that has led to this plan that she'll give up the child. From the demise of their own marriage, Marnie knows that Ben's religious commitments are an immutable subject—that although he was aware from the outset that she lacked religious feeling, that her mother's perfunctory hand-waving about the holidays had left Marnie with no more than a mild sentimental attachment to the rituals, the family seders having seemed as secular as Christmas trees, he couldn't accept her wish after a year of their marriage to cease keeping a kosher home. "Why do I have to participate in your Jewish practice?" Marnie had cried. "Why can't you do that independently of me?" Unable to face another year engaged in traditions that felt meaningless to her, she'd suggested counseling with a woman rabbi from the Columbia Hillel. A week later, she and Ben had sat side by side on the rabbi's chintz couch while the rabbi gently explained that the heart of Judaism is in the home and Marnie felt her own heart miss a beat and then pound out of control as she realized how mistaken she'd been to think that Ben's religious life could, like the printing business he'd taken over from his father and his passion for the track and Miles Davis, be part of his private sphere.

Marnie takes out plates and serving spoons. "And if she keeps the baby, what will you do?"

Ben spears a fried wonton with a chopstick. "I always told her I'd support her and the baby if she wants to keep it. I just won't be the father."

"How can you *not* be the father?"

"I won't live with them. I won't give the baby my name."

Marnie opens the other boxes: chicken with cashews, beef submerged in brown sauce, sesame noodles. Ben eats quickly with his bushy brows furrowed. When the kettle whistles, she pours hot water into mugs and joins him at the table.

"I told her, I told her before I even slept with her, that I could only marry a Jewish woman. She laughed and said I'd be an old man before she was ready to marry and what made me think she'd ever marry me."

Marnie smiles. On the one occasion she met Ellie, she'd liked her—a skinny girl with a long red braid and a SLAUGHTER THE POLYESTER button who'd come to New York to study with the Feld dance troupe, worked nights in a copy shop on upper Broadway, and rode Rollerblades to work. The only way Marnie can imagine Ellie eight months pregnant is as a child's line drawing with sticks for arms and legs and a striped beach ball for a belly.

Ben puts down his fork and wipes his mouth with a paper napkin. His eyes trace Marnie's skin from the vee in her robe up to her forehead. He purses his lips as though to say, *See, look what you set in motion*, and then reaches out to touch Marnie's cheek.

•

Marnie wakes in the middle of the night. Ben breathes heavily, a shade short of a snore. Without looking at the clock, she knows it's 3:52—the insomniac's witching hour. All week, she's bolted awake at exactly this time, a sudden waking without dream fragments or the residue of sleep. Instead, there have been a flood of memories, as if her mother's coma (the jellied surface of Raya's brain having been shaken so hard, the neurologist explained, it was left bruised and bleeding), falling less than a year after the death of Marnie's father, Thomas, has unleashed a swarm of images from a hidden fold in Marnie's own cortex.

Tonight, the memory is of a painting her brother, Alan, made some twenty years ago of the family as a table setting. It was the one year they had all been in high school together, spaced like stepping-stones across the grades: David and Alan, with nearly two years between them but due to quirks of the district's age rules only one grade, then Sam, fourteen months younger than Alan, and finally Marnie, who'd tagged along by skipping a grade so she'd landed a year behind Sam. In Alan's painting, her mother had been the plate, her eyes and nose rising from the white expanse like the woman in the moon, her hair still thick and black. Her father, dressed in a brown suit, jagged on one side to form the serrated edge of the blade, was the knife. David, then a senior, brainy and always brooding, either about his college applications or an argument with Nancy, his girlfriend who was already planning their wedding for four years hence, was the fork, set off far to the left of the canvas. Sam, whom everyone still called Sama, had been a long-legged soup spoon with a haze of marijuana smoke billowing around her hair and an arm draped over Marnie, cast as a plump cross-legged teaspoon with her nose in a book. Alan had painted himself as a goblet with a hollowed-out, oversized head filled with milk. Without a word about its implications, her mother framed the painting and hung it in the dining room, where Marnie had felt compelled each dinner to examine it anew.

Now Marnie can't recall when the picture disappeared. Perhaps the year after Alan's suicide, when Marnie was the only kid left in the house (David by then a junior at Princeton, Sam in her first year at Berkeley) and her mother threw herself into redecorating: tearing down the original fireplace mantel, ripping up the kitchen linoleum, turning the three empty bedrooms into a library, guest room, and ironing room, and then painting all the walls a brutal white that she left bare of photographs and pictures.

Ben moves onto his stomach, his head turned toward Marnie. He blinks his eyes, shuts them, and then opens them wide. "What's the matter?"

"I can't sleep."

He reaches a hand onto Marnie's hip, rubs little circles with his thumb.

"I'm taking the nine o'clock bus to Rapahu and Sam's flying down from Boston so we can have a meeting about what to do with my mother."

"What to do?"

"David says we're going to have to move her to a nursing home—that the hospital won't keep her more than a hundred and twenty days. Sam wants to talk about how long we'll keep her alive on the tubes."

Ben turns onto his back, props a pillow under his neck, and switches on the light. Marnie feels a surge of love for him; even Decembers when Ben would work until midnight for weeks on end printing holiday cards, he'd always welcomed her words, always made her feel that nothing was more important.

"It's going to be a mess. David sees this through his doctor eyes: we have to use all measures to keep our mother alive. And you know Sam. She defends radical ideas like they're starving children. When she was at Berkeley, she was a research assistant for this feminist political science professor, Hildie Something-or-other, who wrote an article about a feminist interpretation of the politics of dying. She keeps quoting this professor about the medical-slash-patriarchal oppression of women."

"This is why people write living wills."

"She'd been trying to get my mother to write one, but it obviously didn't happen in time." Marnie shifts onto her side. "Sam thinks this professor's son is some sort of legal expert on the subject and might be able to advise us on what to do when there isn't anything in writing, but she's been dragging her feet contacting him."

"Why's that?"

"God knows. Maybe he's one of her spurned lovers or maybe she's delaying the fight with David."

"Did your mother ever talk about what she'd want?"

Marnie feels irritated: Is she imagining this or is Ben interrogating her? She leans back, presses her eyes with the flats of her fingers. Her mother's face floats into her mind. She's dangling a plastic rain bonnet like the ones sold in restroom vending machines. The rain bonnet is not a mystery. With David handling Raya's doctors, Marnie has taken over the indomitable paperwork for the insurance claim. This week, a second police report arrived in a mustard envelope. In the report, a boy described Raya as wearing a plastic scarf over her hair.

Marnie thinks about telling Ben about the report and what the boy wrote but Ben is stroking her arm and saying, "Shhh, try to go back to sleep," and her limbs are growing heavy and her thoughts drift like clouds past Ellie with her beach-ball belly, past her father in his jagged brown suit, past her mother and the dangling bonnet.

•

Marnie scans the waiting room of the Rapahu station half expecting to see someone she knows, but only the blind man who runs the newsstand looks familiar. Yesterday, on the phone, she'd tussled with David about wanting to take a cab to his house rather than having him pick her up—this being a classic interaction with David, who snatches at any opportunity to give something tangible to his sisters while avoiding knowing too much about either of them. Now, with the sun breaking through the white winter sky, Marnie decides to walk the mile and a half to David and Nancy's house.

In the eighteen years since Marnie graduated from high school and moved away, Rapahu has changed very little. Main Street still sports the florist shop owned by her now-sister-in-law Nancy's parents and run these days with the help of Nancy's younger sister; the pharmacy owned by the Stephens family, whose son had for a while been one of Sam's many boyfriends (at sixteen, he'd been renowned for his Milk Duds box filled with Seconals, Darvocets, and Valium, but is now, Nancy has hinted, "very into his recovery"); the appliance store where Marnie's parents and Nancy's parents and, more recently, David and Nancy bought their dishwashers, refrigerators, and stoves.

Despite its familiarity, Marnie has always experienced the town as alien: the expectation of enthusiasm for Masonic raffles and Girl Scout cookie drives, the tinsel and spray-painted pine-cone wreaths wrapped around the lampposts and the town's two stoplights the Monday that follows Thanksgiving, the low buildings dwarfed by the expanse of the sky. Not until the summer after she turned eleven—a lonely stretch when Sam had a boy-friend from David's class with whom she spent her waking hours learning to smoke cigarettes and roll joints, and David started a lawn-mowing business with Alan as his assistant and the goal of buying his own stereo by the fall—had Marnie understood that her feeling of being a foreigner accidentally laid-over in Rapahu was connected to her mother.

At the beginning of the summer, Marnie had fallen into a routine, sleeping each day until noon, spending the afternoons stretched out on a beach blanket in the backyard listening to the radio and tanning her legs, reading late into the night. This dreamy pattern broke midsummer when Raya announced that she and Marnie were going to paint the upstairs bedrooms. Each morning at six thirty, Raya would shake Marnie awake so they could work in the early cool: laying tarps, sanding wood-work, rolling and rerolling walls, painting trim with an array of small slanted brushes.

While they painted, Raya talked—first in snatches as she had always done when any of her children would ask about her past, but then, as the days went on and the paint seeped into their skin and the heat rose in August and Marnie mastered painting even window frames, in longer and longer stretches. Each episode of her mother's life attached itself to the place they were working. In Alan's room, there was the story of how Marnie's parents had made the move from the Upper West Side to Rapahu on her father's insistence shortly after his promotion to director of sales at Little Falls Paper, where he'd clawed his way from a salesman in the Bronx to the top of his heap.

"How come Daddy didn't like the city?" It was late morning and Raya was standing on a stepladder to reach the strip of wall over Alan's closet while Marnie sat on the floor painting the radiator.

"It goes way back. When your father was a boy, he and Grandma Mary lived in a tiny apartment over what's now the pharmacy. Grandma Mary would cry and cry about no longer having a house. Ever since, your father has felt that apartment living is only for poor people."

While rolling the walls in Sam's room, Marnie learned how Grandma Mary had to sell her house after her husband, Marnie's father's father, angry that Grandma Mary's claims about her family's wealth had been vastly exaggerated, took off with the three hundred dollars they had in their checking account to make a life by himself in Florida, leaving Grandma Mary with a one-year-old and a household of expensive wedding presents but no income except what she was able to earn as a switchboard operator for the telephone company.

The most spectacular story had come when they reached Marnie's room and her mother had told Marnie that she'd been married before: to Harvey Miller, a painter and a Communist who three months after their wedding left Raya in their Manhattan railroad flat while he headed with a friend to Mexico, Party business, he hinted, a possible meeting with Diego Rivera and Frida Kahlo, but, Raya knew, really an opportunity for a lot of drinking and whoring (would her mother have said *whoring?*—no, probably, not, Marnie thinks), where he died of a spider bite. A twenty-year-old widow, Raya turned a deaf ear to her parents' pleas that she move back to St. Louis. Instead, she found a job as an assistant to one of the curators of Meso-American art at the Metropolitan Museum of Art and began attending City College at night.

Raya had been almost thirty and at work on a catalogue of Kahlo's paintings when she first met Thomas. How does Marnie know that her mother hadn't loved her father at the time of his proposal but correctly surmised that she would grow to love him for his devotion to her, his hardworking nature, and his appreciation of beauty, acquired from his own mother? Did her mother talk about it that summer while they painted the bedrooms? Probably what she said was that she had wanted children. Indeed, two months after her marriage to Thomas, Raya was pregnant with David, and within five years Alan, Sam, and Marnie followed.

"If we'd stayed in the city," her mother said with a sigh (they were painting the trim in David's room), "I would have gone back to work. Old Mr. Klopfer was still the head curator and he told me when I left, right before David was born, that as long as he was there, I'd always have a job."

Marnie turns at the brick ramparts that mark Grant Street, formerly the drive to an estate where Ulysses S. Grant is said to have summered during his presidency, and now a residential street canopied with elms and lined with three-story center-hall Colonial houses. Neither she nor Sam was surprised when, after his residency, David bought the practice of Rapahu's retiring gastroenterologist, making him the third generation of their family to live in the town. She hasn't been to her brother's house since the first week after Raya's accident, when she and Sam shared the guest room. The stay ended badly after Sam, whose temper was even shorter than usual, exploded following Nancy's insistence that they all—Nancy, David, their five-year-old Kyle, Marnie, and Sam—join hands before dinner to say the Serenity Prayer, which Nancy had recently learned as part of what she referred to as her recovery with Adult Children of Alcoholics. "What kind of voodoo crock of shit is this?" Sam yelled—alone with Marnie but loudly enough, Marnie was certain, for David and Nancy to hear. "Neither of Nancy's parents is an alcoholic. They didn't drink any more than Mom and Dad or anyone else's parents."

"She thinks that they interacted with her like alcoholics and that the meetings are helping her to stop enabling those behaviors."

Sam tapped a cigarette out of her pack and put it under her nose. She inhaled deeply. "She probably thinks it was the plan of Señor Higher Power for a bread truck to hit Mom."

As she approaches the house, Marnie can see Kyle sitting in the circular driveway poking with a stick at a patch of gravel a few feet behind David's BMW. He's a silent child who rarely cries or whines or asks for things and spends most of his time digging holes in the ground. It has taken Marnie a long time to understand that unlike her own visits to an imaginary world, her nephew, bored by his parents' patter (*brush your teeth, eat more chicken, get your backpack*), resides full-time in this alternate reality. Of late, Kyle has taken to feigning intermittent deafness; now he ignores the crunch of Marnie's feet on the drive.

Stopping a few steps away, Marnie quietly watches her nephew. After a minute or two, he glances at her boots.

"Could I take a look?"

Kyle makes a tiny nod. Marnie moves closer and lowers herself onto her haunches. She examines the hole in the frozen ground. Around the edges, Kyle has placed a circle of stones.

"It's a secret tunnel."

Marnie remains squatting. Kyle has rubbed dirt into the thighs of his pants. In the weak light, his thin hair looks electric. "A secret tunnel," she repeats.

"It goes under the house and then down a million billion miles to the middle of the earth."

"That's far. What's down there?"

"Lots and lots of people," Kyle says, his eyes fixed on the hole.

"Anyone I know?"

"That's where all the people who die go." Kyle keeps digging. Marnie wonders if this is where he thinks his grandmother is now. For Kyle's fifth birthday, only a week before her mother's accident, Marnie had written a rhyming book that Raya illustrated with watercolors. There were ten pages: *Once in a while, you meet a Kyle. Kyle walks a mile. There's Kyle, in the aisle. Kyle is on trial. Kyle knows how to dial. Kyle has a file. Kyle makes a pile. Kyle dresses in style. Kyle meets a crocodile. Kyle likes to smile.* For the last page, her mother had wanted to paste in a photograph of Kyle. To no avail, she searched her packets of photographs and even called Nancy's mother to see if she had a picture of Kyle with a smile. "Just like Alan," Raya said, surprising Marnie, since her mother rarely mentioned Alan's name. "Your father could never get a picture of him when he wasn't lost in thought."

Marnie hears the front door open, and looks up to see David standing at the top of the stairs. He scowls. "What? You couldn't get a cab?"

"No, I wanted to walk."

"You should have called. Sam took the early shuttle so she could visit Mom. We've been back already half an hour."

Marnie hugs David. In the past year, his hair has turned from bluish black to salt-and-pepper. "I wanted to walk."

"Go in, go in. Nancy and Sam are in the kitchen making lunch." On the front door, a yellow bow that signals support for the troops in Iraq hangs next to a NO SMOKING PLEASE sign. Marnie wipes her feet, wondering which will have irritated Sam more: the yellow ribbon or the sign. Outside she can hear David telling Kyle to come in for lunch, and then his annoyance when he receives no reply. "Kyle, answer me. I've told you a hundred times that you're to answer when people talk to you."

In the kitchen, Nancy is laying out cold cuts wrapped in wax paper and spooning deli salads into serving bowls. Sam sits at the counter, tapping her fingers in the way that she does when she's dying for a cigarette. As usual, Nancy is dressed in overly coordinated clothes: baby blue for her corduroy pants and headband, brown suede for her flats and belt. She looks prissy next to Sam, who with Raya's height but their father's delicate bone structure has for twenty years been wrecking men with her look of careless semi-dishabille—collarbone sticking out from a T-shirt, delicate ankles perched over work boots, long neck exposed by the short crop of her hair. Now Sam sports jeans and an oversized flannel shirt that probably belongs to her most recent boyfriend, Matt, a professor of sociology at MIT who, Sam confided in Marnie, first captured her interest due to rumors of his IRA connections and who writes on rhetoric and culture—dense, theoretical stuff with words like *autochthonous* and *de-realizing* that Sam refuses to read and that even David, the most intellectual of the three of them, has proclaimed impenetrable.

Marnie blows Sam a kiss and gives Nancy a hug. "What can I do to help?"

"Nothing, nothing. Just sit down, everything's organized." Sam winks. She and Nancy had been in the same grade in the Rapahu schools; by sixth grade, Nancy had color-coded notebooks for each subject and a plaid address book with each of her friends' phone numbers, birth dates, and clothing sizes written inside. "I bet she even poops on schedule," Sam used to joke.

"How was Mom?" Marnie asks.

"She got up, did a tango, and then just lay back down, eyes closed, in the same position." Sam grins her toothy Joni Mitchell smile. Nancy looks up from slicing a tomato. She purses her lips. *The joking's good,* Marnie wants to say, *it keeps Raya alive for us, it's what she would want,* and then, for the first time today, it hits her, why they're all here: to figure out what her mother would want.

•

They eat on lavender paper plates in the Queen Anne dining room. In the middle of the table there's a centerpiece from Nancy's parents' florist shop: red, white, and blue carnations with miniature American flags interspersed and a yellow ribbon wrapped around the container.

"Looks like your folks have quite a business in war propaganda," Sam says.

Marnie pinches Sam's leg under the table, but Nancy is deaf to derision. "Oh, yes," Nancy says between delicate bites of her sandwich. "They've used a thousand yards of yellow ribbon since the war began. My father says you can't get a flag anywhere in the county."

Nancy goes on to tell them who from Rapahu is in the Gulf and about the letter-writing campaign at the middle school. David eats quickly and a lot, as if tranquilizing himself with the macaroni salad. Kyle nibbles at the crust of his sandwich, peels back the top slice of bread to inspect what's underneath, turns the bread upside down so that the mayonnaise is on the outside, and then pokes a hole with his forefinger through the center.

Looking across the table, Marnie can see that Sam has also abandoned her sandwich, her tapping resumed. Before they sat down, David had whispered that Nancy would take Kyle to visit her parents after lunch and that they'd be able to talk freely about Raya then. Sam looks at her watch. *Damn*, Marnie thinks about her sister, *she's literally counting the minutes until Nancy and Kyle will leave and she can head out the back door to smoke.*

•

Forty minutes later—after Sam has returned smelling of cigarettes from her trip to the yard and Marnie has cleared the table and refilled their coffee cups with the weak decaf that Nancy serves and David has headed upstairs for pencils and notepads with the name of a pharmaceutical company printed on top—they sit back down at the dining room table: David and Sam at each of the ends, Marnie on one of the sides, the American flags standing like sentries in the middle. "Let's lay some ground rules," David begins.

David has always loved parliamentary rules; in high school, he and Nancy had met on the student council, where David had been first treasurer and then vice president. At times Marnie has thought that what most shook David about Alan's suicide was the way it shattered all family order: their father rushed to the emergency room with a gripping sensation around his heart the morning of the funeral, Sam never crying, David fainting at the funeral parlor at the sight of Alan dressed in a turtleneck so as to hide the rope burns on his throat, Marnie pummeling her mother's chest and screaming, *Liar*, when Raya told her the news, Raya's heroic calm—her eyes shielded like Jackie Kennedy behind dark glasses, as though she were clinging to those television images of the beautiful First Lady and her two small children as a guide for how to walk through the meetings with the president of Amherst (the woods where Alan had been found were, it turned out, part of the campus), the negotiations with the town of Amherst police to release her son's body for interstate transfer, the instructions to the funeral parlor director, the talk with the rabbi, who had never met any of them before.

"I think," David says, glancing at Sam, "that we should each state our opinion fully without interruption."

Sam leans over to take off her boots. She draws her knees up to her chest, resting her socks on the seat of the chair. "Fine," she says. There's something biting in the way she lingers on the word that reminds Marnie of her father and the rage that would at times break through in his arguments with Sam. Her father had hated unions, welfare programs, war protesters, and (this said only in the privacy of his home, even her father having realized by the mid-seventies that overt bigotry was passé in the middle classes) "hippies, homos, and all those Negroes promoted on affirmative action," but he'd recognized in Sam a formidable opponent. Once, after a screaming battle between them about the inherent immorality of capitalism, Sam citing figures about the number of babies killed in Africa from Nestlé's campaign to convert women from breast-feeding to the use of their baby formula, her father jerked the kitchen table as he stood, sending a water glass crashing to the floor. During the ensuing silence, he stared at Sam. When he finally spoke, it was calmly and quietly. "Too bad you're on the *un*-American side."

Sam runs her fingers through her hair. "Go ahead," she says, looking straight at David and leaving Marnie with the distinct impression that this must be a tactic: always let your opponent speak first so your argument can include a rebuttal to theirs.

David begins in the balanced but slightly shrill cadence of an eldest child forced too early to abdicate cuteness for responsibility. (*"Bossy, bossy,"* Sam used to taunt when David, left in charge by their mother at the swimming pool, would refuse to spend the lunch money he'd been given for the four of them at the Good Humor truck.)

Marnie has trouble paying full attention to David's long-winded speech. Today—David pauses for dramatic emphasis—makes eighty-eight days their mother has been in a coma. Yes, it is true, very few people have come out of a coma lasting that long. This, however, is beside the point. Even if *no one* has ever regained consciousness after a head injury such as Raya sustained, it is impossible to predict the course that any individual's illness might take or, for that matter, what treatment innovations might be discovered. A hundred years ago, no one would have believed you could transplant a heart.

Marnie pours milk into the pallid decaf. We are not God, David continues. It is not our job to determine another person's D-day. Rather, it is our duty to care for our mother as long as she remains alive and to do everything in our power to make her comfortable in the meantime.

David folds his hands and scowls, annoyed, it seems, that anything more need be said.

Sam counters in short staccato sentences. David is simply paraphrasing the Hippocratic oath. He's approaching this like a doctor. But Raya is not their patient. As a family, they have an obligation to make choices that honor her personhood, that don't place their own sentimental needs over those of the community. It is their own sentimental need to keep her heart pumping even if she has effectively died.

"It's not a kindness to her," Sam continues. "Raya was a woman of great dignity." Sam's voice catches, and Marnie can see her sister swallowing to keep herself under control. "She can't talk, she can't move, she can't even breathe by herself."

"That sounds like social engineering," David says, circling back through Sam's words for the kill. "Like you're advocating that a council determine who should live and who should die."

"That's exactly what we do," Sam says, her voice rising. "What do you think it means that we pay for heart transplants for two thousand people a year and leave millions of others shut out from hospital care because they have no insurance?"

They go on, her sister and brother at opposite ends of the

table, Marnie seated in between, superfluous to their argument, the shape of which she could have predicted: David's devotion to his doctorly humanism where value lies in any life, no matter the condition or cost, versus Sam's devotion to the defense of the powerless over the powerful such that each drip of Raya's IV is simultaneously an affront to Raya's autonomy and a school lunch wrenched from a child.

As their father would have forecast, Sam is the stronger rhetorician, with each of her arguments prompting David to greater and greater grandstanding.

"And *who*," David says with exaggerated slowness, "*who* should decide how many days Mom gets to use a respirator?"

Marnie feels her neck muscles tighten and cramp. They seem too small, too intimate, the three of them. She wishes that someone else—Ben or even Nancy—were here with them.

"You?" David says, his finger cutting the air, fast like a metronome set for a march. "And, just to take the hypothetical situation, what if you had ulterior motives for not wanting her alive?"

Marnie breathes deeply; perhaps if she could relax herself it would calm David too. And then, *sharp*, like someone stomping on her foot, she realizes who it is that's missing. Alan, who will have been dead twenty years in two days. She covers her eyes, trying to ward off Alan's painting of the six of them as a table setting, the wooden box filled with letters to God that she and Raya found under Alan's bed the summer they painted his room, Alan's face in the coffin, waxy and older-looking as if the passage into death had catapulted his body ten years forward in time.

David and Sam stop talking. Marnie squeezes her dripping nose between two fingers and bats at a tear rolling off her cheek.

"Damn it," Sam says, "damn it to hell," and then hides her own face. David gets up and awkwardly wraps his arms around the back of Marnie's chair. He stands huddled over Marnie until she gently pushes away from the table, disengaging her body. "I'm okay, I'm okay," she says.

David goes to the half bath by the kitchen and brings back a ceramic box with Kleenex inside. Marnie and Sam blow their noses on Nancy's scented tissues.

"I'm sorry," Marnie says. "Just the two of you have gotten so far astray."

Marnie blows her nose again and then looks up at her brother and sister. "Can we start over?"

David sits. He chews on a cuticle. Sam taps on the table. Marnie exhales loudly. "The issue, it seems to me," she says, "is what Mom would want. I know she never did a living will, but that doesn't mean we can't make our best guess about what she would have said."

"She was in excellent health," David says. "I'm sure she never expected to be in this situation for at least another decade. But, even if she had told us clearly what she wanted, it's unclear whether the hospital administration would abide by our verbal report."

"That," Sam says, "is the legal question. Marnie's right. The real question is do we have any clues as to how Mom felt about all of this?"

"I've been thinking about it," Marnie says. "I really don't."

When Marnie last visited Raya, she'd been struck by the sounds: the whir of the respirator, the drip of the IV, the hum that seemed to come from the walls, the occasional clang from the hallway of a metal cart hitting a doorjamb. Only Raya had been perfectly quiet.

David has sunk low in his chair at the head of the table. He looks lost, as though the move away from the medical-ethical domain has left him without bearings.

Marnie has the uncomfortable feeling that there's something she's leaving out, something she should be telling her brother and sister. She closes her eyes to concentrate, and again the plastic rain bonnet, unfolded and drifting loose in space like a kite broken free from its owner, enters her mind. The mustard envelope. The mustard envelope with the second police report.

In the first report, the driver of the bread truck claimed that Raya had darted out in front of the truck. They'd all dismissed this as the driver's desperate attempt not to lose his job. Now, though, the bakery's insurance company has found a witness—the boy onto whose parked car Raya had flown. Sixteen and stunned by the blood, he'd bolted around the corner to vomit, not returning until after the ambulance and police had left. A second police report has been filed in which the boy states that he saw the whole thing. She had a newspaper under one arm and a plastic scarf tied over her hair, the boy is quoted as saying. The truck was coming one way and she was walking the other. Suddenly she walked right in front of it. It was like she didn't even look.

"It's not the kind of thing you talk about in once-a-week phone calls," Sam says, "whether you'd want the plug pulled if you were in a coma."

"Listen," Marnie says, so softly she's unsure if she's actually spoken out loud or if the word has been drowned out by the screech of Sam's chair legs.

Standing, Sam stretches her arms overhead, fingers laced, balancing for a moment on her toes. "I could use a drink," she says. David slumps farther into his chair. Marnie raises her brows and points at the centerpiece.

"Shit. I forgot about Higher Power here."

David jerks himself upright. He looks at his watch. "Fuck it," he says, "let's go to the Millhouse. I could use a double scotch myself."

•

Marnie hasn't been to the Millhouse since high school, when a boyfriend supplied her with his sister's ID so she could get served. Except for the video poker screen over the bar and a CD juke player, the place is unchanged: a cavernous room with a long wooden bar on one side, a dance floor and pool table on the other side, tables covered with green-checked cloths in between. As they walk in, Marnie examines the faces of the people at the bar. Three men, young, in gray work clothes, maybe guys from the tire plant in the next town, are downing beers. An obese woman with pale wispy hair nurses a drink while her companion, a small mustachioed man, punches something on a remote-control box he points at the poker screen. He looks up at the screen, grins, and claps silently.

Marnie and Sam order wine, and David orders a double scotch. Sam takes out a pack of Marlboros. "You mind?" she asks, almost desperately. Both Marnie and David shake their heads no.

"When was the last time you were here?" Marnie says, looking at Sam.

"It's been decades. Probably one summer when I was home from college."

"And you?" Marnie asks David.

David sips his scotch and touches the Marlboro pack. "Can I have one?"

Sam makes a low whistle. "Just don't tell Nancy it was mine if she smells smoke on you."

"I come here on occasion." David smiles. "After an afternoon of too many little old ladies complaining of flatulence and irregularity."

Sam stares over David's shoulder in the direction of the bar. "That woman," she says. "She looks so familiar."

Marnie glances up. The obese woman is walking toward them. When she nears the table, she stops a few feet back, as though taking into account her girth. "Excuse me," she says. "Aren't you the"—she touches a damp upper lip—"the Kleins?"

Marnie and Sam look at David.

"David, David Klein. And you're . . . ?"

"Laura Mulvaney. That's my married name. But I was Laura Preston."

Sam's eyes open wide. "Laura! Laura Preston. Oh my God."

Laura Preston had been Alan's girlfriend. She pushes back a strand of her wispy hair. "I've put on a lot of weight."

Sam, who never turns red, turns red.

"It's okay," Laura says. "No one recognizes me anymore."

Marnie pulls out the fourth chair at the table. She touches Laura's hand above the wrist. Soft flesh rests like a pillow over the bone. "Please," Marnie says. "Join us."

When Alan first met Laura, she'd been in Sam's biology class, a year younger than Alan, with white-blond hair that reached her waist and pale droopy eyes. Every night, Alan would interrogate Sam about anything she might have learned about Laura, but all Sam ever had to tell was that Laura never said anything and always got the highest grade in the class. It had taken Alan two months to get up the nerve to call Laura and ask her out. Sam coached Alan on what to say. Then David wrote him out a script. In the end, Alan had Marnie role-play the call with him. He was dumbfounded when Laura immediately said yes. Until Alan left for college, they'd been inseparable. Once he was at Amherst, they talked every night on the phone. At Thanksgiving—only a week before his suicide— he told David he was going to have to get a part-time job to pay the bills.

"David, Sama, and Marnie," Laura says.

"Right," Marnie says. "Only now Sama is Sam."

"Sam," Laura repeats. She wheezes slightly, and Marnie wonders if this is normal for her or if she's upset at seeing them. "I'm sorry about your mother."

David raises an eyebrow.

"I read about it in the local paper," Laura says. Her eyes are lost in folds of skin and it's hard to tell what she might be feeling.

Thinking about it now, Marnie realizes that she hasn't spoken with Laura since the last Thanksgiving Alan was alive. After Laura had eaten with her own family, she'd come over to join them for dessert. Marnie can still picture the table: her parents at the two ends; Sam and David on the side by the window; Alan, Laura, and herself opposite them. When David asked Laura where she was planning to apply to colleges, Alan answered for her: Smith, Mount Holyoke, the University of Massachusetts. All places near Amherst.

Raya inquired if Laura knew what she wanted to study.

"Paleontology," Laura whispered.

"What's that?" Sam asked.

"Bones," David said. "Bones and fossils."

Raya shot David a sharp look. "Let Laura speak."

They all turned to look at Laura, and Marnie remembers now the way Laura pushed a clump of her hair behind an ear only to have it cascade back over her cheek as she murmured, "The study of the origin of life."

Ten days later, when the phone call came about Alan, Marnie's first thought was about Laura. Raya called Laura's mother to have her tell Laura. Marnie had been shocked when neither Laura nor her parents came to the funeral. Later, when Marnie would see her in the hallways at the high school, Laura would lower her head. Then, after New Year's, she hadn't come back to school.

"Would you like a drink?" David asks Laura.

Laura looks over at her companion at the bar. She waves in his direction but he's staring at the video screen and doesn't notice her.

"Sure," she says. "He can play that thing for hours."

"Invite him to join us," Marnie says.

"Best just leave him be. Jimmie's not much of a conversationalist."

David beckons the waitress and orders more wine for Sam and Marnie, a sea breeze for Laura, and another scotch for himself. He takes a second of Sam's cigarettes, and begins the catch-up with Laura, exchanging his family and job details for hers: married to Jimmie over there, no children, bookkeeper at the Pontiac dealership.

Marnie finishes her first glass of wine. Unaccustomed to drinking in the afternoon, she can feel the effects—the slowing of her thoughts, the widening gulf between what's in her head and what can be put into words. Across the room, there's a table of older people having some sort of celebration. One of the women, short and plump with a reddish bouffant and a maroon pants suit, gets up and puts some coins in the CD player, and soon something that sounds like the Benny Goodman big band comes over the speakers. The woman pulls one of the men to his feet and onto the dance floor. They move like people who've been dancing together for decades, in a polished synchrony, smiling gently at each other; within seconds, the years, the pounds, the wrinkles drop off and they're spinning like Fred and Ginger.

"Remember Mom and Dad?" Sam says.

Thomas—tall, dapper, and precise—had been a great dancer. Raya had always looked awkward on the dance floor—her horsiness accentuated by Thomas's slender elegance—but she had loved the fun of it. Before they'd all become teenagers and started going off to do their own things, Saturday nights had been dance night. Raya would wear a Mexican peasant skirt with a ruffle on the edge (my Frida Kahlo skirt, she called it), David and Alan would roll up the rug, and Thomas would select the records for the night. David and Sam were always partners, both of them quick and graceful like Thomas. Marnie was Alan's partner. Alan had never been able to remember the steps and, as the night wore on, Marnie would feel his back under her fingers growing stiffer and stiffer as their father's corrections would escalate to sharp comments and, usually by the end of the night, to a bark: "Alan, goddammit, count, it's *one*-two-three, *one*-two-three."

Sam smashes out her cigarette, winks at Marnie, and raps David on the forehead. "Come on, partner," she says. The older couple smiles as Sam leads David onto the dance floor. Like their father, David keeps his back and shoulders perfectly still, leading Sam, it seems, from the pit of his stomach.

Laura twists her neck to watch David and Sam. "They're terrific."

Marnie feels annoyed with Sam for having left her alone with Laura. Laura sips her drink. "Terrific," she repeats, her eyes focused now on the bottom of her glass.

That last Thanksgiving, Alan had talked about taking classes over the summer so he could graduate a semester early so when Laura did the study-abroad program she hoped to do at the Leakey Foundation, he could go with her. Now Marnie wonders if Laura ever finished high school.

"I saw your mother," Laura says.

"In the hospital?"

"No, before."

Marnie is surprised and vaguely hurt. Her mother had never mentioned seeing Laura.

"It was a year ago. Almost exactly."

From the look on Laura face, Marnie is certain that she

means on the anniversary of Alan's suicide. For a long time, they had always telephoned each other on that day. Then, during the past decade, they stopped. It had begun to seem morbid to mark the date of a suicide. Last year, though, the first time Raya would have faced the day without Thomas, Marnie did call her mother. It was evening and they talked for a good while, and although neither of them mentioned Alan, Marnie had been certain that her mother knew why she had called.

"I hadn't seen her since before . . ." Laura pauses.

"Before Alan killed himself," Marnie says. She hadn't intended the sharp note in her voice.

Laura peeks up at Marnie. "Except for those first few weeks before I left school when I used to see you and Sama, I . . . I guess I haven't seen any of you since then. Well, that's not quite true. I've seen David a couple of times around town but I always turned my face and he never recognized me."

"Why did you go see my mother?"

"I wanted to tell her something about Alan." Laura puts a hand on her chest, which moves up and down as she breathes.

Marnie feels her jaw clench and a surge of anger welling up inside. She imagines rolling up a newspaper and whacking Laura on the side of her head. "What did you tell her?"

Laura leaks. A tear slides down her cheek. She reaches into a pocket and pulls out a wad of tissues. "I'm sorry," she says. "It's just that it's been such a weight on me and I was so grateful to your mother for letting me talk with her."

She dabs at her eyes with the tissues. "It was about that last time, when Alan was home. We were intimate—I mean, we tried to be."

She hesitates, unsure, it seems, if it's okay to go on. Marnie feels her stomach turn. She really does not want to hear any more.

"We'd planned it for a long time. Alan didn't want me to take any risks, about getting pregnant, so we'd decided I'd get something first. I went to Planned Parenthood and they had me do all of these counseling sessions because I was under eighteen, and then they gave me . . ."

Laura glances over at her husband, then turns back to Marnie. "I told Alan on the phone and he worked out this plan that we could be alone the Saturday after Thanksgiving because David would have left already to go back to Princeton and you and Sama would go with your parents to visit your grandmother."

Like everything about Alan's last trip home, Marnie has gone over that Saturday so many times in her mind that the events are permanently logged in her memory: her father sniping at both David and Alan about their not coming along to visit Grandma Mary, David storming out without saying goodbye to any of them, Alan insisting that he had to use the afternoon to study.

The friends of the red-bouffanted woman and her husband have joined them on the dance floor. The other man, broad as he is tall, laughs as he spins his wife into a series of double turns. Laura finishes her sea breeze. "We tried, but Alan couldn't." Her eyes well. "I told him it didn't matter—there'd be lots of other times. That I'd read in one of the books I saw at Planned Parenthood that this happens to lots of guys the first time, but he wouldn't listen to me."

Laura gives up trying to hold back from crying. Her shoulders heave, tiny dots of black mascara speckle her cheeks and then gather into black streaks that avalanche toward her chin. "He put the pillow over his head and refused to look at me. He just kept telling me to go away. All he'd say was, Go away, I just want you to go away."

Marnie sees Alan's face when Thomas would yell, "Goddammit, count": Alan's eyes cast downward, his teeth ground into his lower lip. She knows that she should reach out and touch Laura's hand or arm, but she can't.

After a bit, Laura's shoulders still. She blows her nose loudly like a foghorn. "Your mother was wonderful. She held my hand and made me tea and said that I mustn't blame myself, that she'd felt that way after her first husband died in Mexico and that she was sure Alan hadn't killed himself because of what happened that Saturday—and that even if it was in some way connected, I wasn't to blame, because that would mean something was wrong long before then. I told her how afterwards I'd wanted to kill myself too, and how my parents ended up calling a psychiatrist, who had them call the police to take me to the Carrier Clinic." Laura runs a finger under her nose. "They kept me there almost a year."

Marnie feels stunned. Stunned that she'd never wondered what happened to Laura. Stunned that her mother had talked with Laura so openly.

All of these years, none of them had ever talked with Raya about Alan. At first it had seemed impossible: her mother so brusque and businesslike about everything to be done. Then, at night, she would disappear early, usually by eight, into her bedroom. In the fall Sam moved to Berkeley, and only Marnie and her parents were left in the house. Evenings, Marnie would sit in the den with her father—Marnie doing her homework, her father reading the paper or reports from work between trips to the kitchen to top off his gin and tonic.

"What else did my mother say?"

"Just that she understood about my having not wanted to go on. That she'd felt that way since your father's death—not that she would ever do anything, just that she wouldn't be unhappy if her end came sooner rather than later."

Marnie shudders.

Laura gasps. She grabs Marnie's arm. "Oh my God. I'm such an asshole." She squeezes so hard it hurts.

Marnie can see Laura's husband scowling in their direction

and pointing in an exaggerated way at his wristwatch. "Your husband. I think he's trying to get your attention."

Laura looks at the bar, and then back at Marnie.

"It's all right. You can go."

"I guess I better. Jimmie's diabetic and can't eat too late."

Laura opens her purse and Marnie holds up her hand to stop Laura from pulling out her wallet.

Laura stands. "I'm such a jerk." She points toward the dance floor. "Tell them goodbye for me, okay?" she says and then heads to the door, where her husband is standing with his windbreaker already on.

On the dance floor, David and Sam have switched partners. David is guiding the woman with the red bouffant into a demi-turn and Sam is doing a three-step with the woman's husband.

Marnie drinks the rest of David's scotch. She knows she should be letting what Laura told her about Alan, a pillow over his head, about herself, a year in the Carrier Clinic, sink in, but all she can focus on is how could her mother have said she wouldn't be unhappy if her end came sooner rather than later? What about David, Sam, and her? Didn't her mother want to be with them? Didn't her mother want to see if she and Sam have children, how Kyle turns out?

She wonders if what Laura told her constitutes evidence of Raya's wishes. Or was it nothing more than Raya trying to be nice to Laura—one woman comforting another with half-truths?

As she had with Alan, Raya had handled Thomas's funeral arrangements by herself. She'd refused both David and Nancy's and Marnie's offer to come stay with them for a couple of weeks instead of being alone in the house. Except for neglecting the flowers and tomatoes that Thomas had planted (according to Nancy, Raya let the tomatoes rot on the vine), she'd seemed to be adjusting to living alone just fine.

It was like she didn't even look.

Marnie wishes she could talk with Ben, ask him what she should do. Ben relishes these kinds of questions: "The interpretive decision," he'd once explained, "is at the heart of Jewish thought."

Maybe she would get Sam's friend's phone number and call him herself. At least then they would have a legal opinion.

The music stops. David shakes his dance partner's hand. Sam gives the husband a peck on the cheek.

Marnie tracks David and Sam as they approach her from opposite corners of the dance floor—Sam waving and smiling from all the spinning and twirling; David dabbing the beads of perspiration on his forehead, glancing at his watch, already, it seems, thinking of Nancy and her opprobrium. For a moment she can see it from above: the three of them as the end points of a triangle etched into the floor of the tavern, Nancy and Kyle and Ben hovering moons, Alan and Thomas and Raya distant stars.

1992

Parachute

She called him on the eighty-ninth day her mother was in a coma. Her sister, Sam, thought he knew something about the legality of dying—living wills, how families could make these kinds of decisions without documents—but aside from a summer when he was in law school working with his mother, whom he called by her first name, Hildie, on a paper on the topic, a paper more grounded in Hildie's feminist politics of death than in actual case law, he knew no more about the subject than the rest of the Boston secondary markets team, mostly MBAs, not lawyers, that he'd recently joined or, for that matter, than her ex-husband, a guy who ran a printing shop. The mistake embarrassed her, and she found herself flushed and damp at the armpits on the other end of the line, a response that returned when, four months later, after he'd moved back to New York, he called wondering if they might have coffee, a beer . . . his voice dropped off. A few days later, sitting across from her in an Afghani restaurant at a table covered with an oilcloth laid over a miniature rug, he talked mostly about Guatemala: a blue lake, Atitlán, a quarter-mile deep with three ancient volcanoes looming overhead like an extra-titted animal, an Indian village nestled at each of the inlets, the villages like abandoned eggs with only a mail boat that left the largest of the hamlets, Panajachel, each morning at dawn to connect them.

The children had gawked, he told her, at his then-long blond hair, at his height (a foot taller than their stooped, dark fathers), at his skin the color of the mountain clouds that blew in each dusk. They'd called him *Jesus con un camión*, Jesus with a truck, and would gather around because he gave them oranges. Watching this big man debone a chicken breast in three deft cuts, a banker's suit draped over the filled-out chest of what she could imagine had once been a lean California boy, the fingers that had grazed her shoulder as they moved to the table, his stories like an intoxicant rising between them, she felt what she'd long thought of as her tiny dried-up heart erupt, tumbling like lava down one of those three ashen slopes.

She (her name is Marnie Klein) was thirty-six, a children's book writer who had buried half her family—her brother two decades ago after he'd looped a rope around his neck, her father nineteen months ago after his heart turned into a backed-up drain, her mother a week after she'd called this *Jesus con un camión* with her misguided questions—as well as a marriage to a man she'd adored but whose Orthodox Judaism she'd been unable to abide.

He (his name is Andrew Stackhouse) was thirty-nine, divorced too—a brief marriage that seemed to have left him largely untouched. After an aborted beginning as a community organizer, the trip to Guatemala having been in part to put together a collective of weavers, he'd wandered east with greater deliberation than his demeanor suggested to law school at NYU, where he'd had an affair with a moody girl named Louisa that ended badly when a vamp named Cat-Sue put her panties inside his contracts course textbook.

Now, a year and a half after they met, they are married, with Marnie nearly three months pregnant, seated thigh to thigh thirty-five thousand feet above land en route to Berkeley for what will be Marnie's first visit with Andrew's parents.

Through the window, Marnie can see a blanket of clouds shimmering and opalescent beneath the belly of the plane, so near that one of her storybook characters could jump from the tip of the wing and somersault to a gentle stop. Andrew is asleep, his fingers still curled on the edges of his newspaper. In Guatemala, he told her, he had gone to villages so high in the mountains, he'd driven through clouds to get there. The children would grab on to the door handles and the side mirrors, damp with the condensation of the thin air, to beg for the oranges he'd pass out the window.

They didn't even know how to peel them, he told her. *They'd bite right through the skin.*

•

"Andrew Stackhouse," her sister, Sam, had said with a laugh when Marnie called to say that he'd moved back to New York and wanted to meet her.

"He didn't know a damn thing about living wills. How well, exactly, *do* you know him?"

"He's one of those people you've known forever but you never really get to know and as the years pass you keep thinking you must know them better than in fact you do. I told you, he's the son of that professor I worked for when I was at Berkeley, Hildie Willis."

Sam laughed again, her nervous laugh, and suddenly Marnie could imagine it: her sister, with her beautiful teeth and her gorgeous boy's hips that no man Marnie has known has not wanted to grab.

"He's a year or two older than me, Alan's age." Sam stopped, caught in one of the culs-de-sac that halt so many of their conversations.

"I know what you mean. The age Alan would be."

"When we met, he was taking a year off from college, hanging out at his parents' house while he looked for a job. We went to a concert together."

"You mean you slept together."

"I can't remember. I know that's disgusting, but I honestly can't. It was a couple of months after I met him and he'd moved into the city and someone had given him tickets for one of those mega-concerts at the Fillmore West—I think it was Grace Slick with the Jefferson Airplane and Quicksilver Messenger Service. All I clearly remember is that we smoked so much pot, I never made it back over the bridge to Berkeley."

Marnie could hear foil crinkling as her sister pulled out a cigarette.

"Thank God there wasn't AIDS in those years," Sam continued. "I bumped into him a couple of times after that, while I was still living out west. I think it was at a meeting for groups sending medical supplies to Nicaragua. Something like that. He'd just come back from Guatemala. Then, last year, when I was working with the Boston Clean Air Coalition, we decided to try to get some money from the local business community."

The hilarity was draining from her sister's story, Marnie thought, in the way it does as people move from their twenties into their thirties.

"I was having a hell of a time, since conservatives like to make their charitable donations for genetic diseases—cystic fibrosis, muscular dystrophy—ailments where it's hard to see capitalism as the culprit. Those hideous telethons where they drag out a poor kid with braces on his arms and legs and everyone can feel good about giving for research to discover the defective gene because no one's going to turn around and say, like they can about a kid who falls down an elevator shaft, who's *responsible* for this?"

Marnie pictured her sister closing her eyes for the first long inhale.

"When I called him, it was awkward, awkward, awkward. He was embarrassed about having become this financial guy with all of these rationalizations about how he'd realized with the Guatemalan cooperative that he'd never be able to help them if he didn't understand how to work within the existing legal system and how he'd gone to law school with the idea of learning the law applying to cooperatives and private support of third world development, but after he got his degree there hadn't been any NGO jobs and then he'd had his student loans to pay, blah blah blah, all the time not getting it that I was psyched that he'd done what he had because I could hit him up for a whopper corporate donation."

Not until Marnie had hung up with Sam and run a bath and put on a recording of Ella Fitzgerald her ex-husband had given her and then poured a glass of sparkling water to bring into the tub with a book she never opened did she admit to herself her curiosity about her sister's long-ago discarded lover.

•

Marnie is quite sure that Andrew's mother won't remember that they met years ago at the Berkeley Co-op. (Marnie hadn't recalled herself until after the dinner at the Afghan restaurant when Andrew had delivered his irony-inflected portrait of Hildie and George.) It was the summer before Marnie's junior year of college and Sam's last year at Berkeley (ahhh, Marnie thinks, Sam was with her old boyfriend Peter then, so she'd probably already slept with and discarded Andrew) when Marnie made her first trip to California to visit Sam. Sam and Peter had been at the apex of their harmony-with-the-earth phase. They'd given their leather shoes and belts to Goodwill, brushed their teeth with baking soda, and taken up a method of natural birth control that involved an instructor named Mahiana Devi who offered counseling sessions at the co-op and sold Sam a year's worth of charts for recording her basal body temperature, her dreams, the consistency of her vaginal mucus, and the cycles of the moon.

On the second day of Marnie's visit, she and Sam walked the half mile to the co-op with Sam's chart rolled in a tube. Mahiana sat behind a card table with an ashtray of burning frankincense in front of her. Despite her Arabian pants and embroidered Mexican blouse, Mahiana looked to Marnie like a girl from Short Hills who could have used some electrolysis. For half an hour she talked to Sam about the Karezza method of Tantric sex practiced by a nineteenth-century Oneida community and a Czechoslovakian psychiatrist's research on cosmic fertility.

Afterward, maneuvering their cart through the sawdust-covered aisles, they bumped into Hildie scooping brown rice into a paper bag. With everyone else in Birkenstocks and Indian shirts and Army Surplus pants, Hildie in her navy suit and black pumps with her thunderous calves and bright red lips looked like she was in drag. She kissed Sam on the cheek, held out a hand to Marnie—"Another Klein"—and then, hardly missing a beat, launched an account of the conference she'd attended that day at San Francisco State on third world women and feminism, how much more advanced the students there were than at Berkeley, how she was off the next day to give a paper at the University of Michigan but would Sam come by on Monday, she needed Sam to do some research for the talk she was giving next month at the International Women's Conference on Western responses to clitoridectomies—cultural centrism or anti-violence advocacy?

"You should see their house," Sam whispered once Hildie headed to the checkout line. "It's in the hills overlooking the bay, handmade out of redwood, with a Spanish-tiled lap pool at the end of which there's a humongous Jacuzzi."

"On a professor's salary?"

"About ten years ago, her husband, George, lost a finger in a chain saw accident. Her son told me they got a three-million-dollar settlement from the chain saw manufacturer and bought the house with cash."

According to Andrew, since the accident, George has never left the Berkeley municipality; approaching the Oakland city line, he'll break into a sweat and scamper back to Telegraph Avenue. George's panic attacks, Andrew claims, are necessary for the survival of his parents' marriage, allowing them time apart while Hildie rides out the crest of her now nearly twenty-year academic stardom, the more elaborate trips to China and India subsidized by George's lost finger. When, in January, Marnie and Andrew had decided to get married, they'd let George save face by saying that it was silly for Hildie and him to fly so far for what would be, after all, a small wedding, when Andrew and Marnie were planning in any case to visit them in September.

Now Marnie feels nervous about meeting George, afraid of what his hand will look like. Or is it Hildie she's nervous about seeing, Hildie with her volumes to say about everything and enough personality, it seems from Andrew's accounts, for all of them? From what Marnie can piece together, as a child Andrew had thought of himself as a member of Hildie's audience. Unable to compete for the stage or even, at times, to make it backstage, he'd opted by fifteen for escape—a job as a bicycle messenger in the San Francisco financial district, where he'd earned enough money to launch his own life: girlfriends, marijuana bought in the Haight; by sixteen, a very used Peugeot and a beginning cache of his own stories. At times, listening to Andrew's adventures—the months in Guatemala, trekking in South America, a boat trip through Indonesia—she sees Hildie reincarnate in her son, Marnie cast now as the awestruck child.

Marnie places her hand over her belly and presses her nose to the window. Outside, it's pale and murky, like the fluid she imagines inside where her baby lies curled. For the past six weeks, since she told Andrew about the baby, they've slept without touching. Were she to ask him about it, he would, she feels certain, say that he hadn't noticed.

•

Andrew wakes when the pilot announces that they are beginning their descent into Dallas, where the temperature is ninety-three degrees. It's an hour-and-fifty-minute layover, Marnie's first time in Texas. Walking from the arrivals gate, they pass through the usual airport shopping mall augmented by Texas-themed goods intended to evoke the fantasy Texas: cowboy hats, string neckties, coffee mugs painted with cows—the Texas Marnie can see out the window looking indistinguishable from the runway at Kennedy where they'd taken off three hours ago.

Passing a raw bar with oysters and clams laid out on ice, Andrew suggests a drink. Marnie looks at her watch. It's noon, one o'clock New York time. Before they were married, she'd never thought about Andrew's drinking. Since she's been pregnant, though, she has been preoccupied with the subject—not worry that Andrew is an alcoholic but rather a nagging awareness that drinking is important to him in the same way it had been important to her father during the long evenings after Alan's suicide when Marnie would sit with him while he read his newspapers and work reports and refilled his gin and tonic three, maybe more, times in a night.

Andrew heads for a table to the right of the bar. For the most part, she's left morning sickness behind; now, though, the processed air and the perfumed candles bring on a wave of queasiness. She pulls out a small plastic bag of saltines from her purse and begins to nibble, dusting off the crumbs from her sweater.

A waitress with sea-green eyelids approaches, a pad of checks perched on her ample hips. Andrew orders a screwdriver and a plate of oysters. Marnie asks for an apple juice on ice.

The waitress squints at Marnie. "Expecting?"

Marnie is startled. She's abandoned clothing with waistbands, but has not thought she was showing yet.

"The saltines. With my first, I lived on crackers. Couldn't keep a darn thing else down. With my others, I ate like a horse starting day one."

When the drinks come, Andrew downs half of his in one go.

"Are you nervous about introducing me to your parents?"

"No."

"It's not like you to drink so early in the day."

Andrew stiffens. "It's vacation. I'm unwinding." Except for a long weekend in Miami, this is, in fact, their first vacation since they've been married. After Marnie learned she was pregnant, they'd canceled their delayed honeymoon, a safari in the Masai Mara—a disappointment for Andrew, Marnie knows (though he'd been careful not to grumble), the travel adventures his attempt to compensate for the sliver of the financial world to which he fixes his attention the other forty-eight weeks.

Marnie grasps for a way to redirect the conversation. "Have you been in Texas before?"

"Once, on my way to Guatemala. We crossed into Mexico at Nuevo Laredo." Andrew angles his chair so he can stretch out his legs. He pauses, debating, Marnie imagines, whether to oblige her by letting go of her jab about his drinking, and then, as Marnie had gambled he would, continues. "The border station made Tijuana seem tame—a lot of guys with silver belt buckles and scars on their faces. It was the middle of the night when we got there and they were officially closed, but a truck driver told us you could get through if you greased enough palms."

Marnie folds her hands over her belly, and leans back so her shoulder blades rest on the padded leather of the chair. It's too early to feel the baby moving, but it pleases her to have her hands only an inch away from her growing child. "Sounds dangerous," she says.

"Not compared to what we encountered later. We used to joke that Laredo was the GO square you had to pass through to get to the real tamale."

Andrew is vague about who the *we* is. Shortly after they met, he'd shown her a shoe box filled with packets of photos from the time he'd spent in Guatemala. Sorting through the pictures, he passed quickly over several of them. In a voice that sounded brittle even to her own ears and that reminded her that she had not yet asked if he and Sam had been lovers, she'd said, "You don't have to hide that you had a girlfriend there." Reluctantly, Andrew stopped censoring the pictures. Many were of a girl with a thick blond braid and leather sandals, someone, he told Marnie, he'd met in Panajachel who'd then traveled with him for a while. In one picture, she was lying without a shirt on a rock overlooking Lake Atitlán, her large breasts lazy and pink, the lake an unreal blue like a photographer's backdrop.

Since then, Marnie has heard many of Andrew's Guatemala stories: how the villages had been like tiny nation-states; how for years the government had tried to break their tribal order but were, as Andrew put it, so goddamned brutal about it, they'd only succeeded in alienating the Indians further; how, looking back, he'd been in the eye of a storm in those highlands without realizing how soon the hurricane would hit. At times, Marnie has wanted to say, *Enough, you've told me enough*, but now, feeling remorseful about the drinking bait, she raises an eyebrow to encourage him to go on.

"A week before I got to Totonicapán, a Peace Corps worker was killed. That felt dangerous. Rumors were that an army officer had offed the guy, a hippie American kid. The police claimed he'd been shot by a student activist from Guatemala City, but the weavers told me no one believed it—that the charges had been trumped up to turn American politicians against the leftists."

Andrew makes a little snort. "As though that were necessary. We were already training the Guatemalan military."

At these times, Marnie wishes she had known Andrew when he had hair to his shoulders and hippie paraphernalia. Had the cynicism been there even then? Once, she'd asked Sam, who said that Andrew had always maintained a hairsbreadth of ironic distance from whatever he did. "His jeans were faded but never frayed. His backpack was made of leather."

"Did you know that then? That the CIA was there?"

"There was talk—particularly around Todos Santos."

The waitress arrives with a plate of oysters. Looking at the gelatinous bodies, Marnie feels a new wave of nausea. She raises her hand to cover her nose. The waitress catches her eye, and places the plate as far as possible from Marnie, with a basket of bread in front. "Thought you might like something bland," she says to Marnie. "Anything else?"

Marnie shakes her head no. She wants to say thank you but fears that if she doesn't stay perfectly still she'll be sick. "I'll have another," Andrew says, pointing to his drink.

Marnie closes her eyes and inhales cautiously. In the past, when Andrew has talked about Todos Santos, it's been about a mountain village reached by roads too rutted and steep for his van to navigate. To get there, they'd had to take the bus—unheated with baskets on the roof and animals everywhere. There'd been only two buses out each week, leaving at some ungodly hour like three in the morning so the Indians could get to the market in time to set up their goods. Now, "doing a Todos" has become a joke between them: the way that Marnie occasionally cajoles Andrew, whose hand will shoot over his head to hail a cab before he's two steps outside, to rough it by taking the subway or bus.

The queasiness about the oysters lifts and Marnie opens her eyes. Andrew has a shell at his lips. He sucks the salt water and blue-gray body into his mouth, swallows, and then washes it down with his drink. With the vodka in his bloodstream, the corrugated lines in his brow have begun a pale pink dissolve.

"Todos was the Guatemalan version of the Wild Wild West. The men drank like fish. They were small even for the highland Indians: short legs, hunched shoulders, nasty tempers. On festival days, they'd hang live chickens from ropes at each end of the village and race back and forth bareback on their horses through the streets and alleyways, betting on who could pull off the most heads without falling from his horse."

She spreads her hands wide and flat over her stomach. If her baby can hear already, she does not want him or her hearing this story.

"I saw it once. It was gruesome: drunken men howling and blood pouring onto the dirt from the necks of these decapitated chickens."

In Andrew's photos of Todos, the men had feet callused as mule hooves and cropped pants like the pedal pushers American women wore in the fifties. There was only one picture of a woman—a tiny figure with long braids, a stiff embroidered blouse, and a face that looked sixty but, Andrew said, had probably been barely thirty. Widowed, with children to feed, she rented cots to travelers, a dollar per night with a quarter extra for each blanket. Everyone, the travelers, the woman, her six or seven children (one died that year), slept in the same one-room thatched-roof hut.

The waitress arrives with Andrew's second screwdriver. Andrew reaches immediately for the glass, and then, as if sensing Marnie's scrutiny, waits a moment before taking two long sips.

The biggest problem, Andrew had told her, was food. Because of the altitude, they could only grow corn. For months on end, the only food in the village would be eggs and beans and tortillas and cans of juice so supersaturated with sugar it left grit on your teeth. When there were travelers in the village, the widow's sister would set up a table outside her stall in the marketplace and cook whatever she had. At night, the men who lived nearby would gather there to drink.

"Would you drink with them?" Marnie asks.

"Not during the festival. But sometimes at night, sitting with them in the market, I'd have a shot of quetzalteca." Andrew sucks on an ice cube. His eyes, usually darting from place to place, are now still, almost glassy. "Most of the men spoke only K'iche', but there'd usually be someone who could translate into Spanish for me. After a while, after I'd bought a lot of the woven bags from them at a price higher than they could sell them at the Huehuetenango market and then started to talk with them about how to form a *cooperativa*, they began to almost trust me."

Andrew pats his shirt pocket as if searching for a cigarette. Marnie watches him and wonders if he has forgotten that he stopped smoking before their wedding or if he has continued smoking in secret. It occurs to Marnie now that Sam and Andrew had probably smoked together.

"There was a weaver who lived outside of Todos, a man named Teofilo who spoke pretty good Spanish and interpreted for the others when I bought their goods. He'd told me that the year before, one of his cousins who'd sold some corn to a guerrilla band had been found with his throat slashed. Someone had painted the letters for the revolutionary party on his jacket with blood."

Marnie wishes her mother could have met Andrew. With her admiration of the people-first politics of Rivera and her idol, Kahlo, she would have enjoyed Andrew's stories.

Andrew plays with his now empty glass. His eyes drift to

the bar and then back to Marnie. "One night, maybe the fourth or fifth time I came to Todos, I was sitting outside the market stall with Teofilo and about a half dozen other men. It was a few days before festival week, and they were drinking this liquor they made each year for the festival from corn—beginning the bacchanal early. Some of them had skipped going to the Wednesday market in Huehuetenango so they could drag the vats of this stuff up from the storage cellar, which was—they saw no contradiction in this—under the church."

Andrew takes another oyster, his Adam's apple bobbing in his throat as he swallows. "It was about ten o'clock, and a boy, maybe fourteen or fifteen, came running into the market. He was the son of one of the men and he began talking, more yelling than talking, in K'iche'. When I asked Teofilo what was going on, he told me the boy had spotted the villager they thought had ratted on Teofilo's cousin. The morning before Teofilo's cousin was found murdered, this man had left with the others for Huehuetenango and had then never come back. Now the boy had seen him get off the bus and head across the square to the path leading to his mother's hut."

Marnie looks at the clock on the wall—an hour still until the plane to Oakland. "What happened?"

"They all got up, with the boy following behind. Two of the men unhooked the machetes that always hung from their belts. Another took a tarnished pistol from under his jacket. I was surprised since I'd never seen any of the Indians with a gun. I'll never forget the way he blew on the barrel and then spit into his palms."

Marnie feels her brows squeeze together. "What happened?" she repeats.

Andrew laughs. "What do you think? They killed the guy."

"You *saw* them?"

"I heard screams, probably while they were hacking at him with the machetes, and then, after a while, two shots."

Her hand moves from her belly to her chest, where her heart pounds wildly. "You didn't try to stop them?"

Andrew looks at her coolly. A bead of salt water lingers on his lower lip. "The man was a *gusano*, a worm—he'd ratted on one of his *compadres*."

"You don't *know* that. You don't *know* that *for sure*." Her voice is thin, almost shrill. On Andrew's face—disdain, as though she's beneath being called an idiot.

"I should have chased after half a dozen Indian men, all of them with machetes, at least one with a gun, only one of them able to understand a word I spoke, and tried to convince them not to kill a man they thought was responsible for the death of their friend?"

Marnie feels like a car whose idle has suddenly shot too high. Her ears are ringing and she is afraid that she is going to do something out of control: scream or slap Andrew. Only once, the night they learned about Alan's suicide, has she ever done anything like that. Her parents had called Sam and her into the living room. Her father was unable to speak. When her mother told them, Marnie lunged at her, batting her fists at her mother's chest. *Liar, liar, liar.*

Yes, she wants to yell. *Yes, you should have.* But her stomach saves her. Her gurgling stomach rising into her esophagus, her stomach that remembers the four oysters Andrew slurped whole and the two that still float in a cloudy fluid behind the bread basket. She stands, pressing on her breastbone, willing the contents of her stomach to stay below her palm until she makes it to a bathroom.

•

While the others had rolled like billiard balls from their senior years of high school into their excellent colleges, Marnie, in her first act of defiance (of all of them, she had been the most compliant, trailing behind Sam, bringing home report cards with only As, rarely ever even getting sick), had the June before she was scheduled to start Barnard refused to go. She'd told her father first, one night after dinner when the two of them sat together with Thomas's gin and tonic between them. Her father had reacted in the only way he knew: to insist on a kind of corporate obedience, to remind Marnie that the deposit securing her position in that September's class had already been sent.

"I'm not going," Marnie said, shocking even herself with the quiet certainty with which she delivered these words. In the morning, when Marnie told her mother, Raya lifted her hooded eyes, looked squarely at Marnie, and then said with neither bitterness nor disappointment, "Fine." Marnie had felt an empty, hollow feeling. She sputtered explanations: she wanted to defer for a year, her friend Janyce had told her about an organization that would arrange for her to work as an au pair in Paris . . . She started to cry, her first tears in front of her mother since Alan's funeral. Raya pulled her close and although neither of them said so, Marnie was certain that her mother was thinking that perhaps if Alan hadn't tumbled off to Amherst like the shadow of David he'd always tried to be, he wouldn't have three months later hung himself from a tree.

In Paris, she'd lost her virginity with a Polish photographer named Wojtek—a huge man with coarse hair, a belly that hung over his belt, and a booming laugh that Marnie imagined must put at ease the birdish runway models he spent his days shooting for a showroom off the Place Vendôme. At first Marnie could hardly understand his Polish-accented French. His voice would tickle the inside of her ear with what sounded like *mon petit, shhh*. It took her two weeks to summon the courage to ask him what did he mean. Sitting cross-legged on the bed like an oversized Buddha, he laughed and laughed, pantomiming something that looked like a beach ball, finally getting up to find a piece of paper on which he wrote, *Mon petit chou*, my little cab-bage. At other times, he'd pat her bottom and tell her, *Il faut que tu gardes la ligne*, you need to watch your figure, and then, as if unaware that her *ligne* had anything to do with the mounds of food he loved to prepare, would insist that she stay under the covers while he lit the water heater that stood in a corner of his drafty studio and, dressed in a red tartan bathrobe, scrambled eggs with a kielbasa he bought at a charcuterie on the Rue d'Odessa, as good as any in Kraków, he'd say.

In bed, Wojtek would sweat and grunt and Marnie would catch herself curiously watching—as though he were letting her see something very important about himself. Although she knew from her high school class in human sexuality that she was supposed to feel something more than curiosity and that Wojtek should be more concerned that she didn't, these thoughts seemed to belong to a different universe than Wojtek, who at sixteen had left a small town west of Kraków where his parents, whom he'd not seen since, still lived with chickens in the yard.

In the third month that she'd known him, Marnie, finding herself late one Saturday afternoon on Wojtek's street, rang his bell. Wojtek answered the door with the red tartan bathrobe wrapped like a towel around his prominent middle. "Not now, *mon chouchou*," he said, kissing her on the forehead as Marnie, hearing a girl's voice, *Qui est là?*, froze. The next day, he came to get her in his old Renault. He squeezed her arms and hugged her and called her his pudgy baby and pointed to the back seat and the bags he'd prepared for a picnic in the Bois de Boulogne. *Du pain, du vin, du fromage, du saucisson*, he boomed. In the Bois, he unfolded a blanket from his bed and laid out the food. He stroked her hair and explained that she needed to know other men, that having slept only with him, she was like a soup made with only one vegetable.

It all seemed very sensible, the way Wojtek put it. Whereas

Marnie knew she wasn't—had never been, would never be—beautiful or sexy in Sam's way, she was nonetheless eighteen with clear pale skin, large breasts, and a pensive expression that suggested something mysterious and undiscovered inside. For months she'd ridden the Métro, walked through the Jardin du Luxembourg, read in the cafés on the Boulevard du Montparnasse with her eyes downcast, fearful of catching anyone's gaze. Having been able to count the dates she'd had before Wojtek on one hand, raising her eyelids was dizzying: Francisco from Mexico City, who followed her from Le Drugstore on the Champs-Élysées and worked at a factory in a *banlieue*; Hans, a Norwegian student reading philosophy at the Université Paris; Benoit, an engineer from Belgium with two children in Bruges and a lot of ideas about free love; Anouar, a wealthy Egyptian working for a few months in an uncle's import-export business on the Avenue de Wagram. They took her to restaurants, to the nightspots their meager or in some cases not so meager salaries would allow, to meet cousins or brothers or friends, and inevitably to their walk-up apartments with stopped sinks or their chic apartments with glasses that clinked. Marnie followed, driven not by her body (that she wouldn't understand until years later with Ben) but by a greed for experience, not just the experience of men and how their machinery worked—erections that came too fast or left too soon or woke them in the middle of the night or as light filtered in through venetian blinds, lace curtains, garret windows—but also the experience of herself unbound, an apparition broken free from the self, the self she'd patched together from the pieces left after her siblings had grabbed all the goodies from the box of character traits, leaving her with only the scraps.

She'd met Ben four years later, during her last semester of college. When he'd interrogated her about her past involvements, she'd been able to say, Nothing, there's really been nothing, some brief adventures in Paris, never mentioning Anouar since Ben would be tormented if he knew she'd slept with an Arab man.

Their marriage lasted thirteen months, the end arriving on a Friday night when Marnie went to light the Shabbat candles that Ben took as a given and halted in the doorway with matches in hand and the sudden awareness that this, the chicken roasting in the oven, the two sets of dishes, were for her like acting in a play she'd never even wanted to see. Her mother too had lived on someone else's stage set, moving to suburban Rapahu, where she'd valiantly tried to make a home, but always with a sense of alienation from the very land itself (the mowed lawns, the manicured hedges, the black tar driveways)—the beloved Manhattan to which she'd fled from St. Louis and had then fashioned into a place for herself with a railroad flat in Hell's Kitchen and a job under old Mr. Klopfer in the Meso-American collection left behind. The candles unlit, Marnie and Ben sat up most of the night, both of them crying at the realization that there was no solution to Marnie's lack of faith: she could no more make herself take the practices that were so meaningful to Ben into her heart than he could give up his belief that as his wife she should.

A decade later, when she told Ben about Andrew, they both cried again, Ben's face buried between her breasts, her hands stroking his thick black hair as she held him tight and told him that she would always love him but that since their divorce she'd been in a kind of prolonged sleep and as she began to stir she could see that she had been misguided in thinking that writing books for children required her to forswear being a parent (as though having to socialize a child into the world would erode her ability to see through a child's eyes). That now, at night, as she lay in bed, she imagined her ovaries shriveling and that before they turned into fossils, she wanted one of the eggs she'd been shedding month after month for nearly a quarter of a century to grow into a baby. There were women who could do it on their own, maybe Sam, who claimed that the connection of love and procreation was a false idea created by capitalism's need for the family to rear and then feed and shelter labor, but Marnie wanted her baby to have a father, and now—she paused, tears streaming down her cheeks—she had met someone with whom she thought a good life might be made, *but how will I know*— and Ben, though his face was crumpled in grief, nodded in agreement—*if I keep sleeping with you?*

•

Once inside the bathroom, Marnie vomits: saltines, apple juice, the breakfast sandwich from the plane. Afterward, she sits on the toilet seat with her knees pulled up to her chest and her forehead resting on her kneecaps.

The room reverberates with the sounds of sinks turning on and off and the racket of the hand dryer. A few stalls down, a woman is talking to a child. "No, sweetie, let Mommy finish before you open the door."

"I want to go out," the child whines.

"Stop it," the woman hisses. The child starts to cry (has the woman slapped her hand?) and Marnie hears her own mother's voice the night they learned about Alan, Raya bellowing over Marnie's screams of, *Liar, Liar*, bellowing from the chest that Marnie pummeled, from lips blue with shock: *Stop it, you're acting crazy. Stop it, Marnie, stop.*

There's vomit on the sleeve of her sweater and she wonders if she's going to be sick again. She stands, leaning over the toilet bowl, but her stomach is hard and still.

She waits for the woman and child to leave before exiting the stall. At the sink area, she dabs at her sleeve with a wet paper towel and then picks off the specks of paper that stick to the fabric. In the mirror, her skin looks pale and blotchy. She takes a travel toothbrush from her tote and brushes her teeth.

Back in the corridor, she feels panicked, as though knowing about the murdered man—what had Andrew called him? a *gusano?*—has placed her, her and her baby, in danger. She imagines making a dash to the terminal exit, hailing a cab, having the cab take her to the train station, taking a train to wherever it is that trains go in Texas. Hiding in a motel. Waiting there until her child is born.

A parade of people roll their luggage toward the gates. She looks at her watch. It's been twenty minutes since she left the bar. She wonders if Andrew seized the opportunity to order a third drink or if he is scowling (even worse, standing) at the entrance to the bar, his mouth filled with barbs for her return.

•

Marnie listens to the long passage of a song by an Irish heavy metal band Matt follows that constitutes the greeting on Sam and Matt's answering machine. She's in the middle of an attempt to leave a cheerful message, "Hi, it's your sister, I'm calling from Dallas, just wanted to say hello . . ." when Sam picks up.

"What the hell are you doing in Dallas?"

"We're on a layover to Oakland."

"You sound funny. Is something the matter?"

Marnie wells up with tears. She's afraid that if she talks, she'll begin to sob.

"Marnie, are you okay? What's the matter?"

Sam sounds frantic and Marnie feels guilty about burdening her sister. Since their mother's death, they've been increasingly reliant on each other and yet also more cautious, as though so many deaths have left them more aware of each other's fragility.

"Marnie, *tell me*—what happened?"

Marnie shudders. Her neck is clammy and her mouth tastes like she's been sucking on a copper spool.

"Is it the baby? Is there something wrong with the baby?"

"No, no," she says, and then she begins to cry: rivulets of tears that run down her face, long gulping heaves.

Sam coos into the phone: *All right, shhh, just take a deep breath.*

Marnie fishes in her bag for a tissue. She wipes her eyes. "It's Andrew. He told me something that freaked me out."

Marnie struggles to tell Sam the story the way Andrew had, correcting herself every sentence or so to say, no, those weren't his words, I think what he said was . . . When she gets to the part where Andrew said that of course they killed the man who had ratted, she tells Sam about Andrew hearing the man's screams and the gunshot, and then she pauses, ashamed to tell even Sam about Andrew's smirk.

"I thought I was going to be sick. I got up and went to a bathroom on a floor below so he wouldn't follow me."

Again Marnie feels queasy. She holds on to the metal shelf under the pay phone. On the other end of the line, she can hear her sister lighting a cigarette and then exhaling the first satisfying mouthful of smoke.

"Look," Sam says. "Let's back up here. What do you think Andrew should have done?"

Marnie leans against the back wall of the cubicle. "I don't know. He could have tried to convince them not to kill the man. He could have run after them to try to stop them. He could have reported it to the police or the embassy or something."

"It doesn't sound like a sit-down-and-talk-it-over kind of situation. As far as running after them, I don't know."

Sam pauses. Marnie pictures her sister drawing her slender wrist to her mouth, the cigarette glowing red at the tip. "I'm not defending Andrew, but just try to imagine it. What would have happened if he'd run after them? A remote village without paved roads or lights, a group of drunken men with machetes and a gun. It's hard to know what Andrew was thinking then—if he was just too stunned to know what to do or if he was scared shitless that they'd turn around and butcher him too."

"What would you have done?"

"At twenty-two, like Andrew was then? Six months after a Peace Corps volunteer had been shot? I honestly can't say. I hope I'd have run after them and pleaded with them to stop. But you know, these villages have their own rules. It's not like Andrew could have argued with them not to take the law into their own hands, to go to the police and have the man arrested. The guy who ratted was probably in cahoots with the police."

"But couldn't he have at least reported what he'd witnessed?"

"Who to? If he'd gone back to Guatemala City and reported it to the American embassy, they would have written down everything and then turned the file over to either the province police for that area or the military. And *then* what? Who else would have been killed?"

Listening to Sam, Marnie feels like she's chewing and chewing on something that won't go down. Although she can recognize the reasonableness of what Sam is saying, her sister's words seem oddly peripheral, as though Marnie were telling her that her chest hurts and Sam were inspecting her feet.

Marnie digs through her tote for another tissue. It's not what Andrew did or didn't do, she thinks, it's the way he seemed to enjoy the story, as though it were an action movie where everyone looks forward to the moment when the villain is felled in a flurry of gunfire.

She blows her nose. "He laughed. Why did he laugh when he told me?"

Sam sighs as though running out of steam. "I don't know," she says. "Maybe he was nervous telling you the story?"

•

At the bar, the waitress hands Marnie a note from Andrew: *Where have you been? If you don't get your butt in gear, we're going to miss the flight. Meet me at the gate.*

On the plane, Marnie holds her limbs close to her body, careful not to touch Andrew's arm or leg. The video with the safety instructions begins. Andrew watches attentively. She leans her head against the window and looks out at the Dallas lights.

When Marnie wakes, the card with the life jacket diagrams is on Andrew's tray table, next to a cup of coffee. Andrew is reading a copy of *The Dallas Morning News*. She peers over his shoulder at the article he is looking at: weak polling results for local boy George H. W. Bush—the war hero, she's read, who at twenty parachuted from the burning plane he'd piloted over the Pacific without confirmation that his two crewmen, whose bodies were never found, had heard his command to jump.

She wiggles her shoulders and her legs and imagines her baby doing the same. *Baby, you've been to Texas now*, she says, silently talking to the little amphibian swimming inside her.

Lowering the newspaper, Andrew looks shyly at her. He hands her the plastic bag of saltines she'd left behind in the bar, then slowly, cautiously, places the flat of his hand over her belly.

2001

Conchita

"Conchita, Conchita, princesita," PK, her father, would sing as he opened the door. Then, we were living in Dorado, twenty miles west of San Juan in a villa with a cook and a maid and a gardener-chauffeur who tended the beach roses, gardenias, and impatiens, polished PK's leased black Mercedes, and drove PK to the construction site where he and his two partners were putting up what was to be the grandest hotel on the island with what I thought must be the shadiest money south of Miami. I was thirty-four, with dirty-blond hair that once touched my ass and that my best friend Louisa had massacred four years before cutting out the knots on the morning of my first daughter Lily's funeral.

"*Ven, salsa rubia, mi rubia,*" come, blond salsa, my blondie, PK had whispered when he first saw me outside the San Juan airport, me laden with backpack and duffel, trying to arrange a taxi to the language school where I had enrolled for a three-week immersion course, Louisa and my brother having convinced me that I had to do something other than braiding the pink and orange and purple mops of Lily's trolls. With his kinked black hair and narrow hips and perfect Spanish (I didn't know that afternoon that PK's excessively rolled *r*'s were his "tell": no Puerto Rican man would loll them around on his tongue), I assumed he was a local. "My driver will take you, we go right by the Calle Fortaleza," he said, the address gleaned by leaning over my shoulder to read the piece of paper in my hand, the street name inflected with the slightest of sneers as though it were the location of a nursery school or a children's camp. All I knew was he felt like a drug, the promise of mystery and adventure in his voice and his eyes and the way his pelvis jutted forward, and if I couldn't be curled up in Lily's bed where I could still smell her breath, all I wanted was to be transported a zillion miles outside my own skin.

"*Ven, Ven*," come, come, he said, and I came.

•

When, fifteen years later, Conchita sinks a cake knife into my arm, two inches on an angle until the tip scrapes bone, a wind comes up from my lungs, bottlenecking near my breastbone and then at the base of my throat. "Bitch, you little bitch," I scream as fingernails go for her neck so that I see, with my arm raised, blood streaming down my elbow, a river of bruised love between my second daughter and me.

By the time the paramedics arrive with a red flashing ambulette, lots of noise in the stairwell and banging on the door, there is blood mottled on my hands, spotted on my shoes, streaked on the floor. Conchita sits at the kitchen table next to the poppy-seed cake with orange icing I'd brought home from the bakery Louisa and I now own together, smoking a cigarette, her lower lip pushed out, her look that says, *You're not the boss of me, you failed, husbandless woman, I'll do what I want.* Still, when the paramedics ask what happened, what I say before they descend with bandages and morphine is, "An accident. The cake. My daughter turned suddenly from cutting."

•

PK, I would learn once Jorge, whom he'd introduced as his personal assistant, had loaded my duffel inside PK's leased Mercedes, was Peter Kantor. The rest took months to piece together. Yes, he could speak Spanish like a local, but he couldn't spell a goddamned sentence correctly start to finish. Yes, he could pick out nearly any song on a piano, but he couldn't read a note of music. Maybe his father was a New York real estate developer. Maybe his mother was the niece of a Roman contessa. It did seem, at the very least, that she was Italian and had given him his Latin looks. Unlikely that he'd once sung backup vocals for Joni Mitchell at a gig she did with Herbie Hancock, and highly improbable that he'd slept with her as he hinted. As for growing up in a ten-room apartment on Park Avenue and summering in Newport, Tom—Louisa's cousin Jay's college roommate, who'd known PK when they'd both attended the Horace Mann School—snorted when Jay repeated this story. And PK had most definitely *not* gone to Cornell, Tom reported—maybe somewhere upstate, but wherever it had been, he'd been kicked out after his first year for brokering term papers for sale.

Conchita was three weeks old when PK and I married in a small dark church two blocks from Jorge's San Juan barrio flat. Jorge, who had morphed into PK's partner, insisted. "Your daughter must have a father," Jorge proclaimed. PK, who I'd learned by then was a bit scared of Jorge, never challenged Jorge's authority on the matter. As for me, with a breast infection and leaking milk, I could not muster forces to object nor courage to telephone anyone other than Louisa to announce either Conchita's arrival or the upside-down marriage plans.

Conchita wore a tiny white lace dress that Jorge's wife, Maria, had made. Maria and Louisa, who'd come for the wedding, took turns holding her while Jorge snapped Polaroid pictures.

"*Mira, mira, rubia, rubia,*" look, look, blondie, blondie, Jorge would yell as each picture emerged, our forms and faces floating up through the dark paper, like bodies rising from the bottom of a deep black sea.

•

Julie, my neighbor, drives me back from the hospital. Even Julie, who has had her daughter, Angie, arrested after finding a crack pipe in Angie's purse, doesn't know what to say about Conchita sinking a knife into my arm. I am groggy from morphine. Julie pats my good arm and asks about pain, how many stitches, if I can shower with my bandage on. When we pull up to our apartment complex, a twenties brick building off Pelham Parkway, once respectable but now, with most of us on rent subsidies, only a half step better than public housing, she asks, "Do you want me to come in? Make you some tea? Help you clean up?"

I shake my head no, mutter thank-you's, and make my way toward the Tudor arched door.

Inside, it is silent. I survey the apartment for clues of Conchita's whereabouts: jeans splotched with blood crumpled on her bedroom floor, her closet door ajar with shoes every which way, mascara, hair spray, cotton balls strewn on the bathroom counter. In the kitchen, there is an ashtray with three cigarette butts, the poppy-seed cake still on the table, the bloodstained knife.

I lie on the couch with a blanket pulled up to my armpits and try Conchita's cell. It rings from her room. I turn on the TV, look without watching: *MacNeil/Lehrer*, *Law & Order*, the eleven o'clock news. I pick up our phone to check that the line is open, then fear that she's tried to call during that second, hang up, and pick it up again to see if a message has come through.

My daughter is out there in the night. I cannot remember when it was that we ceased feeling like extensions of each other, intertwined orbits, the moon and the earth. A nice-looking man announces that medical waste is washing ashore at Rockaway. I close my eyes, grateful that this time it is my blood on the towels.

•

PK left two days after Conchita's first birthday. I asked him to leave because I feared what I might do after six months with his new partners (by then Jorge was no longer working with him, which I knew was a bad sign but not how bad) and their middle-of-the-night calls that drew him from our bed to the shower to the drive to a silver limousine that would arrive, never shutting the engine, the windows sealed with black shades behind which I imagined hell and paradise bound in conjugal embrace—leggy prostitutes from the San Juan nightspots, fluted glasses of French champagne, machine parts in transit from Panama, each cylinder packed with the powder they called their white gold.

It was an early, early morning, the trees and the vines damp and drained of their color, little lapping sounds rising from the sea behind us. Even though I lost my nerve, weeping as he stood at the door, PK must have known I was right, that if he didn't heed what I'd said and leave, the mother of his child might be a woman who brought herself to shame.

By night, a frenzied panic set in. I telephoned everyone whom I had ever seen with PK, finally bundling Conchita into the car, driving with beaded eyes and rough breath the twenty miles to San Juan, tearing through Maria and Jorge's little house, looking under beds and inside closets even though I knew it made no sense, and then flinging myself wailing and crying into their arms, demanding that they tell me where the father of my child had gone.

Afterward, there was the lap, lap of the sea. There were Conchita's cries, starless nights rocking her back to sleep, gray dawns rising to feed her. There were the questions: Would I have put rat poison in PK's coffee, a call to the authorities, a gun to his dream-filled temple? Was there anything I wouldn't have done?

•

Conchita fumbles with the lock. By raising my eyelids slightly, I can see her tiptoe in with her wedge sandals dangling from one hand. There is the too-sweet smell of beer on a child's breath. I keep my eyelids lowered and let my drunken daughter pass by.

In the morning, I am stiff and depressed. My arm throbs and my throat is sandpaper. There is nothing I want, no tastes or smells or activities that draw me, only habit that compels feet to floor. Saran wrapped around my arm the way the nurse at the hospital showed me, I climb into a shower crowded with Conchita's stuff: apricot body scrub, loofah sponge, razor, shaving lotion, a waterproof radio that hangs on a strap from the showerhead. I am already dreading tomorrow, going to work at the bakery Louisa and I opened when Conchita was nine—Louisa the culinary force, the business side left to me, Louisa's cousin Lizzy the liaison with the psychiatric halfway house where most of our staff reside. Crazy ladies, as Lizzy had promised, make damn good bakers, but they are also so attached to Louisa and me that the sight of my bandaged arm will undoubtedly lead one of them to a meltdown.

At eleven, Conchita moves from bedroom to kitchen table. She's wearing a T-shirt and bikini panties.

I pour her a mug of half warmed milk, half coffee, and add two teaspoons of sugar. She holds the calf-colored concoction between her hands, blows gently on the top, and then nuzzles low into the steamy cup.

I am afraid to say anything.

Conchita keeps her nose buried in the mug. It is unclear if she is sniffing or drinking. After Lily died, the crisis counselor had told me to count ten breaths when I thought I couldn't stand being alive one more second. I count two breaths and then reach for Conchita's cigarette pack.

•

The week before PK left, I started to count ten breaths and then thought fuck it and threw a cup of what was thankfully luke-warm coffee in his face. He was in the shower, just in from a night trip to Ponce, the silver limousine having pulled into our drive as I rose to give Conchita her bottle. Conchita and her bottle in my arms, I was screaming through the shower curtain, "I can't go on, I can't live like this anymore, never knowing where you are or when you'll be home, it's not a life," while PK hummed along with the water about whatever victory had transpired during the night.

"You're not listening to me," I yelled. "I'm trying to talk to you, and you're not even listening."

"You listen to me, bitch. Either stop shouting or get out of my bathroom."

I think it was *my bathroom* that did it. The lid must have blown off some tucked-away box of rage. Who the hell was this man to talk to me this way? I'd had a hundred men before PK, and never had any of them talked to me this way. I put down Conchita's bottle and reached for something, for anything, to put in my hand, to hurtle, to smash—Conchita starting to wail as I found it, PK's coffee perched on the edge of the sink.

"You bitch. You fucking whore," PK screamed after the coffee hit his face.

He pushed back the shower curtain and I ran. Out the door with Conchita in my arms, down the road, and then behind a bush, my hand stuffed over Conchita's wailing mouth, saved only by PK's nakedness—no man raised by an Italian mother, whether or not she was niece to a contessa or lived on Park Avenue, would show his genitals to the world—and by the seconds it took him to find his gym shorts and pull them over his dripping legs.

•

At twelve, Julie calls. "Let's go to the beach," she says. "You and Angie and Conchita and me. I'll pack a picnic."

"I'm not up for it."

"You can't sit in the apartment all day. I'll put Angie on to talk to Conchita."

After Conchita gets off the phone, she looks at me shyly like I am a stranger who has moved into her home.

"Can we go?" she asks. She opens her eyes wide and pulls on her lower lip. She's one of those girls whose features don't gel until late in their teens. At twenty-five she'll be beautiful.

"I'd like to go, Mom."

The *Mom* takes up all the room in my chest, and for a moment I can't breathe. Lily was ten days short of her tenth birthday when she died. She'd just let go of *Mommy* and begun to call me *Mom*. I bite the nail on my little finger and focus on that to keep everything else still.

•

The girls vote for Jones Beach, where they can display their flat golden tummies to the boys who hang out by the boardwalk there. Julie, who used to live in New Haven, votes for Hammonasset, where there are dunes and wild grasses and slick rocks to clamber over.

"Hammonasset is so far," Angie, a year older than Conchita, complains, leaning over the back seat and her mother's and my shoulders to finish outlining her lips in the rearview mirror.

"And there's no boardwalk," Conchita pipes in.

"It's a tie, since you two are pipsqueaks and your votes count only a half."

The girls make grunting noises.

"I'm the driver, so I get to decide," Julie says.

"Then let me drive," Angie says.

"Not until you pass the test," Julie says.

"Which won't ever happen if it's up to you," Angie says.

The two of them keep this up until Julie passes the exit for Rye Playland, the second place the girls have lobbied for. Then Angie settles into the back seat—beach bags, magazines, cans of soda, and snacks piled high in the center, Conchita asleep with her head propped on the door.

•

My first thought when Conchita mentioned the genealogy assignment for her American history class was what an insensitive thing to ask this group of fifteen-year-olds, most of them from tangled-up families like ours, to do—and at the end of the school year, to boot. I was wrapped in a towel, slathering on lotion, and it crossed my mind that I should call her teacher to object, but then the phone rang and it was Oona, the bipolar nighttime baker, talking so fast that I'd wondered if she was breaking through her lithium—the air-conditioning had died and, *screw all of yous*, she couldn't get the cakes iced in a kitchen hot as an oven—and I didn't think about the assignment again until I got home the next day, Friday afternoon, and there it was on the kitchen table, in front of Conchita: a piece of paper with the beginning of a family tree. On one side, my parents, my brother, his wife, their three children, Lily (d. 1982). On the other, an empty white space.

When Conchita was old enough to ask questions, I had told her that she had been born in Puerto Rico, her father had loved her, but the marriage was foolish and brief. Over time, she made specific inquiries, but actually many fewer than I had worried she would make: What did her father look like? How long had we known each other before we got married? How old was she when he last saw her? Had I heard from him since the divorce?

I unpacked the poppy-seed cake from the bakery box and took out the cake knife and two plates. Conchita pushed the paper toward me. "What should I fill in here?" she asked, pointing to the empty white space.

There'd been a time, it now seemed a lifetime ago, when, seeing an empty white space, I would have imagined a painting, but when Lily died, I'd lost the ability to conjure images. "Let me first get this box in the garbage and out of these clothes," I said.

"I deserve to know. It's my right to know."

Cake box in one hand, milk carton in the other, I faced my daughter, who was now standing, bouncing on her toes and flailing the paper through the air. I handed her the milk carton. "Pour us some milk while I change into my shorts and we'll sit down with some cake and talk about it."

"I want to know." Conchita's voice was losing the bass and her face was starting to bloat. "Where is he? Where is my father?"

I stood with the cake box still in my hand and my shirt stuck to my back staring at my daughter who rarely cries and had never before asked for her father. Conchita pounded on the counter, the paper now a crumpled ball in the palm of her hand. "Tell me," she yelled. "NOW!"

With that imperious NOW, it was as if PK was in the room. *Come here NOW*, he would order, prone on the bed, his erection in his hand. And then later, after the imperiousness had been dosed with a two-day heroin binge and no sleep, *Stop that goddamn baby's crying. NOW.*

Sob after sob, Conchita was swallowing up what was left of the precious little air. I leaned on the counter. "Your father is dead."

I closed my eyes, immediately regretting having blurted out the words. I'd learned about PK's death four years ago from Lizzy, who'd heard from her brother's roommate Tom, who'd read about it in the Horace Mann class notes. Tom had sent me a copy of the announcement. The way the cause of death was unspecified, a long illness, had suggested AIDS.

With my eyes closed, I could see the cove in the back of the Dorado villa: the blue water that turned purple and then green as the sun fell into the sea. At first, after I'd learned about PK's death, I'd imagined telling Conchita when she was fourteen or fifteen, but then when she turned fifteen, I'd imagined sixteen or seventeen. Lately, I'd been thinking when she leaves for college.

When I opened my eyes, what I saw was Conchita with the knife from the cake and what I thought was, like father, like daughter, PK had a sweet tooth too.

•

At the beach, the girls slather themselves with baby oil, rubbing each other's backs and then the backs of each other's legs. Plastic shopping bag wrapped around my arm, I feel too slovenly to bother with the rituals of suntanning. Angie fiddles with her radio until she finds the rock station she wants, and Conchita stretches out with a T-shirt over her eyes. Soon she is asleep again, her mouth ajar. My own eyelids feel heavy and they too drop, the sun blazing red through the lids as I join my daughter in sleep.

When I wake, Julie and Angie and Conchita are tossing a Frisbee at the edge of the water. I watch them throw and bend and jump—Conchita wiry like a cat, Angie and Julie with bouncing breasts and full thighs. Julie makes a high soaring throw, and Conchita leaps, her black hair wild and curly from the wet and the salt. I imagine her hiss as she nabs the Frisbee between two fingers.

Lily was still a little girl when she died, still young enough to have me wash her hair in the tub, to crawl into my bed when I didn't have the door locked on account of some guy, which in those days was too frequently. I never saw her on the verge of womanhood, as Conchita is now, though I imagine she would not have been like Conchita. A dreamer, she moved at half of Conchita's speed: slow and thoughtful and careful, not like Conchita, for whom everything is absorbed in a nanosecond, her rev set high like a race car's.

Julie has left a half-drunk beer in the sand between our chairs. I gulp, the bottle damp and cool between my hands. I rub the bottle over my face and down my neck and I think of PK withered from AIDS and his parents—Conchita's grandparents—still alive and living in Queens, Tom has told me, and whether Conchita will want to meet them and, if so, whether they will welcome her, and I think of me, middle-aged and damaged, all grace washed away. And I think of our daughter, a wet, salty cat with a Frisbee curled into her arm, and then of Lily, buried now for nearly twice as many years as she lived, and how, in the end, this is everyone's fate: our remains outstrip our lives.

•

In the car on the way home, Julie tunes in an oldies-but-goodies station. She and Angie sing along with the Drifters and "Up on the Roof," and then the Association and "Cherish."

"Cherish," they sing, Julie a decent alto, Angie an off-tune second soprano, "Cherish is the word I use to *descreye-ibe*, all the love I have for you *inseye-ide* . . ." Conchita, who has inherited her father's pure voice, joins in, lifting the song into a heavenly register. PK had liked to sing "Woodstock"—We are stardust / Billion year old carbon / We are golden / Caught in the devil's bargain—and even though I know that Joni Mitchell sang this song solo, for this moment I believe PK's claim that he'd once sung backup for her.

Julie and the girls are in the midst of assisting Paul Simon with "Mrs. Robinson" when Conchita leans forward to prop her elbows on the back of my seat. We've not touched since it happened. I stare straight ahead at the highway, watching the pattern of dashed and then long yellow lines as Conchita starts to play with my hair, twirling it between her fingers, pushing it up into a ponytail, and then letting it fall heavily down, the hairdresser's game she's played with me since she was a small girl.

"And here's to you, Mrs. Robinson," Julie and Angie sing, "Jesus loves you more you than you can know, *wo, wo, wo.*"

"Remember squirmy little Dustin Hoffman in that scene?" I say to Julie, my scalp alert to each of Conchita's twists and twirls.

"Yeah." Julie smiles. "And that leopard-print bra Anne Bancroft wore!"

When Conchita takes out her brush and begins to untangle my hair, I lean back so that my head rests against the top of the seat. My sandy hair drops over the back and a sigh escapes. Conchita brushes gently from my forehead to my nape, the way Louisa must have tried to do the morning of Lily's funeral, and for the first time I see that it is not only her father Conchita is missing but also her sister, who she never met but has always been with us.

On the chorus, Conchita joins Julie and Angie in the "*wo, wo, wo.*" Angie raises her Coke can with the "Here's to you" and I sit up. Soon we are four toasting Mrs. Robinson, the sun sinking low to our right, the windows open, the dusky air blowing on our faces, the golden daughters leaning over the seat, the wounded mothers sailing first into the night.

2003

Barberini Princess

For fourteen years, César Punto had cleaned Ilana Green's office on Saturday. The first weekend of each month she left him a check written in her precise handwriting, handwriting that matched her small frame and bob cut. On occasion, she left a note, a gentle reminder to vacuum under the chair cushions or dust her books. Two or three times a year, she called him to announce her absence from the office and request that he water her plants. During the first few years she'd had the office, she'd seen César often. Then, she'd still been settling in—installing shades, hanging pictures—and he'd helped her with various things. Over the past few years, she hadn't laid eyes on him at all.

Ilana Green was a psychologist and a mother. She thought of herself in that order, perhaps because she'd been a psychologist before she became a mother, perhaps because seeing patients felt entirely natural, whereas she had moments with her daughters, nine and eleven, sturdy redheaded beauties, when she felt awkward, as though she were playing the part of a mother in a stiff unbelievable manner. Her husband, Bill, was one of the alpha New York men who when they first met had still been called by his Wall Street buddies by the nickname, Bear, they'd given him when they were at Princeton together. For a while, Bill had campaigned to have her join the majority ranks of the mothers of the children who attended her daughters' private school, women who had exchanged going back to work after their second was born for the position of full-time domestic CEO and part-time school volunteer. There were former anesthesiologists and corporate tax attorneys stuffing envelopes for the spring benefit. Women who'd once managed trading offices in Singapore gave tours to kindergarten applicants.

She knew that her children would have liked to have her, rather than Nona, their housekeeper, home on the numerous days they had off from school, but it frightened Ilana to give up her professional life. It was hard enough with a doctor before her name to muster a sufficiently firm voice to address plumbers and taxicab drivers, much less her husband, who seemed to grow more remote and irritable with each passing year: the relentless strain of getting up at 3:00 a.m. for the Far East markets, the exile from an essential part of himself left long ago on a beach somewhere. Without her work, she imagined that she would be more vulnerable to Bill, he would sleep with one of the bank trainees, a girl with luminous highlights and sultry lowlights, her daughters would fight more than they already did. Most important, Ilana liked her work, which remained a never-completed puzzle. Each psychotherapy session was a one-act play that she variously directed, performed in, and observed. Each patient who got better, and most of Ilana's did, was a missive of good sent into the world. It was sacred work—an amazement to her that she, raised by a father who believed human nature could be reduced to self-interest, altruism a sentimental myth, had ended up able to give at all.

•

It was a Monday morning, the first balmy day of the year. Ilana walked across the park to work, the paths and lawns littered with the fallen petals of cherry blossoms, the air pungent with the perfume of blooms balanced between perfection and decay. As a child, she'd been terrified of anything in a state of decomposition, going blocks out of her way to avoid a dead bird or a gardener's compost or even a pile of raked leaves, each withering object bringing to mind a vision of what had happened to the remains of her mother, whose lung cancer had been mistaken for recalcitrant bronchitis so that by the time she'd been diagnosed, her demise was too far along to halt. Ilana had ridden to the cemetery with her three aunts, her face pressed against her plumpest aunt's upper arm to block glimpsing the horrid shiny casket or the horrid shiny hearse inside which her father had insisted on riding and from which he had mysteriously disappeared by the time they reached the grave site.

Arriving at her office, she listened to her messages. The last one was from César. He'd lost his set of her keys. They'd fallen out of a hole in his jacket pocket on the subway, somewhere between Columbus Circle and his stop in Queens.

He was so despondent, there was no room for her to be annoyed. "I feel terrible," he said in the message. "All night, I cannot sleep, I feel so upset about this."

With her first patient already waiting for her, she called César with the intention of—quickly—reassuring him that he should not worry.

"I cannot believe this could happen. I try so hard to please you, and now this."

"I'll make you a new set and leave it with the doorman."

"I feel so bad. I only want you to be happy with me."

"I am happy with your work, César. I would let you know if I wasn't."

César didn't say anything. Had he been one of her patients, Ilana would have encouraged him to unpack the silence. But he wasn't, and no benefit would come of it. She crossed her fingers, a wish that, as is the way with everything—beauty, love, hatred, even, she'd come to think, wisdom—his remorse would disintegrate.

•

The following morning, she woke thinking about César. It was strange that she had forgotten that she'd actually had quite a bit to do with him when they'd first met. Then, he'd been the boy-friend of Evelyne, the nanny who worked for the family across the hall. Ilana and her neighbor, Jen, had plunged into one of those quick, intense friendships born of the intimacy of shared circumstances and filled with the pleasure of padding in socks and pajamas in and out of each other's apartments. It was before Ilana had her own children, at the end of her fellowship and the beginning of her private practice, when she'd begun to yearn for a baby, but Bill, with his thoughts returning always, during movies, during sex, to a trading scheme he was working out, couldn't even talk about it. During the brief period of her friend-ship with Jen, they'd fit like lock and key. Holding Jen's baby, Ilana could taste the sensuality, the profundity of raising a child, while Jen, still carrying fifteen pounds from the pregnancy, her clothes yellowed from baby spit-up, could feel for a moment that her life was enviable, not a stupid mistake.

Every night, as Evelyne finished work, César would be in the lobby waiting for her. It was clear to anyone seeing them to-gether that César was in love with Evelyne in a sticky, suspicious way and that it was only a matter of time before she would dump him. When she did, he became so depressed it scared Eve-lyne, who confided in Jen, who asked Ilana's advice. Ilana gave Jen the number for a low-fee clinic and the name of an intake worker César could contact there.

A year later, after Jen and family decamped to Westchester, the friendship unraveling as quickly as it had been knitted, Ilana bumped into Evelyne in the park with her new babysitting ward.

Ilana inquired about César. They were still broken up, Evelyne said, but they remained friends. He'd gone to the clinic Ilana had recommended and he was a lot better, but the store where he'd cleaned at night had gone out of business. He'd found a few small cleaning jobs, Evelyne reported, but was looking for more work. Did Ilana know anyone?

Ilana took his number. She'd keep her ears open, she promised. A few weeks later, she signed a lease on a small suite in a building on West End Avenue. She hired a painter, picked a butter cream for the room where she would see her patients, okra for the windowless waiting room, and a silvery gray for the small patient bath and tiny kitchen. The painter did an excellent job but left a big mess. Remembering César, she called him.

"My God, I cannot believe you called me. Evelyne told me she saw you, but I never think you would really call me."

He'd seen a social worker at the clinic for a few months and one of the doctors had given him some medicine, which he'd taken for a while. "So many times I think to write you a letter to tell you how much you help me. So many times."

"You're most welcome. I'm glad to have been able to help."

"You help me more than anyone ever help me."

An uncomfortable feeling descended over Ilana. Too much was never good. When her patients went on too long about the travails of their journey to her office, she knew they were late because there was something they did not want to discuss. When, right before they got married, Bill had bought her a too-expensive watch, she'd known it was expiation. At first she'd thought he'd slept with one of the high-low-lighted trainees, but a week later he'd confessed that he'd bumped into his ex-girlfriend Louisa.

"For chrissake, it was only a drink. She was in New York to visit some guy."

"A drink? A single drink?"

"That's not what I meant and you know it. We never left the bar. Just old friends talking over a couple of drinks."

Once, Ilana had screwed up her courage to ask one of Bill's college buddies about Louisa. "Louisa, Louisa." He'd laughed. "None of us knew her. Couldn't tell if she was shy or stuck-up. But man, she was good-looking. Had that sylph smoke-in-your-eyes thing going with Bear." Ilana had left the watch on Bill's dresser with a note that if it happened again, if he saw Louisa again without telling her, she would have to leave, and although he'd pained her many times since in other ways, she'd never again had cause to suspect he'd been in touch with Louisa or that there had been a breach of fidelity of any sort.

César arrived within the hour. He cleaned the new office while she went back to the old one to finish packing. The next day, after the movers delivered her things, he helped her unpack her books and files, during which time he told her how much he still loved Evelyne but that his sister had told him to forget her, that Evelyne would never marry a guy who cleaned toilets. He thanked Ilana excessively when she paid him for the two days' work, nodded solemnly when she then offered him the Saturday cleaning job.

Unfazed by blizzards or transit disruptions, César had never missed a week, the only exception when his grandmother died. Now Ilana could not remember exactly when that was, perhaps seven, eight years ago, only that he'd called her to say he had to go back to Colombia for three weeks.

"If you need to hire someone else, I understand."

"Of course not. Don't worry at all about that."

It had sounded as though César was crying. Ilana had been uncertain if he was crying because of his grandmother or because she'd said she would not give away his job.

•

Thursday afternoon, Ilana stopped at a locksmith to copy her keys for César.

The locksmith pointed at the larger key. "Where's the card for this one?"

Ilana stared at the locksmith. A card, a card . . . When she and Bill had bought their apartment, Bill had insisted on changing all of the locks to the expensive sort that require a computerized card to copy the keys. He'd made a fuss about finding a location to store the card. With her office, she could no longer remember who had given her the keys, much less whether there had ever been a card.

"Is there any other option?"

"Change the lock."

"How much would that cost?"

"Two-fifty for labor. Plus the cost of the cylinder."

It was a lot of money, but she had no confidence that she'd ever find the card and didn't want to make more complicated arrangements with César, arrangements that would mean more contact with him. "When could you do it?"

The man looked in a smudged notebook. He put on his glasses and turned the page. "I could do it tomorrow nine to eleven, three to five . . ."

Ilana studied her pocket calendar. Her schedule was so tight between her patient hours and picking up the girls two afternoons a week, any deviation plunged her into what felt like a crisis. She knew it was an absurd arrangement, since nearly every week brought disruptions: the girls' illnesses with the need for doctor's visits and then pharmacy trips, leaks, broken appliances, events at her daughters' school or business dinners she was expected to attend with Bill. Had she been her own patient, she would have said that there was something sadistic about her expectation that life adhere to the schedule she'd made.

"I can't. I see patients Friday morning, and I need to pick up my kids at school at three."

"Well, lady, it's your door. I can only come when I can come."

"There's no other possibility?"

The man turned the page of his notebook. "Saturday, nine to eleven. Time and a half."

•

At her mother's grave site, there'd been a discussion with the rabbi as to whether they should proceed without her father. The gravediggers had a strong union, it was said. Their lunch hour, a full sixty minutes, began at twelve. If the grave-site service did not start soon, they would have to wait until the gravediggers returned from lunch.

It was February. The earth was frozen and the air was damp. The women, their legs covered with only nylon stockings, were shivering. Her mother's eldest sister told the rabbi to proceed.

The casket, bound with green straps, was lowered by a machine into the already dug grave. The dirt that had been removed before they arrived was covered by a tarp, as though it would make the huge mound next to the hole seem less grotesque.

When the coffin reached the bottom of the pit, the gravediggers took off the straps. Ilana wiggled her hands free of her aunts' hold so as to edge nearer to the grave. The casket, viewed from above, appeared monstrously large, way too big for her tiny cancer-consumed mother. It was inconceivable that they were going to leave her mother in this freezing pit.

The rabbi threw the first shovelful of dirt. It made a thud as it landed, spattering across the top of the coffin. In her head, Ilana screamed. Outside, in the frigid air, it was silent.

•

On Saturdays, Ilana usually took Sarah to softball while Bill read the paper and Janey watched cartoons, a habit Janey should have outgrown but had not. Now Bill would have to take both girls with him and stand on the edge of the ratty field making small talk with the other parents. Had he been a character on Janey's show, there would have been a sizzling hiss as she touched his arm.

"I have to meet a repairman at my office," she said. "I'll meet you at the game. You can leave as soon as I get there." Ilana hated her apologetic tone, the implication that she should feel badly that Bill would be spending more time than usual with their children.

Not until the cab was halfway across the park did Ilana wonder if César would be at her office. She'd always left it up to him when he came on Saturdays. She closed her eyes. "Please, no," she said to herself. She wanted to sink into her chair and drink her take-out coffee and read from the volume of Chekhov stories she was carrying in her bag, stories she found more illuminating than most of her professional journals or the conventions she'd long ago stopped attending. She wanted to leave behind her thoughts about her patients and Bill and her children, let her mind rest on the desolate landscapes and exquisite manners of another time. Afterward, she'd be happy to see her family again. By then, Bill's foul mood would have dissolved into three cups of sweetened black coffee and the weekend pleasure of wearing jeans and sneakers and anticipating his afternoon run. The girls, buoyed by the Krispy Kreme donuts he would have bought them and the fresh air, would be giggly, touching her shoulders and hands and hips like they were toddlers again.

Yesterday afternoon, as she'd left, she'd given her own keys to the door staff for César. When the Saturday doorman told her the cleaning person had taken them upstairs, her hopes for the morning evaporated.

The outer door to the suite was unlocked. Ilana could hear the vacuum cleaner. She carried her coffee into the waiting room.

César was working bare-chested. A spray of black hair fanned out from his navel, surrounding his surprisingly pink nipples.

"Jesus. Dr. Ilana. I am so sorry." César reached for his sweatshirt, pulling it over his head, then leaning down to shut off the vacuum.

Standing up, César was beet red. "I take off the sweatshirt because I get so hot. I didn't know you were coming. I am so embarrassed."

"I came to meet the locksmith. I need to change one of the cylinders."

César sat down in one of the waiting room chairs. He doubled over his knees. "Jesus Christ. Look at all the trouble I cause you. You have to come in on Saturday. All because I did such a stupid thing."

Ilana perched on the chair across from César.

"You've done an excellent job all these years. Everyone makes a mistake on occasion."

The truth was, he'd done a good-enough but not excellent job—not, she thought, because he was lazy but because he didn't have the sensibility to think on his own to do the things Nona did automatically: wiping out the inside of the refrigerator, dusting the tops of the picture frames, polishing the spots from the bathroom faucets. The notes Ilana left suggesting extra attention to certain tasks never seemed to have an impact beyond the week they were received.

With César in the suite, she couldn't read. She puttered around in her office until the locksmith arrived. It took him ten minutes to change the cylinder. She wrote him a check for four hundred and sixty-three dollars and threw out her coffee.

César was in the patient bath, scrubbing the outside of the toilet with a rag she didn't recognize having provided.

"It's all fixed. I left the new set of keys for you on my desk."

César stood up. Beads of sweat dotted his hairline.

"Do we need anything? More cleaning products, vacuum cleaner bags?"

"I buy. Don't worry."

All of these years, she'd kept track of the supplies and bought them as needed. It would be easier if she let César do it. One less item on her to-do list. "But you shouldn't be paying for the supplies. Let me get some money to give you."

Ilana went back to her office for an envelope. She put fifty dollars inside and wrote César's name on the outside with a green felt-tip pen. She gave him the envelope. "Pay yourself back for whatever you buy. You can put the receipts inside. Just leave me a note when you need more cash."

César waved his hand. "No, no. You give me a check already each month."

"That's for you. For the work you do. This is for the supplies."

César looked at the floor. A puddle of Mr. Clean had dripped onto the tiles from the rag in his hand. "I just want to make you happy."

•

Before her August break, a trip this year with Bill and the girls to Italy, she left a message for César that she would be out of the office until Labor Day. Could he please water the plants and perhaps use the time to defrost the refrigerator?

In the morning, there was a message from César: *I do my very best with your plants and your refrigerator. I hope I please you. I wish you a good vacation with your family.*

She'd planned their trip so they would begin with five days in Rome, then move on to a villa with a pool and some nearby picturesque villages. She'd been to Rome only once before, the year before she started graduate school, a year during which she worked as a personal assistant for an eccentric art dealer. Her employer had owned an apartment in Rome, and she'd accompanied him on a trip he'd made to procure some paintings. Driving in from the airport, she'd pressed her face to the window, her heart springing open as they passed the Colosseum and the acres of white Brescian marble of the Victor Emmanuel. "If only we could see these wonders freshly," her employer said, with a wan movement of his hand. He rested his head on the back seat of the taxi. "Not painted and filmed and written about so many times that all that's left is the art about the art." She'd wanted to argue with him, but the very act of arguing would have tarnished the moment.

On this second trip, Bill was the scrim through which she and the girls experienced the city. He'd been to Rome twice before, with an old girlfriend, not Louisa, but another Princeton girl whose parents owned a villa outside the city. From what Ilana could gather, those visits had involved a driver taking him and the girlfriend and her parents into the city for the afternoon during which he'd wandered around uncertain of what he was seeing and slayed by the heat while the girlfriend and her mother went shopping and her father went off to meetings that everyone knew were euphemisms for visits to his mistress. Afterward, there had been expensive dinners at restaurants where the girlfriend's father would be greeted by name and Bill would wish he'd worn proper shoes instead of his sneakers.

Now, here with the girls and her, it again seemed that it was the Roman heat that made the strongest impression on Bill, so that Ilana found herself thinking more about organizing their days to include the rare air-conditioned interior than what they would see. Then too there was the limit of his patience. He was interested in the maps at the Vatican Museums and the Roman baths Michelangelo had turned into a church, but was done with the busts in the Museo Nazionale in a quarter hour and baldly refused to climb the stairs to see the Caravaggios at the Borghese.

By their fourth morning in Rome, Ilana woke dreading another day navigating between the places that she wanted to show the girls and Bill's irritability. "Sleep in," she whispered in his ear. "We'll be back after lunch."

"Dress quietly," she told her daughters when she woke them. "We're going to let Daddy rest."

Janey's brow furrowed. With any hint of marital discord, she could dissolve into tears.

"He's just tired, sweet pea." Ilana kissed Janey on the forehead. "We'll have fun."

Breakfast in the hotel dining room without their father transformed the girls into Eloises at the Plaza. Sarah ordered ginger ale with her "bread and jam, *grazie, signore*," which Janey echoed with a "Me too," escaping Sarah's usual refrain of *copycat, copycat*, Ilana imagined, only because Sarah was afraid a quarrel would cause her to veto soda.

Outside, in the fragile morning air, Ilana linked arms with her daughters, the three of them able to walk abreast. They crossed the Tiber, pausing on the tiny island that seemed like part of the bridge to watch a dog running in circles on the bow of a fishing boat. With the girls still laughing about the dog, they made their way to the church of Santa Cecilia, where Ilana remembered her employer having shown her the sculpture of Cecilia lying on her side, the position, he'd explained, in which her miraculously preserved body was viewed by the sculptor on its disinterment a thousand years past her martyrdom.

When they exited the church, it was into the blaze of the midday sun. They took a taxi back across the river, to the Via del Corso, half of the stores the same ones they could find on Madison Avenue but more exotic for Sarah and Janey here. Too hot for lunch and with the girls still infected with the excitement of their purchases and all of them with the sense that Bill's absence made the day a busman's holiday, they went to a gelateria, where the girls ordered ice-cream sundaes and Ilana had an iced coffee in a tall frosted glass.

"One more stop," Ilana perkily announced as her daughters spooned the last drops from their silver bowls. "It's a church with a crypt full of bones."

"I don't want to see any more churches," Janey said. "I want to go back and watch TV."

"Mom just bought you a pair of jeans and a skirt," Sarah instructed in the Austenish tone she'd recently adopted toward her sister, a tone that infuriated Janey. "And you can't even spare two minutes to do something *she* would like?"

Sarah smiled sweetly at her mother. She was already as tall as Ilana and could wear Ilana's shoes. She hadn't done too badly herself on the shopping expedition, with a pair of Italian Pumas and a studded denim jacket.

Ilana read aloud from one of her guidebooks. She'd not seen the Santa Maria della Concezione on her first trip, but both of her guidebooks listed it under their recommendations for children. "For several hundred years, the church's order of monks decorated the crypt with bones." She looked up at the girls. "It sounds like a Halloween art show."

"That's disgusting," Janey said.

"I'd love to go, Mother," Sarah said, tipping her chin into the air.

•

A bald monk with a big belly sat at the entrance to the crypt selling postcards. He wagged his finger at the camera hanging around Sarah's neck.

Entering the first chapel, both girls gasped and Ilana had to control herself not to do the same. Hundreds of skulls were piled one atop the other, a backdrop for three skeletons dressed in hooded robes. On the ceiling, femur bones and hip sockets and vertebrae had been fashioned into a crown and cross.

Janey squeezed Ilana's hand and Sarah sidled close to her sister as they walked deeper into the crypt. In another of the chapels, a canopy of pelvises and a rosette of shoulder blades presided over more robed skeletons. At the end of the corridor, the wired bones of a Barberini princess who'd died as a child hung from the ceiling surrounded by other skeletons, some hanging, some impressed on the stone walls. Janey buried her face in Ilana's arm.

Back outside, the girls were silent. They walked past the shops of the Via Veneto without a single request to go inside to look at anything.

Ilana felt horrid. She'd expected the crypts to be cartoonish, not genuinely creepy. For years after her mother's death, the words of a camp song—*the worms crawl in, the worms crawl out*—had made an endless loop through her head. She would wonder if water had seeped into her mother's coffin and rotted the flesh, if the bones were still in place.

When they reached the hotel, she led the girls to a couch in the lobby. It seemed better to talk to them here, not in front of Bill. She patted the cushions on her two sides.

"So, let's talk about what we saw. What did you think?"

Janey shuddered. "It was scary. I didn't like that princess at the end."

Sarah had refound her Austenish air, the occasion ripe with the opportunity to assert her superiority over her sister and impress her mother. "She was beautiful. Now everyone who comes to that place will know about her. When I die, I want to be kept that way."

"You are so gross."

Ilana took a hand from each girl to hold in her own. "There was an inscription at the end in Latin. It's translated in one of the guidebooks: *What you are, we used to be. What we are, you will be.* What do you think they meant?"

Janey looked confused, torn, Ilana was sure, between her wish to have her mother explain and not wanting to admit her incomprehension to her sister.

"It's obvious," Sarah said. "The bones were once people. Someday we'll be just bones."

"I knew that."

"Liar, liar, pants on fire."

"Hush." Ilana lifted her daughters' hands to her lips. "Hush, my darlings."

Upstairs, they found Bill on the balcony of their suite, reading the *Herald Tribune* and drinking a bottle of water. He was still in his running clothes, his mood boosted by the endorphins released from the exercise and, Ilana imagined, the long sleep he'd had before. The girls went out to show him their purchases. He put Janey on his knee and told Sarah she was going to knock everyone at her school off the planet in that jacket. He smiled at Ilana. That night, he ran his fingers down her spine, the tiny bones that had adorned the crypt like strands of sea cockles, and cupped the points of her hips.

•

When Ilana returned to the office, her plants were dry and droopy and it appeared that César had not been there. She watered the plants and quickly ran the vacuum before her first patient arrived. It was a hard day, all of her patients having saved their crises and anger at her absence for her return.

The week was so busy that Ilana forgot to call César to inquire what had happened. The following Monday, though, it was obvious that he'd been in, cleaning, in fact, more thoroughly than usual: the pictures askew from having been dusted, the windows washed from the inside. In September and October,

César missed two more Saturdays, each absence followed by an intensive cleaning as it had the first time. With each missed Saturday, Ilana intended to telephone César to inquire what was the problem, but each time she felt a hesitation, and then, after the office had been cleaned again, it seemed superfluous.

This year, instead of feeling that the months were racing out of control, the winter holidays and all of their busyness only a blink after summer, what she felt was that the skeletons were taunting her: *What we are, you will be.*

•

On the Monday after Thanksgiving, Sarah came down with a 102-degree fever and a raging sore throat. "Of all mornings," Ilana said to Bill with a sigh. "After I've been out of the office since last Wednesday. My first patient has been holding on by a thread for five days, counting the hours until she could see me."

Bill was shaving. "I can't get into it. I have three guys coming in from L.A. to meet about a six-hundred-mil transaction. You'll have to deal."

Ilana rescheduled her first two patients and took Sarah to the pediatrician. Afterward, Sarah threw up on the curb outside the doctor's office. Ilana sent Nona out to pick up the antibiotic at the pharmacy and helped Sarah back into her pajamas. "Brush your teeth, honey," she instructed through the bathroom door. Sarah stumbled out of the bathroom and lay on her bed. Her mouth smelled foul.

"Did you brush your teeth?"

"I couldn't." Sarah turned on her side. Ilana got Sarah's toothbrush and filled a cup with water. She brushed her daughter's teeth and had her spit in the cup. She smoothed Sarah's hair back from her forehead, cooling now from the Motrin she'd taken earlier. Sarah shut her eyes.

"When Nona gets back, I have to go into the office. I'll be home by six. Nona's going to give you your medicine and she can make you something to eat if you feel like it."

Sarah nodded. She was already more asleep than not.

•

Ilana unlocked the suite door. She had twenty minutes before her first session. As always, she went into the waiting room to turn on the lights before going into her office. From the empty trash can and tidy piles of magazines, she could tell that César had been in.

There was an unpleasant smell, though, in the suite, like something rotting. Ilana deposited a yogurt in the refrigerator of the tiny kitchen. She stuck her head in the fridge, wondering if the smell might be coming from inside. Could an animal, a mouse, or, God forbid, a rat, have gotten in and died hidden behind something?

A feeling of dread came over her. She clutched her keys as she walked back toward her office. The smell was definitely coming from that direction.

Her office door was ajar. She pushed it open. The smell washed so strongly over her that her hand flew to pinch her nose. She gagged. Then she screamed.

César was lying on her office floor. His eyes were rolled back and he was curled on his side. Blood had come out of his mouth and had dried in a rivulet across his chin. The smell was feces.

She shut the door. Unable to stand, she sank to the floor. Her heart was pounding so hard she could feel it in her back, resting now against the wall. She dug inside her bag and found her cell phone to call the police.

•

Not wanting to traumatize her patient, an accountant who traveled uptown every Monday to discuss the panic he felt when a woman touched him, Ilana went down to the lobby to intercept him. As the elevator doors opened, she saw him crossing the lobby. She motioned for him to step aside with her. Someone had grown ill in her office, she explained, careful not to brush his arm. She would call him in the evening to find a time for later in the week.

After her patient left, Ilana told James, the weekday doorman, what had happened. His usually skittering eyes opened wide. "I've never seen anyone dead."

She could hear the sputtering siren of the squad car pulling in front of the building.

"You won't see anything." She touched his shoulder. Her hand was shaking. "The police will cover the body."

Two officers entered the lobby, an older one with a thumb looped under his holster, a younger one with a clipboard tucked in his armpit and a staticky radio on his belt. James breathed in so his chest filled out, torn between his desire to be part of the story—the doorman working when the body was removed—and his terror of the corpse itself.

Ilana led the officers up to her office. She unlocked the suite with the still-shiny key, remaining in the doorway while they bent over to examine the body.

"He worked for you?" the older one asked.

"He cleaned my office, once a week, on Saturdays."

"Yup. Looks like he's been dead about forty-eight. You can call it in," he said to the younger man. "Nasty-smelling, that's for sure."

He stood up. "We need to wait for someone from the medical examiner's office. They'll do their report and then we can cart this out of here. Can we go into that other room?"

Ilana nodded. She followed the two men into her waiting

room, perching on the chair across from them. The younger one rested the clipboard on his knees. She gave him César's name and phone number, then felt embarrassed when she had to say that she did not know César's address.

"Any relatives?"

"There might be a sister here in New York, but the rest, I think, are in Colombia."

"Medical problems you were aware of?"

"No. Well, he had a history of depression. That was, let me see, about eighteen years ago."

"Need to write that down?" the younger one asked the older one.

"Everything the doctor says goes in the report."

"History of suicidal behaviors?"

"No. Not that I know of."

Ilana canceled the rest of her morning patients. Half an hour later, a woman arrived from the medical examiner's office. She put on a mask, squeezing her thick fingers, one by one, into disposable gloves. She looked in César's mouth and listened to his chest with a stethoscope. She pulled off his socks and shoes and examined his feet. Then she nodded at the officers. "Okay, guys, we can get him out of here. I'll radio down to the driver to send us up a stretcher and a bag."

Working together, the two policemen maneuvered a plastic bag under César and zipped it shut. "Don't want anything falling out," the older one said, crinkling his nose. They lifted César's body onto the stretcher and covered it with an army blanket.

After they left, Ilana went to the supply closet to get a bottle of disinfectant. For a strange moment, the thought crossed her mind that she should call César to help her clean up. To her relief, no feces or blood had touched the rug, but, nonetheless, she sprayed Mr. Clean on the area where César had been, letting it soak in while she went back to the closet for a cloth. A shopping bag stuffed with rags cut from what appeared to be César's old T-shirts hung from a hook. She dumped the bag onto the floor, looking for the largest one.

At the bottom was the envelope she'd given César with his name written on the outside in her green felt-tip pen. Surrounding his name, César had written her name—*Ilana Ilana Ilana Ilana*—over and over in the same ink.

She held the envelope the way she imagined César having once done. He must have taken it to her desk, then sat in her chair and used the pen she'd just put back. She imagined him inhaling the envelope, brushing the pen across his lips. Writing her name over and over until the envelope was covered, she saw now, front and back, and then hiding it at the bottom of the bag.

The fifty dollars was still inside.

•

Not until she was in college had she learned that it is Jewish custom to wait to place a headstone over the grave until after the one-year anniversary of a death. She called her favorite aunt, the one with the plump arms, to inquire.

"Your other aunts and I, we bought a headstone. A beautiful granite headstone. We didn't ask your father for a penny toward it, but still he would not come for the unveiling. He was polite, but he basically flat-out refused. She's dead, he told me. We all die, every leaf, every tree, every bug, every bird, mongrel dog, human being dies and rots. There is nothing about dying to make a fuss over, that's what your father said."

Her aunt tsk-tsked. "We thought about asking to bring you to the cemetery," she said, "but we were afraid of your father, afraid he would make a scene and make it harder for you."

Ilana had found the name of the cemetery in the copy of the obituary she'd pasted into her childhood diary, brought to her

dorm room with her few other favorite childhood possessions—
a gold locket her mother had given her, a lithograph of a Mother
Goose ditty, a framed photograph of her mother and her reading together in a hammock. She'd taken a bus from her college
to the town nearest to the cemetery, and then a taxi she could ill
afford. At the cemetery office, a woman looked up her mother's
name in a set of file cabinets and marked an X on a map.

It was a ten-minute trudge through fields of Cohens, Blau-
steins, Goldbergs, Kapinskis, some of the headstones crumbling
and untended, others massive mausoleums of marble, before she
found her mother's headstone, bare save for her name and the
dates of her birth and death.

She'd not gone back.

•

In the evening, after the children were settled in their beds,
Sarah with another dose of Motrin, Janey with permission to
read to herself for ten minutes, a Detective Forbes came to the
apartment. Ilana led him into the living room, away from Bill
watching TV in the family room.

Had she noticed anything strange about César? he asked.

"I hardly saw him. The last time was in April, when I came
in on a weekend to meet a locksmith, but it had been several
years before that."

"How did he seem?"

"Fine. I mean, it was hard to tell. He was vacuuming."

"Did he talk with you?"

The sound from the TV stopped and Bill came into the
room, taking a seat opposite her. There was a look of disapproval
on his face, as though he deemed her too forthcoming or not
forthcoming enough.

"We talked about the keys. He'd lost his set. One of them
needed a card to make a copy and I couldn't find it so I had to

change the cylinder. He was very upset about it. I tried to reassure him that mistakes happen, but he seemed inconsolable."

Bill's stare hardened. She hadn't mentioned what sort of repair she was having done that morning because it hadn't concerned him, but also because she hadn't wanted to hear him tell her that she should have been more careful with the card and César should have been more careful with the keys. Now she felt a surge of anger at Bill's disapproval—that the cylinder and César were none of Bill's business, that they were both, literally, her business, paid for out of her business account. That she'd had it with walking on eggshells not to stir his ire.

"What was the cause of death?" she asked.

"Can't say until the autopsy. Looks either like a coronary or an overdose."

Ilana absorbed the information. The vacuum cleaner had been out in her office. All afternoon, while she'd seen her patients, the question had moved in and out of her mind: Had César had a heart attack while cleaning or had he cleaned her office and then killed himself?

Either way, it occurred to her now, there'd been a broken heart.

Forbes looked at his shoes. She wondered if he'd been trained to allow a few minutes to pass after delivering this kind of news. He glanced at her, proceeding, perhaps, because she was dry-eyed. "Do you know anyone else who knew him?"

"He had a girlfriend when I first met him, but I don't know her last name or how to reach her."

"Maybe Jen knows," Bill said.

With Bill's intrusion, Ilana again felt a surge of anger. It was insulting that Bill would think she hadn't already considered whether Jen would know how to contact Evelyne. Nearly two decades had passed since Evelyne had been Jen's sitter, a job that had hardly lasted a year. It struck Ilana as invasive, almost aggressive, after all of this time of not talking with Jen herself, to subject Jen to a call from the detective. Now with Bill's comment, though, Ilana was obligated to give the detective the phone number she had from years ago for Jen.

After the detective left, Ilana checked on her daughters and then returned to the dinner dishes, caked now with food detritus. Her aunts had debated whether anyone had actually seen her father get into the hearse or if he'd instructed the driver to let him out before they reached the cemetery. All anyone knew for certain was that by the time he showed up back at the house, long after the relatives and other funeral guests had eaten the platters of smoked fish and pastrami her aunts had provided, he was smashed.

•

Three weeks later, the detective called her office. It was one of the two days she worked late, and she was just packing up her things to go home.

"Dr. Green?"

"Yes?"

"Detective Forbes, about César Punto. I'm sorry to disturb you again, but rules and regs require I check with you. No one's come to claim the body. I reached your former neighbor, but as you thought, she didn't know how to reach the ex-girlfriend or anyone else who'd known Mr. Punto."

Forbes hesitated. "If no one shows up by next Friday, we'll have to remove the body from the morgue."

Ilana could hear Forbes's discomfort, his wish to protect her. People who didn't know her often felt this way with her, as though emotional hardiness correlated with body size.

"What does that mean?"

"Well, I don't want to be too graphic about it, but basically we discard the corpse."

"I hardly knew him."

"I'm not suggesting. We just have to inform you."

•

When she got home, Nona had already given the girls dinner. Ilana put Janey in front of a video, settled Sarah at her piano practice, and ran a bath. In the nine years they'd lived in the apartment, she'd never taken a bath.

On their honeymoon, she and Bill had taken a bath together in the claw-foot tub in their Paris hotel room. Bill had washed her fine hair and told her how adorable she was. Even then, on her honeymoon, she'd been aware that he'd not said *beautiful*, the way she imagined he would have with Louisa in response to what she envisioned to be Louisa's Botticelli face and dancer's body. Their sex life, by then well established, was tender and mutually satisfying, but never had she felt that Bill deeply wanted her. He admired her for being a workhorse like himself, he cared about her and had grown, she was certain, to love her, but never had he fallen in love with her, never, as she was certain had happened with Louisa, could she have broken his heart.

She'd not asked the detective what claiming the body would entail. She assumed it meant making arrangements with a funeral home to pick it up and to then have a burial. Money aside, it seemed bizarre that she would bury someone she'd hardly known. And yet, how could she let the body be treated as trash?

The crypts beneath the Santa Maria church had been decorated, she'd read, with the remains of over six thousand persons: Roman paupers and Capuchin friars whose bones had been transported from one church to another following the financial woes and triumphs of various orders of monks. Other than the Barberini princess, no individual was identified. The bones had not even been kept together, pelvises and shoulder blades and

vertebrae joining other pelvises and shoulder blades and vertebrae to form hourglasses and rosettes and crowns.

•

After the girls were asleep, Ilana sat at the kitchen table with a
pencil and pad and opened the yellow pages. In some of the ads,
the prices were listed: interment, cremation, domestic shipping,
international shipping. MasterCard, Visa, American Express,
Major Insurance Plans Accepted.

Would César have wanted interment or cremation? He'd
taken off his shirt because he was hot. Was there a clue in that?

She thought about the pit where her mother's body had been
left. How barbaric it had seemed. Yet, if she had César's body
cremated, what would she do with the remains? It seemed inconceivable to her that she would keep them. But what if a relative did eventually appear from Colombia? How could she say
there was nothing left of César?

She selected Package C: pickup from the morgue, a pine
coffin, transportation to the cemetery, a ten-minute graveside
service.

"Do I need to be there?" she asked the woman taking the
information.

"You're the customer. We do the job either way."

•

When Bill arrived home, he found her still at the kitchen table
with the yellow pages opened to funeral parlors.

"What are you doing?"

"I'm going to bury César." There was a steeliness in her
voice that surprised even her.

Bill sat down. He put his elbows on the table and leaned in
to look at the open phone book. She thought about his college
nickname, Bear. Always she'd associated it with his size, with

something endearing about him. Now she saw that it also captured something intimidating about him, an underlying growl
that was always there.

"He loved me. More than my father ever has. More than you
ever have."

Bill reached for her hands but she crossed them over her
chest and tucked them in her armpits. He placed his own hands
flat on the table. In the bright kitchen light, she could see the
thicket of veins branching out from his wrist.

"Do you want me to come with you?"

"I'm not going."

She pushed back her chair and stood. It seemed to her the
first time that she'd ever looked down at Bill, at the white circle
of scalp visible at the crown of his head. "César's dead. I have living people to take care of."

Her father believed that there was nothing rational about
commemorating death. It either happens at an expected time, in
a way that surprises no one, or it does not. Her father felt the
same way about birthdays, which he refused to acknowledge.
What's to celebrate about the calendar cycling through another
year? There's no accomplishment in that. After her mother died,
her own birthday had disappeared. It had taken her a long time
to understand that the corollary to her father's logic is that life
merits no special consideration.

She slept on the living room couch. Had she slept in their
bed, Bill would have wrapped his arms around her and kissed
her hair and told her it was not true that César had loved her
more than he did. If she had to live with his saying that, she
knew she would not be able to stay with him, with her girls, to
continue doing what she had already decided she had to and
wanted to and would in fact do.

2009

Nate in Bed

You would be surprised to learn that I am happily married, and have been for twenty-two years. I married a few months after I last saw you. My cousin Lizzy—do you remember her? she had a baby not long after we met, a daughter she gave up for adoption—and Corrine—you won't have forgotten her— walked me down the aisle after my father canceled coming east. Corrine's daughter, Conchita, just one, sprinkled rose petals from a white basket. Esther, my mother-in-law, baked the wedding cake: eight tiers with edible silver beads and pink freesia on top.

When we last saw each other, you were bolting east across Columbus Avenue toward Central Park for a Saturday afternoon run and I was walking west, toward the Italian glass store on Amsterdam where I'd bought you a pen for your twentieth birthday, the first birthday we celebrated together. You stopped, right in the middle of the street, and grinned at me. It was winter but you were in only a loose parka, without hat or gloves, and you put your bare hand under my elbow, abandoning your run to guide me the rest of the way across the street, ducking your head slightly, as though you were smelling my hair. You didn't ask me, you just led me to a back table at the café catty-corner from the Museum of Natural History. You ordered a scotch for yourself and a spritzer for me, as though you were certain despite the four years that had passed since you'd last seen me that you still knew what I drank.

Every life contains a watershed moment. This was mine: tipsy from two wine spritzers and you leaning forward on your elbows to push my hair off my forehead and tilt my chin up. If, as you do, I could believe in a benevolent God, he or she must have been watching over me, guiding me so that I veered back into my lane. Did not go to a hotel with you, you betraying a woman to whom you were then engaged, me betraying Paul, my future husband, though I did not know that at the time, whom I'd come across the country to visit, still doubting it possible that anyone as talented and funny and good-looking-enough could be so big-hearted.

What I would not have told you, even if I had gone to bed with you that afternoon, is how on the day Paul walked with his sax case under his arm into the Berkeley bookstore where I had been working since I left you and graduate school and moved in with Corrine, I could sense the joy within him. It was not your guys' guy enthusiasm for everything carnal: for greasy sausage sandwiches, for your racing heart as you caught a football or dove your bare torso into an oncoming wave, for, at one time, me—an enthusiasm that turned itself inside out into brooding, vengeful rage. No, my husband-to-be emanated a deeply settled happiness, granted to him from parents who do not consider personal ambition worth tending. A father, Herb, who for half a century has run a business—helping home owners after fires, rectifying smoke and water damage, renovating with sprinklers and fireproof drywall so the people whose houses he salvages can sleep with peace of mind—that he now shares with his son. A mother—*Esther Sweetie*, his father has always called her—who believes a home requires a freshly baked cake on the kitchen counter, children need to lick icing bowls, and husbands must have warm cookies with their evening tea.

•

You are on my mind this morning as I unlock my apartment door, too early for the Sunday *Times*—it is not yet six—but intent on checking nonetheless. Perhaps it is Paul's absence, in Great Neck to stay with his mother while his father is in the hospital for the first time in his eighty-two years, perhaps a dream fragment wiped out between bed and door. Either way, it surprises me, since I rarely think about you these days, decades having passed since I thought about you all the time, all day long, every experience narrated to the you that had taken up residence in my mind as I debated whether I'd saved or ruined my life with my move three thousand miles away from you, the answer shifting in those first weeks almost hour to hour and you not helping by at first refusing my calls or, if I reached you on the trading floor, the only place where you would answer the phone, saying in your husky voice, "Louisa, can I call you right back?"

I would lie there, in Lily's old bed with her lavender sheets that Corrine had insisted on keeping and that I'd washed six times to remove the vomit and bloodstains and her troll collection on a shelf mounted on the wall, waiting and waiting for your call. And then, maybe ten hours later, after you'd been out with the coworkers you played basketball with at nights—Irish boys who'd gone to Catholic colleges and night school for their MBAs, *the Toddlers*, you called them, feeling yourself more like them in their grit and hunger to make it than the guys from your Princeton eating club who'd had every door opened for them—your muscles still taut and pulsing from the exercise and your skin warm from two beers and a steak and creamed spinach, you'd sprawl on what had been our bed, naked save for a towel wrapped around your middle, and then call. *Baby, I miss you, just come back,* you'd say in your gravelly bedroom voice.

How long did that go on? A few months before you were swept back into your anger at me, for the time I'd gone off with Andrew when, you'd told me in our lowest moments, your longing for me had left you feeling like a dog sniffing a bitch's backside. You shut the door in my face with a finality that had not wavered, I'd assumed, until that afternoon in the bar.

You downed your first drink and ordered a second. You told me about your work, how you had a corner on a certain set of bonds that gave you the long end of the stick and the promise of a killing by summer. And then you told me about Ilana, your fiancé, finishing her training to be a psychologist, smart enough and strong enough, I could tell from the way you described her, to manage you, the only problem being, though you never would have said it, that you could not fall in love with her.

The spritzer had too much wine and too little spritz, but I was drinking it out of nervousness anyway, the alcohol making my thoughts hard to harness, which you would have known: cheap date, you used to call me when I couldn't make it through a glass of wine without becoming silly or sleepy so you would carry me to bed, undressing me, which I felt you doing that afternoon with your eyes.

"What does she look like?" I asked about the woman you were going to marry.

"She's small and fair, with an athletic build and hazel eyes." And then you touched my hair and I put my finger across your lips so you wouldn't say *not a long drink of water,* which is what you'd always called me.

•

I open the door, looking for the newspaper usually left on the doormat, thinking that it must have been in my dream, something about a long drink of water. It's January and the hallway is cold, and I remember with a little shiver the way I sometimes felt almost frightened in bed with you, as though what was human in you might be overtaken by what was animal. How far away that life where my body mattered—how it looked, how it felt, your response to it—seems to me now at fifty-three. In the twenty-two years since that afternoon, I've lost not only my vanity but my feeling of mind-body identity, so that I no longer believe, as you did about me, that elegance of form is elegance of being. I do my best to keep the numbers on the scale where I want them and my skin and hair well tended, but my body is now essentially the vehicle for carting around what I think of as my self. Not that Paul and I don't have sex, we do, and it has always been good, never a battlefield, but it is for both of us simply one of life's many pleasures, which as we've aged and grown have expanded to include new pleasures—bird-watching and stargazing, chamber music and Flemish paintings—and an even stronger sense that the crown jewels are those moments of communion that if we're lucky humans sometimes experience with one another and the bonds of love that get us through the forest the rest of the time.

For a moment, in that bar, with the dark wood and the wine pulsing through my veins and your fingers touching my hair, I felt you wanting me in a way no one else ever had or, I felt certain, ever would. It was as powerful as any drug I'd sampled with Andrew from his pharmacy of esoteric leaves and powders, as powerful as any emotion I would experience until I had Nate and a whole other world of feelings opened to me that left what we'd had together faded juvenilia.

Had I let go of the wheel for just a nanosecond, you would have left some bills on the table and put your hand on the small of my back and shepherded me somewhere with an enormous bed and a sea of pillows and plush towels. Am I wrong? And here is the watershed, or perhaps I should say miracle, given who I was then: having just months before met Paul, who while I nearly torpedoed my future was watching tennis with his father in the Great Neck house where he'd grown up, awaiting my call about which train I would take to come meet his parents for the first time, there was a faint but already beating awareness that the moment had arrived when I could choose happiness and, amazingly, because nothing in my past would ever have predicted such a thing, I did.

•

When Corrine and I first opened Esther Sweetie, my bakery named after my mother-in-law, who'd taught me during Paul and my Sunday visits to her house how to make coconut cake and hamantaschen and plum tarts and lemon squares, on the site of a former East Harlem bread factory Paul had discovered after the original place burned to the ground, I thought what I was trading was creating something no one really wanted, my poems, for something everyone wants. "It's not true," Paul argued with me. "How can you say that about your poems? You've published at least two dozen, right? You've won awards. You had a poem in *The Atlantic*. How many people can say that?"

"Twenty-some poems in literary journals that no one other than other people who publish in literary journals ever reads, a few awards, and a poem in *The Atlantic* is not a life's work."

"What about art for art's sake? I thought you believed in that."

"Maybe for the rare genius. But I'm not Emily Dickinson or Wallace Stevens. The culture will survive without my poems. My work is unwanted. I don't mean that in a self-pitying way. I mean it in an utterly descriptive way. Regardless of whether my poems are brilliant or lousy, there is not an audience for them. I don't want to spend my life creating something that sits in my computer hard drive and does nothing for anyone except make me miserable."

Paul took my hands between his.

I started to cry. It would break my heart to give up on writing poems. But it had come to feel wrong that I would have whatever talents I'd been bequeathed from my father's beloved nucleotides and all the benefits of my fine education and then do nothing but create misery for myself.

Paul looked as anguished as I felt, anguished that he could not fix my pain the way he and his father did with their clients' fire-ravaged homes.

"Look," I said, wiping my tears on the back of my hand. "It was you who taught me that we make our own happiness. Not all of it, of course. We can't control earthquakes or cancer or death. But when I let you into my life, I turned it around."

My husband rarely wears anything aside from Levi's and T-shirts, but like his father he always carries a pressed white handkerchief. He handed it to me.

I blew my nose. "I still remember the first time I met your parents. I took the train to their house. You and your father were sitting side by side on the couch, watching a tennis match, enjoying each other's company. Your mother had three pans of red velvet cake in the oven. She was sifting confectioner's sugar for the cream cheese icing. You and your father could smell the cake and were looking forward to eating it after dinner."

Paul studied me, perhaps remembering the afternoon, the cake, perhaps knowing in some inchoate way the import of that day. "Imagine if your mother only baked cakes that pleased her, if she didn't care whether you and your father liked them. That's the situation with my poems. I'm done with making something only for myself."

•

Having stayed up late waiting for Nate to get home, I want to drink a glass of juice and eat a slice of the cranberry bread I brought home last night from the bakery and read the paper and hopefully get heavy eyes and be able to go back to sleep. The *Times*, though, is not yet here. I look around as if it might have been tossed under the shoe rack we keep by the door, a silly sign still on our door from when Nate was little: OUR FLOORS AND OUR CHILD WHO LIVES ON OUR FLOOR / APPRECIATE YOUR LEAVING YOUR SHOES BY THE DOOR. "À la Japonaise," I used to joke because women hate to mar their outfits by removing their footwear and men worry about holes in their socks or unpleasant smells emanating from their feet, but you would have known the real reason, you'd taught it to me when you left your collection of running shoes outside our door because you abhorred the idea of street dirt being trekked through our rooms.

On the shoe rack, placed neatly next to Nate's basketball sneakers, is a pair of burgundy ballet flats, elasticized along the edges to grip the foot, with a small black bow on the top, the kind of shoes worn barefoot with skinny jeans even in winter by the girls at Nate's school. I stare at the shoes, as though they might be a forgotten pair of mine, as though they might have been left by our housekeeper, whose bunioned feet would never fit in a shoe so tiny and delicate, my heart pounding out of control as I try to come up with some other explanation than what I know to be true.

•

Closing the door, I review in my mind Nate's arrival home last night. As always, I'd waited up for him. He'd come home at our agreed-upon time and I'd kissed him, checking for the smell of alcohol or smoke. He blew his breath into my face. "Nothing, Mom, nothing," his voice a mixture of resentment at the intrusion and resignation that it was justified since there had been two nights this past year, one only five months ago, when he'd come home drunk and vomiting, so sick I'd sat on the bathroom floor with him until three in the morning holding his old beach bucket under his chin while he moaned, calling his pediatrician in the middle of the night to ask about alcohol poisoning, slipping ice chips through his cracked lips and then, after we'd managed to get him cleaned up enough to get into his bed, sleeping next to him on the floor to make sure if he got sick again he didn't aspirate vomit into his lungs.

Before these nights, I'd thought of my son as a good boy, sweet and smart and hardworking and, when he's happy, funny and at times kind of goofy like his father, soft in the way of boys who have been well loved by their fathers. Not like you, who lived in fear of the dark moods your father had brought home along with a never properly healed bullet wound from a war. Like his own father, Paul had taken Nate to the park every day weather would possibly permit. Winters, they'd arrive home in ski jackets and hats, pink-cheeked with freezing noses ready for steaming hot chocolate and sugar cookies; summers they'd come in sweaty and parched, gulping glasses of water and devouring the ice-cream cake or cherry pie or whatever else I had made that afternoon.

I put one of Paul's corduroy shirts on over my pajamas and walk back to Nate's room. I pause before his closed bedroom door. I knock, wait a few seconds, and then turn the handle.

For a moment, in the dim light of the room, I cannot take in what I am seeing. Two heads in my son's single bed. Nate, sprawled on his back with his mouth slightly open, his face oily from sleep, a musky scent emanating from his skin. Next to him, on her side with her back against the wall, a girl with a mess of curly red hair and her full breasts exposed.

I stare at the girl, at her pink nipples, the beauty mark on her collarbone. Even though she's lying down, I can see that she's short but with some meat on her. There's a condom wrapper thrown on the floor and a wad of tissues inside which must be the used thing.

The girl opens her eyes. She has a sweet round face with big brown eyes and full lips, and a fleeting thought passes through my mind that I am proud of my son for choosing a girl outside the emaciated blond mold that is the ideal of his group. A look of terror forms on her face. She yanks the sheet up to her shoulders and hides in the pillow.

I shake my son, as I do every morning, and he moans. He turns his back to me, as he has every school morning since he was three.

"Nate," I say, first softly, then, a second time, louder.

"Mmmm."

"Nate, wake up."

"Just let me sleep, Mom. I'm still tired."

I shake harder. "Nate. You have to wake up."

My son shifts back toward me. He opens his eyes, shuts them, and then opens them again.

"Oh, fu-uck."

"Nate, what is going on here?"

"Mom, get out of here, okay? Give me a minute. Fuck." He pounds the mattress with his fist, then turns to the girl, her face still buried in the pillow. "The alarm didn't go off," he tells her.

"You both have two minutes to get your clothes on and meet me in the kitchen. Two minutes. I'm serious."

I walk back to the kitchen. My temples pound, my blood pressure soaring. I take a deep breath, irritated that I can't call Paul, his cell off while he sleeps due to the work calls that come at all hours, Esther panicking about Herb if the house phone were to ring so early.

I fill the coffee carafe with water and measure the ground

beans into the basket. Then I fill the teakettle and start it boiling in case the girl wants tea, take the Saran off the cranberry bread, put out plates. I can't get the girl's face out of my mind. Something about it seems familiar, as though I knew her when she was younger, perhaps from one of Nate's camps or even preschool, the face utterly altered but with the individual features essentially the same.

Nate pokes his head into the kitchen. He's put on sweatpants and a T-shirt and his hair is sticking up. There's a rangy scent to him, and I'm not happy that it reminds me of you in the mornings when you'd reach for me and I'd push you away, teasing, *Go shower, I mean it,* you nuzzling your face in my neck, telling me I smelled like a shell or beach grass or something else from the sea.

Behind Nate is the girl, dressed now.

"Okay, Mom, she's going to leave. I'm just going to walk her to the elevator."

"Oh, no, you're not," I say, my voice sharper than I intend. "This is not a joke. You both come in here and sit down."

"No, Mom."

"Yes, Nate." My jaw clenches. I am grinding my teeth. Over the past few months, Nate and I have on a couple of occasions approached this treacherous place: the awareness that he no longer has to do what I say. On each occasion, he has moved back from the precipice, both of us desperately hoping that we will eventually be able to cross that chasm without a disaster.

Nate rolls his eyes and comes into the kitchen. The girl follows, looking at the floor. She's wearing leggings with a white peasant shirt and a long cardigan. In the light, her hair is amazing: pumpkin-colored, with corkscrew curls that cascade down her back. I pour two glasses of juice and hand them each one.

"Would you like some coffee or tea?" I ask the girl.

"Coffee, please."

"Milk and sugar?"

"Yes, please."

I heat some milk in a pitcher in the microwave and bring the pitcher and the sugar bowl to the table. Nate and the girl are still standing, Nate with a hip against the counter, the girl shifting awkwardly from foot to foot.

"Sit."

Nate gives me his dead-eyes look, his way of telling me that he refuses to engage and if I insist he will foil me by turning himself into a zombie. The girl perches gingerly on the edge of one of the kitchen chairs, stirring two spoons of sugar into the mug of coffee I've handed her. From the diamond studs in her ears, the cashmere cardigan, the Coach purse, it looks like she comes from an affluent family, but that she carries her privilege lightly, does not, as do some of the kids from Nate's school, think it makes her special. Our apartment, overlooking Morningside Park—when we first moved here a scary place littered with broken glass and discarded needles, now a haven with terraced esplanades and enormous weeping trees but still dangerous after dark so that I shudder wondering how she arrived here in the middle of the night—must seem foreign and bohemian: bookshelves overflowing with Paul's LP collection and my poetry volumes, walls covered with paintings done by artist friends, no lady decorator fabrics and fussy kitchen tiles.

I start to cut slices of cranberry bread, then, thinking of the condom wrapper, catch myself, leaving it to these two not-children. My son, who'd not served his own food until he was fourteen, waiting always for his father or me to place his plate in front of him until I'd had to tell him it was too babyish for a boy his age, cuts himself a large jagged slice.

"Take some," I say to the girl.

She cuts a sliver, and for a moment I worry that she is one of those girls who are afraid of food, who won't eat in front of boys.

She eats a forkful as though to be polite, gagging slightly from anxiety, it seems, and then takes a second bite with what I can see is real hunger.

"This is delicious. Nate told me you own a bakery in Harlem."

"I do."

"He told me that you were a poet and that you gave up poems to bake cakes."

"I did."

"I write poems," she says. A funny sound comes from her throat, almost a burp.

She covers her mouth. "Excuse me. I'm sorry. I'm kind of nervous."

"She won a Scholastic Gold Key for one of her poems last year," Nate says.

"Congratulations."

"And she went to the writing program at Skidmore last summer."

I've run a business now for twelve years, but there are still moments like this, with these two kids, one my own flesh and blood, who've wronged me in ways I can't yet articulate—some twisted combination of putting themselves in danger and violating my home, sneaking behind my back and yet under my roof—when I can't seize control of a situation. The first summer I lived with you when we'd have a fight and you would raise your voice, I would burst into tears. Jesus Christ, Louisa, I recall you once saying, don't you know how to fight back? But I didn't. My mother had either endured my father's condescensions or taken revenge in her own subterranean ways.

I clear my throat and fold my hands on the table. "Okay, so what happened here?"

Nate peers at me. He's discarded the dead-eyes look. "Mom, you know what happened."

"No, I don't." I study the girl. For the first time, she looks directly at me, and again I feel a disturbing sense, a déjà vu but not exactly, of having somehow already met her. "Where do you go to school?" I ask.

She glances at Nate.

"What does that matter?" Nate answers for her.

"Listen, we're going to work together on this, or . . ." I pause, catching myself before I make some kind of wild threat—call the police, boarding school, roads Nate knows I would never take.

What I want to do is to call Corrine, who has come through the other side of some pretty awful experiences with her daughter, but I'm afraid that if I get up, even just to pee, Nate will quickly usher the girl out or, even worse, slither away with her to disappear into one of the teenage lairs these kids with their constant phone access to one another can always find.

What I want to ask Corrine is whether I need to call the girl's parents. Is that the stupid conventional course or the adult thing that I have to find the backbone to do?

"Chapin," the girl says. "I'm in eleventh grade, like Nate."

Nate cuts himself a second piece of cranberry bread, and a wave of ridiculous relief that at least he's eating washes over me. Over the summer, after we'd grounded him for the second drinking incident, he'd gone on a health kick, rejecting anything from my bakery, relishing the power of being in control of his own body after having been spoon-fed his entire life. When his stomach turned concave, I'd insisted he go to the pediatrician to be weighed. He'd lost twenty-three pounds. We'd spent a miserable two weeks in August in Italy while I anxiously registered every half-eaten panini, every meal at which he ordered only a salad, until finally, in Venice, he began to really eat again: first gelatos, then fried artichokes, then plates of spaghettini, his appetite slowly returning and a reasonable amount of the weight.

He yawns. What my son wants to do is go back to sleep.

The girl takes another bite. "This is so good," she says, her voice a little too loud, as though she thinks if she just keeps filling the room with sound everything will be okay. "My mother hates to cook. Our housekeeper does all the cooking, but my dad doesn't like her food so we have a lot of takeout too."

"Do I know your mother?"

The girl looks at Nate. He shrugs his shoulders. "I don't think so."

Her voice drops in volume. "She's a therapist."

I know that I am now on thin ice and that I have to quickly skate forward. "And what's your name?"

My son wipes the cranberry bread crumbs from his mouth. "Mom, what the fuck? Why are you going there?"

I put my hand over his. "Because I am going to call her parents, to let them know she's here. They have a right to know where their daughter is at six in the morning."

Nate glares at me. Pure hatred. As a young child, he'd been so easy and reasonable, no storms of *I hate you* and *You're the worst mother on the entire planet*, neither of us was prepared for this past year when he's had to break away to become himself.

"I am not going to tell them the details. That's your business. I am just going to say that when I woke up this morning, she was here in our apartment."

The girl looks at me with horror, as though I have told her that in three minutes she will be executed.

"Sarah," she whispers. "Sarah Callahan."

My eyes open wide and my hand clamps my mouth, muffling a gasp. Unable to stop myself, I stare at your daughter with her gorgeous red hair, her ballet flats outside my front door, the beauty mark on her collarbone that you bathed or perhaps you did not do the baths, that her mother bathed, covered by the blouse your wife bought her or you gave her a credit card to buy herself, seated now at my kitchen table, eating the cranberry bread from the bakery I run with Corrine, who you hated because you thought she was too wild and loose.

Your daughter is crying. "My father will kill me," she says. "You don't know him. He'll ground me for the rest of my life."

"I do know him. William Callahan." I do not say, *Yes, he will ground you for the rest of your life.*

"How did you know that?" Nate demands. "Her father's first name?"

"We went to college together."

Your daughter rests her arms on the table and lays her face on top of them. She cries into the pillow of her folded arms. I open her purse and take out her cell phone. I scroll through her recent calls until I see "Home."

My son touches your daughter's heaving shoulder. He rubs her back. I am glad he is kind to her.

•

I lie on my bed with your daughter's phone in its hot pink case on my chest, your face across that table twenty-two years ago as clear in my mind as if it were last night.

I wonder what you look like now, if you have lost your thick hair, if you have a gut.

A lifetime ago, you told me that you could imagine me at fifty. "You'll still be beautiful," you said, and it was the nicest compliment anyone had ever given me, your faith that time would treat me well. This, though, had been the heart of the sickness between us that I did not understand until the afternoon in the bar with you, filled with excitement at the strength of your desire for me but with enough distance after our four years apart to be able to recognize that there was a higher order of love. I had fallen in love with how you made me feel about myself more than with you. Yes, I loved your determination, the way you catapulted yourself from your plumber father's two-family house in Cincinnati to Princeton, the way you'd insisted on forging your own way, escaping the dull grind of your father's work, the smashed dreams of your hockey player brother-in-law, the deprivations of your sister's life. And yes, I loved your exuberance, your enormous joie de vivre—but mostly, if I was honest, I loved the way you made me feel: like an exquisite prize, not the overlooked afterthought I'd always been for my father, too peripheral from my mother's deepest dramas to keep her from driving her car through a guardrail and down an embankment.

Not until I met Paul had I understood what it means to love someone for himself, to love him independently of what he does for me—where he takes me, to use Corrine's phrase from our girlhood together, from before Lily died, after which, in order to survive, Corrine had to become a grown-up, which I understand now very few people do. With your daughter here, crying in my kitchen, I can see why you came to hate me—I was using you, using you to feel better about myself—and why you had to get away from me. Your love for me left you feeling degraded, and you dug me out of you, in those months after Lily's death, like a dog scratching out a tick.

I push the call button on your daughter's phone, listen to the ring on your home line. I do not know what I will say if your wife picks up.

"Sarah," you mumble, reading your daughter's name on your caller ID, the alarm seeping into your sleep voice by the second syllable of her name. I see your mussed hair, your deer's eyes that you gave your daughter, and in that moment I know that you are a good father even if you react more with your heart than your head, so that it will be my one task with you, what I owe your daughter for my son having snuck her into his bed, to slow you down enough to think about how to respond to your child.

"It's me."

I think back thirty-four years to the night we met, you trying to smell me through the Princeton drizzle, my cousin Lizzy pregnant with the baby she named Brianna and then let go, before I met Andrew or found him in bed with Cat-Sue, before Lily or your parents died, before I understood that jaguars don't kiss horses or you became rich or Corrine and I opened our bakery.

"Louisa?"

I see you swinging your runner's legs over the side of the bed, sitting up, your tiny psychologist wife who doesn't know how to cook curled at your side.

I see my husband asleep in his childhood bed, his silenced cell phone next to the notebook he keeps with his clients' names and the addresses of their damaged homes printed in block letters, his father sleepless in his hospital bed, his mother awake by now, poking through her cabinets as she decides what she'll bake for her husband's return home today.

"Louisa? Is that you?"

I inhale deeply before I speak, taking stock of the gifts in my life and the soil of sadness out of which each has grown.

"Bear," I whisper.

"Oh, Bear."

Acknowledgments

Thank you to the editors of *Agni*, *Confrontation*, *Kansas Quarterly*, *The Ledge*, *The Massachusetts Review*, *Prairie Schooner*, and *Slice*, where earlier versions of eight of these stories first appeared; to the editors of *Glimmer Train* and the Summer Literary Seminars for awards granted to "Barberini Princess"; and to the editors of the *Best American Short Stories* for the selection of "Instructions to Participant" as a Distinguished Story of the Year.

Again, thank you to my sage literary agent, Geri Thoma, who found this collection its home, and to my brilliant editor, Sarah Crichton, and her über-competent assistant, Marsha Sasmor, who brought it to life.

These stories stretch back many years, and were generously supported by many friends and teachers including: Mickey Appleman, Peter Carey, E. L. Doctorow, Terry Eicher, Mark Epstein, Claire Flavigny, Alejandro Gomez, Amy Kaplan, Christina Baker Kline, Philip Lopate, Jenny McPhee, Shira Nayman, Jane Pollock, Caran Ruga, Arlene Shechet, Jill Smolowe, Ana Sousa, Nancy Star, Barbara Weisberg, Mary Kay Zuravleff, and the talented and bighearted women of the Montclair Writers Group.

Acknowledgments

Finally, my gratitude to my extended family of Gornicks and Hollenbecks, to my husband, Ken, who knows these stories from the inside, and to my sons, Zack and Damon, for whom my love has no horizon.

A Note About the Author

Lisa Gornick is the author of the novels *Tinderbox* and *A Private Sorcery*. Her stories and essays have appeared widely, including in *AGNI*, *Prairie Schooner*, and *Slate*, and have received many honors, including Distinguished Story in the *Best American Short Stories* anthology. She holds a B.A. from Princeton and a Ph.D. in clinical psychology from Yale, and is a graduate of the writing program at New York University as well as the psychoanalytic training program at Columbia. She lives in New York City with her husband and two sons.